John Brandon was raised on the Gulf Coast of Florida, and worked in various warehouses while writing his first novel. He has been the Grisham Fellow in Creative Writing at the University of Mississippi, and the Tickner Fellow at the Gilman School in Baltimore.

Also by John Brandon

Arkansas
Citrus County

A MILLION HEAVENS

JOHN BRANDON

ABACUS

ABACUS

First published in the United States in 2012 by McSweeney's,
a privately held company with wildly fluctuating resources.

First published in Great Britain in 2013 by Abacus

A CIP catalogue record for this book
is available from the British Library.

ISBN 978-0-349-13886-2

Typeset in Garamond by M Rules
Printed and bound in Great Britain by
Clays Ltd, St Ives plc

Papers used by Abacus are from well-managed forests
and other responsible sources.

MIX
Paper from
responsible sources
FSC
www.fsc.org   FSC® C104740

The author thanks Paul Winner, Bess Reed Currence,
Brett Martin, and Heather Brandon.

THE WOLF

The nighttime clouds were slipping across the sky as if summoned. The wolf was near the old market, a place he remembered enjoying, but he resolved not to go inside, resolved to maintain his pace, an upright trot he could've sustained for days. He was off his regular route. He had passed several lots of broken machines that weren't even guarded by dogs and now he was crossing kept grounds – the trees in rows, the hedges tidy, the signs sturdy and sponged. He cleared the first wing of a well-lit building, catching his trotting reflection in the mirrored windows. His head jerked sidelong toward a parking lot and there he saw the quiet humans.

The wolf understood that he had stopped short in some sort of courtyard and he understood that these humans had snuck up on him, or he had snuck up on them without meaning to, which was the same. He retreated into the shadows. The humans hadn't spotted him. They seemed lost to the world. They sat with their legs folded beneath them. Not a whisper. Not a sigh. The wolf couldn't tell what these humans were doing. A lot of knowledge was obvious to the wolf and hidden from humans, but they had their own wisdom – deductions they'd been refining for centuries, beliefs they would cling to until they could prove them.

The wolf slipped into the neighboring truck dealership and crept under a row of huge-tired 4×4s. He snuck around behind the humans, who were all concentrating on the building in front of them. Not one of them was eating or drinking. Their hands were empty of telephones. The wolf could tell this had happened before. This gathering had occurred untold times, and the wolf had known nothing about it. He resisted the urge to clear his snout and break the quiet. The humans. They were even more vulnerable in the night than in the day. They'd convinced themselves they were in their element by raising buildings and planting trees, but the wolf knew that seas existed and that humans belonged near those seas and eventually would return to them. These humans were stranded in the desert and above them hung a moon that was also a desert.

This domain, this fin of the poor neighborhoods south of town, had not been part of the wolf's rounds for many seasons. He checked in down here from time to time and the area seldom changed. The clinic had been built, the wolf didn't remember when, and the market had shut down. The wolf would've liked to explore the old market, cruise the sharp-turning passageways of trapped air, but he could not pull himself away from these humans. He was putting himself behind schedule. The wolf could not have named any specific entity that threatened his territory, but that was irrelevant. He had rounds. The wolf was as trained as the terriers that slept in the humans' beds. The wolf had been trained by his instincts, by forefathers he'd never known. He didn't roll over or beg, but his trick was rounds, starting each evening near Golden and veering below Albuquerque to the loud safe flats near the airport. Up to the windless park where the humans' ancestors had drawn on the rocks, then farther to Rio Rancho, where the scents from the restaurants were milder and children on glinting bikes coasted the hills. Bernalillo. The big river. The property where the Indians were kept. With plenty of time before dawn, the wolf would pick his way around the base of Sandia Mountain, winding up near Lofte, the northern outpost of the eastern basin, and there he would watch the new sun turn Lofte's handful of buildings, which from a distance appeared to be holding hands like human children, the urgent red of hour-old blood.

The wolf's paws were planted, his senses directed at the humans. Whatever they were doing, it wasn't in order to have fun. Maybe they were deciding something, piling up their thoughts. Or perhaps they were waiting. The wolf knew about waiting. But humans, unlike the wolf, rarely waited without knowing what they were waiting for.

It was dangerous and without profit for the wolf to get intrigued with human affairs. At present he was huddled into the wheel well of a hulking pickup truck, putting himself behind schedule, because he wanted to hear the humans speak, wanted them to break their silence, because he wanted an explanation. He stood in continual anticipation of hearing a voice. A question asked. Human laughter. He worked his tongue around his teeth, tasting nothing, tasting his own warm breath. An involuntary growl was idling in his throat and he stifled it. The wolf could wait no longer. He perked his ears one last time, the wind dying out for him – still nothing to be heard. He forced himself to back out from between the two trucks that were hiding him and forced himself to skip the old market and make for the airport. He cleared his snout decisively. He resumed trotting, but after three or four blocks, while passing some weedy basketball courts that stood empty behind a high fence, he broke into a flat run and the scents he smelled then came mostly from the furnace of his own body.

SOREN'S FATHER

He of course hadn't run his lunch truck route since he and Soren had arrived at the clinic, and his route was where he'd always sorted out his troubles, paltry as his old troubles seemed now with his son lying here in creepy serenity day after day. On his route – the traffic swelling and subsiding, the billboards sailing above with their slogans, the hungry awaiting him at the next stop – Soren's father had counseled himself through the workaday decisions of parenting and running his small business. He was a creature of habit and his habits were now mostly wrecked. He still knocked out his pushups, four sets of fifty, right down on the linoleum floor of the clinic room. The floor was perfectly clean, waxed to hell and back, and Soren's father, if he dropped a crumb from his food tray, always knelt down and picked it up and dropped it into the little wastebasket that was continually empty. The final ten pushups of the final set brought grunts out of Soren's father that he could not stifle, and sometimes Nurse Lula came and peeked in the door and saw Soren's father flat on his front. Nurse Lula was the one who'd shown Soren's father the secret smoking spot, so he didn't have to descend all the way to the ground floor and walk out front and stand under the carport. There was a landing that jutted from the sixth floor staircase. The door to the landing was marked DO NOT OPEN ALARM WILL SOUND, but this wasn't true. You could walk right out there and see in every direction. There was a casino in the middle distance, and way off a spine of maroon peaks. Soren's father didn't enjoy cigarettes as much as he had before, the smoke chugging out his half-open truck window as he navigated the city; now he used smoking to take breaks from the clinic room the way the folks he served on his route used smoking to take breaks from their factory jobs. Sometimes Lula was out on the landing. She had wide-set eyes and a gentle manner that made her seem holy. When she spoke to Soren's father she avoided talking about her children but sometimes she slipped. They were girls and the younger one was taller than the older one.

Soren's father was losing weight already, but it wasn't because of the hospital food. Everyone complained about the food, but Soren's father was used to eating from his truck – a soft, odorless sandwich or half-stale apple fritter or limp hot dog. He'd always fed Soren well enough, taking him down to the fancy grocery store with the hot bar and letting him point out what he wanted, but as for himself, he couldn't see wasting the leftovers from the truck. He was accustomed to eating in traffic, so when he ate his dinner in the clinic room his chewing sounded monstrous against the quiet. He was eating as much as he ever had, so it must've been pure worry that was taking the pounds off him. There'd been a scale in the room and Soren's father had Lula take it away.

It was hard to know what to do with the quiet. Soren's father couldn't get used to it. The quiet was impure, same as if you were up in the woods somewhere. The woods had chipmunks and falling pinecones and tunneling beetles and in the clinic there were machines beeping and whirring and nurses shuffling around in their chunky white sneakers and the rattling of carts. Soren's father had never watched much TV and Soren, back when he was awake, hadn't shown any interest in it either. Soren's father used to try putting cartoons on their living room set and Soren would stare at the screen suspiciously for a minute and then move on to something else. Soren's father had long since stopped trying to watch the news, which was both depressing and uninformative. He was a reader of science fiction, a habit he'd picked up to fill downtime between stops on his route, and now he read in the room, occasionally aloud, wanting Soren to hear his voice. Soren's father's interest in interstellar goings-on was waning, but with a paperback in his hands he was not completely at the mercy of the clinic's busy, endless hush. He could put words into his mind and, when he felt like it, into the still air of his son's room. One of the characters Soren's father was reading about had been cast into a trance by means of a dark art that was part science and part magic, and Soren's father had begun to skip those passages. He didn't want to reach the end of the book, where the noble young trooper would predictably awaken.

It was Wednesday, and evening now, so the vigil had begun. Soren's father hadn't heard them gathering but they were down there. Soren's father's mental state was one of being acutely aware that he was in a fog, and the vigils weren't helping clear that fog. He parted the blinds. This was the third Wednesday and their numbers were growing. They were far below, most of them bowing their heads, and it disconcerted Soren's father that he couldn't see any of their faces. They were like those schools of tiny fish he remembered from boyhood filmstrips that moved in concert like a single inscrutable organism. They seemed practiced, experienced, but where would they have gotten experience at this sort of thing? Nurse Lula said there had been vigils at the clinic before but it was usually a one-time thing. She remembered last year a cop had been shot in the abdomen during a traffic stop and a crew of folks in uniforms had come one night with candles and had each slurped down one bottle of the cop's favorite beer. These people showing up for Soren didn't light candles and they didn't drink. Soren's father didn't know how he was supposed to feel about them. He worried that they knew something he didn't, that they had access to a gravity of spirit that was beyond him. And the vigilers made him feel exposed too, onstage, so whenever they were gathered out there he stayed hidden behind the meticulously dusted blinds.

Soren's father had seen them arriving that first Wednesday, before he knew they would become a vigil, when they were merely a half-dozen people loitering in the corner of the parking lot. A security guard had approached that first week and looked them over and elected to leave them be. Last week, with close to fifty people in the troop, a news van had rolled into the lot and a girl in an orange scarf had tried to talk to the vigilers. She didn't get a thing out of them. Not one word. They didn't stay long, the news folks. Nobody was beating drums or getting drunk or holding signs. No one was crying. Nobody was doing anything that could be readily mocked.

THE PIANO TEACHER

The lie she had come up with was that a library branch on the other side of town was screening old monster movies each Wednesday evening. She couldn't tell her daughter she was going to sit outside a defunct flea market half the night, watching people a football field away as they vigiled. Her daughter wouldn't understand vigiling and she certainly wouldn't understand spying on a vigil from the high ground of an adjacent lot. And she also couldn't tell her daughter she wanted to be near the boy. The piano teacher had climbed into the car her daughter had given her as a hand-me-up, a high-riding silver station wagon, and had sat at swaying red light after swaying red light and crossed Route 66 and now she slowed passing the clinic, which was out of place here on the edge of town, the only tall building in sight. The vigilers huddling in the parking lot were like cattle awaiting a storm.

The piano teacher passed them by and rolled onto the grounds of the market. She didn't feel she was superior to the other vigilers, and in fact observed the rules she knew they followed – didn't speak during the vigils, or turn the car radio on – but she was more than a vigiler. She was one of the forces that had *put* them in the parking lot of that clinic. She could do what they did, could open her windows and endure the chill air rather than running the heater in her car, but the vigilers could never do what she'd done, which was to halt a miracle. The others, hugging themselves loosely in the sand-swept parking lot, were hoping to gain something, but the piano teacher was only hoping to feel sorry enough.

So here she was in the dark in a part of town she wouldn't have visited in a hundred years. The moon was strong and the piano teacher could see the writing on the market stalls, all in Spanish, cartoonish drawings of vegetables and shoes. Between the market and the clinic was a used car lot full of tall gleaming pickups. From this distance the clinic looked like a spaceship that had run out of gas. Or like a miniature of itself, a toy.

The piano teacher had thought for sure she'd seen something moving in the shadows, and now she saw a creature ambling across the parking lot that must've been an enormous coyote. He was big for a coyote. The creature seemed male, though the piano teacher wasn't sure why. He moved with a strut. The piano teacher watched him pick his way along the fence, which he probably could've jumped at any time. He came into the moonlight and passed back out of it and was gone in one complete moment, and the piano teacher, after the fact, thought of rolling up her windows. The piano teacher could not have said what color the animal was, one of those dark shades of the desert that was more a feeling than a color. He hadn't even glanced at her. The piano teacher looked at the sky, at the clinic, down at her hands, at the buttons that locked the doors and ran the windows up and down. The boy had really played that music, had written it or channeled it or who knew where it had come from. He had played his soul, without ever having previously touched a piano. If he'd stayed conscious there would've been calls coming in from all over to hear the boy play, from the wealthy craving a novelty and maybe even from conservatories wanting another prodigy. But the boy didn't know how to play. The boy had played what he'd played but he had no idea about piano. He was in a coma now, so instead of a prodigy many thought of him as some sort of angel, though they were afraid to use that word. He didn't know how to play piano but he was an instrument himself, they believed. And of course many were firm that there had to be a medical explanation, folks who would cling to their practicality to the end. And none of these people had even heard the music. They knew it had been played and that experts had deemed it original, but only about a dozen people had heard the music and the piano teacher was one of them, and she was the only one who'd heard it that first time, who'd heard the boy play it live. If anyone knew the truth it was the piano teacher, but she knew nothing. She was a dumb witness. There wasn't a thing wrong with Soren physically, the newspaper had been clear about that until they'd finally let the story drop because there were no new developments. There was nothing at all wrong with him except he was not conscious.

The piano teacher had decided she would always depart last. She would remain until every last vigiler down in the parking lot was headed back to regular life. She would wait for the exodus that would occur between one and two in the morning, and after the last car had left the clinic and the wind was the only sound again, she would turn her key and leave the market and steal the last faraway glance at Soren's blank window up on the top floor.

CECELIA

She stayed in line with a convoy of cars leaving the clinic until the interstate loomed up. Car after car pulled onto the west ramp, heading toward other parts of the city, and only Cecelia broke off and climbed the ramp going east. She was already on the outskirts, and after she cleared the jutting foot of Sandia she would be clear of town entirely. She lived out in Lofte, a stagnant outpost on the once-lively Turquoise Trail, about a twenty-minute drive into the desert and then another ten minutes on the state road. She had a stop to make before home, at the cemetery that served Lofte and the other basin towns – Golden, Hill City, Cromartie. There were few other cars on the road this late, and they either screamed past like rockets or drifted around in the right lane. Though it was nowhere near morning, light was bleeding up from the corners of the sky.

When Cecelia reached the grounds of the cemetery she couldn't help but feel like she was trespassing, like she was going to get run off by a rent-a-cop, but the gate was wide open and the streetlights along the lane were burning. She pulled around a curve, assuring herself that she was using the cemetery precisely as it was meant to be used. No one could say what the right or wrong time was to visit the dead. The place was absolutely still. Going this slow, Cecelia could hear her engine gargling and hacking and she felt rude. She let the car cruise without touching the gas or brake. She didn't hear any birds, didn't hear an airplane in the sky. The place likely didn't have a night security guard and Cecelia didn't see any cameras on the lampposts, and in short order she went from fearing surveillance to feeling too *un*watched. She wasn't being monitored and she wasn't being looked out for. She could do anything, but what she was going to do was absolutely nothing, just like the last time she'd been here. When she'd come to Reggie's funeral almost a month ago she'd lost her nerve and stayed in her car, and the same thing was happening tonight. She had the same feeling, helpless and unhinged. She parked at the curb in the same spot as before and wound her window all the way down like before. She tipped her head toward the sky. There was no weather, not even the ambitious little clouds that had been blowing over the vigils.

There was a modest hill between Cecelia and the gravesite over which, the day of the funeral, she'd seen the tops of the tall men's heads – Reggie's father and uncles probably, men Cecelia had never met. The funeral party had been partially shaded by the cottonwood trees. The cut grass sprawling in every direction had struck Cecelia as the greenest thing she'd ever seen, the fresh flowers around the headstones jarring bursts of color. Even with the engine and the radio off, she hadn't heard anything that was said about Reggie, any of the eulogy. She'd heard only a reasonable daytime wind that had little to whistle against. She'd been unable to raise herself from her car that day, unable to shut the door as gently as possible and blend into the group at the gravesite to cry and pray like everyone else. She'd sat behind the steering wheel in a black dress she'd picked up that day at a consignment shop. When the ceremony was over and the bereaved had begun descending toward the parking lot, Cecelia had fired up her engine and fled. And it had been only a couple hollow days later that Cecelia found herself at a vigil for a boy in a coma, part of a mild crowd hungry for unspoken rules. *That* she knew how to do. She knew how to vigil. She knew how to sit passively. She'd logged hours and hours down below the sixth floor of the clinic but after a month had still not laid eyes on her friend's grave.

Reggie sometimes didn't seem gone. He did but he didn't. Cecelia had never met anyone like him and she had thought that even before he'd passed away. When Reggie had been doing nothing he never seemed to be wasting time, and when he was doing a lot he never seemed to rush. He'd spent his energy and his money and his mind at the correct rate, never hoarding or throwing to the wind. His temper was rare and expertly wielded. And yes, Cecelia had admired his hard-earned tan and his loose-limbed mannerisms and his arresting jawline. She had watched him with more than the curiosity of the bored as he did everyday tasks like making coffee or changing his shoes, and she'd listened with more than a band-mate's professional interest each time he'd shared a new song in rehearsal. She was glad she and Reggie had never succumbed to any demoralizing trysts or clumsy grope sessions. Truly. Now that he was gone, she was grateful she'd be able to miss him in a straightforward way, as a fallen ally. She didn't know how to grieve him, only how to miss him, as if he'd only moved away rather than died.

Cecelia breathed the night air, smelling neither flowers nor cut grass. She smelled her car. She didn't want to go home yet, didn't want to face her mother or the stupid chickens her mother kept in the yard. The chickens were all her mother cared about any more. Her mother wasn't well. Mess around with chickens and watch television, that's what the woman did. She didn't do anything else. Cecelia didn't want to think about it, didn't want to walk into that house that always stank of the elk stew her uncle liked to drop off on the doorstep. Chickens. TV. Elk stew. Cecelia squinted. It was the middle of the night but she could see everything around her, like the whole cemetery had moved off and left a shadow of itself. The upholstery was sagging from the roof of Cecelia's car and she reached and pressed it back into place.

With the loss of Reggie, Cecelia had lost her band. She had been in a band and now that band did not exist. It was no more. No more rehearsal. No more arguing with Nate, the drummer. No more going to the tragic little gigs. Cecelia's ears would ring no more. She would sing no harmony. She wouldn't wear that men's dress shirt with the wide collar that she always wore to shows. Was it a big deal, no more band? She couldn't tell. Was school a big deal? Or the shell her mother was retreating into these days? Cecelia was a dormant guitar player. She was probably a dormant daughter.

The upholstery sagged down again, and this time Cecelia pushed it back in place with both hands, pressing upward on the roof of her car and pressing herself down into her seat. She pressed until her arms began to quake.

REGGIE

The piano sat in the center of what Reggie was calling the main hall. The room was spacious, but still the piano dominated it. The piano looked disapproving, dauntingly formal, like pianos often did in unfamiliar places. The instrument was ancient and well kept, of a dark but faded wood, and its bench was upholstered with leather the color of a radish. There was no ceiling to the hall Reggie was being kept in, or else it was too lofty to be seen. The place was blanketed in uniform shadow. It seemed alive, the hall, or at least not dead. If Reggie held his breath there was true quiet, pure of electricity running its course, of insect industry, of breezes.

Reggie had a mat to lie down on, even though he didn't sleep. He rested, like a great fish might. There was no way to track time, so Reggie rested when he felt tired of not resting. He remembered real sleep, back in life, black and hard and oblivious to everything but dreams. He remembered waking full of unhurried purpose. His mat was right down on the floor, like a monk or a drug addict. It smelled worn and tidy.

After Reggie had been in the hall what felt like a couple weeks, a library appeared. It didn't contain a desk, so it was a library rather than a study. It was attached to the main hall but the light was cleaner in the library, bright enough to read comfortably. Reggie didn't read, though. He sat bolt upright in the library's grand, creaky chair, which was covered in the same red leather as the piano bench, and flipped backward and forward through the ornate volumes, listening to the pages and smelling the bindings. He didn't have what it took to read one of the books. It wasn't a crisis of energy; it was that Reggie knew none of the books could help him. Reading a book seemed local and desperate. And the fact that people had sat down and *written* the books instead of doing pretty much anything else with their time on earth – taking a walk with a friend, eating chocolate, tinkering with a weed whacker in an oil-smelling shed – made Reggie sad. The thought of all the songs he'd written made him sad. All any writer could do was either document what was known or speculate. Reggie didn't need to imagine a different world because he was in one. He didn't want to celebrate or complain about the world he'd been snatched from, which was now so fathomable. It was easy for him to see now that the living world had always given him what he needed. This new place had no idea what to do with him. He sat in the big chair and ran his fingers over the rough cloth of the book covers. He shuffled through the pages with his thumb, picking out random words. When he needed to break the quiet, he snapped the books shut.

Reggie didn't believe he was being punished, but it was possible he was awaiting punishment. He wasn't religious, but of course he was aware of purgatory, familiar with the concept of the afterlife utilizing a waiting room. He didn't think he'd committed any acts that warranted eternal justice, that warranted Hell or whatever, but he also knew sometimes you broke rules without knowing it. Or sometimes you were supposed to do something and did nothing instead, a sin of omission. And now and then, he wouldn't have been surprised, your paperwork got lost or the person you needed to speak to was on vacation or whoever was in charge just didn't like the look of you. At least this particular waiting room wasn't cramped or foul-smelling. It didn't matter how long he had to wait, Reggie reasoned – it wasn't like he had to be somewhere. It wasn't like he was going to be late to band practice or run out of daylight working on a yard.

The trouble was the solitude. In life, Reggie had never minded being alone, but this was different. Back in life, solitude was temporary. Even if a person was in jail, not that Reggie had been, there were guards and other inmates. If you were driving across the empty desert, you were on your way to see someone. If you were a child banished to your bedroom, you would accidentally fall asleep and before you knew it the morning was underway and here was Mom making pancakes. There was no waking up for Reggie because there was no sleep. There were no other inmates. No pancakes. No map on which to track his progress.

Reggie walked laps around the main hall, managing at times to feel like he was strolling instead of pacing. He felt he had very little peripheral vision, though he couldn't be sure about this. He had no aches or itches to ground him, no hunger that could rise up and concern him. He still had his scars. He could feel that his tooth was still chipped from when an edger had shot a pebble up at him. He found himself fretting over the yards he'd tended back in the living world. He imagined them growing dumpy. It took more skill to keep a desert yard presentable than to run a mower over a lawn of

St Augustine grass. Not many people knew what they were doing with desert yards. Most guys dumped weed killer everywhere and plopped down some pots. Most guys did whatever was quickest and cheapest.

Once in a while Reggie stood in front of the piano and wondered if he felt like playing it. He didn't. He didn't want to play. He hadn't even sat down on the bench. Reggie existed in a gray area and the keys of the piano were the whitest and blackest things he'd ever seen. He rested his finger on a low B-flat and pushed it down so gently that it didn't make a sound.

MAYOR CABERA

His town was dying and its last best chance, it seemed, was a group of religious yahoos headed by a guy named Ran. Ran had told Mayor Cabrera over the phone that the group had 170 members. More importantly, they had enough money – their endowment, Ran called it – to build a facility and then sustain themselves in that facility for a hundred years. They were going to erect one plain building that would include housing, worship space, a gym, a cafeteria. Not being fancy was important to Ran's group. Mayor Cabrera didn't understand their religion. They started with the Bible but had no problem revising it whenever science proved it wrong. They thought one should be devout for moral reasons, not to cash in on everlasting life. They considered confession childish. They thought talking about Hell was wrongheaded. They never, under any circumstance, recruited. It was the opposite, Ran had told Mayor Cabrera. If someone wanted to join the group, that person had to be voted in. That person had to convince the members that he belonged, then survive a probationary period. These people were going to make their home either in Lofte or in some town in Oklahoma.

SOREN'S FATHER

Some of Soren's clothes were hanging in the closet of the clinic room, and Soren's father pulled the doors shut so he wouldn't have to look at them. He made a point to flip back the blanket every morning and put socks and shoes on his son, and he liked to be the one to remove the shoes when night fell. It was a habit, and habits were what he'd always counted on. The sight of the tiny polo shirts in their garish colors, adorned with dinosaurs and airplanes and tractors, made Soren's father think of specific days he'd spent with Soren – at the zoo, at the plaza where the Indians sold toys, at that church where the old lady read stories – but the shoes were plain and brown and not particularly beat-up. They were any kid's shoes.

There had been days when Soren's father was convinced Soren was gaining color and had expected to return from a smoke on the secret landing to find his son blinking into the steady pale light from the window, but that was delusion. His son was absent as ever. He was elsewhere. He wasn't recuperating. He was just elsewhere and nobody could guess when he might return. The doctors didn't have a clue. In the first days of the coma they'd been comforted by their charts and tests, their metabolic abnormalities and cerebral cortices and CAT scans and MRIs and they even had a fancy name for the fact that Soren's arms were bent at the elbows, hands resting on his chest, rather than straight down by his sides. 'What does that mean?' Soren's father had asked. 'What does that mean that his arms are bent?' The doctor had clicked his tongue earnestly and said, 'A lot of times it doesn't mean anything at all.' They couldn't say what had put Soren in a coma. Soren's father wasn't accustomed to medical doubletalk. This was the first medical problem of Soren's life. He didn't have allergies. He hadn't even caught those ear infections all kids were supposed to catch.

Soren's father made a point not to ask the doctors any more questions. It was up to him to consider questions he didn't want to consider, like whether Soren was supposed to keep growing, how long it would take for Soren to lose all his coordination. Soren's father didn't know how much time had to pass before his son would have to relearn the alphabet and choose a different favorite animal and a different favorite food. Would he still know what an opposite was, a rhyme? Soren's father didn't even know if his son was dreaming.

He wished he'd been present when his son had fallen into his coma. Not that his presence would've changed anything, but he wished he'd seen the start of this ordeal. He felt sorry for the piano teacher. Poor woman. Soren's father didn't care a lick about music. He'd signed Soren up for piano because it was supposed to be good for a kid's brain. Soren's father never listened to music in his truck. When he'd driven his route he'd listened to the wind rasping in the half-open windows and to the sound of his tires against the road and he'd been content. Music had always seemed irrelevant to him, and the cause of Soren's coma, he had to admit, was irrelevant too. He just wished he'd been there.

THE PIANO TEACHER

She had suffered a failure of courage in the only moment of her life when courage had been called for. She had stopped the boy from playing and no one knew it. They thought he'd stopped on his own because that's what she'd told them back when she was telling anybody anything. She'd done something wrong and then she'd lied about it. And so no one faulted her. Not her daughter. Not the boy's father.

The boy, that day, had listened almost too patiently, alert and without a word to say, while the piano teacher pointed out the parts of the piano and explained their functions. She'd sat him down on the bench and they'd flipped through the primer, a resource more for study at home than for lessons, and then she went over and pulled the curtains because the sun was angling in at eye level and she grabbed a pecan cookie to bring over to the boy, a trick she always employed with new students, a simple way to start on good terms. He was toying around on the keys, hitting them at random, softly at first and then surer. The piano teacher gently set the lid of the cookie jar back in place. She stood a moment and listened to the boy's tinkering, envying him the experience of sitting at a piano for the first time. She could almost hear something organized in what the boy was banging out, an accident of the keys. She made her way across the room to him and when she was a step from the boy, holding out the cookie and reaching with her other hand to tap his shoulder, five gallant notes cut purposefully through the air and then were trampled under by a slow cavalry of low, weighted notes. The piano teacher lost herself. She couldn't tell if the music she was hearing was fast or slow, angry or sad. She'd never heard this piece of music. There was surrender in it. Surrender to forces the boy knew nothing about. She couldn't move again until the boy's hands rested, a fraught pause in the song, and it was all she could do not to slam the fall down on the boy's fingers. A breath rushed in through her nose and she smelled the pecan cookie, she smelled the boy's hair which smelled of a clean attic, she smelled the hot dust on the windowsill cooling along with the ocean of sand outside. She lurched forward, her knee on the bench beside the boy, and pressed her palms onto the backs of his hands. The piano released a startled croak, and with that croak ringing on the air the piano teacher found herself catching the boy so he wouldn't topple straight back off the bench and bust his head.

She had not asked for this type of student. She hadn't even asked to have a *good* student. She'd been perfectly pleased with regular children who learned slowly and sensibly at thirty dollars per seventy-minute session until their parents decided they'd given piano a good enough try and let them take up high-diving or painting. She had not asked to hear music like that, the notes dragging with impotent hope. She had not asked to live in Albuquerque. She was never supposed to be in this damn desert and it wasn't her that should've been the boy's teacher. She had not asked for her gas-guzzling car. She had not asked to grow old.

In her wood-floored den, the room she'd been using for lessons, she approached the piano from a wary angle and sat on the bench without surrendering her full weight. She didn't want to press the soles of her bare feet against the pedals, and so she kept on an old pair of sandals she wore around the house. The piano teacher turned her head and gazed out the big window that looked out into the backyard. There was an orange tree that had come with the house and that had its own private sprinkler that flipped on for twenty minutes each night. The tree kept getting bigger, but the fruits it produced were tiny and sour.

Twice in her life a piano had been taken from her. This one, though she was sitting at it, had been stolen from her by the incident with the boy, and long ago her childhood piano had been sold. The piano teacher's father had once had money but then the piano teacher's stepmother had come along and spent it. Her father had allowed this to happen, had downsized their house twice and given up his hunting trips. Eventually her father had to move them to Albuquerque and come out of retirement, and that was when the piano, a lovingly maintained Bösendorfer, had been liquidated. There was still a lake in Oklahoma that bore the piano teacher's maiden name, but she had no claim to it.

She had never decided anything for herself. She'd been handed off from her father to her daughter. She wasn't from this desert. She belonged in this desert as much as the orange tree in the yard. She'd once had piano, at least. Now she had the vigils but the vigils were not hers. She didn't belong. The vigilers were more of these lost desert people, trying not to be lost. As long as you were in the desert, you were lost. You could forget for a time, but you were still lost. The piano teacher felt the same at the vigils as anyplace else. She felt separate always. She had a stale secret, she had *stopped* the boy playing, a secret she would never tell and was already tired of keeping.

DANNIE

She was up early, making breakfast for Arn, frying a pound of bacon and cutting up fruit. She had coffee brewing and she was going to put out an expensive bar of chocolate. The sliding door stood wide open, dry air washing in. Soon light would pour over the horizon and find Dannie's balcony. The sun would arrive after the dawn was long done, dopey, drifting upward like a child's balloon.

Dannie had moved to New Mexico about a year ago. She had lived in Los Angeles and now she lived in a town called Lofte in the middle of a desert basin, on a road once known as the Turquoise Trail, in the condo of a trucker. The condo was full of the trucker's belongings – books about addiction, auto racing memorabilia. The trucker was around fifty, Dannie gathered from the pictures on the walls. The condo had a bunch of magnifying glasses and pairs of binoculars and a telescope. The telescope had been out on the balcony when Dannie had moved in and she'd left it out there, slumping toward the scruffy fairways of the golf course that bordered the condo complex. The course was out of business and full of rabbit holes. Dannie sometimes gazed at the sky, but often she zeroed in on abandoned golf balls and read the tiny print on them, the handwritten initials.

Dannie had come to New Mexico after her divorce was final. She didn't know whether to feel sensible or insane. She'd come to the desert planning to stay a month and return to California recharged, but a month had passed and then eleven more had slipped away and Dannie couldn't bring herself to go back to her old life. Her old life wasn't there anymore. She had a job she could do anywhere and a balcony to linger on and she was getting enough sleep, which all seemed sensible, but she was doing one thing in particular that a sensible woman did not do: she was trying to get impregnated by some young kid she barely knew. She'd gone off the pill and she hadn't told Arn. She'd met this guy two months ago and he was practically a teenager and now they were living together and she was trying to conceive his child. Of course, it didn't ever have to be *his* child. If Dannie got pregnant and didn't want Arn to know anything about it, she could always break up with him and leave the area. She doubted Arn was attached to her. He was dazzled because she was older, but he wasn't attached. He did whatever Dannie told him to do, but there wasn't much he'd do *without* being told. He would rub her feet for a full hour if she told him to. He was attending a vigil with Dannie for a boy genius who'd fallen into a coma, spending one of the two nights off work he had each week in a parking lot because Dannie had told him she wanted company, because she couldn't stand to lose a night with him. Dannie couldn't tell what Arn thought of the vigils and she wasn't going to ask. There was no talking at the vigils, and talking *about* them on some mundane Thursday afternoon wasn't something Dannie was going to do. Arn didn't like for anyone to be upset, and if he quit, he knew, Dannie would be upset. He would probably attend every vigil till kingdom come rather than get into an argument.

Dannie pulled the last of the bacon out of the pan and rested the strips on top of the others, a paper towel layered in between. She got syrup and ketchup out. What Arn did was put the bacon in the middle and put a saucer of syrup on one side and a saucer of ketchup on the other and alternate strip for strip. Arn struck Dannie as a carrier of desirable sperm not because he had lots of dazzling positive attributes, but because he had no negative ones. Dannie had come to believe it was more important to not be an asshole than it was to set the world on fire. Arn wasn't stubborn, moody, jealous, fickle.

It was a few minutes till six. Dannie missed Arn in an embarrassing way, the way teenage girls and old women missed men. Lately she'd been breaking down crying at songs on the radio. And she craved gossip all of a sudden, something she had no dependable way to get because she no longer had any friends. She'd had friends in L.A. but she hadn't spoken to any of them since moving to New Mexico. She wasn't angry with them, hadn't gotten into a spat or anything. She'd simply stopped calling them back or answering their e-mails. She'd opened a new e-mail account and had stopped checking her old one. Dannie had felt powerful and brisk, being able to stop friendships in their tracks like that. She'd isolated herself, had broken ties with L.A. Now, she knew, she was approaching the point of no return. If she didn't get in touch with her friends to let them know she'd met a twenty-year-old kid and was trying to get knocked up, she'd never be close to any of them again.

She knew she was not going to call them. Something was wrong with her. She was going to let her friendships dry up and blow off. She was going to stand by and allow that to happen.

CECELIA

Professor Rose's door was open a crack. He was Cecelia's music history teacher. She peeked in and saw him at his computer, clicking around with the mouse. He was looking at women. Cecelia knocked and he shoved off from his desk, rolling across the small office on his chair. He pulled the door all the way open.

'Office hours?' said Cecelia.

Professor Rose frowned. 'By all means.'

He opened a folding chair for Cecelia, then he sat back down. He didn't get rid of what was on the computer screen, a couple dozen girls in bikinis.

'I need to drop your class,' Cecelia told him.

'Isn't it too late?'

'Today's the last day.'

'It's not a demanding class, is it?'

'I can't study. I can't listen to music right now.'

Professor Rose scratched the corner of his mouth.

'It's Reggie,' Cecelia said.

'I know you guys were close.'

'We had a band.'

'I see.'

'We used to listen to the music for this class together.'

Each girl on the computer screen had her hometown and occupation under her picture. Three of them were from Scottsdale, Arizona. Professor Rose's office was cramped with record albums. He had a well-trimmed beard that somehow made him appear more troubled than if he'd had an unruly beard.

'I'm sorry you lost your friend,' he said. 'He seemed like a good guy. I don't think I've ever had a friend die on me. I've had a couple betray me. I don't know what I should say to you. I never know what to say.' He looked amused, not genuinely. 'People just stop living. They're alive one day and not the next. It's very weird, when you think about it. Isn't it? It's so strange. See, I'm terrible at this.'

'No,' Cecelia said. 'You're not terrible.'

Professor Rose opened a drawer, closed it. 'What instrument do you play?' he asked.

'Just guitar.'

'What do you mean, *just* guitar?'

'Guitar,' Cecelia said.

'That's better.'

Professor Rose unhurriedly ran his eyes over the shelves and shelves of records. His screensaver popped on, obliterating the women.

'Drop my class if you wish,' he told Cecelia, 'but you should still listen to the music. If you've really got music, then music is all you've got. Look at *me*. I could've been playing in bands the last five years or I could've been teaching at this shithole. They let me stay here for five years, using me on the cheap.'

Cecelia nodded, not really understanding what Professor Rose was talking about. She didn't like feeling sorry for Professor Rose. She didn't feel like she needed to feel sorry for anyone.

'I'm not going back to giving lessons,' he said. 'No more teaching of any kind. They say it's satisfying, but I have to disagree.'

Cecelia sensed she needed to make her escape. She should've dropped the class over the computer and been done with it. It had seemed like the right thing to do, to let your professor know to his face you were quitting his class, but Cecelia now suspected that was an outdated custom. She suspected she'd always been too concerned with following the customs.

THE WOLF

On his rounds, the moon high and shrunken above him, he encountered an injured bird. The bird was young and its wing was cleanly broken and when the wolf nosed in to examine, his breath on the bird, it did not wail in alarm. It was proud, perhaps. It shivered though there was never any wind over in this park, in this enclave where humans of bygone centuries had drawn their fears and their gratitude on the rocks. The young bird, the wolf knew, was likely the victim of young humans of the current century practicing at fun, young humans who were not afraid of nor grateful for anything. The wolf was stuck. He was trying to hear his instincts but if his instincts had been working he wouldn't have to *try* to hear them. Normally he would've passed the bird without a thought, but he found himself considering the suffering of the little creature, found himself considering that the bird was young and proud and quiet. The wolf had to kill the bird. He wasn't going to eat it because it would be a choke of feathers and brittle bones, but he had to kill it. The wolf gave himself a shake as if after a rain had caught him out in the open. There was no wind so the scent of the bird was gathering. The wolf looked up at the moon and it was even smaller. The bird's eyes were set on the wolf. It had never seen a wolf and was never meant to see one. This bird was none of the wolf's business. Its beak was a vivid yet translucent orange. Its feet looked disposable, not like they were meant to last a whole lifetime. They had, though – the bird's life was at a close. The bird finally looked away. It was smaller than the wolf's paw. The wolf realized suddenly that the bird, though tiny, was not young. The bird was fully grown and had survived a lot and that's why it was proud. The bird was old like the wolf.

The wolf moved away a stride at a time, staring ahead at the silhouettes of the broken hills that marked the edge of the park, waiting for a new scent, and he even began to trot before he slowed and stopped again. He'd moved his body away but some other part of him was still standing over the bird. He turned, backtracking. He never backtracked. But he did now. He returned to the bird and without looking at the tiny animal he crushed the life out of it with his paw and shoved the carcass under a rock and fled.

The wolf darted through several clusters of half-built houses and then to make up time he cut through a vast shopping complex that had been built in the northern part of Albuquerque. He swiftly passed a bank of loading docks and then an area where plants were kept in pots and then a bunch of dumpsters that smelled like nothing, that smelled of steel and cardboard. There was a shop that reeked of cut hair and then the wolf rounded a restaurant and as he passed the back of it he noticed a radio sitting on an overturned crate. There were a bunch of other overturned crates and an ashtray that was empty because of the wind. The wolf smelled the humans inside the building. He smelled singular harsh liquids. The wolf did not know this area well and should not have been loitering. He sidled up to the dormant radio and tried to make sense of it. It was plugged into the wall and was producing only static. The back door of the restaurant was propped open and the wolf could see down a long, empty hall. He began nosing the big flat buttons on the radio and he found the one that changed the numbers on the screen. He was changing the station. The radio smelled like grease, which to the wolf was a clean smell. He changed the station and changed it again, trying to be gentle because each time he nudged the front of the radio it teetered. He heard voices and deeper voices and he heard human laughter. He heard music but it was drowned in static. He heard an organ, and a woman singing softly, and blocks of wood being tonked together. The static came in waves. The wolf didn't understand enough about the radio. He looked behind him, into the open, and saw the parking lot give way to a pebbly field of nothing and he knew that beyond what he could see from this vantage the pebbly field gave way to a low road that led to the great, raised road. The wolf was far behind schedule. The business with the bird and now this radio. If the wolf was stopping here it should've been because he smelled food the humans had discarded. His rounds had once been his life, a duty that defined him, the most important part of him. The night had been everything and the day only a time in between that had to be tolerated. The wolf began poking all the buttons with his snout. There had been one red light on the radio's front and now there were three. The noise was louder but still mostly hissing. There was chatter in several languages. Only when the radio clattered backward off the crate, skittering a bottle hard into the wall, did the wolf breathe full again. He knew what to do finally, knew to run away, to push himself to a righteous sprint that might get him to where he needed to go.

SOREN'S FATHER

When Soren had played that music and fallen into his coma, his father, along with his piano teacher, had been attacked as frauds. Among the attackers were the Catholic Church and also a big atheist who had a show on cable TV. Neither party had heard the music, but instead of tempering their positions, that fact only made them more vociferous. They said the fact that the music had not been released to the public was more proof that a scam had been perpetrated. The Catholics had released a tougher-than-usual statement that referred to Soren's case specifically and then went on to condemn all false miracles. The atheist, who always had sweat on his brow and called himself a *humanist*, implored Soren's father to come clean, implored him to admit Soren didn't write the music, to admit that Soren's father and the piano teacher had seen an opportunity when Soren had fallen unconscious and had swiftly, ruthlessly capitalized on it. Soren's father had never done anything ruthless in his whole life, and had rarely done anything swift. And he'd said about a dozen words total to that piano teacher. He'd seen her briefly at the hospital when Soren was brought in and hadn't heard a peep from her since – probably scared into hiding by that first rush of media harassment. They'd been gone a long time now, the news people, and Soren's father hoped the piano teacher was okay. He remembered her clothes, a dressy kind of T-shirt and slacks that didn't go all the way down to her ankles. She'd seemed frustrated, angry even.

The piano teacher taped all her sessions and she'd turned the tape of Soren's session over to Soren's father and to the authorities. The music was sixteen seconds long and then you could hear Soren falling and the piano teacher catching him. All that fuss over sixteen seconds of music. There'd been a meeting where three experts offered up their opinions. Only one believed it was possible that Soren had written the music, but all three agreed they'd never heard it before. Soren's father had let it be known that he would not be selling the music or allowing it to be used for any commercial purpose, that it was Soren's music and he could decide what to do with it when he woke up, and this was viewed by Soren's father's detractors as a strategy, a way to build mystery and hold out for a higher price when he finally did sell the music. Soren's father was not going to sell the music. He hadn't even listened to it but once. There wasn't a whole lot to it. It was certainly sad, but most slow piano music was. He had the original tape somewhere safe and he tried not to think about whether or not his son was a genius. He didn't know him as a genius. He knew him as his son, whose favorite food was olives, who couldn't stand having a comb run through his hair, who enjoyed folding the laundry and making perfect squares out of T-shirts.

In the weeks following the lesson, about a dozen lawyers called Soren's father. They called wanting him to reconsider his position regarding the music, wanting him to entertain offers, wanting to represent him if he was going to do any television appearances, wanting to know if he felt he was being slandered.

Thankfully, because Soren's father had *not* gone on TV, had *not* accused anyone of slandering him, because he had stayed in the clinic and mostly out of view and in his worn jeans and windbreaker didn't impress anyone as a mastermind, the media hoopla had died down. In place of attention from reporters, the weekly vigil had emerged. Soren's father was not comfortable being the object of attention, whether the attention came from churches or TV hosts or anonymous Albuquerqueans, and he'd hoped the vigil would be a one-time thing, then a two-time thing, three-time, but it had been going for a month now and the attendees had grown from half a dozen the first night to close to a hundred. These people seemed to be on Soren's side, but still they made Soren's father self-conscious, down there peering six stories up. They made him feel there were things he ought to be doing that he wasn't. On one level they were simply well-wishers, but they also had wishes for themselves that probably weren't simple at all, hopes to *get* something out of Soren, and Soren didn't seem to have anything to give. Apparently Soren had turned over everything when he wrote that music, music the vigilers had of course not even heard. The vigilers were shivering campers, and Soren was their fire. These people were cold in their souls, and if being near Soren offered them comfort then Soren's father supposed that was okay. The vigils only meant Soren's father had to close the blinds each Wednesday evening and that for a few hours he couldn't go out to the landing and smoke. Soren's father felt bad for the vigilers, really. They were waiting and didn't know what for. Soren's father knew what he was waiting for. He was waiting to get his son back.

DANNIE

Arn's night off, and no vigil. Dannie was sitting with him at the kitchen table, the oven light casting shadows. Dannie had a bowl of cut fruit out, picking at it.

'I'm not going to start sleeping all day like you do.'

'I don't think you should,' said Arn.

'Then how are we going to see each other more?'

'Quality, right?' said Arn. 'Not quantity.'

'I want you to go to sleep right now. I don't care if you're not tired. Tomorrow we're spending the entire day together. We're going around doing normal-people activities in the sunshine.'

'Like what?'

'The zoo, for one. And we're going to happy hour.'

'What if I don't feel happy?'

'You go to happy hour to *get* happy,' Dannie said.

'Oh, I see.'

'Eat some of this fruit.'

'No way.'

'It'll go bad.'

'You can say the word "fruit" all you want. Those are still just sugar-veggies.'

Dannie didn't laugh. She gently chewed a grape. 'I was lying when I said I was twenty-seven.'

Arn stuck his chin out.

'I didn't want you to think I was old. I'm really twenty-nine.'

'Okay,' Arn said. 'Lying doesn't bother me. It's not a pet peeve of mine.'

'The idea of dating an older woman. I was letting you . . .'

'You didn't need to, but it's okay you did.'

'Not a pet peeve?'

'Lies. The truth. What's the big difference, really?'

Arn's face was sober and untroubled.

'You're not going to be mad at me, not even for thirty seconds?'

'The issue's dead as Doris Day. Whoever that is. Or was.'

'But I was dishonest. It's a betrayal.'

'You weren't honest, but I don't feel betrayed. Takes more than that to make me feel like someone betrayed me.'

'So you accept my apology?'

Arn nodded. 'Twenty-seven, twenty-nine – either way you're a broken-down old lady.'

REGGIE

A guitar materialized, leaning in a stand right next to the piano. Reggie picked the guitar up and it felt at home in his hands, but he didn't play it. He put it back on the stand. Whoever was running this show knew he was a musician, and maybe was trying to be hospitable to Reggie, giving him a way to pacify himself, but he didn't want pacification. He hoped he wasn't offending anyone – it was a gorgeous guitar, made of unstained white oak that smelled of broken nutshells – but in his predicament happy music seemed mocking and unhappy music indulgent. And writing music, making something out of nothing in the context of this void, would require optimism that Reggie did not at the moment possess. Reggie wasn't ignorant anymore. There was plenty that was being kept from him, but he wasn't ignorant enough to believe that writing a song had any point.

The guitar appeared, and then sometime after that, down at the dimmest end of the main hall, Reggie found a bar – a full bar with stools and all the paddles jutting up that showed what beers you could choose from. The liquor bottles were a wave of color against the back wall. There was a bowl of lemons and a bowl of limes and a cutting board and paring knife. All the little tools and shakers and specially shaped glasses. Reggie had never been behind a bar, and he stood back there but didn't touch anything. He leaned with his hip against the back counter. Tending bar had always looked pleasant to him, a job that required practice but not originality, much like tending yards. The beer paddles were arresting in their variety but Reggie wasn't thirsty for a beer. He'd never been much of a drinker. At parties he'd nurse from the same plastic cup for hours, and he'd rarely tried hard liquor. He slid open the drawers one by one and in the very last drawer found a baggie of marijuana and a small, heavy pipe. Like alcohol, Reggie partook in pot now and then but didn't much enjoy it. It made him more talkative, he supposed, but that was about it. He slid the drawer closed. Reggie turned and looked the bottles over. Many of the brands he'd never heard of. There was a mirror on the wall behind the bottles and for the first time since he'd arrived in this place he saw his face. It was the same. It was an empty street that could've been either lazy or desolate.

Reggie went and stood in the center of the main hall and peered up into the perpetual dusk, or maybe it was dawn. It was like looking into a weak headlight on a foggy night. Reggie kept doing his laps, trying not to pay attention to the speed at which he walked. He was barefoot and the floor was perfectly clean.

He tried to piece together his accident, but could not remember what might have caused it. He had a quick clip of the moment after, the tart smells of the wrecked truck, the glare of the sun off the scattered glass, his blood leaking out of him onto the seat. And he had the moment just before. He'd been humming a new song, had felt excited like always, and calm, and there'd been no one in his mirrors, not one car up ahead. He couldn't call up one note of that song now, like it had been stolen. Not one note.

Reggie thought of women, and it felt different than when he thought about food. Food gave him no feeling at all, which wound up making him frustrated, but imagining women gave him solace. The feeling was simpler than when he'd fantasized in the living world, because now there was no pressure. There were no women around. He could think of them as a benevolent, plural entity. He wouldn't have to approach a particular girl and say the correct thing. He didn't have to feel hollow about the countless women he would never possess. Thinking of women was like thinking of sunny prairies. The backs of their knees. The tops of their feet. Reggie didn't have to worry that he was wasting time with his reveries. Both waste and time were dead notions.

CECELIA

Cecelia agreed to meet Nate, the drummer, for dinner. He'd wanted to pick up sandwiches and eat in the barn behind his house, but that was where they used to hold band practice and Cecelia didn't care to ever enter that barn again. It wasn't really a barn. It was a spiffy backyard cabin. A brand new hot tub hung from its rafters on ropes because Nate's dad hadn't gotten around to having the thing installed. Whenever they'd played loudly, the hot tub would sway above them.

Cecelia met Nate at a diner on Route 66, his backup idea. The only people who enjoyed the whole Route 66 thing were rich people who didn't *have* to stay in seedy hotels and eat at crappy diners, people like Nate who found the idea of migrating because you were down on your luck quaint. Nate had a thirty-year-old car that was in gorgeous condition and Cecelia had a thirteen-year-old car that was an absolute piece of shit, and they both fit right in on Route 66.

Nate was waiting for Cecelia when she got there, out in front of the diner, leaning against a phone booth. Cecelia felt like Nate was already a complete stranger. They'd spoken only once since Reggie died. Nate had tried to explain why he wasn't going to the funeral, and Cecelia had explained why she was. Nate didn't know Cecelia had chickened out and sat in her car in the parking lot.

They went in and ordered burgers with green chiles. The table had a dozen condiments on it, a huddle of syrups and hot sauces. Nate looked cheated. The band had been his project. Reggie had been about as close to a friend as Nate could come.

'I wanted to meet because I need to know what your thoughts are concerning the band.' Nate struggled to get his straw out of its paper tube.

'Meaning what?'

'We need a new member. You got any ideas?'

Cecelia drew an impatient breath.

'You heard me,' said Nate. 'This is what bands do. They reconstitute.'

'Another one-of-a-kind songwriter?'

'They're around.'

'Reggie *was* the band. He was the architect and we were brick-layers.'

'You were his apprentice. Maybe it's time to ply the trade. Maybe you're the answer, right here under our noses.'

This was how Nate's mind worked. Everything could be fixed by hustling. Nate had booked all the gigs and gotten local critics to review the band and had bought a bunch of equipment with his own money.

'I'm presently not touching my guitar,' Cecelia said. 'That'll make things tricky.'

'You're going to stop playing music?' Nate asked. 'You're going to take up jogging or collect stamps? Just keep going to those vigil things and waste away? That's what Reggie would want?'

'Let's leave Reggie out of it,' said Cecelia.

'I'll put it this way. I'm keeping the band going and I'm retaining the name. So what I'm really asking is if you're quitting.'

'Then, yes. I'm quitting.'

'Think it over. Let your emotions settle. Or better yet, leave your emotions out of it.' Nate looked out the window. There wasn't much out behind the diner – some dumpsters and a sagging fence. Somehow you could tell the wind was blowing. 'Our name has some recognition factor in this town, you know.'

'With a dozen people.'

'You're underestimating us and you know it.'

'No one wants to hear us without Reggie and you know *that*.'

'They'd get over it. Just like us, they need to get over it. We can mourn Reggie the person, but Reggie the band member we've got to move on without. Lots of bands have lost a member.'

'Not one I've been in.'

They were quiet for a while, resting their cases, each testily examining a menu even though they'd already ordered. Eventually the waitress showed back up. She dropped off their food and Nate asked her if she'd heard of a band called Shirt of Apes.

'Shit of Apes?' said the waitress.

'*Shirt* of Apes,' Nate pronounced.

'I don't think so. Y'all need anything else?'

Nate shook his head and the waitress left.

'That doesn't mean anything,' he said.

Cecelia didn't believe there was any decision to be made. Even if she'd wanted to keep the band going, where would they get songs from without Reggie? Nate had never written a note in his life and Cecelia was just another chick who had some complaints she put to guitar.

'Just have an open mind,' Nate said. 'Can you at least do that?'

'My mind is open,' said Cecelia. 'It's the topic that's closed.'

When they were done eating, Nate paid the bill and they went outside. The air smelled cheap, like sand and rubber. Cecelia didn't want to make plans to see Nate again. Without the band their paths might not cross, and that was fine. They said goodbye and Cecelia moved toward her car, but Nate followed her, trailing a few feet behind. Cecelia slowed and Nate caught up and walked her backward a step like they were dancing. He put her against her car with his body and leaned in with the unmistakable intent of kissing her. Cecelia squirmed, her breath misplaced, Nate's eyes close to hers, the chemical smell of his hair all around. Cecelia could not stop their lips from brushing. She couldn't stop a kiss of sorts from occurring before she jerked herself back against her Scirocco, her elbow banging the window. She was flabbergasted. She looked at Nate, hoping for an explanation, but the look that came over his face meant that he had nothing to be sorry about. Cecelia tried to duck into her car but then remembered the driver door handle was broken. Nate didn't give any ground and Cecelia had to sidestep away from him and circle around to the passenger door. She glanced over the top of the car toward Nate, and he was still standing there, almost jaunty, smirking at Cecelia uncharitably as she fumbled with her keys.

DANNIE

She needed to convince her body that she was settled in New Mexico for the long haul, so she finally started putting away all the trucker's things. She carried armload after armload of clutter to the extra bedroom, a room she rarely entered, and loaded up the closet until it was spilling. She stacked pictures on the bed, constructed mounds of knickknacks on the floor. Soon the window was blocked with extra chairs and wall racks. Dannie thought it odd that a person who lived in the desert owned a mirror with a cactus and a wolf on it. That's what people did, though. People who lived near the beach filled their cottages with shells. In cities, people jammed their lofts with sharp, efficient gadgets.

Dannie got the idea that the trucker, like her, had moved to New Mexico to escape. In his case it was probably alcohol or pills, in her case the wreckage of a failed marriage and a mother who'd found religion and was impossible to talk to. As Dannie piled all the trucker's belongings into the extra bedroom, she wondered if he would miss any of it. Dannie wished she could throw it all out, take it to the dump and keep the extra room for a study or a gym. Maybe the trucker wanted rid of all this shit but didn't have the guts to do something about it, to turn it all over to the gulls at the landfill. Dannie wished she could mail every picture and bookend and paper towel holder to people she used to know. She was likely missing a staggering number of showers and weddings and housewarmings. She was way behind on gifts. She took a photo off the wall in which the trucker was skydiving, his thick gray hair popping out of his helmet, and carried it down the hall and tossed it on the pile.

Later in the day, tired from rearranging the condo, she sat on her balcony with two rock-hard avocados in her lap. It was finally chilly enough to wear a sweater. Dannie was considering returning the avocados. The idea would either burn off over the course of the day, like the desert haze, or it would gather. She'd bought the avocados the day before. They were nowhere near ripe, and she wanted guacamole. She could always buy guacamole at the restaurant where she bought her little batches of sopapilla, but there was nothing like spanking fresh guacamole. If she were in L.A. and had bought the avocados at the supermarket she would've returned them in a heartbeat, but the store in Lofte was a mom-and-pop place and they needed every sale they could get. Mom and Pop were old. Their store was failing.

Dannie, as sometimes happened when she was alone at the condo, was having dark thoughts about Arn. She suspected he was using her for a place to stay. There was circumstantial evidence, namely that he didn't seem to have had a place of his own when they'd met. He had a topper on his pickup and Dannie was pretty sure he'd been sleeping in the bed of the truck and keeping his stuff in the cab. She'd never asked him to move in. He'd slept over for several nights, taking sick days off work, then one day he'd stayed at the condo all day when Dannie went out, then before she knew it there was a stack of his shirts on the dresser and bacon in the fridge. He was fully moved in and had never had to bring stuff from anywhere else, hadn't carried in any lamps or books or spoken of a broken lease. Dannie didn't have grounds to be indignant, since she was basically stealing Arn's sperm, but she had grounds for good old romantic worry because she'd grown to like the kid. She imagined him up at that sonic observatory where he worked, and hoped he was imagining her at the condo. The owner of the observatory kept a huge poetry book up there, like 700 pages. No novels, no magazines, no puzzle books. The idea was that when the aliens contacted us, the first thing they would hear was our poetry, our most worthy expression. Dannie pictured Arn vacantly leafing through the humungous tome, letting the stanzas drift into and out of his mind, preoccupied with thoughts about her.

She sniffed the avocados. They smelled like California. She didn't want to live in California ever again, but she thought she'd like to take Arn there. For all she knew, he'd never been out of New Mexico. He was a good guy. She wouldn't be worrying about his motives, she knew, if they were the same age. She doubted a kid his age could genuinely be interested in her, knew *how* to be interested in her. She had lied and told him she was twenty-seven, then come clean and told him she was twenty-nine, but really she was thirty-three. She was thinking of taking Arn to where she grew up and she couldn't even be honest with him about her age. Every relationship Dannie had ever been in had been farcical, and this one was no exception. What had ever led her to believe she could be married? In Los Angeles, to a guy from Los Angeles? Dannie was glad she hadn't had a baby there. The baby would've turned out like her, thirty-three years old and with no idea who she was. She wanted to have a baby in a place where it could grow up to be itself, where it could take each morning and afternoon and night as it came, where it could live like Arn, relying on instinct rather than twisting itself in knots with scheming.

Arn worked nights, at a place where they monitored outer space for sonic anomalies. It was a rip-off of a government site in another part of the state called Very Large Array. All Arn did was sit in a chair all night and watch meters. Arn felt this job suited him because he didn't care whether aliens existed. He didn't mind solitude. Arn went to work with a gallon jug of water every night and drank the whole thing before morning. He had a taut bulbous belly, like a toddler. He had two nights a week off, and Wednesday nights he went with Dannie to the vigils. In a way, those were their most intimate times, right next to each other in a drawn-out silence – no sex or suspicion or anything else. The vigils were a sanctuary, where no one had a past or a plan. It seemed like bad form to show affection at the vigils, but sometimes Arn would take Dannie's hand and hide it in his jacket pocket so he could hold it, like something valuable he'd found on the street, a good luck charm, and this reminded Dannie of misbehaving in high school. Dannie hadn't noticed many other couples. There was a pair who looked like grad students, the guy in a flannel shirt and studded belt and the girl always wearing tights and scarves that didn't match. Then there was a lesbian couple who sat with their knees touching. At first Dannie had dragged Arn down to the clinic, but now he didn't seem to mind going. He wasn't a vigiler in his own right, not yet anyway, but if you went to the vigils you went to the vigils. No vigiler was above any other. No one was on probation, no one received gold stars. No one had to give explanations or listen to them. It was enough to simply want the vigils to continue, and Dannie wanted them to continue forever, wanted to keep meeting these same strangers smack in the middle of each week until the weeks ran out. She knew for that to happen, Soren had to stay in his coma. She wanted the vigils to continue *and* she wanted Soren to wake up healthy. The vigils were good news in Dannie's life and they could only be stopped by other good news.

Dannie stood and positioned herself behind the telescope. She aimed it down the street, whisked past the Javelina, past all four stoplights, until she found the market. The old couple was out front, eating their lunch. They were talking, and then the old woman noticed something at her feet. Her shoelace was untied. The old man unhurriedly set his plate beside him on the bench and went down to one knee. The woman smiled faintly. He was tying her shoe. He was tying her goddamn shoe. There was no way Dannie was going to return the avocados. She couldn't. She knew what she'd do instead. She'd break them open and get the pits out and plant them down below her balcony. She could water them from up here. She could root for them. Root for them to root. They'd be something to wait for, to invest herself in. This was another way she could convince her body she was settled.

THE GAS STATION OWNER

He turned off the radio, which always went to static this time of day. He had the disassembled parts of an old pricing gun on the counter, and he finally gave up on the thing and scraped the parts into a cardboard box with his forearm. From his stool behind the register he saw a slick sedan with California plates roll up to the nearside pump. It was that gal who was renting out Terrence's place. She had on a cream-colored coat with a city look to it that she buttoned up as she stood by and watched a kid about young enough to be her son select low-octane and get the pump chugging. It wasn't her son. The gas station owner already knew it wasn't her son but after the kid got the nozzle set up the gal leaned him against the car and planted one on him. The gas station owner had seen the gal around but had never laid eyes on the kid. If he had his own car, he got gas for it elsewhere. The pair of them were still smooching, so the gas station owner averted his eyes. He idly tapped the keys of his adding machine, thumping out a nonsense sum. The truth was, it was nice to have a new couple in Lofte. The town didn't get new couples. It didn't get new anything. When the gas station owner had moved here, all those decades ago, it had been as lively and hopeful as any place. The turquoise trade had still been humming. Families couldn't wait to take car trips across the desert in their station wagons. The gas station owner had thought he was making a bold change, making his own way in life, moving from predictable, peopled Albuquerque to this spirited basin outpost. The spirit was gone now. The money was gone. If the gas station owner tried to sell his house now he'd get about enough for a steak dinner and a beer. And he hadn't even escaped anything. He was in the same old desert, living by the desert's rules – still, in his heart, afraid of the desert. He'd never challenged it. He'd only taken an elk or two from the desert when an elk was offered.

When the Audi was full up, the couple came into the store. The gal asked for the restrooms and the gas station owner pointed the way. He got a jolt of pride about once a week when a lady asked to use his restroom because he kept it spotless. The gal disappeared into the back hall and the kid stepped to the counter with cash wadded in his hand. He stood there without saying anything, squinting against the light of the big window behind the gas station owner.

'What brings you all from California?'

The kid glanced out toward the car. 'She's the one from California,' he said.

'Oh,' said the gas station owner. 'What about you then? What lucky burg has the pleasure of claiming you?'

'I'm from all over,' the kid said. 'I guess I was born in Ohio or something.'

'Ohio. Never been. Is it nice?'

'Every place is the same,' the kid said. He wasn't squinting any- more. 'Some places it rains a lot and some places it doesn't rain at all. Other than that, every place is exactly the same.'

'How are they the same?'

'Bunch of people acting like they know what they're doing when really they don't know shit.'

'I never heard it put like that before.' The gas station owner stood up off the stool. His knees weren't what they used to be. He wanted to ask the kid more questions because the kid obviously didn't want to answer them. 'Did you all move out here for work?'

'I work at that observatory,' the kid said.

The kid counted out the money owed for the gas and put coins with it. He set it on the counter and the gas station owner left it sit- ting there.

'That place where they listen to the stars?' he asked the kid.

The kid nodded.

'Aliens were trying to get hold of me, I don't believe I'd take that call.'

'I want this too.' The kid picked up a bulky chocolate bar off a rack and put another dollar with the money.

'I'm Mr Fair,' the gas station owner said. He offered his hand and the kid set his jaw and reluctantly shook.

The kid didn't give a name, so the gas station owner asked him for it.

'Why do you want my name? What's the point?'

'I'm a curious old codger. I'm a curious old codger and you're a respectful young man. When we run into each other on the street, we'll know what to say.'

'I could give you a fake name,' the kid said. 'Give me a minute to think.'

'Everybody's got a name and everybody's from somewhere. And I don't believe you're from Ohio.'

The kid started unwrapping the chocolate. Without looking up, he said, 'If I had a cozy spot in the world like this I'd never leave it, either. I'd stay nested in all day and wait for people with things to do to stop by so I could talk their ears off.'

The gas station owner chuckled. 'Nobody *gave* me this station, you know. It wasn't a gift.'

'I'm just saying, you're really good at sitting inside it.'

'Thank you.'

'You got a talent.'

'And how about you? What's your talent?'

'I'm a people person,' the kid said.

'Yeah, I was picking up on that.'

'Everyone's got to make a cozy place, don't they? Whatever way they can. You got your ways, I got mine.'

The gas station owner was impressed. The kid was like a plucky raccoon poking back at an old bear. The gas station owner tried to think of something else to say, something to confuse the kid, but then the gal came back out from the restroom, a placid look on her face. The kid broke the chocolate bar and gave the gal half, and she nuzzled his cheek. She said goodbye to the gas station owner and then the kid held the door open for her. The gas station owner watched the pair all the way to their car, leaning into each other and gnawing on their candy, but neither looked back at him. He lowered himself back down onto his stool and then sat still, his back straight, nothing moving inside the station except settling dust.

MAYOR CABRERA

He sat in the basement of the motel he ran, the Javelina, watching a movie about a mayor who slaughtered all the new people who moved to his town. The psychotic mayor looked like Colonel Sanders, and this was making Mayor Cabrera hungry for fried chicken. Fried chicken wasn't something he cooked himself, and Lofte's lone restaurant didn't offer it.

The motel had two guests, two single men, and they were probably settling in for the night. They wouldn't bother Mayor Cabrera. He wanted fried chicken but his nose was full of the scent of elk stew. He was sick of elk stew. The mayor on TV was holding a big cookout in the town square. Whenever he spoke loudly, addressing the crowd, his accent got Southern. The whole premise of the movie, to Mayor Cabrera, rang false. As mayor of a small town, you needed every new citizen you could get. You would never murder your own tax base, your own economy. If there dwelled within you homicidal urges that could not be suppressed, you would drive a couple towns over to do your killing.

Mayor Cabrera's town, Lofte, was in trouble. Two guests? The business at the Javelina told volumes about the health of the town, and two guests in a night was not enough to break even. Mayor Cabrera didn't want to be mayor anymore. Being the mayor of a healthy town was one thing, but being in charge of a doomed town, going down with the ship and barely being compensated for it, was another. Usually being mayor didn't mean much more than sitting at the head of the table during town council meetings. The other members kept the budget, brought items up for votes. Soon enough, though, Mayor Cabrera would be called upon to lead. He would be looked to.

Mayor Cabrera stood and stirred the elk stew. He took his shirt off and sat back down in his undershirt. Mayor Cabrera wore button-front shirts adorned with Western scenes because out-of-towners seemed to like it. For town meetings or when the occasional Turquoise Trail bus tour came through, he even donned a cowboy hat. No one could pin down Mayor Cabrera's ethnic background, not even him. He had some United States Indian in him and some Mexican Indian and some regular Mexican and probably some regular American. Lofte, which was mostly poor white, had elected him, he believed, because they considered his murky blend of heritage to be perfectly New Mexican.

The psychotic mayor in the movie was spying on a young couple playing tennis, licking his lips. Maybe the mayor was a cannibal.

Maybe he was going to have another cookout and feed the towns-people their neighbors. The phone rang and Mayor Cabrera picked it up and said, 'Javelina.'

'I'm in nineteen. I was wondering what the story was on room service.'

'That's a very short story. Your best bet is the diner down the street. They're usually open till midnight. Or maybe eleven.'

'I'm watching this movie. I'm kind of in for the night. You don't have *anything* down there? Any food I could buy off you?'

'I have some stew I could bring up.'

'Is it good? I got cash.'

'It tastes like stew.'

'I don't want to miss what happens here. The guy who was Freddie in *Nightmare on Elm Street* is this crazy mayor. You ever seen this thing?'

'I think I have.'

'He's wearing some kind of sash.'

'Why don't I bring you by a bowl in a few minutes? There's no charge.'

'I appreciate that. I got plenty of cash, but I sure like to hang on to it. I like to keep it right here with me.'

Mayor Cabrera saw the commercials ending and then the man told him as much. They got off the phone. Mayor Cabrera opened a cabinet and began hunting for some plastic bowls, wishing he hadn't mentioned the stew, feeling suddenly uncharitable, feeling that every little thing he did every day of his life he did out of some pathetic idea of professionalism. He did what people asked because it was easier than thinking about what he really ought to be doing. He served and served.

CECELIA

For days the sky had looked like rain, but only this morning had it begun grumbling. Cecelia and her mother were in the living room, the windows open, the TV on.

'Driving the birds crazy,' Cecelia's mother said. Her wheelchair was positioned in a way that allowed her to look through the kitchen and out the back screen door, toward her chickens. She didn't need the wheelchair. It had once been her sister's, Cecelia's Aunt Tam's, in the months before she'd died. Cecelia's mother had taken it out of the hall closet where it had been folded quietly for ages and had opened it up and polished the hardware and buffed the leather. That was all fine, but when she was done she hadn't put the chair back in the closet. She'd started sitting in it now and then, to watch TV, and in time it became the only chair she'd use. The husband Cecelia's Aunt Tam had left behind still lived in Lofte. He was the mayor, in fact. He and Cecelia's mother had once been thick as thieves, but now they rarely spoke.

'You ever think of getting a dog?' Cecelia said. She didn't say, *Like a normal person.*

Her mother made a face. 'They kill little critters and leave the carcasses on your porch.'

'Because they want to impress you and show gratitude.'

'With a dead chipmunk?'

Cecelia knew why her mother couldn't get a dog. A dog was an actual personality to engage; the chickens were merely a presence, something other than nothing. They generated a busy, low warbling that sounded like far-off weather.

'Can I make you breakfast?' Cecelia asked.

Her mother again made a face.

'How about oatmeal?' Cecelia started to get up.

'Not yet,' Cecelia's mother said. 'I'll have something at lunchtime.'

'I'll make you a bowl and if you don't like it we'll throw it out.'

Lately Cecelia's mother barely ate. Cecelia saw her pick at dry cereal, but no real food. Her mother's loss of appetite seemed planned. It was too abrupt, like she was making a statement.

A woman on TV laughed. The Home Shopping Network. The woman was brushing a cat. She had a big wad of fur in her hand, and was proud of it.

'What class you got today?' Cecelia's mother asked.

'Poetry.'

Cecelia's mother raised an eyebrow. 'Did they tell you the secret yet?'

'What secret?'

'Of how to write poetry. There's a secret to everything, you know. They don't want you to think so, but there is. There's a trick.' Cecelia's mother held still, looking upward. Cecelia thought she was thinking about artists and their esoteric know-how until she clicked her cheek and said, 'They're not making a peep.' The chickens.

'I took the class so I could write good song lyrics,' Cecelia offered. She would've dropped the class when she'd dropped music history, because writing song lyrics was no longer in her plans, but she needed nine credits in order to keep her scholarship.

'I don't care for lyrics,' Cecelia's mother said. 'Or people banging on drums. I like it when you play your guitar.'

'I know you do.'

'Why don't you play something sugary sweet for me? Play it loud so the birds can hear it.'

'I'll play for *you*,' Cecelia said. 'I don't perform for pets.'

Cecelia made herself get up and go to her room. She opened her closet and grasped the guitar by the neck. She would turn her brain off and let her fingers strum as she'd trained them to. Playing a song or two on her guitar was a small chore compared to explaining to her mother why she *didn't* want to play, explaining about Reggie, explaining about the band being over and the class she'd dropped and the stunt Nate had pulled at the diner, making a pass at her, and the vigils she'd been going to where she would sit for hours with cold hands and a stiff neck thinking about fairness and fate, and that her piece of shit car, since Cecelia could now hear the rain finally falling, was going to leak and Cecelia would have to take towels out with her the next time she drove somewhere.

REGGIE

An oversized belt buckle showed up, sitting on the piano, and he recognized it immediately. It had been a gift from his uncle when he was seven years old. Reggie had worn the buckle for months and then finally his uncle had come to visit from Phoenix. Reggie's uncle didn't have kids. He was laid-back, unlike Reggie's father with all his rules and his chart that kept track of chores and the little bank he'd given Reggie for the paltry pay he was awarded for the chores. Reggie's uncle drank beer like he was in a commercial. He had a tan. Reggie's uncle had cruised into town in a Corvette and parked it prominently in Reggie's family's driveway for the neighbors to gawk at. And Reggie gawked at it too, later, when everyone was inside, his uncle telling a long story about getting lost on a hike. Reggie went outside and looked in the open driver-side window of the low black car, and never had he seen or even imagined such a dashboard. The inside of the Corvette was a cockpit, like something out of *Star Wars*. There were a hundred controls. The driver's seat was sunk down among the buttons and levers and displays. Reggie reached in and stroked the leather of the seat and then gripped the steering wheel. An air-freshener in the shape of a nude woman dangled from the rearview and Reggie leaned in the car trying to smell it. He didn't dare open the door. His uncle came out of the house then to get something from the car and Reggie straightened up and took a step back. His uncle approached with that grin and rested his hand on Reggie's shoulder, but as he went to pull the door open he stiffened. He stepped away from Reggie and pressed his eyes closed and then pointed to the door so Reggie would look. His grin was long gone. On the door were four or five neat scratches. It took a moment before Reggie realized the scratches were at the height of his belt buckle and understood what had happened. Reggie's uncle was cursing under his breath. It occurred to Reggie to say he was sorry but he couldn't because he'd never seen his uncle angry before. His uncle thumbed the scratches and shook his head, seeming to forget Reggie was there, and Reggie escaped around the house and sulked in the backyard.

Now Reggie touched the belt buckle but didn't lift it off the polished wood of the piano. The buckle was a skull with wings, the skull smiling deviously. The next time Reggie had seen his uncle, the next big holiday, his uncle hadn't had the Corvette and he didn't seem as tan or carefree. It was easy for Reggie to see that he'd turned out a lot more like his father than his uncle. Reggie liked to work and didn't care to impress anyone except the people closest to him. When he'd died he'd been driving an old Dodge truck his father had handed down to him.

Reggie turned away from the piano with the intention of leaving the main hall and almost walked into a bureau, broad and hunched-looking, close enough to the piano that when Reggie backed up a step they seemed like a set. He knew this bureau. It didn't tower like it had when he was a kid, but he recognized it. It was his father's. And here it was. His parents had new furniture now, but the bureau squatting mutely in Reggie's space had been his father's years ago. As a kid, Reggie used to sneak into his parents' bedroom and creak the bureau drawers open and pore over the contents. There were boxes in the bureau and boxes inside those boxes. Jewelry that probably wasn't worth much but that Reggie could think of as pirate treasure. Photos of relatives Reggie had never met. Car titles and birth certificates in baroque script. Tie pins and cigar cutters.

Reggie had stolen a buffalo nickel. He had no idea why he hadn't simply asked for it, but instead he'd filched the old coin and taken it back to his room and after that he'd never again picked through the bureau. The nickel had been old when Reggie had taken it and it was older now. Reggie had no idea where his father had gotten the nickel or what meaning it held. His father, if he'd noticed it missing, had never said anything about it. Of course he'd noticed it missing. Reggie, as he'd grown older, had often wanted to confess, to clear his conscience and have a laugh about it, but he never had. Now it was too late. He wondered if, when his parents were finally ready to sift through *his* possessions, they'd find the nickel in the old fire engine bank.

Next was a program from a chorus recital Reggie had performed in, perched in the piano's music holder, which to that point had sat empty. Reggie didn't touch the program or even look closely. He knew it by the yellow-winged birds on the cover. The program marked the first experience Reggie'd had with a girl. His memory was a plaything, he gathered. He'd known his afterlife was a plaything, but apparently his history on earth was too. Kimmy Susteran. She'd never spoken to Reggie before that day on the bus when she took his hand firmly in hers and guided it up under her white polo shirt. Reggie wasn't going to indulge in this recollection. Someone wanted him to indulge, so he was refusing. He wanted to think about what *he* wanted to think about. He wanted to think about nothing and wait in peace for whatever he was waiting for.

THE WOLF

The wolf had begun his rounds early in order to see the humans gather outside the clinic building. He wanted to witness their arrival, and so he had crossed over from Golden to the outskirts of Albuquerque with the shadows still strong. This was an excellent way to get shot, but getting shot seemed a far-off fear, too obvious a fear. He padded past the old market and bellied under one of the trucks on the adjacent lot and saw as the first humans found their places under the weak, lofty lights. One at a time or in clutches they entered the quiet and hunkered in it, intensifying it. The wolf didn't know what he'd wanted to learn, beating the humans to this spot. Soon enough he was waiting again, like last time. The cars appeared in a slow flurry and then everything was still. The wolf could hear confused lizards scuttling around outside the perimeter of the human presence, wondering what was going on. The wolf could hear a noise the moon was making.

The wolf did not enjoy these meetings. He did not enjoy watching the humans stifle their sneezes to preserve the quiet. They were young and old, these humans, men and women. None of them would laugh or cry. This parking lot, this hush, made the silly serious and the weak strong, but none of these humans would ever be as serious as the wolf. He was fascinated because the humans weren't acting like humans, but there was nothing in this for him. And probably the humans *were* acting like humans – probably they were intentionally acting unlike themselves, which only humans would do. In some way the wolf could not detect, they were competing or bargaining.

It was not a struggle for the wolf to leave this time. He shimmied out from under the truck and galloped vacantly in the direction he always went. Like the moon, he saw everything, and seeing everything was the same as seeing nothing.

He galloped until he heard drumming, and when he snapped back into the moment he was startled to be in Rio Rancho. He could not recall his journey up the western flank of the city but he felt the fatigue of the journey. He tracked toward the drums, soon hearing other instruments too. This was music being made by live humans right this moment, deep in the night. He knew if he got close enough he would *feel* the music. It was the jubilant soundtrack of parades. The wolf was nearing the high school. He leapt a fence and crossed a grass field where he'd seen humans attempt to outrun each other. He snuck through a courtyard crowded with a thousand tiny locked doors and smelled the glue of books and smelled cotton and salt and the plant the young humans burned and inhaled.

When the wolf emerged from the school buildings he was socked by the thump of the drums and rising blasts of the horns and by the fragrance of the lush grass getting chewed under the boots of the band members as they pivoted this way and that. He took cover behind a closed-up concession stand. The bleachers were empty. The leader would stop the playing and raise his voice and then motion for the show to resume. The leader wasn't wearing a hat like the others but he was wearing white gloves that seemed to glow. The wolf was enthralled and had no sense of what was behind him or whether he was obeying or defying his instincts. The music was so loud that for a moment he didn't pay attention to the scents on the air. These arranged yet wild sounds would outlive the instruments that produced them and certainly outlive the young humans that played the instruments and the music would exist, somewhere, after even the wolf was dead and gone.

SOREN'S FATHER

After peeking to make sure all the vigilers had gone, he raised the blinds to the dark, petering foothills. His coffee had gone cold. It was hard to stand up straight. His back had begun to ache from the orange-upholstered armchair in the clinic room, but going out and locating a store and talking to a salesman and choosing and purchasing his own chair and having it brought up to his son's room on the sixth floor was not something he was going to do. Everything was daunting. He had even been skipping his pushups. He wasn't going to do them unless he could do the full two hundred, and when the time came to do them, after breakfast, light swelling into the window, he found that he was unable to get himself down on the floor. He thought he could already tell a difference, that his triceps were succumbing to atrophy. It didn't take long at his age. He was even smoking less – one around midday and one after dinner and one late at night when he couldn't sleep. The nurse who'd shown him the smoking spot, Lula, had switched shifts and the new nurse was too young and businesslike and made Soren's father nervous when she came in, flashing her practiced smile, and shifted Soren so he wouldn't get bedsores. Soren's father had quit putting socks and shoes on his son each morning. He had stalled out on his science fiction novel, and he told himself it was because the shoddy sleep he'd been getting made his eyes ache. That wasn't really it. The problem was that all the crises of the galaxy seemed either too large to fathom or too small to worry about. Things would work out in the book, and he didn't feel he needed to know exactly how.

He knew how bad it was for him that he wasn't running his lunch truck route. He had always run the route. It was the spine of his days. Everyone looked forward to seeing him on their breaks, waited for him and saluted him and marveled at how fast he made change. There were five trucks in his fleet, and only four were in use right now. Soren's father's truck was sitting in the parking lot, sand blowing into the grill and collecting around the tires.

Still nothing was wrong with Soren other than his coma. His vitals were strong. His skin was fine. No colds. No seizures. There would be no drama, no lesser trouble that might offer relief or distraction.

CECELIA

She was up in the booth. She had a view of four auditoriums, but only one was used at this hour, a class about architecture. This particular professor never needed anything complicated from

Cecelia. He used an old-fashioned slide projector that never broke. The professor was very old, kindly. He was exactly what Cecelia believed a professor should be. He had white, mussed hair and patches on his sleeves.

A lot of the younger professors had latched on to the idea that they were doing something wrong if they didn't utilize all available technology. They wanted to incorporate the Internet and show everything on big projectors that hung from the ceilings and could only be operated by remote control. They wanted every kid to have a laptop and have them all networked and downloading and everyone was supposed to wear headphones and use thumb drives. Despite her A/V job, Cecelia was not savvy in these matters. Whenever a professor had a problem that was over her head, she would go through the same routine. She'd shut the whole system down and power it back up, duck down and mess with some wires underneath the cabinet, press a few random buttons, put her hand to her chin and shake her head and say, 'I've never seen it act this way before. Something's really wrong with it. They'll have to get a technician out here in the morning.' Usually the professors were understanding, but occasionally one would say, 'I thought you *were* the technician.' So far, Cecelia's boss seemed not to have caught on that she didn't know the first thing about high-tech computer equipment.

Cecelia cracked open her poetry anthology and read a couple verses about small boys playing in backyards. The poems were hushed and reasonable and made Cecelia drowsy. There was another girl who was supposed to be in the booth with her this hour, who always helped keep Cecelia awake, but she hadn't shown. The girl had a lot of friends and always came in with a different hairstyle. Her name was Marie.

Cecelia closed her eyes for a few minutes and then a knock came at the booth door. She looked down at the architecture class. Nothing was amiss. The professor was still pointing and lecturing.

'It's open,' Cecelia said. She sat up straight and tucked her hair behind her ear.

A guy holding a pizza pushed the door back. He had a ponytail. 'This is from Marie,' he said. 'She felt bad about leaving you alone in here.' His T-shirt was bright yellow and it said YELLOW SHIRT across the front.

Cecelia was starving. She wondered if the pizza was meant as a bribe, so Cecelia wouldn't tell their boss that Marie wasn't showing up.

'She didn't have to buy me a pizza,' Cecelia said.

'She didn't,' said the guy. 'I owed her a favor. I had some other deliveries on campus.'

'How do you know Marie?' Cecelia asked.

'Lots of ways,' said the guy. 'She couldn't make it because she came down with temporary fatigue syndrome.'

'Oh,' Cecelia said.

'People are always trying to be funny, aren't they?'

Cecelia nodded.

'I won't accept a tip from you because you didn't order the pizza. No tipping on gift pizzas. That's my policy.' The guy turned quickly, swooshing his ponytail, and was gone.

Cecelia slid the pizza box in front of her and opened it. She ate two wide greasy slices and felt like she'd never want to eat again. Now that she was full, the pizza didn't smell good, so she set it outside the door. The architecture class was winding up. Next there would be a biology class in the east auditorium and a political science class in the north.

The phone rang. Cecelia got up and carried it over near her chair and set it on the counter. It was so loud it was ringing itself hoarse. Cecelia lifted the receiver.

'A/V booth,' she said.

'Amway.'

'Hello?'

'It's Nate.'

Cecelia hadn't spoken to Nate since the incident at the diner. 'How'd you get this number?' she asked.

Nate breathed sharply. 'Isn't that a boring job?'

Cecelia had noticed that whenever Nate felt guilty he acted meaner than usual.

'What do you make, like nine dollars an hour?'

'Look,' Cecelia said. 'Don't worry about the other day. It's a weird time. No big deal.'

'Why would I worry about the other day?'

'No reason, that's what I'm saying.' She wanted to be civil. Nate was probably more messed up than he would ever let on over Reggie. Reggie had been the kind of person who, though he was good at everything, didn't inspire jealousy. He made people feel satisfied with themselves.

'Thought you'd be happy to know, I'm giving up the name Shirt of Apes,' Nate announced. 'I decided I better take the opportunity to shake the old fans – try to get some new ones, normal ones, maybe people with money to spend.'

'Uh-huh,' Cecelia said.

'You probably won't be as happy to hear I've decided I'm going

to use our old songs for my new band. I'm having tryouts this weekend and whoever I pick, I'm going to teach them our songs and
we're going to perform them live for pay. As part of a new, currently
unnamed band. Just to be clear.'

'You mean *Reggie's* songs.'

'Since you're on sabbatical or whatever, and I don't suppose
Reggie needs them for anything.'

'You mean you're going to steal Reggie's songs because you can't
write your own.'

'Call it what you like.'

'I am. I call it stealing.'

'I could justify taking the songs until the cows come home.
Anybody can justify anything. It's what separates us from animals.
It's a waste of time, though, isn't it – sitting around justifying when
there's so much to be done? It's not easy starting a band, you know?'

Cecelia felt frozen up inside, but she heard herself talking.
'There's got to be a way I can stop you,' she said. 'Legally.'

Nate snorted. 'You won't do that. You won't get a lawyer. Reggie
didn't have the songs copyrighted or anything.'

'Copyrighted?'

'Yeah, that's what you do if you're smart. You copyright intellectual property.'

'You're an evil person, Nate. I know that's not news to you. I'm
pretty disgusted I was ever in a band with you.'

'You needed my capital and hustle. Power, I call it. You needed
my power.'

Cecelia didn't say anything. If she had said something, she
would've expressed her wish that Nate had died, not Reggie. She
wasn't going to say something like that. It was true, of course. If

someone had to get in a bad car accident, it should have been Nate.

'You didn't have to quit,' Nate said. 'I'm not going to be penalized because you don't feel like playing anymore. I invested a lot.'

Cecelia's heart wouldn't slow down. The only victory she could salvage, at the moment, was not letting Nate know how badly he'd upset her. She was telling herself, almost in a chant, that she wasn't going to let Nate have the songs without a fight, but right now she wanted to appear calm, merely disappointed. She wasn't going to get a lawyer, true, but she also wasn't going to do nothing. Nate would probably get the songs, she could already see that, but she wasn't going to let him out of this unscathed. She was tired of being above things, of putting up with things. She saw that there were people who attacked and people who got attacked, and that the only way to keep from being a victim, like Cecelia perpetually was, was to do some attacking.

MAYOR CABRERA

Once a month he went to visit a professional lady named Dana. Dana was semi-retired. She had a few steady clients and rarely tried a new one. Dana was the only woman Mayor Cabrera wanted. He certainly didn't want a young woman. Dana had short, straight hair and prim little feet that Mayor Cabrera liked to hold in his hands. She was always wearing a different pair of glasses and when she laughed she straightened her back and crinkled her nose. She didn't laugh a lot. She always seemed vaguely pleased but if you wanted her to laugh you had to earn it. Mayor Cabrera dreaded the day Dana would say she was quitting the business and he would have nothing to look forward to, nothing bright to think about while he passed the hours at the motel. He shouldn't think about her quitting, he knew. These monthly jaunts were meant for relaxation, not fretting. It wasn't only being with Dana in bed; it was getting out on this empty, pebble-shouldered road and absorbing the slaps of the rushing air, doing something that might be wrong, something strictly for himself. It was skipping dinner and accepting one of Dana's cigarettes and staying up until the stars faded swapping stories.

Mayor Cabrera was driving in the opposite direction of his worries, away from Lofte, where more and more people seemed to sense the town was going under. People were sniffing it on the wind. Some would move away, get out while the getting was good, and this would accelerate the town's demise. The lifers, the ones who'd raised children in Lofte, would stay. They'd expect Mayor Cabrera to work a miracle. They'd think that since he had reddish skin and smelled earthy, he'd know how to fix everything. But the only fix was money, and no one had any. The truth was the town had been in decline for twenty-five years. Longer. Denial was the only defense against it, and denial was finally running low. Maybe Mayor Cabrera would work a miracle. Maybe Ran and his followers would move to Lofte.

The old racing grounds loomed up, nothing left but two sets of weathered bleachers staring each other down over a weedy flat. Mayor Cabrera remembered when they'd raced dogs, even horses. Now the place was a ruin. Compared to other ruins it was brand new, but it was a ruin. Mayor Cabrera was still five minutes from Dana's villa and he felt his worries losing steam already, their urgency flagging. He felt his neck loosening up, his breaths filling his whole chest. When he was with Dana, he felt that being alive was enough. Being alive was an achievement and a reward and an end in itself. Maybe that religious group would come to Lofte and save the town and maybe they wouldn't. What if they spurned Mayor Cabrera and went elsewhere, to Oklahoma or wherever? Would he have another date with Dana? Yes, he would. What if the motel went under? Would he still get to press his mouth against Dana's ear? Yes, he would. No matter what happened, nothing was going to stop him from sitting up with Dana after the rest of the world was asleep, Mayor Cabrera peacefully spent, a happy cliché, nursing the tart gin drinks Dana mixed and telling and hearing of times before he and Dana had known each other, enjoying the old stories all the more because he was in a story that moment.

REGGIE

Sometimes he jogged, like a person concerned with health, and sometimes he slowed to a despondent shuffle. His laps didn't mean anything but that didn't seem like a reason not to do them. On the bar one day he noticed a box, a slim green box sitting there where a drink would've sat if Reggie ever drank. He opened the box and a harmonica was inside. He took the harmonica in his hand and turned it in the weak light, the instrument winking at him. It was more lustrous than the bar implements and it was the perfect weight. Reggie breathed neutrally into it and it produced a whimper.

Reggie carried the harmonica back over where the piano and guitar were and set it down in its own space on the floor. Here was something else, sitting up on the body of the piano – a framed picture. Reggie turned the picture toward him and took it in. His chest felt crowded. It was a picture of a house but more importantly it was a picture of a yard. Mr Dunsmore's yard. He was a friend of Reggie's parents who lived down the street. When Reggie had gotten old enough and realized what he wanted to do for a living, this man had given Reggie reign over his almost-acre. The deal was that Mr Dunsmore would not pay Reggie, but Reggie had an unlimited budget to put toward the property. Mr Dunsmore added Reggie's name to his tab at the nursery. Mr Dunsmore had never had a son, just a string of daughters, and he taught Reggie to play chess and taught him some things about grilling. Mr Dunsmore tried to let Reggie win at chess, but Reggie had no aptitude for the game. He wasn't strategic and didn't like to think about more than one thing at a time.

Reggie leaned against the piano and examined the picture, picking over the landscaping choices he'd made like someone picking friends out of an old graduation photo. This yard was his masterpiece, his pride. A yard wasn't like a song; it wasn't catching lightning in a bottle. A yard was like a person. It could grow distinguished. It could be dragged down by its flaws. Mr Dunsmore would let the yard go now. He wouldn't let anyone lay a hand on it. The yard was surely in disrepair already, but in this photo it was perfect: hemmed at each side by hand-watered ironwoods, a smoke tree hiding the shed, arrow-straight pathways through the blackbrush, an agave guarding the porch steps, pebbles of cloud-gray surrounding the garnet pumice in the flower beds. Reggie could smell each plant. He remembered the smell of Mr Dunsmore's deck shoes and remembered the perfume Mr Dunsmore's youngest daughter wore, home on weekends from school down in Las Cruces.

Reggie was letting it happen again. He was being manipulated, his emotions guided and coaxed. Someone wanted him to think about Mr Dunsmore and his yard. Reggie looked at the bureau. He'd stashed the chorus program and the belt buckle from his uncle in the top drawer. He looked at the guitar and harmonica. The bar had appeared. Before all that, the library. Of course, the piano. It had been here waiting on Reggie when he arrived and it was still waiting. Reggie slid the picture of Mr Dunsmore's yard out of the way and folded his top half forward onto the piano, resting his cheek against the wood. It looked grainy but was slick as a car hood. Reggie closed his eyes and went limp. He was supposed to write songs. That's what he was being nudged and nudged toward. It was songs. *He* wasn't waiting. Whoever was in charge was the one waiting. Whoever was in charge had been trying to tease songs out of Reggie, to trick him into writing. That was it. Reggie had a talent and someone wanted to exploit it or exhaust it. Reggie wasn't waiting, he was being held captive. The instruments weren't meant to comfort him. They weren't hospitality. Even the afterlife wanted something from you. The only thing of value you had left.

Reggie took the picture of Mr Dunsmore's yard and placed it in the top drawer of the bureau with the other items. He stood in front of the open drawer. There was something bubbling up in him that he'd rarely felt in the living world. It was anger. Anger at injustice. At powerlessness. He picked up the harmonica and squeezed it almost hard enough to break it. Inspiration was being engineered in Reggie. He was a cow and his udders had been getting massaged since the moment he arrived. Reggie tipped his head back and gazed up into the inscrutable low sky that constituted the roof of his quarters. He wasn't even sure he had more songs. What if he didn't? Reggie wondered if the songs were a simple bribe – his music in exchange for a pleasant eternity. Maybe heaven was like a third-world country, you had to grease a few palms. Reggie had died free of debts and he didn't owe anyone anything now. He wasn't going to be bullied. He hated a bully. His anger was everywhere, in his organs. He felt that something inside him had been wound and wound as he completed lap after lap around the main hall and now that something was spinning loose. That's how he felt on the inside but he concentrated on keeping his outward bearing calm and deliberate. It was easy to forget, until something reminded him, that he was being watched, and he wanted whoever was watching to be startled by what he was about to do. He put a shoulder to the bureau and gently moved it away a few paces and then carried the guitar in its stand to a safe distance. He ran his hand over the piano and then hoisted and propped its heavy lid. He got hold of the bench and raised it over his head. It felt neither heavy nor light, same as the harmonica had felt to Reggie, same as a good gun had always felt, back in life. Reggie sidled around and gathered his breath and brought the bench down with all the force he could muster into the innards of the piano, and a sour shout filled the room. Reggie felt good about what he was doing, relieved, after walking in circles for ages, at the physical decisiveness of the action he was taking. He disentangled the bench, drawing moans from the piano, and posed with his weapon above his head before crashing it down over and over into the delicate workings of the colossal instrument, splintering the soundboards and bashing loose the bass strings and then the treble strings and jarring the bridges loose at painful angles. The red leather of the bench was scuffed and in two places torn open. Reggie was sweating lightly. He took a couple more whacks and then tossed the bench into the piano, where it rested on top of the rubble it had created, legs sticking into the air.

CECELIA

She opened her passenger door and reached through the car and pushed open the driver's door, which was still broken and was going to stay broken, then she walked around and got into the driver's seat and rested her forehead against the steering wheel. Crossing campus, she'd seen a flyer Nate had pinned up. He was calling his new band Thus Poke Sarah's Thruster. His tryouts were in two days. Cecelia opened her window and reclined her seat, not ready to be in traffic. She looked at the white sky, the sun stuck up there like the bottom of a pail. She hadn't done anything about Nate, hadn't taken any action, hadn't begun to figure out what action she could take. She was afraid, was the truth. At times her anger felt stronger than her fear, but other times she felt paralyzed. And sometimes she wondered if it was Nate she was angry with or if she was fed up with the whole world and frustrated with herself. She had too many enemies. She needed to find some mindless courage. People said bullies were cowards but that wasn't true. It was the victims who had no courage. And she'd only been Nate's victim since she'd refused to keep on with the band. Before that, she'd benefited from his single-mindedness and from his resources. She'd been afforded the chance to perform music, to play Reggie's songs for people who lived to hear them. Maybe in a weird way Cecelia missed Nate. She missed the gigs. She missed the band's following, roughly a dozen fans who'd been committed enough to seem deranged. The twelve fans had been nervous around Reggie but spoke easily to Cecelia and Nate. They treated Cecelia and Nate like they were fans themselves, fans that got to play in the band. These people were overqualified community college types who showed their devotion by holding their heads against the speakers during the upbeat songs and solemnly swaying, eyes shut, during the slow numbers. They wore gloves to the shows – driving gloves, brightly colored mittens, fingerless gym gloves. They had a way of intimidating strangers who wandered into the venues. Nate had tried booking gigs in secret, with little or no publicity, but there was no escaping these fans. They had told Cecelia and Nate that if Shirt of Apes ever had T-shirts or bumper stickers or key chains made, the items would be rounded up and destroyed. The items would be confiscated and burned.

Cecelia started her car with the normal clattering of the engine and drove to the cemetery. The roads were quiet and the cemetery was quieter. She brought her car to a stop in the spot she'd sat during Reggie's funeral. The breeze leaning in the windows carried the scent of flowers – all the bunches of cut, surviving flowers lying this way and that in every corner of the cemetery.

This time Cecelia got out of her car and walked out around the hill. She was finally going to pay her respects. She passed a pickup truck with an open trailer of lawn equipment, and half-a-dozen men were eating sandwiches, using the pickup's hood as a table. They nodded as Cecelia passed. She looked at all the flowers everywhere. It wasn't a normal amount. The bouquets looked like a mob that had been mowed down with machine guns.

Reggie's grave, this time of day, was not in reach of the shade, and Cecelia was able to single it out because the stone was so shiny. The glare gave him away as recently deceased. The stone was simple, not small. It seemed like Reggie himself, no interest in pride or regret. Cecelia's heart, for a moment, did not feel crowded in her chest. She wanted something to do with her hands. She saw now why you brought an offering, why flowers covered the entire grounds. It was so you could make a living action, be responsible for an alteration to the scene you'd entered, *do* something.

Cecelia stepped up to the gravestone and put her fingers to it and it wasn't as cold as it should've been, like the skin of a snake. Seeing Reggie's full name there, recorded in the most permanent way, sunk the idea of his being dead further into Cecelia's heart. Once your name was engraved, you couldn't do anything else. Your file was closed. No more accomplishments or kind lies. No more people to meet for the first time who might think you were interesting or merely nice or that you might rub the wrong way. No more books to read. No more midnight snacks. No more songs. Cecelia wanted to talk to Reggie. No, she wanted him to talk to her. She wanted to hear his voice, but she would've settled for watching him do something, anything – wrap up extension cords or tune a guitar. She owed him. It was easy to feel that. Cecelia owed Reggie.

She looked at the year of Reggie's birth and at the other year. She knew a century from now someone would stop at this grave and feel nothing more than the broad sadness anyone felt at the death of a young person they'd never met. This someone would shake his head, thinking of himself at this age, thinking of himself when he was poised to come into his own. It didn't have to be a century from now, Cecelia knew. It could happen tomorrow.

SOREN'S FATHER

A strange thing had happened – strange to him, anyway. Women were interested in him. Soren's father had his cell phone number changed but the women still called the clinic asking for him, sometimes lying to try to get to him, claiming to be his sister or niece. It wasn't a bunch of women, but the same persistent handful over and over. They left baked goods and smokes at the nurses' station. Women did this sort of thing, Soren's father knew; they fell in love with prisoners and movie stars and other men they'd never met.

He hadn't been with a woman since Soren's mother, and he knew that was not a good thing. It was proof of cowardice, if anything, and usually there was a price to pay for cowardice. He knew he ought to spend less time in the clinic room. He ought to spend less time with no one for company but his indisposed child. It was much worse than being alone, being in the clinic room. He panicked at the idea of thinking of things to say to some woman, topics to bring up on a date or whatever. As things were, at least he never had to worry about what some woman felt like eating for dinner, about what time some woman wanted to go to bed, about what offended or placated some woman. He had enough to worry about and he could do his worrying on his own. These women were primarily interested in his son, he knew, and he didn't want to discuss his son with anyone, especially anyone in high heels, but he kept catching himself drifting off at Soren's bedside thinking about these women, imagining what they looked like – their legs and supple necks and petite hands. He went over and stood at his son's bedside, feeling unsure of anything. Soren had a wild hair sticking out from his eyebrow. A coarse gray hair that wasn't lying flat with all the others. What was he doing with a gray hair? Soren's father thought of plucking it but he didn't want to. He smoothed it with his fingertip over and over until it stayed in place.

DANNIE

She'd discovered a worthwhile use for the telescope on the balcony. In some craggy hills beyond the wrecked golf course, probably over a mile away, was a stretch of hiking trail. Dannie tracked the hikers in and out of shadows, staying with them as they passed behind bristlecone thickets or permanent dunes and emerged on the other side. She had seen women take dumps, men toss beer cans into the brush. Today she had three males, about twenty-five, stoners but outdoorsmen. They had their shirts off and all of them were skinny like rock stars. One had a booklet and he kept reading passages out of it that made the other two laugh. They were the types of guys who had no one to answer to, no bosses or girlfriends or account- ants or coaches. They were walking through life without shirts, cracking themselves up.

She went in and opened her old e-mail account, the one she'd used when she lived in L.A. She could close the thing, cancel the account's existence, rid the universe of it, but she hadn't yet. That was too final. The number next to the word INBOX was in paren- thesis and was very high. Maybe it was full. Dannie, looking at this e-mail page, felt a perfect mixture of curiosity and dread. She didn't genuinely care who had gotten married or who else had gotten divorced or who was moving to New York or New Zealand or who was going back to school for interior design or who had breast cancer or whose parents had died or who wanted to be sponsored for a charity 10-K or who'd opened a Pan Asian restaurant in an up-and-coming neighborhood or who'd worked on a movie that was going to Sundance or who'd gone fishing in Mexico. And Dannie had especially low interest in hearing any news about her ex-husband – whether he was dating someone or was in jail or gay or what. Dannie pretended he no longer walked the earth, and it worked for her and she was going to keep pretending that.

She hit CHECK ALL and slid the cursor to the DELETE button and then she waited. She couldn't tell what all was going through her mind. She stared straight into the screen and the next thing she knew her fingertip pressed down. She hadn't given herself permission to do this. Her hand had taken it upon itself. It couldn't have, though. It didn't work that way. Dannie had made a choice. It was easy for her to do the rest of the pages. CHECK ALL, DELETE. Over and over. Dannie kept going until she had zero new messages. She guided the arrow up the screen and signed off, then set the computer aside and stood unsteadily, feeling worried but proud. She found some things to straighten, some things to dust, kept her arms and legs moving as long as she could. There would be nothing on TV. She didn't feel like reading.

A vacant hour passed, lost. Maybe two hours. Dannie's fertile time of the month had come and gone and she was not pregnant. Nothing had happened inside her, she could tell. Nothing in her body. In her mind, though, things were happening that should not have been. Sometimes Dannie could not elude the thought that Arn might not be real. He might not be a real person. He had no e-mail account and no phone number. Dannie and Arn never went out and so she never saw other people talk to him. He had clothes and

75

some possessions, but Dannie could've planted that stuff. When your mind put itself to work on a delusion, it built in reasonable explanations for things, for why you might not be able to go out in public with a person and see other people talk to him. The person could work nights and be a homebody who was perfectly happy to spend his time only with you. There would be a reason why you couldn't remember getting to know the person, why you could only remember not knowing him at all and then knowing him as you did now. Dannie could've dreamed Arn up and then loaded her fridge with bacon.

THE GAS STATION OWNER

He closed at nine each evening and then, before he went home, spent a couple hours out behind the station drinking whisky on ice. There was a nice view from behind the station, and sometimes when he was too sober his house made him lonely. The moon was out and the desert floor seemed to glow. It was near midnight and still the silhouettes of the mountains that buffered Sandia could be seen. The gas station owner used less ice as the night wore on. The aching in his joints had subsided.

The gas station owner, earlier that day, had been reading a book about Oppenheimer and his gang, the atomic set, all the scientists who had been assembled from Europe. The gas station owner was jealous of people who got consumed with something, who could fall prey to an obsession of the mind, some intellectual entanglement that kept them up at night. The gas station owner was a practical person. He could think abstractly, but not in a productive way. He wished he could wander around in a stupor, his body lost but his mind focused, neglecting food and all hygiene. The gas station owner was currently drunk. That much was sure. If he was going to walk around in a stupor, it was going to be from Evan Williams.

The ice in the cooler was frozen together in one big chunk. The gas station owner arose and ambled into the back of the station and retrieved a butter knife. He sat and chopped at the ice until enough was broken off to make another drink – at this point, a few shards. Every night he told himself he needed an ice pick and every day he failed to endeavor to locate one.

The gas station owner had decided he wanted his nickname to be Shade Tree. These were the thoughts the whisky gave him. He didn't want to be addressed as Shade Tree; he wanted it on his gravestone, and wanted to be buried under a big cottonwood. A suburb called Rio Rancho had sprung up north of Albuquerque and the gas station owner had seen in the paper that they were getting ready to dedicate a cemetery. It was not easy, in the desert, to find unbought gravesites under consequential trees. The gas station owner made a plan to call the place in the morning.

He heard a car pull in out front. It happened a couple times a night. The driver would get out and examine the pump, searching for a place to slide a credit card, then curse a bit and maybe spit, then continue on down the road because that was all that could be done. The gas station owner liked to think, in this day and age, that people still ran out of gas. He wanted to live in a world where that still happened. The gas station owner did not fool around with credit cards. This hurt his business, but not that much. He hadn't heard a door slam, hadn't heard the car out front pull off. In a minute he'd have to walk around and check it out, make sure some idiot kid wasn't vandalizing the place, make sure it wasn't a drunk who'd pulled off and passed out. The gas station owner slurped some whisky. It tasted like sugar-water. It tasted like stale tea. Clouds passed in front of the moon and the desert floor lost its luminescence. The gas station owner turned his head and someone was standing not ten feet from him, a tall man with thick hair and a baseball cap. The cap was sitting up on top of the hair. The gas station owner stood spryly, sloshing whisky on his sleeve. He faced the man, letting the man know he was alert, drunk but not *too* drunk.

'Help you, friend?'

The man looked over as if he'd just noticed the gas station owner, as if he'd sleepwalked out here. 'I doubt it,' he said.

The gas station owner was not shaken. He was prepared to gently guide this man back to his vehicle or to fight him. The guy had on some kind of khaki outfit. There was a patch on his sleeve.

'You own this station?' he asked.

'Free and clear.'

'You Jay Fair?'

'People call me *Mr* Fair when they're standing on my land.'

'I'm here about the illegal shooting of some elk, Mr Fair. Seems not everybody respects the seasons. Not everybody in the world follows the laws passed by their legislators. That may come as a shock to you.' The man still wasn't looking at the gas station owner. He was looking off at the desert night. 'You know anything enlightening about that topic?' he asked. 'The topic of elk poaching?'

'I've never seen a rent-a-cop up close,' the gas station owner said. 'I never go to the mall, so . . .'

The man wanted to smirk. He tapped the patch on his sleeve,

which said FISH & GAME. The guy had something tied around his wrist, some type of animal call.

'Is that a whistle?' the gas station owner asked. 'Do you have a whistle?'

The man had turned his head farther away. He was looking in the opposite direction of the gas station owner.

'What's so interesting out there?'

'Nothing,' said the man. 'I don't like looking at poachers, is all. It makes me sick to look at a poacher.'

The gas station owner performed a sigh. 'Poacher' seemed a trumped-up term for somebody who caused an occasional tres-passing elk to become dinner. Obviously this ranger guy thought he was something special. That was why he was poking around in the middle of the night instead of during business hours. He thought he was some desert hero. The gas station owner wasn't going to ask about the late hour. He was going to pretend it was noon instead of midnight. 'Look, I'm pretty busy with my whisky. How does this go? How long do you keep staring into space and making accusations? I could get insulted and demand a duel, if that'll speed things along.'

'You're not permitted to mention fighting a duel to me,' said the man. 'That's threatening a state employee.'

'Your checks say State of New Mexico on them and you're proud of that?'

'You got a nice setup here.' The man took his hat off his hair then squeezed it back on. 'Real nice.'

'So I've been told.'

The man cleared his throat in a way he believed was meaning-ful and walked off. After he turned on his heel the gas station owner only heard his first few steps. He wanted to call after the man, but kept his peace. After a minute, the car could be heard. It ran smooth – a well-kept government car. The gas station owner sat back down, not sure he wanted more whisky. Maybe he was done for the night. Maybe it was time to head home. That ranger or whatever he was probably wouldn't be back. He'd wanted to let the gas station owner know he was aware, wanted to scare the gas station owner. And maybe it had worked. The gas station owner didn't hate the idea of getting mixed up with the law, but he also didn't *love* elk meat. He'd taken it because it was there. That's how he lived his life – accepting what came along – and now they were hassling him even for that. He was tucked away, living a nothing existence, and the world still couldn't leave him be. The desert wasn't aiding or abetting him. It was goading him. The desert couldn't wait to give him up, even to some uniform from the city. There was no man the gas station owner feared, but the desert could put a shudder into him. That true loneliness, that *lack* of ill will. The desert had no respect for him. It wasn't goading him. It was going to stay quiet and unfathomable. It was a distracted murderer, this land they all lived on. The gas station owner was drunk, but these were the right thoughts.

SOREN'S FATHER

He'd let the mail build and now was reading it all in one afternoon. Mostly crazy people – a woman claiming to have conceived her daughter immaculately, a young man from Japan who'd written a song for Soren. Several were professional requests. A lady at a college in California was doing a study. A guy in Boston was working on a book about extraordinary children and wanted to focus a chapter on Soren *before* the coma, on his everyday habits and personality. Of course, support groups had sent literature. And someone had sent a prayer shawl, though Soren's father didn't know what religion it was for or how it worked.

Women told their winding stories, some calling Soren's father an inspiration and deeming Soren an angel. These women considered themselves mystics, considered themselves misunderstood. And then there was one that seemed different, succinct and confident, from a woman in Santa Fe who thought Soren's father might need a break from the clinic and wanted to keep him company when he took that break. This woman's way of wording things was neither rash nor sappy and she didn't say much about herself except that she would be around when Soren's father decided he wanted a comrade for a couple hours – someone with whom, she said, to duck away from the gusts and flash floods of life. *I'm not going to claim to be normal,* she'd written, *but I will report that this is the first letter I've written in years.*

Soren's father slipped this woman's letter under a sweater that was folded on the dresser, and the rest of the mail he carried down the hall and dumped into the trash chute. He walked down to the nurses' station and told the nurse behind the desk, a plump gal with perfect fingernails, that he didn't want any more of his mail, that he wanted it thrown out. The nurse drifted back from the counter in her rolling chair and slipped a blank sheet out of a printer. She told Soren's father to write his request out and sign it, and he did so, his fingers feeling untrained, childlike.

'I'm not sure if we're allowed to dispose of mail,' the nurse said. 'I hope we are. For some reason, that sounds like fun.'

CECELIA

The wind had done something to the TV antenna, leaving Cecelia and her mother with one fuzzy network and two religious stations. Cecelia wasn't about to mess with it. Her mother was the one who sat in front of the set all day, and apparently losing the bulk of her viewing options wasn't going to change that. Cecelia wanted her to show some interest in getting the antenna fixed – even calling Cecelia's uncle, even getting out the phonebook and nipping to TV repair, even just getting upset about it. Her mother almost never watched the network. She watched the church channels. On one people were always giving testimonials and asking the viewers to sow a financial seed, and on the other scores of black folks in robes sang all day, their arms outstretched to the heavens. Cecelia's mother had received brochures from these channels. She'd mailed off for them. The brochures sat in a tall pocket on the side of the wheelchair. They were gaily colored, on heavy paper. Once you were on the mailing list they had their hooks in you.

Cecelia went into her bedroom and closed the door. The semester was winding up and she was not excited about the prospect of having nowhere to go for three weeks, of having to manufacture excuses to leave the house. She could say she had band practice, since her mother still had no idea that her band was gone. She could say a lot of things. It wasn't like her mother was going to give her the third degree. So long as she had her stupid chickens and her unnecessary wheelchair, Cecelia's mother wasn't going to do much detective work concerning her daughter.

Cecelia cleared some things off her floor, then began taking down each one of her postcards, a steady line of them that spanned all four walls at about head height. There were over a hundred. Cubist prints. Album covers. A boxing ape. An old lady with an Uzi. The postcards had been meant to inspire Cecelia's songwriting. She didn't need them anymore. She was through creating. She was doing nothing, a tourist in the war of her life. She let the postcards fall, one by one, into a garbage bag, dropping the pins into an old sneaker and then into its mate. The postcards felt like nothing in the garbage bag. They had taken her years to compile and now they were nothing. Cecelia tried not to look at them, tried not to have parting moments with any of them. All the postcards down, her room larger and brighter now, she rested the sneakers, stuffed with pins, inside the garbage bag. She'd won some ribbons when she was young, for debating. She couldn't think of anything less important to her now than debating. She had a couple soccer trophies, though she'd never been any good. There were other items, certificates and plaques. Cecelia took it all in the one bulging bag out to her car and drove up the old Turquoise Trail, the bag next to her in the passenger seat, rippling in the wind.

She got out and toted the bag through the cacti. There wasn't going to be a ravine or a cliff. In the desert you couldn't get rid of anything. The desert held what you gave it until people from a different era came poking around. Everything was a fossil from the first day it existed. Cecelia took the sneakers out and set them aside, then rested the bag under an embittered evergreen shrub. She told her fingers to let the bag go and they obeyed. She loosened the laces of the sneakers, dug a little hole with her foot, and poured the thumbtacks in, covering them back over and ramping like they were seeds.

REGGIE

The main hall shrunk and the library and bar both vanished completely. Even though Reggie had not sat and read a book – had only skimmed them in order to busy his hands and hear the sound of flipping pages and smell the failing glue – he missed the library. It had been a cozy alcove. In the main hall the perpetual dimness was trying, but in the library the same light had seemed soft and drowsy. Reggie hadn't had one single drink at the bar but he missed it now that it was gone. It had been the only color outside the red leather of the piano bench and the big reading chair. He especially missed the perpetually ripe lemons and limes. Where the archway leading into the library had once been there was now concrete painted thickly gray. The library may still have been there for all Reggie knew, just inaccessible now, blocked off. Where the bar had been there was simply empty space. Reggie thought the floor looked faded, but that could've been in his mind. It reminded him of when he'd fix up a rich guy's yard, a *lawn*, irrigated at great expense, and there'd be a kayak or something lying there and when you picked it up the grass underneath was sickly and pale.

Reggie's laps around the hall were shorter now and took up little time, but they helped him empty his mind, a difficult thing to do when you were trying to do it. He walked backward for variety. He marched. One day he came around what he considered the last bend, the stretch where one lap ended and a new one began, and he stopped stock-still when he saw that the piano had been repaired. Reggie stood in silence for a minute and then approached the piano and stood before it like someone who'd worked his way to the front of a line. To be honest, he was dumbstruck. The piano seemed to have been restored to the exact condition it had been in before Reggie destroyed it. It wasn't new now; it was still old but perfect again. Reggie could feel that he was smiling. He couldn't tell if he was amused or if he was smiling in menace like the skull on the belt buckle his uncle had given him. The bench wasn't fixed. The bench was scuffed and gashed. Reggie pushed it out of the way and stood directly in front of the piano. He brought the tip of his finger down on an A-sharp and to his ear it was precisely in tune. Reggie didn't touch another key.

The light in the hall seemed to have dimmed even further, but like the stain left by the bar this could have been in Reggie's mind. Or maybe his eyesight was faltering. Reggie had intermittent success denying it, but almost always now he was frustrated. Frustration was his baseline emotion and there was little to do about it except take it out on the tools. Reggie gripped the harmonica and reared back and hurled it straight up into the shadows and waited the moment or two that passed before it zipped back down and crashed to the floor. The harmonica was broken. Reggie shrugged. He left the thing lying on the ground, knowing it would likely be fixed. Reggie wasn't sending a message this time like with the piano; he was breaking things because it felt good. Reggie was vastly disadvantaged. This was a game of patience and his opponent had an infinite supply. His opponent would win. You couldn't *beat* a higher power. But also, somehow, it made no sense to give in. It made no sense not to extend the fight.

Since the moment Reggie had found himself in this hall – after perishing in the middle of a lovely day while humming a lovely new tune he couldn't now remember – he'd been muttering to himself the way anyone did when alone. But now he got down flat on his back on his mat and openly addressed his captor. He spoke clearly without yelling. What he wanted to know was what bad thing he'd done, what important thing he'd left undone, to be singled out. He'd never once in his life on earth wished to be singled out. Had he wasted a talent? Had he broken sacred rules? What insidious problem had he been a part of? What duty had he shirked? Reggie asked his questions and then listened to the quiet swell up behind them.

He started to hear a buzzing, a low interminable ring, a noise similar to the ringing the morning after a show, but deeper than that, as if it had been planted in his head, as if it would grow rather than dwindle. Reggie was being harassed. He would be shoved and taunted until he gave up his songs.

The hall was shrinking even more and could no longer even be described as a hall. It was a room. Laps were now absurd. Reggie's mat was gone and the floor was cold. There had been no temperature up to now, but the floor was growing chilly under Reggie's bare feet and under his back when he laid down to rest. He rested in the spot where his mat had been, and it didn't take long before he'd be shivering. He would've given anything to sleep like the living, to sleep like he used to, to be warm under a blanket and feel a slight hunger but be unwilling to get up for a snack because the bed was too cozy. He thought of what the morning felt like after a night of sleep, a steamy shower, a big breakfast that required a series of decisions – what kind of toast, how you wanted your eggs, bacon or sausage, hash browns or home fries.If the bar returned Reggie would've had a drink. He'd have an Irish whiskey with one ice cube in it because that's what his father drank on the rare occasions when his father drank.

Reggie had never been stubborn when he was alive and suspected he was only faking stubbornness now. There were a couple things he did well and took pride in, but winning for the sake of winning had never interested him. Winning had never filled him with joy and losing had never devastated him. He'd played chess with Mr Dunsmore to be polite, but had never been invested in the outcome. He'd put forth enough effort in school because everything went smoother if you earned good grades, but receiving a C had never gotten under his skin.

It was principle that was causing him to resist writing songs. Reggie hated bullying. He had never bullied nor allowed himself to be bullied and he didn't want either end of it now, but at the same time he was starting to understand that if ever there were a place where principles were mute, this was it.

He didn't know a thing. He was staggering around in a tight circle, humming. The only way to drown out the buzzing, which seemed to emanate from the direct center of Reggie's brain, was to hum. And what humming led to was not lost on Reggie.

CECELIA

It was Christmas Eve, but nothing in the house would've told you that. Cecelia and her mother had never been huge on holidays, but they usually at least put a ham in the oven and hung a couple wreaths. They hadn't even driven over to the Hispanic outskirts below Albuquerque, a tradition of theirs, to admire all the driveways lit with candles in stiff white bags. Cecelia's uncle, who she hadn't spoken to since last Christmas, wasn't stopping by this year. He had a bunch of guests at the hotel.

Outside it could've been any time of year. The TV was set to the one network they still got, to a show about people who wanted to be inventors. This week the inventions had a holiday theme. The judges were mean to the contestants but nice as pie to one another.

'This teenager on the news.' Cecelia's mother set aside the flimsy basin newspaper that still got delivered to the house every week. 'He tried to commit suicide by drinking Woolite.'

Cecelia was a teenager, for another couple months. She didn't feel like a teenager. She felt, when she was around her mother, like she was the parent and her mother the kid. This woman had taken care of Cecelia for the better part of two decades and now, what, she wanted the favor returned?

'He threw it all up. It was too gentle to do any damage, just like they advertise. Teenage boy.'

Cecelia picked up the Rubik's Cube and gripped it in her lap.

'Teenagers,' Cecelia's mother said. 'You almost have to admire them.'

'Almost,' said Cecelia.

'Last night a bunch of them painted fake petroglyphs in with the real ones.'

'They should go to jail.'

'I've never known the difference between petroglyphs and hiero-glyphics.'

'Hieroglyphics are in Egypt and they tell complex stories. Petroglyphs are here and they look like something high school kids could do.'

'While I'm thinking about it, can you get my yearbook down from the attic?'

'Your yearbook?' said Cecelia.

'They didn't invent high school especially for you, you know?'

'The attic?'

'You'll see it. Pop your head up there and it's over to the left.'

Cecelia placed the Rubik's Cube, already sweaty from her palms, onto a cork coaster. A man on TV was pleading. He was wearing some sort of helmet. Cecelia had been waiting for her mother's spirit to resurface, getting her mother up each morning when she was barely awake herself and half the time running late, and there simply wasn't a course being run. Things didn't even seem to be getting worse. Her mother was going to slouch in the wheelchair of a dead woman, incrementally losing weight and idly making small talk until – until when? Now she wanted to look at her old yearbook? What did that mean?

'Something wrong with you?'

'I'm ship-shape,' Cecelia said.

Her mother made an indignant noise.

'Actually, I've got to go.'

'Where to?'

'I need to be somewhere. Else.'

Cecelia's mother looked at the clock, her eyebrows raised, then resignedly rested her gaze on the TV screen. She wanted to protest, to say Cecelia shouldn't be running off on Christmas Eve, but because she hadn't put up one stocking, didn't receive a channel airing a Christmas special, hadn't had the stove on all day, she didn't have ground to stand on.

'Well,' she said. 'Get my yearbook.'

Cecelia barreled up Route 14, not sure where she was going. She knew that whatever happened during the night, she'd wind up back

89

at that house by morning, dragging her mother out of bed. She felt taken advantage of most every day. The afternoon that Nate had called and harassed her in the A/V booth she'd vowed to go on the offensive, but she hadn't. She hadn't confronted Nate. She hadn't openly confronted her mother. She had her car to escape to, her bedroom, the vigils. She didn't attack. She evaded.

Cecelia pushed the gas pedal down farther. The evening sky was brackish with light. She slowed for some roadkill, then went even faster, as fast as her falling-apart car would go. The more wind she could get whipping in the windows, the less she could hear the cranky noises her engine made, the latest of which sounded like a Styrofoam cup being crumpled. Pebbles were pinging hard against the oil pan. With the speedometer at ninety and the car not willing to push it any higher, Cecelia let off the gas. She slowed rapidly. The noise of the wind evaporated. Soon everything looked familiar again. She saw a stately adobe mailbox in her headlights and pressed the brake and swung onto a driveway. It was one of the unused mansions, low but sprawling, a lot of logs incorporated into the structure. Cecelia kept her lights on. She didn't hit the gas or the brake. She rolled around the back of the house, feeling powerless against the momentum of her car, expecting motion lights or dogs or something. When she shut down the engine, she felt off the grid, away from herself even. She wasn't a normal college girl who got to live on campus and worry about diets and dating. She wasn't a member of a band. She wasn't a daughter in good standing.

She got out of her car and walked up to a huge screened porch and tried the door. It seemed locked at first, but Cecelia kept jiggling the handle and it popped open. She felt like a criminal, an element of the night. Everyone else in the world was ensconced in holiday warmth. The air inside the screened porch was different. Chlorine. Cecelia strolled around the pool and then sat at a dinette set. These people kept a stark pool area. There was a cactus-shaped thermometer hanging up, and a humorous placard about peeing in the pool. The owners had probably never been here. These were the decorations that came with the house, to get you started. Cecelia put her feet up, then set them back down.

She sensed movement. She turned her head and saw a guy descending a flight of shallow steps, and there was nothing to do but stay still and seated and try not to turn red. The guy saw her and made a noise. He was holding something, a lit joint. He looked down on Cecelia with an open expression, like the world was full of reasonable explanations. He was acting cool or he *was* cool. He glanced at the joint in his hand, peered out toward Cecelia's car. It was hard to say who'd been caught in something.

'Evening,' Cecelia said. She was still in the chair. 'No harm meant. Just having a sit-down.'

The guy wasn't much older than Cecelia. He was a little nervous, but mostly he seemed ready to be amused.

'I assume I don't know you,' he said. 'I don't really know anyone around here. Are you a vandal?'

'Not as of yet.'

'Is anyone with you?'

'No, that's the whole point,' Cecelia told him. 'I was looking for a place to be alone.'

He drew on his joint, then settled stiffly into a chair, still peering out through the screen. 'I guess I ruined that for you. I guess you're not alone now.'

'Where's your car?' Cecelia asked.

'Garage. That's where I left it, anyways.'

'I'm not here to steal anything. I was just, you know . . .'

The guy shrugged. He held out the joint and Cecelia declined.

'Our garage is full of my mom's crap,' she said. 'I forgot cars could go in garages.'

'Fortunately, no moms live at this house.'

'I thought these places were all empty.'

The guy squinted, holding in smoke. 'Usually is, but I have an internship.'

'I better get one of those,' Cecelia said. 'Seems like what everybody's doing.'

The guy let the smoke leak from the corner of his mouth until there wasn't any more. 'I believe you. You're harmless. You were looking for a place to chill out. You're not dangerous, I can tell. Either that or, you know, I'm wrong.'

The tension was already drained out of the situation. This guy didn't really know how to be tense. He came from rich, healthy, relaxed stock. Cecelia told the guy her name. She watched him pull a baggy of trail mix from his pocket and drop it on the table. She'd thought it was going to be more pot but it was trail mix.

'I started walking out that way today,' he said, pointing by raising his elbow. He extinguished the joint, then tucked what was left of it behind his ear. 'I guess you'd say I was hiking. The problem with the desert is there's not really a trail and you don't know when to stop. You don't know when it's okay to turn back.'

'You could go until you almost couldn't see your house anymore. That'd be pretty far.'

The guy took a good look at Cecelia, like it was his right. He slouched to the side in his chair in order to see her bottom half. 'I started hearing coyotes,' he said. 'That was the end of the hike.'

Cecelia took a big whiff of the chlorine air. A wind swept through the screen and Cecelia made sure not to show she was cold. She didn't want the guy to get her a blanket or a coat.

'Where's your internship?' she asked.

'This place that puts out a catalog of catalogs.'

'What do you do there?'

'Actually, I don't want to talk about work when I'm high.'

'I bet you don't do much of anything.'

The guy nodded, like he was too adult to take Cecelia's bait. 'You ever see anyone make a citizen's arrest? In real life, I mean. Could I citizen's arrest you for trespassing right now or would I be the one doing something wrong by detaining you?'

'No one's arresting anyone.'

'Is it even a real thing, though? A citizen's arrest.'

'Give me some cash,' Cecelia said.

The guy squinted again, like when he'd been holding in the smoke.

'How much you got in your wallet?'

'A hold-up,' the guy said, coming around to the idea, failing to stifle a grin. 'Like the Old West.'

'They have hold-ups everywhere.' Cecelia stood and put her hand out.

'You're supposed to have a weapon.'

'I don't need one. You're going to give me some money. It doesn't have to be much.'

'I think I got twenty-seven bucks.'

'Hand it over.'

The guy laughed to himself. 'You should be careful. Not everybody thinks it's cute to get mugged on Christmas Eve on their patio.' He went ahead and dug out his wallet. 'I'll give you twenty-five. The place I get coffee in the morning only takes cash.'

'Tomorrow's Christmas.'

'I'm working Christmas. That's how you get ahead.'

'Weren't you born ahead?'

The guy flattened the money and arranged it so it all faced the same way. 'Yeah, but I'm going to get *more* ahead, just like my dad did, and his dad.'

Cecelia took the bills from the guy's hand, his face expectant, like Cecelia was going to do something, like he was going to get a show for his money, some parting words. She turned crisply and walked toward her car, finding it difficult to stride normally. The guy was going to miss her when she was gone. It felt good, finally retaliating against the world a little bit. It was a step. She wrapped the money around her finger and slipped it into her pocket. She didn't know if she wanted to hurry or if she wanted to saunter.

SOREN'S FATHER

Hers had been the only letter he'd responded to. Something in the way she expressed herself failed to make him anxious. She wanted things from Soren's father, she'd admitted, but wasn't going to trick him into giving her any of them. She was going to get them fair and square. She thought it took years to get to know a person, so what did it matter how you met? What difference did it make what caught your attention first? Soren's father felt a sensation that was familiar to him from when his wife had come along, a feeling of being taken in hand, of giving way to a person with superior romantic expertise. He was grateful to be pursued, and even grateful to himself for allowing the pursuer to succeed.

Soren's father had read the letter over and over and then finally called the number at the bottom, the day after Christmas, standing out on the secret smoking landing but not smoking, and only when the woman answered the phone and greeted him did he know that her name, Gee, was pronounced like the letter G. Soren's father normally spoke on the phone only to resolve simple dilemmas related to his lunch truck business, but Gee began asking him questions and, a surprise to himself, he knew how to answer the questions and so she asked him more questions and before he knew it he'd been on the landing forty-five minutes. Gee did not avoid the topic of Soren. She surrendered her belief that there was indeed something magical about him, but in this day and age a person's magic was nobody's business but his own. She mentioned she was divorced, but Soren's father didn't dig for details about that. She lived in Santa Fe. In her younger days, she had been head chef at a Chinese restaurant. As soon as Soren's father had begun to feel a creeping embarrassment at how long their phone conversation was lasting, with the first stars becoming visible in the semblances of holiday dusk, Gee said they should probably get off but that she wanted to take him to dinner the next night. Soren's father had gone back inside then, feeling that the longest Christmas of his life had finally passed. Christmas Eve had been awful, thinking of how excited Soren would've been at bedtime, his head full of Santa Claus. Christmas Day had been grueling, listening to forced celebrations from other rooms, watching his turkey and dressing grow cold on the table. And the feeling had lingered right on into the next day, that feeling of being without happiness while others counted blessings. But at long last, with something new on the horizon, something new to be occupied with, Soren's father felt that Christmas was done.

So here he was, waiting under the carport at the front of the clinic for a white van. It was the time of year most people were with their families, resting up and taking stock. Soren's father's family was on the sixth floor and Soren's father's lunch truck business was suffering without his day-to-day involvement and he was about to go on a date for the first time in years because he knew he needed to. Soren's father could see his truck over against the far fence, lording above the cars. He knew he should go start it and let it run a minute, but he wasn't going to do that. It was the same lack of will he felt when he wanted to do pushups. He didn't want to smell the inside of the truck, the odor of grease and dust, a bad smell that was also comforting. He didn't want to hear the engine knock around and then settle, didn't want to picture Soren sitting on his knees at the other end of the bench seat, his face turned toward a window full of endless faded sky.

Soren's father spotted the van. It was certainly white. It was one of those old vans, not a minivan. Gee was two minutes late. In his business, two minutes late was a crisis, but for most people it was the same as right on time. Soren's father found himself short of breath when the van made the turn and rolled under the carport. He felt rooted to the cement. Gee hopped down from the driver's seat and strode over and hugged Soren's father. His feeling at seeing her was one of muted elation. He'd seen nothing but the sixth-floor nurses for two and a half months. Gee's teeth were white, same as the van. She wore a loose sweater and had cool eyes.

Gee drove them down out of the city, Soren's father watching the clinic until it was a spot of light among many. This was the farthest away he'd been. This was farther from the clinic than his house was. The night would be cold, Soren's father could tell, but his palms were sweating. He looked at Gee, driving with both hands locked onto the wheel like they taught you as a teenager. There were no rear seats in her van and the space was taken with rods and couplers and sacks of bolts. Soren's father asked about the supplies and Gee said she was helping someone set up an art gallery. Her tiny earrings were glittering in the light from the dash.

'I meant to buy you flowers,' Soren's father said. 'I forgot.'

'I don't believe in buying flowers,' Gee said. 'I believe in letting them grow wild and happening upon them.'

She pulled onto a gravel lot next to a tall, restored home. She explained that the chef lived upstairs and used the ground floor as a dining room. The chef's two daughters were the waitstaff. Aside from a potted poinsettia on the front walk, there were no holiday decorations, and this pleased Soren's father. There were no menus either. Small glasses of beer were brought out and Soren's father realized he hadn't had a beer since Soren's coma.

'My only hope for tonight is that you can relax a little,' Gee said. 'You're the kind of father that needs to be forced to worry less, and I'm going to help with that. The first thing is, loosen your grip on that little black phone.'

Soren's father set the phone on the table, and then he picked it up and put it in his pocket.

'Are you supposed to sip this or something?' he said, holding his little beer.

Gee shrugged. 'Chug it if you want.'

Soren's father tipped the glass back and emptied it, then flagged down one of the daughters to bring him another. The beer came out and soon after that an appetizer.

'I should put this on the lunch truck,' Soren's father said. 'See how the guys down at the paper processing plant would like some confit.'

'That's a thing,' Gee said. 'Trucks with gourmet food on them. They drive around the downtown office buildings. It makes the lawyers feel alive, buying a meal in cash off the back of a truck.'

'What makes it a confit, anyway?'

'They cook it in its own fat,' said Gee. 'The French will do anything to an animal. A lot worse things than confit.'

The main plates came forth, trout that had been cooked on a wood plank and a salad of beets and cactus flowers and different puckery cheeses. Gee ordered wine but Soren's father stuck with more beer. The food was ridiculously better than the lunch truck food or the clinic food. No denying it. He had the vague feeling of being in someone else's life. His wife had been good at living, but he could already tell she had nothing on Gee when it came to enjoying things. Soren's father watched Gee cut her fish into too-large bites and then savor each one. Maybe she would enjoy him that way. Maybe she could force herself into a space in his mind. He could think of her while he sat the hours away at the clinic.

'Since I started writing my memoir,' Gee said, 'everything I do feels like a scene from a book.'

'You're going to write about us having dinner? You're going to write about us eating trout with the head on it?'

'I don't know. I have to wait and see if it seems important after some time passes.'

'What made you decide to write a memoir?'

'I noticed a lot of boring people were doing it, and crybabies.'

'You're not a crybaby, are you?' Soren's father asked.

Gee smiled. Soren's father was out of beer again.

'Last Christmas I was in Mexico,' Gee said. 'I went hiking.'

Soren's father had quickly finished his food and he couldn't tell if he was still hungry. He pushed his plate away.

'This year it kind of slipped by,' he said.

'It's pointless without children,' Gee said. 'Most holidays are.'

'I could've put up a little tree in his room and put a gift under it. I got him a bike. It's at home in the garage.'

'When he wakes up, it'll be waiting on him. He won't care he didn't get it on Christmas.'

'It has training wheels.'

'Sounds like my speed. I never learned how to ride a bike.'

'Why not?'

'I never learned. People always say you never forget how to ride a bike, but I never learned. And I never learned how to whistle.'

'Never learned to whistle?' Soren's father said. 'What do you do when you see a pretty girl?'

'I am a pretty girl,' Gee said.

Soren's father drew in a breath like he was going to whistle but then didn't.

'I think I'm getting my wish,' Gee said.

'You are?'

'You're relaxing, just a little.'

Soren's father saw the girls coming around with dessert and coffee. Gee was swirling the last bit of her wine. He saw her trick. Soren's father had never once considered that she might not like him. He wasn't sure how she'd done that. She'd banished all doubt from him without his knowing about it.

'Better finish that,' Soren's father said. 'Coffee's on the way.'

'I never finish the last sip of wine,' Gee said. 'It's too sad.'

MAYOR CABRERA

Two nights in a row without one guest. There'd been a band of three couples on Christmas night, each couple getting their own room, and they'd stayed on for the night of the twenty-sixth, but nothing the night of the twenty-seventh and nothing tonight. No laundry. No questions to answer. No coffee to brew in the lobby. Mayor Cabrera, out of spite, flicked on the 'no' in the sign. NO VACANCY. When things got too slow at the motel, Mayor Cabrera would think of the old days, when he ran a small roofing company. Roofing was something you could do until you stopped, and then you couldn't do it anymore. It was too hot and too hard on the back. In the roofing business you worked some punishing hours but then when you were off you were really off. You felt the work in your hands when you held a beer. In the motel business, Mayor Cabrera was always bored and never felt off-duty. He wished he was still roofing, and that he was doing it for Dana, his professional lady. Being in a higher, hotter spot than everyone else all day helped a man, but you had to do it *for* someone. It was nice to think of Dana when he had a little down-time, but he had nothing but downtime and was thinking about her all the time. He was thinking about her more and harder than he'd ever thought about his wife, back when she was alive. Mayor Cabrera had once had a devoted woman and manual labor, and now he sat in a motel in a dying town, pining for a prostitute.

He went downstairs into the basement. It was a refuge, the basement, but also made him feel closed in. There were a couple high slats of window and now and then the wind would lash sand against the glass. Mayor Cabrera stopped and looked at his calendar, tacked to the wall with a pencil hanging next to it. He used to fill the boxes up with scrunched writing – meetings concerning the town, meetings concerning the motel, his paydays and days off. Lately he left the calendar clean. If he forgot something, he forgot something. Mayor Cabrera cleared some clutter off the old metal desk, scraping a pile of old papers into the trashcan. There were some old granola bars in the pencil drawer and he threw those out too. He paused before pulling open the deep bottom drawer. He knew what was in there. All the potholders his sister-in-law had knitted. There must've been a couple hundred. He'd never attempted to sell them. Who would want potholders while they were drifting through the desert? The old rotary phone rang and Mayor Cabrera plucked it off the desktop.

'What's the word, mayor?'

It was the owner of the motel, Mayor Cabrera's boss. Mayor Cabrera hoped he wasn't calling because he was on his way. He was due for a visit.

'How's shelter renting tonight?'

'Shelter is hardly renting at all,' said Mayor Cabrera.

'That bad?'

Mayor Cabrera knew the motel owner didn't care if the Javelina made money. He had other businesses that made money. Mayor Cabrera could probably stay at the Javelina until the owner died, and maybe even after, if the owner's kids decided not to sell the place. Or the owner could die tomorrow and the place could be on the market next week. Both were deflating thoughts, being out of a job or staying at the motel for years to come.

'Is it snowing there?'

'Not that I've noticed,' said Mayor Cabrera.

'I heard something about it snowing in New Mexico. One time I was in Old Mexico and it snowed. Did you know it snowed down there?'

The motel owner sounded drunk. Arizona had likely played a basketball game. The motel owner donated small fortunes to University of Arizona, and he judged the quality of each year he spent on earth by how the basketball team performed.

'Oh, wait,' said Mayor Cabrera. It took a lot of effort for him to be dishonest, but he wasn't going to have a drawn-out conversation with his drunken boss. 'I think I hear somebody. Better get up to the office.'

'Okay,' said the motel owner. 'Rent that shelter.'

Mayor Cabrera hung up the phone. He stared down at the potholders in their drawer, then picked one up and handled it. It was the ochre color of mountains at noon. Mayor Cabrera always brought stew to his sister-in-law's place when he cooked up a batch. He'd always brought her stew, from way back when her sister was alive, and though he'd quit speaking to his sister-in-law, though he diligently avoided her company because he didn't want to be reminded of his losses, he'd never quit delivering the stew. It was a way to not feel guilty. For all he knew, she dumped it all out. He always left it on her front porch and rang the bell and drove off like a teenager pulling a prank. One day he'd found a mess of potholders in a plastic bag on the step, with a note that read SELL THESE IN THE LOBBY, WE'LL SPLIT THE PROFITS. He'd picked up bag after bag of the stiff, rectangular cloths. She had no way to know when he was coming, so sometimes the potholders must've sat out there for many nights, collecting dew and then drying out and then collecting dew. His sister-in-law had never seemed like a woman to crochet or knit or whatever. She wasn't *that* old. Mayor Cabrera wasn't old. He could clearly recall the days before Cecelia had come along, before his sister-in-law was even his sister-in-law, when she was the spunky sister of his future wife. He thought of a trip the three of them had taken to Taos. They'd gone up in early spring to hike, when the trees would be budding and the streams filling and the birds amorous, and no sooner did they get into town and find a place for breakfast then the sky turned gray and the playful breeze turned into a stiff wind full of icy intent. Mayor Cabrera could remember, like it had happened last weekend, asking the waitress for hot sauce for his hash browns and then becoming aware of the first tiny snowflakes flitting against the windows of the restaurant like confused insects. They couldn't go hiking and weren't about to race the storm back to the basin, so they located the cheapest bar in Taos, which didn't seem all that cheap, and drank the sunless day away. Mayor Cabrera's wife who wasn't yet his wife became easier and easier to convince that another round would be a good idea, and Mayor Cabrera, though he couldn't afford it, kept buying drinks for the locals. At some point what little light had been in the sky was gone and the snow was falling in a perfect endless sheet. The three of them piled into Mayor Cabrera's old El Camino and pulled away from the bar not know-ing where they were headed, using the weather as an excuse to drive slowly. Just outside town they turned down a quiet road lined with identical rental villas, snug-looking, cozy rather than cramped. Mayor Cabrera pulled into an empty driveway and they sat there.

The place was unoccupied. Nowadays a villa like that would have as many cameras and alarms as a bank. No one had protested. He could hear it now, his sister-in-law giggling and giggling, nervous and excited, the unspoken and obvious fact of what they were going to do becoming clear in the cab of the El Camino. They were hidden by the storm. The villa wasn't big but had three or four chimneys. Mayor Cabrera had gotten out and clomped around the back and found a bathroom window he could force open. The three of them had kept the lights off in the villa and the fireplaces cold but they did prepare hot cocoa in the kitchen and click on the space heaters. The cocoa was from Europe or something, in a fancy canister, and his sister-in-law packed it in her bag. They played a few hands of Castle, but once they were warm, the alcohol wearing off, the girls were all yawns. When they heard the banging on the front door the next morning it roused them from a dry-mouthed slumber. They'd fled out the back of the place, coats half on, and tripped out into the white-gowned Ponderosa pines. They circled around and found themselves on a vista from which they could see the restaurant from the day before, and the bar. What was wrong with Mayor Cabrera's memory? It was too good. He could painfully recall how satisfied he'd felt driving back to the basin, barreling through the bright cold with two women sleeping beside him and a fresh adventure under his belt and the desert opening and opening before him.

Mayor Cabrera reached up and removed the calendar from the basement wall. He folded it in half and put it in the trash. He remembered what was in his back pocket and pulled out a Christmas card from Ran. More garbage. It was a *holiday* card, no reference to Jesus, a photo of a farmhouse on the front. Ran had signed the card but hadn't written anything personal. Mayor

Cabrera couldn't figure Ran out. He was some kind of well-meaning con man, but most people meant well and everyone was conning someone. Mayor Cabrera didn't feel he could be conned, at this point. Or maybe he wanted to be conned, which made you immune.

There was a door at the back of the basement that led outside and Mayor Cabrera opened it and stepped out and folded his arms against the wind. It was a low wind, sweeping the desert floor, bothering Mayor Cabrera's pant cuffs. It was coming from the Northwest, like the wind always seemed to this time of year. Mayor Cabrera's stomach felt light and he could feel that he was grinding his teeth. It was his niece. Mayor Cabrera didn't have a child of his own but he had a niece. His absence in her life was a great adult shortfall. Mayor Cabrera never thought this way, and his mind was in a quiet terror. There were the trappings of adulthood, which everyone wound up with, and then there was being an adult. Mayor Cabrera felt dizzy and widened his stance. He'd been managing the regret of neglecting his sister-in-law all these years, but he'd neglected his niece too. He'd held her when she was a baby, taken her for ice cream when she was a toddler, dropped her off at pee-wee soccer practice. And then he'd stopped. He'd bowed out. He'd resigned from unclehood. He closed his eyes for a time until his balance returned. He felt the opposite of how he'd felt after that trip to Taos. The desert didn't seem like an answer but like a hostile maze. Mayor Cabrera hadn't looked after anyone, and there was no other accomplishment worth a damn. And now Cecelia was a young woman and she was a stranger to Mayor Cabrera. He'd allowed himself to indulge in motel troubles and town troubles. He was a few years from fifty. Cecelia deserved a competent uncle, but at this point she wasn't expecting one. Mayor Cabrera had busied himself with the town so he could ignore the shambles of his private life. He'd passed Christmas in the basement of the hotel, staring at action movies. The TV station had arranged a sprig of holly in the corner of the screen and they left it there all day. Mayor Cabrera had eaten leftover pasta salad. He'd drunk a couple beers and then lost interest and switched to ginger ale.

Mayor Cabrera stood facing a multitude of spiny plants and eroding rocks and forced himself to remember when Cecelia was a baby, when his sister-in-law was herself, when Mayor Cabrera's wife was alive. They'd been sure Cecelia would have a better life, though their own lives were far from bad. Nothing had seemed more important than Cecelia growing up happy. Mayor Cabrera didn't know much about his niece at this point, but he was pretty sure she wasn't happy.

THE WOLF

It was a concert of religious guitar music. The wolf had settled under an RV on the edge of the fairgrounds to listen to the reverberating licks and preening voices. At the end of each song a roar rose up from the humans attending the concert that was louder than the music and full of fervor and made the wolf nervous. It was a chilly night, the smells thin. The underside of the RV stank but the wind that buffeted under and rippled the wolf's fur was vacant of worthwhile scents – smoke, birth, another predator.

The musicians kept asking questions of the crowd and the crowd kept combining their voices with certainty. The wolf was afraid of these humans and he also pitied them. They had little soul left and that's why they aggrandized what sliver remained. And what of the wolf's soul? Lately he found himself panting with no cause, while resting on a cool morning under an outcropping. He'd caught himself clamping his jaws down on his own foreleg.

The wolf hastened away from the concert straight toward Sandia Mountain, exhilarated because he'd completely broken off his rounds. They were unrecognizable tonight, his rounds. He didn't feel worried about them. He felt a blessing of strength that needed to be used, so instead of skirting Sandia he began to climb it, the most inefficient and unpleasant route to Lofte, beating up his paws, thirsty, hoping to ensure he'd be able to sleep in the morning, straight up the mountain and then he'd go straight down the other side and he would not avoid anything the remainder of the night nor give way nor hold himself still, meaning that whatever creature fate put in his way before dawn would be subtracted from the living world without any knowledge of what had happened to it.

THE GAS STATION OWNER

As soon as the offices opened back up he called the free paper that covered the basin and ordered a want ad. The next issue wasn't going to press for over a week.

NEEDED: gas station/store managers, lofte, no nights, two positions open, 505-386-2387

The idea of leaving the station put the gas station owner in mind of a young boy shedding a shabby blanket that had always comforted him. The mirror in the back room he peered into when he trimmed his hair. The bills he got to sit and write out, the amounts of which changed by mere pennies from month to month. The short aisles of canned goods he could straighten and straighten – condensed milk, chili, potted sausage, peppers. His radio stations that came and went. His whisky in the evenings. The big window behind the register.

Taking even this small step of placing the ad in the paper agreeably loosened something behind his eyes. Cleared his head. He was going to shed his blanket and face whatever gales the desert could offer. He was going to confront the desert, finally. He wanted to find the middle of it, the still dry heart of the land. He could see himself walking into the wild and could hear that quiet moment already, the rhythmic crunch of his boots and the lisping of the desert wind against his body, the quiet simple sounds of what would be the first brave thing he'd ever done.

DANNIE

The numbers at the vigils had peaked and then in the last couple weeks had declined, but this Wednesday evening it was raining – a musty drizzle that refused to rally into an earnest storm, that kept dampening everyone and then losing steam – and more significantly, the holidays had arrived. This Wednesday they'd lost fully half the group from last week. The fat had been trimmed; Dannie tried to think of it that way. Anyone sitting vigil tonight was staunch. She appreciated these people for being lost like she was and for not wanting to talk about it just like her and for never missing a Wednesday. Maybe this was the perfect size for the group, about thirty.

Arn had been sitting back to back with Dannie and he scooched around and rested his hand on her boot. He was wearing a garbage bag over his clothes like everyone else. The muscular guy with beady eyes had handed them out to everyone off an enormous roll. Arn was soaked anyway. He looked like he was about to grin, but he could look that way for hours. He was a comfort to Dannie because she knew nothing could make him quit. He always kept a reserve, an empty part of him, a reserve of nothing, and it gave him an advantage. He was attending the vigils because Dannie wanted him to and because he wasn't picky about what he did with his time. He was picky about what he ate, but not about his pastimes. He would not grow overwhelmed or lose heart.

And maybe none of these other people here tonight would quit. For the muscular guy the vigils were a discipline, another component of an ascetic program aimed at physical health. There was a man who wore sunglasses and who always had a pen in his hands – nothing to write on, just a pen to fiddle with. There was a red-haired woman who wore homemade earrings. She had a tattoo of a humane, inclusive sun on her foot, and wore sandals no matter the temperature. There was a manic painter, in splotched overalls, constantly tapping his foot or biting his fingernails. Painting seemed like the worst job for him, and vigiling also seemed against his nature. The vigils hadn't helped the painter calm down, but he was still here. There was a guy with a pinched face who wore a trench coat with hundreds of pins on it, like a colorful armor. He would close his eyes for long stretches but it was obvious he wasn't dozing because of his rigid posture, his head propped snobbishly atop his thin neck. He never slouched, even draped with that ten-pound coat. There were a few chubby women, a little older, for whom sympathy was a calling. Of those the group had lost, a significant faction had been college kids, maybe even a couple high school students. One of them was still here, the girl with the doleful eyes who drove that car that made such a racket pulling into the parking lot. Another of the losses had been a very old lady who'd worn a necklace with a bunch of rings on it. Dannie was forced to wonder if she'd passed away. She'd looked decrepit getting all the way down on the ground and then trying to rise. Dannie didn't know which was sadder, to think the lady was deceased or to think she'd quit, to imagine her dead or to face the fact that one could still be making false starts at eighty-five years old.

Dannie had quit a marriage and quit her friends. She had quit her hometown. Quitting had defined the trajectory of her adult life. She didn't want to quit on the other vigilers and she didn't want them to quit on her. She wanted everyone to see it to the end. Dannie wondered about the people who had quit. What were they doing at this moment? Were they disappointed or proud or numb? She wondered if they could eat or do laundry or get lost in a movie, knowing the vigil was going on without them. She wondered how many of them were alone. She wondered if they'd found peace or found something else to take the place of peace.

HISTORY OF ARN I

At ten years of age he was shipped to the Northwest, where he learned not to expect sunny days. People were proud of the dampness. When the sun appeared for a week and the streets and yards and tree branches dried out, people wondered how to act. Summer was an affront. Arn wasn't one of these people. He'd been born in the Midwest. He saw how it was out here. You were supposed to give in to the rain and stay or you were supposed to hate it and want to move away, but Arn had no say about where he went. To someone like him, weather, cloudy or sunny, didn't mean a thing. Weather allowed people who weren't truly sad to play at it, people who weren't happy to go through carefree motions.

Before middle school Arn had moved so often that the houses he'd lived in blended together. All the houses smelled like casserole and had littered lawns patrolled by pets with disappointing names. All the houses contained an adult who was slightly meaner than most or slightly nicer than most and areas that were off-limits and elaborate systems for divvying the chores.

And then Tacoma. There was a foster mother, but it was the father Arn remembered. His name was Ron Darling, like the baseball player. Ron Darling was bald, with a clay-colored beard that blended in with his chest hair and wrapped around to the back of his neck. He told a lot of stories. Arn was old enough to realize that most of the stories hadn't happened to Ron Darling but to someone he knew or had talked to in a bar. The details were exaggerated, the settings plucked from air. But the unlikeliness was what *made* the stories; the fact that the guy was asking you to believe something so outlandish is what made it feel true. This man, Ron Darling, could not have been a houseboy for a pop star. He could not have moved from Chattanooga to California at age eighteen and met some people and then some more people and ended up living at the home of a famous teen heartthrob, refreshing drinks and entertaining guests with his high-dive prowess. 'Different time,' Ron Darling would remark. 'People had houseboys. Closest I come is one of you foster punks.'

Ron Darling had a bunch of other foster kids, all boys, and he hired them out for work. It was like he had a labor agency but didn't have to pay the workers. Or barely pay them – five bucks a day. He could undercut the legitimate agencies and he got paid under the table. He would drive Arn and his brothers to some lumberyard or machine shop and put his feet up and read a crime novel, occasionally looking up to dole out praise. He told the boys that in order to overcome being foster punks, they had to learn how to work hard, that work could save them. And Arn always worked hard.

One of his foster brothers under Ron Darling, a black kid with jutting bottom teeth, constantly annoyed Arn. Arn didn't mind work, but he minded this kid and his grainy, rising voice. The kid would not stop talking. He tried to give Arn tips while they worked, tried to show him shortcuts and reveal the finer points of power tool use, but the kid didn't know any more than Arn did. Every slip Arn made, the kid would be standing over him, wagging his head. He'd click his tongue and say something like, 'Told you – work smart, not hard.' The kid had comments about what Arn ate, about his T-shirts. Arn did not want to bicker with this kid, yet he did. The kid had a way of drawing Arn in. All Arn wanted to do was fistfight and get it over with, but somehow it never came to this. The kid had been at it a long time, irritating people, and was skilled at narrowly avoiding violence.

One day, Ron Darling could not ignore them any longer. Arn had screamed at the kid and the guy who owned the little moldings plant had heard. It was a Sunday. Arn had declared that if the kid spoke again in the next five minutes he was going to kill him, that he was going to hit him in the head with a hammer as many times as it took to make sure the kid could never say another word, and if Arn had to go to jail or juvenile hall that was fine with him. Ron Darling walked over, pointedly not worked up, and asked the black kid to come with him. They left and Arn kept working. He had no idea which one of them was in trouble, he or the black kid. Without the kid's yapping and Ron Darling's oppressive presence, Arn got most of the job done that day.

In the evening, back at the house, the black kid was nowhere to be found. He wasn't going to be there anymore. Ron Darling said they weren't going to discuss it. He wasn't angry with Arn, wasn't pleased with him. A problem had arisen concerning his business and he'd smoothed it out; that was all. Arn saw the value in being a good worker, but also he felt he'd won something not worth winning.

Terrance. That was the black kid's name.

Quickly a replacement was found for Terrance, an Indian kid who claimed to have run away from a reservation. Arn suspected it was a rule; you could only have so many white kids before you had to take a minority. The new kid was surly and weighed his words. Almost instantly upon his arrival, Ron Darling began ridiculing him. His name was Jonathon and Ron Darling pronounced his name in a syrupy lilt, as if the Indian boy were gay. Ron Darling invited the other boys to join in with the ridicule, and most did. Ron Darling said it over and over, the kid's name, and Jonathon went into a determined campaign of avoidance. He read a lot, war histories, and stared out an open window. Arn was friendly to Jonathon whenever he got the chance, when Ron Darling was elsewhere. The kid seemed above conversation but he sometimes spoke lone statements toward Arn. 'My mother descended from the people of Sitting Bull, my father from bridge builders.' Statements like that. 'My honor exists, fully formed. I need only find it and wear it like a fine coat.'

One evening Jonathon refused the dinner Ron Darling served and Ron Darling began calling him names. Jonathon stood and calmly announced that Ron had no grounds to speak even a single word to him, that Ron's babble was but dried thistle in the wind. Ron Darling grew earnest and told Jonathon he ought to be grateful, that he could do a lot worse, and Jonathon replied that Ron Darling understood the nature of true gratitude as well as a hamster understands calculus. Ron Darling, now flustered, said he could see why no reservation would want a useless punk like Jonathon, and Jonathon declared that he would rather die than live on a reservation, that he would rather perish shivering in the wilderness than rest warm and fed but with his heart full of the white man's lies. Ron Darling, no way around it, was losing a verbal confrontation with a twelve-year-old kid. He wanted to hit Jonathon – in fact, he raised a tense arm – but that was the one thing he couldn't do. He couldn't hit a kid and put his business in jeopardy. He could either keep the kid and keep making fun of him and risk being made a fool, or he could do what he'd done with Terrance – invent some infraction worthy of dismissal and send him down the line to the next family. Which was what he did.

Arn, in Jonathon's absence, felt spineless. He felt like Ron Darling's pet. He liked working hard, but he was losing faith in it. For choosing the evil he knew in order to delay the next move, the next upheaval, he felt beaten in spirit.

*

A few weeks before eighth grade was to start, Ron Darling's wife left. It surprised Arn how much this event damaged Ron Darling. He grew sullen and less mean. He ate nothing and played music in the house almost constantly, music without words, music that seemed meant to drown out whatever was going on in his head. His wife had been a negligible presence, not wanting much to do with the boys, but apparently Ron Darling had needed her for something. Maybe her family had money and now Ron Darling would never get it; maybe she'd found someone who would give her kids of her own, though she was kind of old for that. In her absence, Ron Darling began talking almost exclusively of a time – some distant decade – when he'd ridden the crest of a Houston real estate boom, owned a fleet of BMWs, had a hickory tree growing in his living room and a live-in maid. 'I've been a maid and I've had a maid,' he kept saying, almost singing it, like a country song. Arn wondered if Ron Darling had ever even lived in Texas. He never mentioned his wife. He was less mean, but it seemed like he was saving it up, hoarding his ill will for a specific purpose. It even occurred to Arn to comfort him, but he didn't know how. There were a couple other boys who'd been with Ron Darling longer. They were giving him a wide berth, so Arn did the same.

He went to school and people talked to him and he took notes and sneaked a cigarette now and then. He came home and ate snacks and watched TV and chuckled at the jokes of his foster brothers. No more dinners were served. Several weekends came and went with no work, no piling into the pickup and putting on gloves that were too big and toiling the minutes away and then breaking for burgers and then toiling the rest of the minutes away. It took Arn well into the fall semester to realize it: Ron Darling had lost interest in his business and had quit booking jobs. He'd lost interest in much, and one of those things was scuttling around chasing a buck. Arn had been slow on the uptake, and now all the warm weekends had passed.

At school, Arn and his foster brothers were wary of each other. They all had something in common, something to be ashamed of, but that shameful fact could be worked around as long as they weren't together. One of the brothers ran track. One was a nerd. One a suave horn player. Arn decided to try out for basketball and found that it was not a difficult game. All he had to do was hustle and good things happened. It was a school of the whitest kids around. If Arn decided to snare every rebound, he could. If he decided to score a lot, he could. The coach didn't go out of his way to praise Arn, but Arn figured that was because the coach didn't want to show favoritism. The tryouts lasted a week, and by the end of that week Arn knew he'd found an identity as an athlete that might obscure his other identity as a foster kid. Instead of laboring with shovels and drills, he would burn the hours of his weekends practicing free throws and learning to dribble with his left hand.

On Sunday, Arn found an abandoned hoop at an elementary school near his house and shot countless deep jumpers into a steady wind, riding a high. On Monday, he waited until after first period to go to the locker room. He pushed back the door and sidled up to the roster, breathing the foul air that he'd helped taint with his basketball sweat. He belonged in the locker room, had a claim to it. His eyes darted from name to name, too fast to read them. They weren't in alphabetical order. Arn put his hand to the paper. He worked his way down the whole sheet. He was so excited, his eyes wouldn't work. He took a look around. No one was watching him. He started at the bottom this time and worked his way to the top.

Now he felt it in his stomach. His name was not there. The names of a couple kids who were almost as good as Arn were there, and also the names of about ten kids who were clearly inferior. Blood was racing around in Arn's head. He pulled the roster off the wall and checked the back of it, resisted the urge to rip it into pieces. A couple kids came through the door and Arn was instantly embarrassed. They paused and then squeezed past him – not kids who'd been at the tryout, just regular PE kids. All the other basketball players had come before school and found their names. Arn wondered if they'd noticed his absence on the roster, if they'd been confused, if they'd secretly determined which player had made the team who didn't deserve to, which player was the worst of all. Arn pressed the roster back onto the wall.

When lunch period arrived, Arn was not hungry. He returned to the locker room, picked his way through to the offices where the coaches hung out. Coach Shell saw him through the glass and excused himself, stepping over some other coaches who were splitting a pizza. He came and stood in front of Arn, his head tipped to the side. He seemed like he felt guilty but was trying not to show it. Resigned is what he was – to what, Arn didn't know. Coach Shell wasn't saying anything. He was going to make Arn speak. But Arn didn't. He waited it out too. Coach Shell scratched his neck. He looked at Arn like the two of them had suffered a common injustice.

'Ask your dad, or your . . . whatever.' Coach Shell did something to his collar and then scratched his neck harder. 'Ask him why James Shell wouldn't let you on his basketball team. I have my reasons, I guarantee you that.'

Arn did not agree to ask Ron Darling anything. All he wanted to say was that none of this was fair, but he wasn't going to say that.

'If you're trying to piss off Ron Darling, you should've let me *on* the team.'

Coach Shell shrugged his shirt back into place. 'It's not like you have to quit basketball for life. It's just a middle school team. Worst one in the county.'

'Say I was the best player at the tryout. I want to hear you say it. Say I'm the best basketball player at this school.'

At this point Coach Shell must have considered his job, considered the fact that he could get in trouble for unfairly excluding Arn. All he would say was, 'You worked hard out there. You gave a great effort.'

That evening Arn went into the back room of the house, where Ron Darling was sitting in front of his TV, and announced that whatever feud Ron Darling had with Coach Shell, it had cost Arn a spot on the team.

'It's a poor musician who blames his instrument,' Ron Darling slurred.

'I'm not the musician,' Arn said. 'That's Randy. I'm blaming you.'

'James Shell can go to hell.'

'Yeah, he probably will.'

'It rhymes. James Shell can go to hell.'

'And you'll go right along with him, you asshole.'

Ron Darling's breath caught. He looked small in his recliner. His white T-shirt was stained down the front. It didn't take him long – a couple shamed seconds – to understand that he had fully fallen and this was the sort of thing that happened after the fall: your once loyal charges told you to go to hell.

After the basketball episode, things went downhill at the middle school. Arn's PE class did a unit on archery and some kid intentionally shot Arn in the arm with one of the dull wooden arrows. Arn, in frustration, broke the arrow in two, and he was sent to the office for destroying school property. Arn began drinking protein shakes and doing lots of pushups, not even counting the pushups, hoping for fights that never materialized. People seemed afraid of him, not in a way he enjoyed – the girls as well as the guys. He took all the money he had, the multitude of five-dollar bills Ron Darling had given him for each day he'd worked, down to the discount store and bought their cheapest home gym. He dragged it into his room and cleared a space for it, sliced the box open and spread the parts over the worn carpet. The gym didn't use weights, but heavy bands you had to stretch. It was around midnight, five hours after he'd brought the box into his room, this box adorned front and back with pictures of a satisfied man doing curls, that Arn threw in the towel. It wasn't his fault that the thing wasn't coming together. There were missing parts and extra parts. The directions were vague, grammatically incorrect. The assembly, even if it were possible, did not seem a one-man job. Arn leaned down over a flap of the cardboard and drove his fist into the face of the satisfied man doing curls. He collapsed on his bed. The store where he'd bought the gym didn't do returns; if you bought a thing, that thing wasn't their problem anymore. Arn told himself he'd work more on the home gym the next evening, but he didn't.

Close to graduation, Arn tried and failed to pick up smoking as a regular habit. He was relieved middle school was ending, but not hopeful about high school. He skipped the graduation ceremony, of course. He had his own ceremony, which was the cleaning out of his room, the getting rid of everything. The home gym and his basketball sneakers and a half-pack of cigarettes he'd abandoned and report cards and a coin collection he'd forgotten about and a Mariners cap he'd stolen from one of his old foster brothers. There was a lake nearby with a rotting dock and Arn guided wheelbarrow-load after wheelbarrow-load through the woods, over a hard-packed trail full of roots that bumped the wheelbarrow up off the ground, and out to the end of the dock, where he tipped the wheelbarrow forward and wrestled it side to side, dumping every scrap. He pictured the fish under there, not knowing what to think, letting the strange objects settle on the bottom of their world and then nosing closer to investigate.

REGGIE

His room in the afterlife was now roughly the size of his old bedroom in his parents' house, but with the piano and the bureau and the guitar reclining in its stand the place was cramped as a closet. Reggie didn't even pace anymore. He leaned against the walls. He didn't want to think of his room as a cell. This place wasn't prison and had nothing to do with prison. He believed this place had nothing even to do with laws, earthly or biblical, and whether Reggie had broken them. The floor had grown colder and Reggie had given up resting down where his mat used to be. Now he curled up on top of the bureau. With concentration, he could get the noise in his head to dull without the need of whistling or humming, but in time his concentration always gave out. He thought of the desert mornings, so obvious and refreshing. He thought of sleep, of open spaces.

He thought, at long last, of Cecelia, of the way she frowned when happily surprised and smiled when disappointed. He never could've done it consciously, but some wise part of him had kept him from dwelling on Cecelia until now. Some conservative branch of him had saved her for an emergency, and that's what Reggie was in the midst of. That, or the afterlife was now directly controlling Reggie's memory. The afterlife had broken Reggie down emotionally and now was giving him the comfort of a friend. Cecelia was an ace being played.

Before Reggie had met Cecelia, he'd never imagined an audience for his songs, but in time he'd begun judging their quality purely by her reaction. She was adorable and admirable in a way that made Reggie long to protect her rather than exploit or impress her. Not that she needed much protection. She seemed to wish at times to be gullible and thoughtless, but she wasn't. Reggie thought of her tiny pale feet curled up under her when she sat and played guitar. He thought of her sandpaper elbows. The way her face was somehow sharp and soft at once. He thought of their first meeting, at a concert held in the biggest auditorium on campus. About thirteen people had shown up. A woman with buzzed hair had played a deeply resonant wind instrument as tall as she was and a man with braids to his waist had accompanied her on xylophone. The two were married and both worked at a college on the West Coast. Their music sounded like it had been born deep in a mystical woodland. They were unfazed by the comically sparse crowd. They'd played three or four lengthy songs and then bowed and wheeled off their instruments. Reggie had noticed Cecelia during the show, sitting up straight and paying unwavering attention, a lock of hair wrapped around her finger, brow furrowed. When the show was over she remained in her seat and so did Reggie. He watched her as she kept gazing at the stage, empty now. Everyone had left the auditorium and Reggie felt like he would've waited all night for her to make a move and finally she gathered up her satchel and sweater and side-stepped into the aisle. Reggie hurried to get next to her and she wasn't a bit startled by him. He told her his name and she said hers. When they got outside she handed Reggie her bag to carry and then he walked her toward the parking lot. There was a feeling that nothing had to happen, that they didn't have to banter about the concert or identify things they had in common. They walked past the fountains in quiet, part of the hushed soundscape of the campus night, and when they reached Cecelia's car Reggie handed over her bag and thanked her, not knowing what for, and she shook his hand but not like men shook hands – she took one of his whole hands in both of hers and just stood there with it a moment like she was going to tell him something about his future. Reggie was thinking he had to ask for her phone number but for some reason he couldn't. He'd let her adjust her rearview mirror and back out and drive off. The next time he saw her was the first day of the next semester, in a class on early-twentieth-century painting. After class they had lunch together at a place with good stromboli and finally they talked and talked like old friends, breaking a longstanding silence between them, getting up for refills of soda and sipping on them deep into the afternoon.

Reggie thought of a night months after that, the only time he'd come close to kissing Cecelia. They'd been walking through the museum on campus, not paying attention to the art but enjoying the sequestered atmosphere, and a storm had rushed over Albuquerque and knocked out the power at the university. The backup lights had clicked on, barely bright enough to walk by, and Reggie and Cecelia had sat on the floor against a bench, the marble incredibly hard underneath them, feeling like the only two people in the world, or at least in the city, feeling safe in the cloistered caverns of the museum. Reggie had sensed his opening, sensed that at that moment Cecelia would have no grounds or strength to resist his advances.

Sitting on the bureau with his feet dangling down, Reggie felt relief for the first time since he'd died. He felt himself giving in.

SOREN'S FATHER

He spent an entire day with Gee, and though he could tell he was enjoying himself there was nothing he could do about the feeling that anything that happened to him while his son was in a coma didn't truly count. There could be no milestones, no further tragedy. That could've been why he was enjoying himself, he had to consider, not because he was so taken with Gee but because when he was with her reality was suspended. If Soren's father was killing time, that wasn't fair to Gee – if he was using her to speed along the dead stretch of time that would end only when Soren awakened. At the moment, though, he felt powerless against Gee. He wanted to see her, for whatever reason. He wanted to be around her. And anyway, he told himself, they'd met because *she'd* written a stranger a letter. They hadn't even kissed yet. Soren's father was analyzing things, which for someone unpracticed felt like overanalyzing, and maybe he was grateful to Gee even for that, for giving him a matter to over-analyze. Soren's father was good at simple thinking, and his situation, simply thought of, was that time needed to be spent and some ways of spending time were preferable to others and Gee, well, she was pretty damn preferable.

They spent the whole day together and she took him to a studio she kept about halfway between Albuquerque and Santa Fe. The studio was farther from the clinic than the restaurant house had been, and maybe Gee was aware of that. Maybe she was expanding his range little by little. The studio was full of roadrunners Gee had made. They were mostly glass and had oversized heads and spindly legs that made them look like they were going to pitch forward. Gee said that was part of the art, the fact that whoever looked at them was forced to imagine a big crash and a floor full of shards to tiptoe around.

They went to an outdoor restaurant with a bunch of space heaters and Gee got Soren's father to eat raw fish, tuna that had been cubed up and that you scooped with grainy crackers. Soren's father was surprised Gee had convinced him to eat the tuna and more surprised that when she asked him how business was going, he came right out and told her. He told her that he'd lost a driver and didn't have the pep to search for another one right now and so instead he was selling one of the trucks. He was going to lose part of his territory to a competitor.

Gee took a swig of some pomegranate juice she'd ordered and swallowed hard. 'So you think you might lose the whole thing? The whole business, in time?'

Soren's father guffawed. 'Hadn't thought that far ahead,' he said.

'Happens all the time. Lose one business, start another one. This is the United States.'

'Doesn't happen all the time to me.'

'Maybe you and I are meant to throw in our lot together.' Gee let out a triumphant little laugh. 'I have an idea for a restaurant I've been holding on to. Maybe I've been waiting for a partner. Maybe we're supposed to change each others' lives. Maybe a plan is underway that won't be revealed until it's complete.'

Soren's father tried to look amused.

'I think you have more talents than you give yourself credit for,' Gee told him. 'Might be time to use them. Maybe when Soren wakes up he'll have an even better father that before.'

Soren's father had no idea if Gee was serious about the restaurant idea. He did know he didn't care for her suggesting he hadn't always been the best person he could where Soren was concerned, the best possible example for his kid. That probably wasn't how she'd meant it, though. She was concerned about him, was all. Soren's father had no idea how well he knew Gee. He felt like a charmed snake, and like it must be for snakes, most of the charm resided in the charmer's lack of fear. Soren's father was only half-charmed, though. He wasn't a healthy enough snake to get fully charmed. The sun was very bright and the heaters were close and low. Soren's father reached for his water glass but all he had left was ice.

CECELIA

She did not wake her mother. Usually, on days Cecelia went to campus, she got up early in order to have time to get her mother up and out of bed. Her mother would argue against having the blinds opened. She would argue against the making of toast. When Cecelia left the house, she would do so dragging the fresh, oppressive knowledge that whatever she accomplished that day – wherever she went, whoever she met, whatever she learned – her mother was at home listlessly tossing feed out the back door, subsisting on crackers, listening to preachers.

The morning of the first day of the new semester, Cecelia skipped all this, so when she was pulled over crossing the Albuquerque line, she couldn't resist the thought that she was being punished for neglecting her mother. She saw the lights behind her and heard the loudening siren. She drove a couple blocks, making sure she wasn't going to cry unexpectedly, but she was nowhere near crying.

She turned into a plaza anchored at its ends by a battery store and a place that sold dirty magazines. She sifted through the glove box for her registration, then applied some lip gloss, killing the time until the knock would come at her window. She wasn't going to crane her neck. She collected some trash into a pile on the passenger seat, fished a nickel out from under the console.

Here he was. Cecelia wound down her window and handed out her license and registration and her proof of insurance, which she wasn't sure was still valid. The cop was a picture of freshness. He looked like in the past hour he'd gotten a haircut, a shave, a shower, his uniform pressed, nails clipped, shoes shined.

'Know why I pulled you over?'

Cecelia could see the cop's breath. It probably smelled minty. He was standing up straight, way above her.

'I'm not intoxicated. I know I wasn't speeding and I know I wasn't littering. I'm not trafficking any Mexicans. I didn't rob a bank.' Cecelia pulled her seatbelt away from her with her thumb. It didn't really snap back.

'Is this the route you're going? The smartass route?' The cop's tone was not contentious. He wanted to have pulled Cecelia over for her own good.

'Is it because my car's a total piece of shit? Is it not roadworthy?'

The cop wasn't making a move to run Cecelia's license. He was holding her information on his metal clipboard. 'It's your brake light,' he conceded. 'The left.'

Cecelia looked back in that direction.

'You have to get it fixed,' the cop said. 'It's non-optional.'

Cecelia found the cop's eyes with her own and listened.

'So, the question is *where* are you going to get it fixed? Do you have a place you go to?'

'Not anymore. I used to but he moved.'

'I can recommend one: Thomas Imports, up on Paseo Del Norte.'

'Thomas Imports.'

'If you promise me you'll go there, I won't write you a ticket.'

'I promise, then.'

'When?'

'How much does it cost?' Cecelia said.

'Less than a ticket.'

'Not for me, because if you gave me a ticket I wouldn't pay it.'

'Oh, no?'

'Lack of funds. And I guess lack of interest.'

The cop smirked. A guy exited the dirty magazine shop weighed down with several bursting bags, like he'd been to the grocery store. Cecelia and the cop watched him until he was around the corner.

'Look,' the cop said. 'If I tell them you're coming, they'll replace it at cost – couple bucks. I'll tell them Cecelia's coming in this afternoon.'

'Okay,' said Cecelia. 'Thanks.'

'Paseo Del Norte, west of Transom. Thomas Imports. Big blue sign. I'm going to call them.'

'I appreciate that.'

'They'll tell me if you don't show, and I've got your information.

The light needs to be fixed before the other one goes out and somebody hits you.'

'I get it.'

'There's really nothing more dangerous than driving without brake lights. People get hurt. I'm making sure you understand.'

'I do. Fully.'

The cop nodded. He wrote something down, then handed Cecelia back her license and papers. He was happy with himself. He patted the top of Cecelia's car sportily and went back to his cruiser, where he made a show of calling someone on a cell phone.

Cecelia stayed where she was. She wasn't going to pull out first. And she wasn't going to the mechanic on Paseo Del Norte. It wouldn't only be the bulb. It would be fuses and wires and the whole electrical system. The mechanics would compile a list of all the things mortally wrong with Cecelia's car. They would make her aware of every danger. It was that, but also she wasn't going to the mechanic on Paseo Del Norte because she didn't want to accept a favor from some scrubbed cop. She hoped never to take another favor from a person who considered himself good. The world was full of goody-goody jerks and Cecelia did not aspire to inclusion in their ranks, nor did she wish to be fodder for their goodness.

She reached into her school bag and felt around for the inside pocket. She found what she was looking for – the twenty-five dollars she'd taken from the kid with the internship. She rubbed the bills in her fingers. She was never going to spend these bills. She would keep them close, for strength. She saw why she'd been pulled over. It wasn't because she hadn't woken her mother, it was because she'd trespassed and stolen this money. The world didn't want her stepping out of line. It was reacting. Warning her. This cop and

Nate were on the same side – all authority, all rich kids, all whom luck favored. Cecelia had engaged them and they weren't going to let her get away with it.

She looked back and saw the cop still sitting there in his car. He was writing, listening to his dispatcher. Cecelia would wait him out. If he didn't have to hurry off somewhere, neither did she. She'd read a book or something. But she didn't even need a book. If she could sit at the vigils for hours on end, she could outwait this cop. She didn't need to invent a task, didn't need to keep cleaning her car's interior or organizing her glove box. Cecelia was the best vigiler, and this cop was only good at being good. Every week there were fewer people outside the clinic because none of them were as ready as Cecelia was to be absent from their regular lives. Cecelia couldn't wait for the next vigil, to see how many more had dropped out. She didn't miss her mom. She'd never missed her uncle. She didn't need television or home-cooked meals. She didn't miss making music. She didn't miss being a conscientious student, didn't miss any of the old versions of herself she'd left behind. The only thing she missed was no longer in the world.

Cecelia saw the cop pull a computer out from his dashboard and type something into it. He took a gulp from a water bottle and replaced the cap. She'd be late to class if necessary, but she wasn't going to leave first. She rolled down her other window, the passenger window, and let cold pass through the car. She repositioned herself, pulling her legs up into the seat, seeing what was across the street – a big open yard of stone birdbaths. They were endless, like a photograph of crops. Acres of them. There were no birds anywhere. A thousand baths and not one bird. The baths were bone dry. The sky was empty.

THE GAS STATION OWNER

He was training new employees, two of them, to be co-managers and co-clerks and co-stockers and co-janitors. The last time the gas station owner had an employee was five or six years ago, a kid whose father owned a car dealership in Santa Fe. The kid had been carrying on a feud with his old man. He hadn't talked much but he showed up on time, until he hadn't shown up at all and the gas station owner never heard from him again. He hadn't even come back to get his last check. Probably he'd proven his point to his father and the two of them had made up and he was talking someone into a sunroof that very moment. Now the gas station owner had these two sisters, not babies but young – both, they informed the gas station owner, engaged in a correspondence course that would certify them as librarians. They'd be leaving at the end of July. They'd be done with their coursework and would be off to do internships. The internships could be in New York. They could be in Miami, Los Angeles.

'Yeah,' the other replied. 'Or they could be in Las Cruces.'

The gas station owner assured them he'd be back in a month or two. He apologized for their scant training. The sisters were from Golden. They had been hired on as waitresses in Lofte's restaurant just a few weeks ago but business was falling off by the day and the diner couldn't keep them. They were relieved to have these new jobs. They were eager for the chance to organize, to be in charge. The gas station owner gave them a number to call if there was a problem customer.

'Take Sundays off,' he told them. 'Unless you don't believe in taking Sundays off. In that case, open on up.'

He held out a list of vendors, complete with shipment sizes and frequency. The skinny sister leaned forward and took the paper, then handed it to the other.

'What I do is, every time I get five hundred dollars I drop it in the safe.' The gas station owner pointed to the back room.

'We'll do it every three hundred,' said the skinny one.

She was more talkative than her sister. She was notably skinny, and the quiet one was thin to a normal degree. They dressed about the same, with white T-shirts and chopped hair.

'Can we bring our dog?' the skinny one asked. 'A phone number for a thug is one thing, but the dog would be more ...'

'Preventative,' said the other.

'That's the sort of thing I'm going to leave up to you,' the gas station owner said. 'I'll have to tell Mayor Cabrera you think he's a thug. He'll like that.'

The gas station owner lowered the blinds. He came out from behind the register, as if to give a tour, but everything in the shop was in plain view.

'Make sure the oldest dairy stuff is at the front of the case. It's mostly chocolate milk and half-and-half, which takes a while to spoil.'

'Question,' said the skinny sister. 'How come no energy drinks?'

'I don't know,' said the gas station owner.

'Sunglasses,' the other sister said.

'Yup,' resounded the skinny one. 'Put a rack right in that corner. We're in the desert, after all.'

The gas station owner thought of his rucksack, almost fully packed. He hadn't considered sunglasses. He was enjoying the preparation a bit too much, getting packed and rested. He was getting ready to test himself, not go on vacation. And if he were being strict he would've left his whole future to the elements, would've severed ties with the known world, which would've meant leaving the station untended. He was giving the station a fighting chance to survive his absence, he told himself, only because that was better for everyone – these girls, the failing town – not because he cared about the place.

'This is embarrassing,' he said. 'I forgot your names.'

'Don't worry about our real names. We've been Dewey and Binky since we were this high.'

'Do you have a nickname, Mr Fair?'

'Well. Shade Tree.'

'Because he's tall,' said the regular-sized sister.

'Probably other reasons,' replied the skinny one. 'Nicknames say a lot.'

'I can't wait to have a child,' said the regular-sized sister. 'I can't wait to nickname that little sucker.'

Back at home, the gas station owner returned to his rucksack. He was taking a knife, a knife he'd sharpened to the point of being almost too sharp, a knife that if it rubbed enough against its leather sheath would slice right through. He was bringing jerky, dried fruit, nuts, coffee. He was bringing water, many layers of clothing, toilet paper, lip balm, sunscreen, lighters and matches, a hat he'd bought special, a compass, a watch. He was taking a notepad and a pencil, to count the days. He was bringing both a thin hotel room Bible and his bulky Manhattan Project book. He was not taking a shotgun. This was foolhardy, he knew, but he wanted everything to fit in his sack. He was taking a .38 revolver. He did not want to take cash, but probably he would. It seemed like it would sully the endeavor, cash, but probably he would take some. The desert never played by rules or stood on ceremony, and the gas station owner wasn't going to either. He wouldn't leave his station unmanned. He wouldn't set off unarmed or without money. What mattered was getting into the center of something he'd spent his life dawdling on the edge of.

MAYOR CABRERA

He arrived early and Dana shooed him out to the balcony. This had happened before. She didn't want him to see her applying makeup. She didn't want him to stand around and look at her in her jeans and T-shirt. She was in the shower now. Mayor Cabrera could hear the water.

The balcony was tiny. You had to maneuver yourself around the door to get out there. You had to scrape your belly on the doorframe. No room for a table, not by a long shot. There was a pretty stone hill to look at, spiked with sapling evergreens. Mayor Cabrera did not understand why if you were going to bother constructing balconies, if you were going to draw balconies into your blueprints and procure the materials and burn the man-hours, why you wouldn't make the balconies two feet bigger and then a couple could sit out here with a place to put their drinks.

Mayor Cabrera heard the water cut off and then a few minutes later heard clinking sounds from the kitchen. Dana always prepared a snack plate to put near the bed. Mayor Cabrera could picture the look on her face as she sliced up the fruit. He very suddenly felt dizzy and reached his hand to the railing. The balcony felt high up, a lot higher than two stories. Usually, by this stage, Mayor Cabrera was like Pavlov's dog. He should've been at full ready by now, and he was not. He wasn't experiencing a hint of readiness. He felt snuck up on and disoriented and wanted off the porch.

He entered the condo and crossed over the cushy rug in the den and leaned in the archway of the kitchen. Dana paused in her cutting but didn't turn to face him. The kitchen smelled like melon and there was a tiny window through which could be seen a vast canyon view.

'None of this seems in season,' Dana said.

'No?' said Mayor Cabrera. 'Well, it's the desert. The only thing that's ever in season is chile peppers.'

'Where do cantaloupes come from, anyway?'

'Cantaloupes,' said Mayor Cabrera. 'I guess I have no idea.'

Dana resumed her slicing, rising onto the balls of her feet for leverage. Mayor Cabrera examined the back of her, and when it did nothing to help him he looked away. Dana had a bunch of liquor bottles on a high shelf above the window. Mayor Cabrera knew most of the bottles had likely been gifts from clients. Dana only drank gin. He didn't want to ask her about her Christmas, didn't want to know who she'd spent it with. He hoped just with her mother in Abilene.

'What is that thing?' he said.

Dana turned her head to see what he was pointing at. 'Oh, that's a holder for glasses. A glasses rack.'

'How does that work?'

'Eyeglasses, not drinking glasses. It doesn't work, though. The glasses fall off.'

'You've got a lot of glasses,' said Mayor Cabrera.

'Fourteen pairs.'

Dana set the plate she was working on aside and cut into something new. The new smell was stronger, earthy and cloying.

'A kid I used to tutor gave it to me. It doesn't work for glasses but I put mail under it.'

Mayor Cabrera knew Dana had been a tutor for years, all through her twenties. She'd been to a few years of college. She'd told him she'd preferred tutoring girls because the boys always liked her too much. They always showered and put on good clothes for the sessions. She'd had to buy baggy sweat suits to wear. It was math she used to tutor. The sound of her voice seemed like it might be helping Mayor Cabrera with the lack of anything happening in his pants. He felt *something*, he thought.

'How come you didn't finish college, if you don't mind me asking?'

'I don't mind. I never even got close. I went to three different colleges for a year each.'

'I didn't know three.'

'If you count that community college.'

'I didn't get to go at all, so . . .'

'You didn't miss much.'

'No?'

'You can read, right?'

'Passably.'

'And you can drink beer, even when you don't feel like it?'

'Now *that* I can do.'

'That's all it is.'

Dana pulled out a cheeseboard and a small pewter tankard that contained honey. The view out the window was a brush of shadows now. Mayor Cabrera heard the heat kick on.

'I always wanted to work in a high rise,' Dana said. 'People always run that down, working at a big company in a cubicle, but I think it sounds nice. Elevators and casual Fridays.'

Mayor Cabrera adored every part of Dana. Her elbows and her heels. He didn't care what she'd looked like twenty years ago. He adored her now. He could not understand what was wrong with him. His lower half was dead. He felt sweat breaking out under his clothes.

Dana said the lid of the cocktail shaker was stuck and asked Mayor Cabrera to pull it apart. He closed the space between them but instead of reaching for the shaker he pressed himself against Dana. He had nothing to press with, nonetheless she shuddered, her knife blade sunk into a strip of mango. Her head tipped back into his chest. She held the knife as though she were steadying herself with it, the blade static there in the flesh of the fruit.

The scent of her hair alone should have been enough. Her little waist in his grip alone. The suppleness of her ear against his whiskers. But none of it was. Mayor Cabrera felt thoroughly fed up with himself. He knew it was a lost cause. He knew that to keep trying would be swimming in quicksand. This had never happened to him before. Dana was everything and the only thing he desired.

His thoughts quickly switched to protecting her feelings. This wasn't her fault, of course, and he didn't want Dana to feel inadequate. She was nothing of the sort. She would handle this sort of problem like a pro, Mayor Cabrera knew, smooth it over, but it would hurt her pride. Mayor Cabrera had to invent some emergency, some pressing mayoral business that had slipped his mind. The little kitchen window showed only darkness outside now and his nose was full of foreign fruit and Dana's shampoo. He'd say he needed to rush back to Lofte and he'd act annoyed about it, which would be easy because he *was* annoyed. He was not going to wait around to see if Dana bought any of it. He was going to pay her and get his coat and get the hell out of there and catch his breath. People had emergencies. Emergencies were a fact of life.

In his car, headed south, Mayor Cabrera had to face it: he did not want to be a client of Dana's anymore. He didn't want to be a client because he wanted to be more than that. He wanted her body but he wanted the rest too. He wanted Dana to be his and no one else's. He wanted her in her jeans without makeup. He wanted her scarfing greasy McDonald's instead of pressing her lips against a dripping plum. He wanted to watch TV with her, take up jogging with her. He wanted all her gifts to come from him. Mayor Cabrera let up on the gas pedal. There was nobody behind him. He felt rushed in his mind and didn't want to rush down the road. What he was considering was nuts. He squeezed the steering wheel and then honked the horn a half-dozen times, trying to loosen things up in his head. He wanted to know all Dana's problems, but he didn't want to become one of her problems. He was entertaining a fantasy and trying to convince himself the fantasy could be reality. There wasn't an ounce of wisdom in Mayor Cabrera. He was trying to ignore all the roadblocks, and there were plenty. For instance, where would they live? There was that. They wouldn't live at the motel, now would they? Would she be willing to quit her job, to give up a client list that, at her age, would be impossible to recover? Did Mayor Cabrera have enough money, enough prospects, for the both of them? Would she want to be with someone of so little accomplishment? Sure, Mayor Cabrera was a mayor, but he was destined to be the mayor that finally killed off Lofte. Dana might laugh at him. She wouldn't laugh, because they'd known each other too long, but she might not take him seriously, might let him down easy. It was a well-worn way to be pathetic, falling in love with a professional lady. Mayor Cabrera had told himself he'd set their appointments at once a month because he didn't want to get used to Dana, didn't want her to lose her allure, but that had never been the danger. The danger was this, falling for her, and it would've happened no matter how often or seldom he saw her. Normally when he drove this road in this direction, the sun was rising and Mayor Cabrera was gladly exhausted. This time, dawn was far off and if Mayor Cabrera was exhausted it was with himself. His life was off course. He'd taken a bad exit thousands of miles ago. He'd tried to fashion himself into a loner. He wasn't a loner and he wasn't really a mayor. He'd been an uncle and a brother-in-law and he'd once been a hell of a husband. Now he was nothing. Now he was desperate.

CECELIA

Picking her way through the music building, changing batteries and locking up A/V cabinets that professors had left wide open, Cecelia saw Nate's name on the rehearsal space schedule. Space 4. Noon. This was something he'd mentioned from time to time – pursuing a minor in music in order to gain access to the university's rehearsal facilities. He had a perfectly good place to practice – that plush garage behind his house – but he had to go and lay claim to scarce rehearsal space at the school. That was Nate. If he ever thought about other people it was in terms of what he could take from them.

Cecelia strolled herself over to the student union and picked at a muffin, killing time. She flipped through the school newspaper, skimming a story about an African prince that would be attending University of New Mexico. She stood at the windows that looked out onto the field where the band practiced. No band today. Football season was over. Instead, some kind of intramural flag rugby game. It looked like something from a college brochure. Cecelia watched the people collide with each other, watched them laugh, watched them arch their backs as they ran to avoid having their flags pulled off, watched them drink sloppily from a big orange cooler.

She returned to the music building. The card in the slot outside rehearsal space 4 said Thus Poke Sarah's Thruster, and from inside there was noise. Cecelia peeked in the window, knowing that no one inside would spot her because she didn't care if they did. Apathy was her camouflage. Nate was behind his drum set, banging on it, an obnoxious look on his face. He was keeping the beat exactly. He always could do *that*: hold the beat like a metronome. The song they were playing wasn't one of Reggie's. Cecelia had never heard it.

The guy on bass and the guy on guitar looked like brothers, the sort who bicker constantly but never want to be apart. They didn't seem like anything special. There was another guy, on keyboards. He was the talent. He had on a loose-fitting ski cap and no shoes. He didn't have to think about what he was doing, didn't have to contort his soul. Yes, they were a band. No denying it.

Cecelia didn't want to stick around long enough to hear them play one of Reggie's songs. She felt as though she'd gotten a bead on an enemy, and she wasn't sure if hearing Nate and his minions tromp around on the hallowed ground of Reggie's imagination would add fuel to her fire or discourage her. She was shrinking her soul, and discouragement was an indulgence. She backed away from the studio door as if children were sleeping behind it and descended onto the main walk, blending herself in with a late-day stream of amiable young people who were filled, each and every, with vague intentions of making themselves better. Cecelia hid among them, walking how they walked. Her intention was to be worse, and so far what she'd accomplished was stealing twenty-five dollars and mouthing off to a cop. She needed to escalate her tactics. She needed to reach a darker height. If she couldn't, then she was as feckless as any of these girls in their ballerina shoes or these soft-eyed unshaven boys who'd never have it in them to do anything despicable. Cecelia had enemies and now she was learning how to *be* an enemy. This herd of kids Cecelia was walking along with, all hats and fancy cell phones, was on its way nowhere.

SOREN'S FATHER

Soren's birthday came and went. He was a year older. He was aging, at least on paper. Soren's father had not bought his son a gift. The bike he'd bought him for Christmas was still at home, in the utility closet behind the washer. He hadn't gotten Soren a cake or even a card. He hadn't mentioned the birthday to Gee. One of the nurses had stopped by and asked if Soren's father wanted the staff to do anything, to gather and sing or bring up balloons, but he'd declined. Soren had missed his own birthday, and Soren's father had to entertain the possibility that he might miss another. The two of them could be sitting in this same room with the same expressions on their faces a year from now. That wasn't out of the question. It very much *was* the question. Soren could be in a coma a year from now and he could be in a coma a year after that.

Soren had been skinny before but now his legs were sticks. He'd gotten taller but weighed less than before the coma. Soren's father hadn't done a pushup in ages and his arms were feeble. He and his boy were shrinking. Soren's father wondered how many birthday cards had come to the clinic for Soren. Maybe none. Maybe the only strangers still interested in him were the vigilers, and there were only about twenty of them left, the true believers, the zealots — or at least they *wanted* to be those things. Soren's father had sold off another lunch truck, to the same guy who'd bought the first one. He didn't like having a truck sitting outside the clinic waiting for him. Maybe he didn't *want* to resume his route. Maybe he'd been sick of driving that fucking truck. Maybe he'd been sick of smoking cigarettes, sick of the smell of heat-lamp beef tips. Maybe he wanted to blow the cash from the trucks taking Gee out to fancy dinners. Maybe thinking about the future, tomorrow or next month or next year, was the most futile thing a person could engage in.

Soren's father stood at the window of the clinic room looking out at the expanding desert instead of looking at his son, who'd had a haircut that day and didn't look right. The haircut made him look older and dopey, and he was young and sharp. Soren's father gazed out past the quadrant of the parking lot where the vigilers always sat, missing them a little despite himself, looking forward to Wednesday and their mute company. There was an auto body shop and a cell phone store. There was a vacant lot beyond the interstate where a hot-air balloon crew was sitting around munching on apples, waiting for tourists. Above everything was a blue sky, a sky the precise color of a pickup Soren's father had owned when he was young, back when a blue sky meant something.

REGGIE

He sat on the bench at the piano, the gashed upholstery pinching the backs of his legs. He did not feel bound by time. He was free of the burden and crutch of seconds and centuries. He sat on the bench, his feet resting on the pedals instead of on the cold ground and his hands resting in his lap. There was no dust whatsoever on the piano. The air in Reggie's tiny chamber was the purest he'd ever breathed. Reggie removed his shirt, something he'd often done when he wrote songs back when he was alive. He folded the shirt and rested it up on top of the piano.

He was at the mercy of the afterlife whether he surrendered the songs or not. To act like he wielded any leverage was delusional. Reggie told himself he wasn't giving in because of the deteriorating living conditions, nor to squelch the shrill vibration in his brain, nor even because the solitude was too much for him, the lack of answers, the lack of everything – love, hunger, sleep. He was giving in because there was nothing noble about holding out. There was egotism and defiance in holding out, and probably even toughness, he could admit, but nothing truly noble. Reggie had been able to accept in life that he couldn't have all the answers, and he would accept the same in death. He knew that the notion that one got what one deserved was childish and his obstinacy concerning relinquishing his songs had become a form of begging. Begging for answers about the day of his accident, on that straight, familiar road, answers about this new life that wasn't a life at all and wasn't new anymore. Reggie was going to wind up where he wound up. Someone had a plan for him and that plan was none of his business.

Reggie tried not to hold his breath. He raised his hands and let his fingers fall upon the keys and felt a great relief at acting rather than resisting action. He was a man, though a dead man, and what brought him peace was work. The notes were strong and Reggie was not rusty in his playing. The song danced out through his hands, the buzzing in his head subsiding, the notes filling the void that was Reggie's world. He had never cried as a grown person and didn't know how, but he felt the trials he'd endured swelling up in his heart. It was hard not to play too fast. He was finally complaining. The song was a lament. The little room without a ceiling had the most robust acoustics Reggie had ever heard. It felt like he was composing the song as he went, though that could not have been true. He'd been writing the song all along in a secret part of his brain, the part where he'd hidden Cecelia from himself for all that time. As the song opened up before Reggie he wondered what Cecelia would think of it. He wished she could hear it. It was good, he knew. What he wanted was to see Cecelia frown at it, pleased.

CECELIA

She woke up groggy, her throat dry and stomach unsettled. Her mind was as quiet as a closed theater, but there was turmoil in her body, in her midsection and limbs. She felt like she'd been breathing something other than air all night. Cecelia had already gotten used to leaving her mother in bed, leaving her mother to deal with the morning on her own, but this morning she was pointedly thankful at being able to slip into clothes and swish some mouthwash and sneak out of the house unmolested. She felt like she hadn't slept all night but she had.

It wasn't until she was in her car, after pulling up onto the interstate and settling into the right lane as was her habit, that she realized she was humming. She wasn't a person who hummed or whistled, but she was humming and not stopping. Maybe she wasn't stopping because she wanted to know what the song was. She didn't recognize it. It wasn't a finished melody. She could hear notes in her head that corresponded to the notes she was humming. She could've stopped, but for some reason she wasn't. She heard piano, fluttery at first but jostling into a song, and then suddenly decisive. She wanted to speak out but she didn't. She kept her window closed. Cecelia had had songs stuck in her head before, but these notes were way inside, like trace amounts of lovely poison. They continued as she drove and drove, the sky getting clearer along with the music. The discomfort in her body was fading. Her stomach felt okay. Her head didn't feel normal but it didn't ache. The song sounded like it was being played on a very old piano, like a lot of the songs in the History of Music class Cecelia had dropped. This song wasn't from History of Music. Cecelia had never heard it before. She'd never heard anything similar. She wasn't humming anymore. It wasn't necessary. Her throat was quiet and she heard the song all the more clearly.

During her first class, she could barely hear the professor. The song was getting louder and the noises from the outside were falling away. Cecelia found she could slow the song down in her mind, but she couldn't stop it. It was either repeating or it had no end. Cecelia was grinding her teeth. She wished she had gum. There was a pop quiz and Cecelia wrote her name on the paper and handed it back in without answering any of the questions. The forced heat in the classroom was making her eyes water and her sinuses tingle.

When the class was dismissed, she went out and stood under a tree in the liberal arts quad. She could hear singing now, along with the piano. She heard singing and the voice was her own. The lyrics were as unfamiliar as the music, but the voice singing them was hers. She looked around. Sorority girls and a yoga guy and a maintenance man. A professor from the journalism school. They were all going about their days, wishing to be better people. There were no leaves on the tree Cecelia was standing under. The ground beneath her was too soft. She didn't know what to do. She went to the student union and ate lunch off by herself. She tried thinking of another song and couldn't keep straight even the simplest, catchiest pop melody. She picked her sandwich apart and then pushed it away. She put her head down on her bag and tried to sleep and pretended to sleep, but she was nowhere near drowsy. The other kids were finding lines to wait in. They were getting out on the sidewalks and striding toward reasonable destinations. Cecelia couldn't blend in with them any-more. She felt ridiculous. She went to a deserted part of campus and sat under a sculpture that resembled a shipwreck and cried for a time in the shadows down under the hull.

By the time her afternoon class wrapped up Cecelia was way beyond liking or disliking the song. She'd spent a day with it. She knew every note and lyric by heart and she always would. She'd col-lected some handouts her religion professor distributed, but she couldn't remember a word the woman had said. The song was poppy but not upbeat. It groused impalpably, it's underlying tone one of grievance.

Cecelia went to her evening class, a class focused on the city of Paris during certain decades. The song was as clear as ever, but not as insistent as it had been. Or maybe Cecelia was exhausted. The song seemed to have gotten comfortable with her, too-loud background music. Cecelia could almost follow the thread of the lecture. Marie, the girl from the A/V booth who'd sent her the pizza, was in this class. She winked at Cecelia. Cecelia sat in the back and held a pen over a blank sheet of paper as ten minutes passed, then another ten, then another, admitting something to herself, a fact Cecelia had no idea what to do with but could no longer avoid. She knew what Reggie's songs were like and they were precisely like this one. She had the same feeling in her guts, the same apprehensive joy, as when she'd first heard any of Reggie's songs. The structure, the lyrics – none of it was done in a manner that would've occurred to Cecelia or anyone else. Cecelia had written plenty of songs and they were a far cry from this one. This wasn't her style and it wasn't anyone else's in the living world. It was the unmistakable style of Reggie Mercer. A fact was a fact. The Paris professor was going on about plumbing and bearded painters, and Cecelia stared toward him dumbly, nodding as if she appreciated his knowledge, watching the piece of chalk he kept tossing up and catching.

After class, Marie came back and sat in a desk near Cecelia. She had colorful eye makeup on. Marie always invited Cecelia to go out with her at night, and this time Cecelia did not turn her down. Cecelia didn't want to be alone. She didn't want to go back home with this song in her head, didn't want to go back home regardless.

They walked together to the parking lot and then Cecelia followed Marie to a heavily balconied high-rise, where Cecelia parked her car and hopped into Marie's brand new Volkswagen Bug. They drove across town and visited some people who lived in an old church building. There were a handful of young men around who were continually engaged in tasks. There were girls, all of whom had long pink fingernails, and they lolled about on the couches. It was an environment where a conversation would never survive, and Cecelia was glad for that. The young men kept bringing sweating pitchers and the girls kept emptying them into their glasses. Marie sat next to Cecelia with a hand on Cecelia's forearm. None of these people knew Reggie. Marie hadn't known him. Outside of Nate badgering her, Cecelia hadn't spoken about Reggie since his death. She never felt like explaining how she felt about him, explaining the quiet benevolent edginess he'd embodied, explaining what was happening now, his song.

Cecelia looked around at all the stained glass. At the other end of the room was an altar, a pulpit or whatever. A couple rows of pews hadn't been ripped out. They still had the hymnals in the little slots.

'There's no music,' Cecelia said. 'There isn't any music on.' She wasn't sure whether it would help or hurt, to have music going outside of her. Maybe she wanted everyone's voices drowned out. Maybe she didn't like a bunch of people lounging around in a house of God. Cecelia didn't think there was a higher power looking out for her, but this was still disrespectful. It was the kind of thing Reggie never would've done.

'We're trying to cut down on music,' one of the girls told her.

'For purposes of spiritual renewal,' said another.

'Music giveth,' the first girl said. 'But it also taketh away.'

In time, the young men came out with grilled cheese sandwiches. Each girl, Cecelia included, got her own little platter. The girls all had to remove their bare feet from the table. A pickle was on each plate, a handful of chips. The sandwiches were quartered. The young men didn't sit down. They stood by in case the girls needed anything else.

Next they went to a bar with a cowboy theme. The place was closed and the staff had convened out back to drink from a keg and grill hot dogs. Cecelia downed her beer greedily. She had passed most of the day with the feeling of being on a remote plane, but now she felt close to the ground, aware. She could smell the sweat of the busboys, stripping their shirts off in the cold.

Cecelia found herself in the passenger seat of a parked SUV, Marie on the seat with Cecelia, half on her lap. Cecelia recognized the guy in the driver's seat. He was the pizza guy, the one who'd come to the A/V booth. This time he wore a light blue shirt. It said, across the front, LIGHT BLUE SHIRT. He put on some music, soft enough that Cecelia couldn't really hear it.

'It's stuffy in here,' she said.

'All the windows are open.'

'Is this elevator music?' Marie asked.

'This is *my* music,' answered the pizza guy. 'Frankly, I wouldn't mind if it was used in elevators.'

'Cecelia's a musician,' Marie said.

'My bandmate died,' Cecelia said. 'His name was Reggie. He died, so the band is over with, but the notable thing is that last night he sent me a song while I was sleeping. That's the only conclusion I can draw. That's the part that might be worth mentioning to people at a party. A new song of his, one I'd never heard, found its way into my mind while I was sound asleep and it's playing over and over as we speak.'

Everything was still for a moment. Cecelia was relieved to have said what she'd said. She couldn't decide if it sounded crazier or more reasonable, now that she'd put it into words. The pizza guy blew air into his cheeks. He seemed like maybe he'd heard all this before. He tapped his knuckle against the windshield, thinking.

'That's morbid,' he said.

'I agree,' said Cecelia.

'How do you know it's this Reggie guy's song?' Marie asked.

'Because it's *just so*,' Cecelia said. 'It's done the perfect amount – not underdone and not overdone.'

'Sounds like a good name for a really bad album,' said the pizza guy. '*Just So*.'

'You can't tell what the song's trying to do until it does it.' Cecelia could hear the beer in her voice. She was drunker than she felt.

'If you learned to write songs from Reggie, wouldn't your songs naturally sound something like his?' Marie asked.

The pizza guy broke in. 'Doesn't work that way. If you can't write a certain kind of song, you can't write a certain kind of song.'

'That doesn't sound true.' Marie shifted her smooth, soft weight on Cecelia's leg.

'I can tell it's his song,' Cecelia said. 'Like the way you could pick a relative out of a crowd, even if you'd never met them.'

'That doesn't sound true, either.'

'Believe her,' said the pizza kid.

Marie scoffed kindly. 'I say she's not giving herself credit. She wrote a song and for some reason she's not taking the credit. As a rule, songs don't get telepathically transmitted. They get written.'

Cecelia shook her head.

'Maybe that's how geniuses work,' Marie continued. 'The songs appear in dreams. Maybe you're a genius and you didn't know it until today.'

'I wish,' said Cecelia. 'I'm many things, but I'm no genius.'

'What's the first line?' Marie asked. She lit a cigarette. Cecelia had never seen her smoke before.

'The curbs in the suburbs all rhyme with each other.'

'Okay,' said the pizza guy. 'What's the second line?'

'That's why you kick them like you kicked your little brother.'

Finally, at sunrise, Cecelia and Marie arrived back at the high-rise with all the balconies. Cecelia got on the road headed for Lofte and fought to stay awake. This was going to be the first time since she'd started college that she would blow off an entire day. She hadn't missed an hour of work when Reggie died. Today she was going to miss work entirely and the same with all her classes. She drove under a hot air balloon and then could not relocate it in her mirrors. It seemed to climb to a point directly above her whining Scirocco and vanish.

At home, Cecelia snuck inside and went to her bedroom. She could hear the TV in the living room. It was the black gospel singers, their voices like revelers heard from across a lake. 'Tears for all woes,' they sang. 'A heart for every plea.' She could hear the gospel singers and she could hear Reggie's song. Cecelia wondered if her mother knew she was home, wondered if her mother was out of bed. She wondered if her mother had the wherewithal to worry about her. She hadn't told her mother anything important in a long time and she sure didn't want to explain that a guy Cecelia had considered her best friend and who Cecelia's mother had never met had died and then, dead, had written a song Cecelia was now in possession of, a song about a neighborhood that held none of your history and all your pain.

Cecelia sat up and took the Rubik's Cube from the nightstand.

It was cool against her fingertips and against her forehead. When it wasn't cool anymore she set it down and stood up from the bed. She pulled the closet doors open, pulled the string that snapped on the bulb. She reached into the back of the closet and took out her guitar and positioned a chair, pulled an old tape recorder over and plugged it in. Cecelia pressed PLAY and RECORD and began stroking her guitar. It was the same old guitar and these were her same old fingers. It took her a few bars to clear out her throat. She looked around at her bare walls. No postcards, but then she wasn't in need of inspiration. She was in service to someone else's inspiration. She looked at the interminable line of tiny holes where the tacks had been, hitting notes and strumming heavier.

THE WOLF

It was daytime but the moon was out, a tarnished coin in the ozone. The wolf had given up his rounds. His territory was all he had and he'd been patrolling it since before he could remember and he'd forsaken it and wanted nothing more to do with Albuquerque. He haunted the basin now, a lost land that would offer a lost animal no aid, a land where the dunes shifted overnight and scorpions feared their own stinging tails. The wolf frequented old Rattlesnake Park, an area that didn't seem owned by any particular human, a place marked off with NO TRESPASSING signs that had been posted by trespassers. Closer to Lofte there was a copse of doomed pine trees on a defunct golf course and the wolf used the branchless woods as cover. The days were not bright and the nights were not dark. The wolf was subsisting on nothing but butterflies, snapped from the wind and swallowed in fluttery gulps.

There was no reason for the wolf to do rounds. No animal could encroach upon the wolf, and if the humans encroached, which they had and would and did, it was temporary. Their empires fell. Their great cities burned and blew away like cigarette ash. The basin was littered with wind-scorched ghost towns. Many more settlements had perished than survived.

Everyone who lived in Lofte lived on the edge of Lofte. The wolf watched people soap their cars. He watched them run in groups. One house had a backyard full of chickens, and the wolf found himself gazing down at the penned birds from his perch on a hard hill that seemed high in the daytime but at night seemed so far from the stars. The chickens behind the little house were kept in a fence meant to thwart coyotes. The wolf should've slipped down and plucked a few, but he didn't want them to be gone. He was able to imagine loneliness now and he suspected that once the chickens were gone he would feel it. His rounds had been misguided, but they had kept the wolf busy and exercised. The chickens were unwittingly keeping him company and in a way he was guarding them.

Though often there was no car parked at the house with the chickens, the wolf knew there was always a human inside. Sometimes the wolf saw her ease the back door open and spill feed in the yard. Sometimes he saw her through the window, sitting in her kitchen, sometimes in a chair with big wheels and sometimes in a normal chair. He'd seen her lean against her ice box and cry. There was this older one who never left the premises and there was also a girl who came and went. The girl had arrived home a short time ago, in her low, groaning car. The wolf gave up his promontory and eased down the hill toward the house so he could hear the chickens and so he could frighten them a little, put them on edge for their own good. They didn't notice him until he was right there at the fence. They had no pride and precious little cunning, but the wolf felt affection for them. A couple of cars were coming up the street and the wolf hid behind a shed in the next yard. The cars passed and the wolf heard the chickens again, clucking softly, a sound like water dripping on wood.

The wolf saw a window with no blinds toward the front of the house and he saw the form of the girl inside, the one who came and went. He stayed put and after a short time the wind died out altogether and the wolf heard the strumming. It was a guitar. It stopped and the wolf stood still until it started again. The music was coming from behind the window where the girl had been standing. The wolf heard the girl trying out her voice, reedy and full of an emotion the wolf couldn't grasp. He crept out into the open and crossed over from the neighbor's yard and put himself against the wall of the house with the chickens. There was never a way to tell, once music began, how long it would last. He was panting and his breath was out of rhythm with the song. The wolf got right under the window, pinned between the stucco and a line of tough shrubs, and he felt – now that he'd quit his rounds and quit his appetite and quit trying to figure out what power the human music held – now he felt this girl's song pressing on him pleasantly from without and within. He didn't have to discern anything. The song wasn't chasing him or being chased. The song was doing a lap of its own natural rounds, a lap that somehow wouldn't wind up in the same place it had started. The song had a good fate and maybe the wolf did too. He felt the angst that had been building in him begin to evaporate. There was peace in his soul and if he had a brain he didn't hear it. The girl convinced her voice to rise with purpose and the strumming rose with it. The wolf felt quick and dumb. This music could have been anywhere and he could have been anywhere but they were both here. The song was going to end but that didn't matter because whenever it ended would be too soon. If it ended in a human minute that would be too soon and if it ended when morning broke that would be too soon.

DANNIE

She was sitting out on her balcony again, her computer on her lap. She was supposed to be working but was just poking around on websites, doing what she was always doing, which was waiting for Arn to come home. He was late, which meant his boss, the owner of the sonic observatory, had taken him out for breakfast. His boss, as far as Dannie could tell, was very smart and lonely. Dannie herself, she had to admit, did not seem very smart these days, and the only time she wasn't lonely was when Arn was around.

Dannie was a researcher. She got paid by the hour to find things out. While Arn waited for monumental information that would never arrive, Dannie sought out scores of minutia. Mostly, these days, she used the Internet, but she also knew her way around a library, around a hall of records. This morning she was to begin compiling a list of honorary degree recipients. Some guy wanted to know how many honorary degrees had been awarded in each nation, which disciplines the degrees were awarded in, which individuals held the most.

Dannie brought up a search engine but didn't do more than that.

She closed her eyes. The mood she was in felt like someone else's mood, someone younger than Dannie. She felt a rogue craving for drugs. She hadn't done drugs in years, since she and her ex-husband were dating, but this morning she had that itch. She had thought she'd outgrown drugs. Maybe it was the desert. The desert was the perfect locale. Maybe it was because she was trying to get pregnant and knew the fun of the young could soon be behind her. It was almost time for the end of Dannie's cycle and she hadn't felt a hint of a cramp. She didn't feel irritable. Didn't feel bloated. She was trying not to think about it, trying not to jinx anything or obsess over the calendar. She wasn't late yet, after all. When she was late she'd go get a couple tests at a drug store in Albuquerque – until then, she wasn't going to think about it.

She began clicking around, marking websites. She only worked five hours a day, so she wouldn't get carpel tunnel or burn her eyes out. When Dannie had originally discovered New Mexico, years ago, she'd been working for a movie house, scouting sites for a cowboy comedy. She'd spent three weeks up near Santa Fe, and she'd known she would return to the state, although she couldn't have guessed the circumstances. Before the movie thing, Dannie had worked for PBS. Before that, she'd modeled for a home shopping company – coats mostly. For some reason, she looked nice in coats. She guessed it was the hue of her cheeks, which always looked like they'd been rouged by wind. Dannie was grateful for her skin. She'd always thought her skin made her look fertile. She'd never tested the notion until now.

Dannie heard the scratch of Arn's key and then heard him padding through the condo. He came out onto the balcony and plopped down in the other chair, a hand on his belly. His boss had stuffed him full of bacon. He flopped his arm out toward Dannie and she took his hand.

'You ever have your cholesterol checked?' she asked.

He shook his head. 'Not big on doctors.'

Dannie closed up her computer and set it under her chair. She looked at Arn's hair, which was matted to his head. He often went days without showering, but he never smelled bad.

'Which drugs have you tried?' Dannie asked him.

He paused, then said, 'Just pot.'

'Really?'

'What more should I have done?'

'More than *that*.'

'Why?'

'Lots of reasons.'

'Like what?'

'Oh, to lose track of time. To test yourself.'

Arn scrunched his nose.

'To be daring.'

'Yeah, I'm not all that daring. I have been known to lose track of time.'

Dannie squeezed his hand. His T-shirt was drawing up, revealing his little-kid belly.

'Why the sudden interest?' he said. 'Are you going to administer a random drug test?'

Dannie raised herself up and climbed onto Arn's chair. There was a pattern they'd fallen into. Dannie would corner Arn, would chase him down or trap him. She had on a puffy blouse that tied in the front, and she began undoing the straps.

'Anything else you want to know?' Arn said.

Dannie sat straight. 'How many women have you slept with?'

Arn made a face like he'd performed a magic trick. 'You're it,' he said.

'Yeah, I bet.'

'No joke.'

'Sure, Arn.'

'It's the truth.'

'I don't care that you've slept with other women. You don't have to lie. I don't like you because you're supposed to be pristine or something.'

'I'm just answering your question.'

Dannie made a skeptical face, and Arn didn't respond to it.

'Now if you're lying, I am going to be angry,' she told him.

'What would I stand to gain from that lie?'

'I don't know,' said Dannie. 'Something.'

Arn shrugged.

'I'm not like you. Lying *is* a pet peeve of mine.'

'Most people are that way.'

'You're telling me you were a virgin when we met?'

'Affirmative.'

'That's your story? That's your final answer? I took your virginity.'

'Lock it in.'

Dannie felt deceived. She felt like she'd won something she wasn't sure she wanted. It was believable, she supposed. Arn wasn't the type who would need to chase girls in order to prove something. He did have a certain unspoiled exuberance during the act. Maybe it was true and maybe it wasn't. Dannie looked down at Arn. He was a prize the desert had awarded her and she was frightened of him. She was trying to get pregnant by this boy and maybe she already had, trying to turn him from a virgin to a father, and he didn't know a thing about it. She did not feel upset about the thought of doing this and that was more proof she was falling for him. When she'd first gone off birth control she'd told herself if she got pregnant she'd move away and never tell Arn a thing about it, but now she was in deeper than he was. He wasn't a novelty or a dupe.

'What is it?' Arn said.

Dannie shook her head. She reached out and stroked the lumped-up section of his hair as he gazed up toward her with his artless brown eyes.

HISTORY OF ARN II

He bounced around during ninth grade, but before tenth he was placed with a couple way up north of Seattle, almost in Canada. They were strangely close, this couple, and didn't talk much to Arn. The man worked at a candy factory and was always throwing tantrums and the wife was always soothing him, hugging him close and burying her face in his flannel shirt. The man had an exact schedule and when it was thrown off he fumed. If a show he was planning on watching got pushed back because the president was speaking, or if the mechanic didn't have his car ready on time, he would stalk around in tight circles, tossing things against walls. The wife would spring into action. This was her talent, calming him. They had a younger son, too, and he was their own. They had a biological son who was like eight and then they'd gone and taken in a fifteen-year-old foster son too. Arn didn't get it. He had no clue why they wanted him, but he didn't mind living in their house. The days slipped by. The food was tasty and promptly served. The boy, the eight-year-old, was obsessed with baseball and kept to himself. He spent his time taking batting practice at the mini-golf complex down the road or sorting cards into sets in his room.

School was a trial for Arn. He got sent outside most days by his typing teacher. She was a fat, red woman whom Arn kept tormenting long after she let up on him. He felt guilty about giving her a hard time because she was an easy target. She'd started it, always harassing him about hunting and pecking, but still, she was an easy target. It was like he was trying to teach her a lesson, to make an example of her, though he couldn't have said whom the example was for.

In eleventh grade, Arn got his pants pulled down in the lunch line by a big football player, a senior, causing the entire cafeteria to laugh. Arn went out to the parking lot and slashed the tires of the guy's Mustang. He left a note under the windshield explaining to the football player that they were even now but if he chose to give Arn any more trouble, it would end in someone's death. If the football player decided to trade harassments with Arn, Arn explained in the note, he would have to either kill Arn or be killed. *If it's worth all that*, Arn wrote, *go ahead and make the next move.*

Arn got a job at a car wash. It took about one week for the owner to realize Arn was a better worker than any of the other kids, and he was promoted to assistant manager, which meant he got an extra two bucks an hour and he was the one who pulled the cars around and drove them onto the tracks of the car wash. Arn hadn't had his license very long, so driving a bunch of strange cars, even in second gear, was fun for him. His life wasn't bad there for a while. He had a job that wasn't drudgery and soon enough he would graduate and be free.

At the house, the ongoing problem was that Arn's foster father had not been sleeping. He'd been more on edge, and had instituted a bunch of new rules. He gave demonstrations of how to do things quietly, how to make a sandwich without jangling the silverware drawer, how to plug headphones into the television. He'd shown Arn and his real son how to turn a doorknob first and *then* gently pull the door closed, rather than forcing it shut so the knob had to click. The real son, nine or ten at this point, did not heed any of this. Since Arn had moved in, the boy had lost interest in baseball and had started reading a lot. He never had friends over, and took a lot of showers, sometimes three in a day. Arn reminded him over and over to be quiet, wanting to prevent conflict in the house, but conflict avoidance no longer seemed to be this boy's program.

One night Arn awoke to a scuffle, to his foster father's grunts and his foster brother's whimpering. Arn went into the dining room and the father had the son cornered, hemmed in by the china cabinet and the big wooden table, and was kicking him, just booting the shit out of him over and over. Arn froze, though not for long. The situation wasn't complicated. A defenseless kid was getting beaten to a pulp. Arn brushed past his foster mother and into the boy's room, where he got a good grip on an aluminum baseball bat. He returned to the dining room and set his feet and dinged his foster father in the back of the head. Arn didn't swing his hardest, but hard enough. The man stood up straight a moment before slumping to his knees and then the rest of the way down. His son didn't leave the corner. The kid stared at Arn like he thought Arn was coming after him next. The foster father moaned, rocking on the carpet. The mother stared, not at anyone, seeming for once to need comforting herself.

Arn didn't have a chance to take stock until he was on the train. There were probably a hundred reasons why it was hard to admit that he was on the run, but the most prominent was that it felt silly. It was silly to think of himself as some kind of fugitive, as *wanted*, as fleeing justice. It felt surreal, thinking that the cops had been called, a photo of Arn had been turned over, the whole incident in the living room had been recounted, that taxpayer money would be used to track Arn down. Probably all that was happening. Probably the foster mother and foster brother were making Arn out as a dangerous psychopath, pinning the kid's bruises on Arn to spare the father. Probably an upper-level-type cop would be assigned Arn's case, a cop who wore a suit and didn't report to anyone, and if that cop found Arn he would be tried as an adult and would rot in jail. Assault with a deadly weapon. He was only a few short months from eighteen. The family would form a united front against him in court. Arn could see himself in a collared shirt that didn't quite fit, standing before a judge, listening as he was made out to be jealous and angry and ungrateful and everything else foster kids were supposed to be, listening as his foster father was made out to be a saint. He'd have a big bandage on his head, the foster father, or maybe he'd talk with a slur. Arn wouldn't bother telling his side. The judge wouldn't even be disgusted with him; she'd feel pity.

Arn was really on a train. He was really hightailing it out of town.

Arn had his own little area on the train. He had his bag on the seat next to him and his feet up. He watched the river. It wasn't a river anymore. It was a sound or a bay or something. A raffle was announced over the speakers. Whoever had the right number on their ticket would receive a free bowl of oatmeal, fancy oatmeal that came with raisins and brown sugar and cream. Arn pulled out his ticket and listened. He didn't win. There were about nine people on the train, but someone else won the oatmeal. Arn found the restrooms then returned to his seat. He couldn't decide if the train was covering ground or if it was piddling along. At some point, he was going to have to get off. He was going to have to choose a stop. He'd paid enough to get to Portland, Oregon, which would at least get him out of Washington. He was moving again, but this was different than foster moving. Arn was controlling this move. He didn't have anyone to answer to. He had nothing but slack, enough to lasso the world or enough to hang himself.

There was a girl at the other end of Arn's car. He'd gotten a good look at her when he'd gone to the bathroom. All he could see now was her boot, sticking into the aisle. She had a music player and a cell phone and a book and magazines. She wore colorful tights. It heartened Arn to think that this girl did not know him at all. If they were to speak to each other the girl would form opinions about Arn, beliefs about who Arn was, and these beliefs would be wrong. Anyone who passed by Arn could think he was comfortable with his life. They could think he had a bright future, that he was already living his future.

When Arn got to Portland he paid more money and stayed on the train. He didn't feel up to dealing with a city. He stayed on, putting more miles between himself and his past, and finally got off at a town with one small college and one big bakery and stands everywhere that sold expensive coffee and expensive nuts and candles. There were a bunch of wine bars. There didn't seem to be any heavy industry. There were limousine ads posted everywhere, for people who wanted to be driven around to vineyards.

Arn checked himself into a hotel room with a little window. He put the TV on and locked the door and almost slept, thinking of that little shit purposely making noise in the middle of the night, thinking of the oatmeal he hadn't won, thinking of that girl with the tights. She'd gotten off at Portland, toting all her wired, clumsy possessions with her like medical equipment she needed to keep breathing. This town Arn was in was sunny and dry. A different part of the country.

When he awoke it was past lunchtime. He walked down the street and ate a sandwich and then ate another one. He emptied his tray into the trash then pushed out into the sunshine and began asking around for work. He asked at a couple restaurants and had no luck, relieved, despite himself, at being turned down right away instead of having to fill out applications that would ask him for a bunch of information he didn't want to give. He asked about winery work, knowing that migrants often did work like that and that migrants, like himself, weren't able to fill out applications to anyone's satisfaction. But it was the off-season. A time known as The Crush would come along in a few months, but there was nothing doing at the moment. There wasn't a big supermarket in the town, a place Arn might collect carts or stock shelves.

He left the main drag and walked up a hill, walking in order to avoid standing still, and found himself staring at what appeared to be a temp agency. It looked like a house, not a business. The sign was quaint. It said JOBS in large letters and down in the corner it said NEW GARDEN.

From the moment he walked in the front door, he was treated strangely well. The other two guys in the waiting room had red eyes and runny noses, older guys, like forty, and they were being treated

civilly, but Arn was being fawned over. There were three men working in the office. They fetched Arn water and tried to give him a
bagel. They were waiting for someone, a woman named Amber.
Amber would be Arn's liaison. They gave Arn no papers to fill out.
The office was full of flowers and bookshelves.

When Amber arrived, she led Arn to a white back porch and had
a conversation with him. They didn't talk about the past. Amber
could get earnest in a snap and she could throw her head back and
laugh and laugh. She wore a sleeveless shirt and her shoulders flexed
every time she picked something up. Her shoulders looked stronger
than Arn's. Everything Arn said to her was right. Amber seemed to
want Arn to have a secret, and he did. He had a whopper.

They stopped by the hotel in Amber's minivan to pick up Arn's
bag and Amber drove him to a huge complex that was to some
degree a church but was other things too. Arn was installed in a
room in the dormitory. He was fed pizza. He looked out at the parking lot, saw a tow truck patrolling. The whole experience felt cultish,
but this was a small worry. Arn wasn't susceptible to brainwashing,
and felt very favorably about being given pizza and a free place to
stay.

The church grounds were a beehive of activity, but for the first
few days Arn only heard from Amber, like she didn't want anyone
to spook him. She hadn't asked him for his money yet, hadn't asked
for free labor. Arn was not yet a dupe or a slave. Amber began telling
Arn about herself, Arn eating pizza and Amber picking at a salad.
She'd had a muscle condition that had caused her, as a child, to walk
on her toes. At age twelve she'd had surgery to fix the condition and
had needed a bunch of physical therapy. She'd grown close with her
therapist and had fallen in love with working out. Exercise had

changed her life, had given her an identity. Through her twenties, she'd been a competitive fitness professional. She had a closet full of trophies, she told Arn. She'd been asked to appear on the show *American Gladiators*. She had been paid to show up at the grand openings of gyms and vitamin shops. Arn expected a tragic end to this phase of Amber's life, steroids or injuries, something that had pushed her toward religion, but she didn't share anything tragic. She wasn't a zealot. This church job was just a gig for her. Running the branch of this organization that helped troubled youths was her career, like somebody else was a hairdresser or a pharmacist.

She checked on Arn a few times a day, and she did give him papers to fill out, but nothing that seemed official. The papers asked what Arn liked to eat and what music he preferred and what kind of work he excelled at. Arn told Amber his favorite sport was basketball and she showed him the church's indoor court. It was like a high school's – glass backboards, hardwood floors, bleachers. Arn would shoot baskets for hours, then he'd go back to his room and eat pizza. He felt like a beloved dog, fed and allowed to play and sleep as he wished. Amber was his master and he was supposed to wag his tail when she showed up. She wasn't white, Amber, but she talked like a white person. She wore very straight-legged pants. Raised veins ran down her forearms. She had pretty fingernails and she smelled like crisp bed sheets. Whenever Arn smelled her, he felt the feeling he'd felt during his first conversation with her, out on that splendid latticed porch. Arn noticed that Amber was a big hugger but she never hugged *him*. She never rested a hand on his arm, never patted him on the back.

In the time it took for summer to arrive, Arn constructed a new life at the New Garden complex. There were lots of meetings about fostering a full existence and having full relationships and doing other things to the fullest, but Arn could skip the meetings whenever he felt like it. He thought maybe he ought to go to some meetings about addiction – drug, alcohol, gambling – to make it seem like he was damaged and needed more help and should not soon be discharged from the dormitory, but he couldn't bring himself to do this. He felt like he'd be making fun of the people who really needed the meetings. Instead he took jogs around the parking lot, getting a tan, something he'd never had. Other people were installed in the dorms, but they didn't last. There were even some guys about Arn's age, but he avoided them. He only shot baskets when the gym was empty. There was a certain courtyard where people smoked, and Arn considered taking another shot at cigarettes, to pass time, but he didn't want to have to become friends with all the smokers. On Tuesday and Thursday nights movies were shown, mostly comedies. Arn was set up with a job at a warehouse that supplied restaurants. He only worked four days a week, six hours at a time. He did a lot of sweeping, a lot of opening big cases of canned foods to check if the cans were dented. The manager wanted certain cans to be dented because he didn't like that particular vendor and wanted a reason to return their shipments, so sometimes Arn dented these cans himself. He kept waiting for New Garden to ask more of him, but they never did. Sometimes Arn didn't see Amber for days, but when he did she would stare at him and ask where in the world he got his smile from.

There was one weekly meeting Arn never missed. It was a Spanish class taught by two girls who were freshmen at the little college in town. They'd grown up going to New Garden and now they attended the little college, which was also religious, and they taught

Spanish class Saturday mornings in the common room of Arn's dorm building. One was blond and one brunette. They had wavy hair and plump mouths and they managed to construct outfits that were not slutty but still somehow revealed their midriffs. They never tired of flirting with Arn. Amber would not come right out and forbid Arn from going to the Spanish class, but she made no secret of disliking the girls. She disliked them because they were rich and because they were shallow and because they'd always treated her like the help – and, Arn surmised, because they were young. They didn't have to work out or eat right or be nice to people.

'Don't you love his little belly?' one would say, loud enough for Arn to hear. 'He's like a movie star when they go on vacation and let themselves go.'

'I wish I could rest my head on his belly.'

'I wish I could kiss it.'

'It's from all the pizza he eats. That's what the belly's from. We just have to keep the pizza coming.'

Since the girls were churchy and were always in a church when Arn saw them, there was little tension to the flirting. It was sort of hypothetical. These girls were pledged to be virgins when they married and they weren't going to break the pledge nor were they going to marry Arn. They could say whatever they wanted.

'How would you tell me I'm sexy in Spanish?' one of them would say to Arn after class. 'It's a pop quiz. How would you tell me you wanted my body?'

Arn felt guilty going to the Spanish classes, knowing he was being disloyal to Amber. The flirting didn't feel free.

'Wouldn't you like to buzz his hair?' one of them would say. She'd walk over and run her fingers over Arn's head.

One day, one of them rubbed lotion on the other's legs. One day, they traded bras. One had worn a black bra when she should've worn a white one, so the other agreed to trade. They told Arn to close his eyes.

'We're the exact same size,' one said.

'Yeah,' said the other. 'In a dark room you could never tell us apart by our tits.'

It didn't take long before Amber began trying to get the Spanish class cancelled. She did not have the power to do this because the girls' parents were prominent supporters of the church, but she seemed to want to send a message, to let the girls know she wasn't going to let them have Arn without a fight. Amber considered the girls a bad element for reasons that had nothing to do with their flirting. She considered them spiritually bankrupt and hypocritical and spoiled. And Arn knew she was right, but he couldn't help himself. The girls who taught the Spanish class were the type of girls who, a couple short months ago, in Washington, wouldn't have given Arn a second look. The girls in Washington knew Arn as the foster kid who'd gotten pantsed in the lunchroom, who worked at the car wash and didn't play any sports. To these Oregon girls, Arn was a tan mystery.

When Amber couldn't get the class cancelled, she went with the opposite tack. She advertised the class. She tried to get enough people to attend that the girls actually had to teach, had to make a lesson plan and answer questions and grade stacks of vocab quizzes. It wasn't ineffective; it annoyed the girls and interrupted their flirting. They could still hold Arn after class, but other people wanted to stay too; other people wanted special instruction. The girls' retaliation was to institute a final exam. The exam would be administered to each student individually, at the girls' dorm over at the college. The girls could've asked Arn out to a meal or something any time, but they wanted to beat Amber fairly, to stay within the constraints of the contest. They wanted Amber to know she'd had every chance to win.

The last Saturday the class was to be held, the last Saturday before the final exam, on a morning determined to make itself into the summer day it was meant to be, Arn received a curt phone call from Amber telling him he had to come to her house and trim her hedges. She'd let them get too high and now she couldn't reach the tops. Arn stood in the common room where the phone was kept. He'd known it was a matter of time before he'd be mowing and raking people's lawns. Amber was doing this because she was angry with him. She wanted him to miss the Spanish class and do yard work instead.

'What if I can't make it?' Arn said.

'You can make it.'

'Can I do the hedges later, like this afternoon?'

'I'm not a person who threatens or bribes,' Amber said. 'I'm a person who gives of herself to a staggering degree, and then when I need help with something once in a while I like to receive that help without a lot of back-and-forth.'

'I see,' said Arn. And he did. He was going to trim hedges instead of being teased by hot young girls. He was going to hold a pair of shears above his head, sun in his eyes, clippings cascading onto his shoulders. He could handle it. Worse things had happened to people in the history of the world.

Arn walked to Amber's house. He followed the directions she'd given him over the phone. It was seven blocks. There was her minivan. Approaching the house, Arn saw the hedge and let out a chuckle. It was about twenty feet high. The job would've required a bucket truck.

Arn knocked on the door and then stepped back off the porch, taking another look at the hedge, amused. He knocked again. The deadbolt turned over and the door drew open and Amber was standing there in a pose both forward and shy, wearing a complicated nightgown and platform shoes. Arn was overwhelmed. His wish to step inside the house and his wish to flee felt exactly equal. He saw so much of Amber. He'd never seen her hair pinned up. Her calves bulged in the high shoes. She didn't smell like clean sheets. She smelled like something else. Snaps and buttons were everywhere. She was a woman, full-fledged.

'You'll skip the final,' she said.

Arn failed to disagree.

'You'll skip the final and you won't attend any future classes those girls teach or meetings they run or anything they're involved in.'

Arn held onto the doorframe. 'What will I tell them?'

'You don't have to tell them a thing.'

Amber held herself against the half-open door, pushing her front against it.

'The only person you have to answer to is me,' she said.

Arn felt awakened. The Spanish class girls were nothing compared to Amber. They were pretty, that was all. Arn was afraid he was supposed to say something now. He watched, entranced, as Amber took a step back and grinned. Arn could tell she was savoring the fact that he had no idea what he was supposed to do, that his head was spinning. She pulled him inside firmly and guided him to the bedroom. One by one, she tossed about a dozen pillows from the bed onto the floor. She asked Arn to take his shirt off and he felt he would've done anything for her. He would've robbed a bank without a moment's hesitation.

The bed all cleared off, Amber ignored it. She walked over to Arn and pulled him down onto his back on a lavender rug and climbed atop him. She knew what she was doing. No sooner than it dawned upon Arn that he was having sex, he began to realize that it wasn't going to last very long. He had to remind himself that he was allowed to keep his eyes open, that he was allowed to watch this amazing spectacle.

REGGIE

There was a breeze. There were no windows but there was a breeze from somewhere. It carried blatant scents such as chlorine, such as the smell of a heater kicking on for the first time since last winter, but also scents Reggie had to guess at – dollar bills, dead batteries. The breeze was cool and the floor had become comfortably warm, like the floor of the bathroom in that fancy hotel Reggie had stayed in on a trip to Colorado with a friend's family. Reggie's living area was spacious, a hall again, but he made a decision not to recommence his laps. The bar and the library had returned, and Reggie prepared himself Irish whiskeys and perched on a stool like a customer. He'd never been a real customer at a bar because he'd died before turning twenty-one and had never felt compelled to procure a fake ID. He sat across from the bottles and sometimes he looked past them into the mirror and his face didn't show him a barren, lethargic street anymore – maybe, instead, a beat-up stretch of interstate, a stretch of interstate that didn't go anywhere exciting but that the locals appreciated. Reggie had to use more ice in his whiskey than his father did, and couldn't take down an honest gulp until some of the ice had melted. He never carried his drink to another part of the hall and never left a drink unfinished. He sat in the red chair in the library and committed to a novel, a five-hundred-pager by an Italian in which all the characters realized they were characters, understood they were mere artifice, and began hopping trains in every direction to confuse the author. The billowing exhaust from the trains was described in a fancy way and from what Reggie could tell looked exactly like the sluggishly circulating smoke huffs that hung above the main hall. Reggie's mat did not return. Instead, a hammock. Reggie had never been in a hammock before, and it was almost too comfortable. The breeze was stiff enough to rock it. Reggie didn't bring books to the hammock. He drank in the bar and read in the library and rested in the hammock.

Reggie's next song was ready. He started by messing around on the harmonica – warming up, putting some cracks in the quiet – but soon it was time to earnestly compose so he shucked his shirt and picked up the guitar. He had no idea how many songs were in him. Reggie cracked his fingers and began playing. He knew what was coming but it sounded different hearing it on the air than it sounded in his brain, as if the songs were made of an element that enlivened upon contact with oxygen. He was enjoying writing songs again, and would've been doing it whether or not he was rewarded. He hadn't asked for any of the luxuries the afterlife was showering on him. His inclination was to feel bribed, kept, but these were concepts from the world of the living. Of course he was kept. Reggie's earlier refusal to read a book or drink a cocktail had made no difference, and his acceptance of the afterlife's hospitality made no difference. It wasn't a bribe. Reggie was giving the songs away. Nothing he received meant anything, only what he gave.

CECELIA

On her way to the agriculture building for a repair call, walking out around the Natural History museum and then past an acre or so of pepper plants, the next song arrived. Cecelia had been taking her time getting to the building, knowing she was going to go all the way over there and climb stairs and locate the classroom and interrupt the class all for no reason, because there was no way she was going to be able to help – she never could – and she heard it, another song. It seemed to grow out of the wind and quickly became louder than the wind. She smelled the peppers and heard the notes. This song was running the same course as the last, arranging itself, getting organized, but this one was coming together much faster. There was no need for Cecelia to hum. She was already getting the gist of the melody, and could already tell it was unfamiliar. Another song. Cecelia felt the same apprehension, the same spark of joy. Something impossible was happening. Cecelia racked her brain. Maybe Reggie had played the songs while she was asleep sometime and her subconscious had kept them buried until now. But Cecelia had never slept around Reggie. Not once. Maybe what was happening was akin to when mothers lifted pickup trucks off their children. Cecelia missed Reggie so badly she was having an adrenaline rush of the spirit, doing the extraordinary. Maybe the songs weren't being given to her, maybe she was taking them. She felt sweetly defeated. She was living proof that nobody knew anything.

Inside the building, she found 209 and knocked on the open door. The professor was wearing dress shoes and ratty jeans and looked familiar to Cecelia. He looked more familiar than someone would from seeing them around campus, but she couldn't place him. He had his phone hooked up to the A/V cabinet. His images were appearing on the computer screen but nothing was coming through the projector. Cecelia nodded at him confidently, hearing parts of what he was saying but mostly hearing the song, looking at the professor's phone but also looking out at the waiting students, who didn't seem to be rooting for or against Cecelia.

She touched a couple dials under the cabinet, staying down there for what seemed like long enough. When she stood, she said, 'The projector isn't responding at all. That's not a positive sign.'

The professor didn't seem disappointed. He thought it might be the phone's fault. He seemed resigned to malfunction in general. Suddenly Cecelia remembered why he looked familiar. He'd come to the vigils for a few weeks, back at the start of them. That was it. There'd been one night in particular that he'd sat close by her. He'd dropped out. He'd dropped out like all the rest would eventually. At the most recent vigil, two days before, there'd been only a dozen people. The high-strung painter was still sticking it out, but it was only a matter of time for him. The haughty guy with all the pins on his coat was unreadable, a threat. The guy who always hid behind sunglasses even though it was night out and was always playing with a pen – Cecelia hoped he'd be the next to go. There were the middle-aged fat women with their reassuring expressions who seemed to believe that everything wrong with the world wasn't really wrong, that it was all part of some convoluted grace. There was the pretty girl in her thirties and her young boyfriend. Who knew what they were doing? They were trying to prove something to each other or using the vigils as part of their dating or something. The woman seemed rich, from her car and her clothes. Cecelia didn't know why someone with a cute boyfriend and a new car would spend her time in a parking lot. None of the other vigilers had as much right to vigil as Cecelia had. They would all fall away, just like the redheaded hippie woman with the tacky earrings and the weightlifter dude.

'It'll be fixed by the next time this class meets,' Cecelia told the professor. It was what she always said.

'I'm a farmer,' the professor said. 'If it was a tractor, I could fix it.'

Cecelia scribbled down the serial numbers of the machines in the cabinet and the classroom number and departed the agriculture building. There was a bench on the edge of the pepper field and she sat on it. Most of the peppers were a shade of green, except one row that was bright red, the peppers as big as eggplants.

The song was mostly assembled, mostly clear. It was an acoustic punk song. It was short and fast and there wasn't one moment when it slowed down. Each verse was the same. The song was about the sounds a person hears while falling, about flowers with snow on them, about children asleep in their church clothes. There could be another song after this one, and another, and though Cecelia knew the songs were bad for her, she wanted more of them. It was hard to determine when this punk song ended and restarted, but Cecelia could tell. She could sense when it crossed the finish line, which was also the starting line. Cecelia sat up straight against the back of the bench. She didn't know if she was being tormented or rewarded. The sun broke the haze, and a glare settled on each smooth pepper in the field before her, turning the world into endless blinding acreage.

MAYOR CABRERA

Pulling his dirty clothes out of a tall canvas bag and filling one of the washers in the Javelina laundry room, he found himself holding the shirt he'd worn on his last visit to Santa Fe. He peeled a sock off it and held it up by the shoulders. It was blue with a collar of lighter blue, with oversized buttons and a breast pocket that snapped closed. The air in the laundry room wasn't easy to breathe and the overhead light was flickering. Mayor Cabrera set the shirt aside and filled the washer the rest of the way, extracting a mint from the pocket of some pants he must've worn to the diner and a pen from the pocket of another shirt. He dumped in the detergent and started the water running and then turned back to the blue shirt, lifting it and pressing his face into it. It was there, Dana's scent – right in the middle of the chest where she'd nestled her head back into him – a clean, powdery smell but also the smell of something baked, something flaky and not too sweet. He was holding the shirt with his fingertips so he wouldn't ruin the scent. He'd chosen that shirt to wear to Dana's because it was stiff and made his shoulders look broad. He'd worn it up to her place a bunch of times. He'd worn that shirt the time all those bees were on Dana's little balcony and Mayor Cabrera had called over an exterminator and hadn't let Dana pay for it. That meant something, didn't it, that she'd allowed him to pay for that exterminator? The visit after that he'd brought her a stuffed bee, which always sat on a shelf of her entertainment center and stared with its bug eyes out into the living room. This was the shirt Mayor Cabrera had worn the time Dana had let it slip that she wanted to go see this guy named Roderick or Broderick something who was performing in downtown Santa Fe. Dana was sheepish about mentioning the concert because it was Mayor Cabrera's evening, his once-a-month appointment, and she was a professional, but Mayor Cabrera could tell something was on her mind and had dragged it out of her. The show was sold out but a number of tickets were being held at the venue for anyone willing to wait in line, and so Mayor Cabrera overcame Dana's protests and they went down and got seventh and eighth in line and sat along an adobe wall that grew warm after a while against their backs. The strangers they conversed with assumed them to be a couple, and Dana didn't say otherwise. She had stories about other times she'd seen this guy play, down on the Gulf Coast and up in Colorado. Once the doors opened, Dana and Mayor Cabrera went to the bar and then found a cozy spot off to the side. Dana didn't want to sit and she didn't like to be right up front either because she liked to see the audience as well as the band. She liked to see the backs of the people's heads as they nodded along raptly. Afterward they went to a crowded diner. They hadn't gotten home until three in the morning and Dana's eyes had been heavy in the car, so Mayor Cabrera got her to agree to go ahead to sleep and she promised she'd make it up to him the next day, that she'd settle all accounts in the AM. But the next morning Mayor Cabrera had to get back to Lofte early and when he departed Dana was still zonked under her comforter and Mayor Cabrera snuck out without a sound.

THE GAS STATION OWNER

He still had not left. The girls were running the station more than capably and he was supposed to be gone. He had summoned the desert to bring its strife against him, and now he was hiding from it. He was on one knee scrubbing the back of the toilet, his bucket of cleaning supplies propped up on the closed lid of the commode. The girls cleaned the bathroom Monday through Saturday, but nobody could make it gleam like the gas station owner. Nobody else cared that once in a while a sharp-dressed woman from Albuquerque or maybe a much bigger city was forced to use the restroom at this out-of-the-way dive and came in expecting the worst facilities she'd ever laid eyes on and when she walked down the narrow hall and opened the flimsy door she fell into utter shock at the fresh tidiness. This is what the gas station owner cared about, apparently. The water in the commode was blue. The floor was spotless. An impressionist Paris street adorned the wall.

The gas station owner moved on to the mirror, pulled the Windex out of the bucket. The gas station owner had told the girls Sunday was optional, and he was glad they'd turned down that option, because that meant he could come in. He could sit in the station like he always had – his place to be, his something to do. His rucksack had been packed for seventeen days now. Perfectly packed. It was at his house, sitting out on his closed-in porch, collecting dust. He'd had his purposeful fun for a time, taking everything out and repacking, fitting in a little more dried fruit, one more pair of socks. The pack was finished and the gas station owner was avoiding his porch. At this point, laying eyes on the pack shamed him. He had his clothes out on the porch too, the clothes he was going to wear the day he started walking, and a pair of fancy boots he'd driven into the city to purchase. It was the first time since he was a child that he'd had his feet measured. The boots had a lifetime warranty, and the pair the gas station owner had were going to meet that warranty easy because they'd never been worn outside the store.

The gas station owner collected his supplies and put a new bag in the little trashcan and went and perched behind the register.

Maybe he didn't want an adventure, he only wanted to plan for one. Maybe he liked to stay cozy, like that kid who worked at the alien observatory had told him. He liked to be curled up warm and safe. Not only was the gas station owner no better than that kid, he was worse. At least that kid had guts. At least he didn't have to be on his home field and get to make up all the rules. The gas station owner slid a stick of jerky out of a display and after a minute put it back. He was embarrassed he hadn't left yet. He'd told Mayor Cabrera he was going to be gone awhile, had asked him to keep an eye on the station and on the house, and a few days later he'd run into Cabrera picking up lunch at the diner. He'd lied and said he'd postponed his excursion because the girls needed more training at the station. Like it took a whole lot of know-how. And he was embarrassed the girls knew he was still around. When he came in on a Sunday he couldn't help but straighten shelves and clean. They noticed. They knew he hadn't left. He had told himself he was waiting for the right day to leave, for a sign even, waiting to refine his purpose, waiting until he didn't have a choice but to embark. The fact was, he would never fully understand until he was out there and he *did* have a choice.

The gas station owner had his station for comfort and his whisky and he'd even gone back to the Bible. He didn't know what that meant. It was a bunch of knowledge he'd mastered as a kid and then had forgotten. It was the same old Bible he'd carried to church as a tyke, still chock with floods and famine and pestilence and idols and war, full of people with conviction and people without conviction getting punished for it. The gas station owner was doing the opposite of going to church. He was reading scripture six days and then working on Sunday. He wanted Psalms but he needed Proverbs. *How long will you slumber, O sluggard? When will you rise from your sleep? A little sleep, a little slumber, a little folding of the hands – So shall your poverty come on you like a prowler, and your need like an armed man.*

THE WOLF

It was so hazy that he could not tell from the pit of the gully how near sunset was. The sky looked like a stretched old cloth. The floor of the gully was damp and the wolf kept his belly against it. He had been gnawing his foreleg all day, the skin fraying now. He could taste the blood as it quick-dried into the weightless air.

The wolf needed to be this close to the house with the chickens so that when he heard the girl's car he could make it to the window without missing the next song. He'd heard two of them, and the days he'd heard them he'd felt calm, but when he didn't hear one he felt lunatic. He had to stay down in the gully so no one would spot him and he couldn't see anything from down in the gully, couldn't watch the chickens or watch the humans of Lofte as they kept their routines or broke them. All he saw was an occasional airplane passing overhead, leaving a streak behind it whiter than the white sky, a streak that began near the airport in Albuquerque and would end somewhere the wolf would never go even if he lived forever.

The last time the wolf had gone to the window for a song was almost two full days ago. He needed one soon. The first song had come in the morning and the second one in early evening. If the people who lived in the house next door to the house with the chickens had glanced out their little red-tinted kitchen window they would have seen him. They would've reported him.

From the gully the wolf could no longer see the chickens but he could hear them ruffling their feathers and knew when they were asleep. He could hear them bickering, pecking one another's feet. The wolf was not going to take a chicken. He was charmed by their vulnerability. The wolf was effortlessly guarding the chickens from the coyotes, now in the thick of their thin season. The wolf did not want anything to disrupt the delivery of the songs. He wanted the older woman to stay home all day, safe, boiling water on the stove and staring out the window and sometimes weeping, and he wanted the chickens safe in the yard and he wanted the road shushed quiet with the passing of healthy cars until he heard the racket of the girl's injured car and she was back from wherever the songs came from. He wanted to be shimmying under the window, pinned against the wall by those spiny bushes that were at once dying and growing unruly. There was a hunger in the wolf that was also a desire to starve, and the girl's songs were all that could help. He wished he could hear them always and then he could sleep in the day and howl at night like he was meant to.

It had been two days without a song. The sky was losing light. The wolf felt repulsed at the thought of eating, but he had the old itch for a kill. His teeth were sharp and too large for his mouth. He feared he was going to bite his foreleg hard enough to break the bone, and then he'd die stuck in this gully. His own blood was the saltiest he'd ever tasted and it reminded him that some blood was sweet. He would wait until midnight, if he could last that long. If the girl did not return by midnight with a song, he couldn't be held responsible for whatever wickedness his longing drove him to.

DANNIE

Her period arrived. She had believed she might be pregnant and had not allowed herself to think about it because she didn't want to jinx it, but she had thought about it anyway, secretly, and she *had* jinxed it. She stood on the balcony and watched a posse of crows milling about down where she'd planted those avocado pits, their black wings tucked against the wind like men in coats.

She arose and put her eye to the telescope. The town was abandoned, the streets resting. There were wreaths on the lampposts. Eight of them. Dannie had sat out here one day and watched the mayor himself hang them. He had carried his ladder from post to post, had given each wreath a smack before he'd raised it. Dannie was drinking from a bottle of water, and she leaned over the railing and poured some down and it splattered on the desert ground as if on a tabletop. The water wasn't going to sink in. It was going to sit there like a kitchen spill until the night froze it or the day evaporated it.

She went inside, fetched her driver's license, and left it out on the kitchen counter so when Arn awoke he would see it and discover her true age. He still thought she was twenty-nine. She sat curled up on the couch and after a while heard Arn bumbling around in the bathroom. She heard the toilet flush. She heard the noise he made when he stretched, heard him getting into some crackers in the kitchen.

'You left your license in here,' he called.

'I did?'

'On the counter.'

'Notice anything?'

'About your license?' Dannie heard him pick it up. 'The picture doesn't do you justice. That I can notice right off. It doesn't show how your skin is.'

Dannie didn't answer.

'California,' Arn said, distinctly pronouncing each syllable.

'Look at the date of birth.'

Arn clicked his tongue, thinking, doing math. 'I get it, you're older than you said.'

'By how much?'

'You're thirty-three.'

'I'll be thirty-four in three weeks.'

'Shoot,' Arn said. 'In that case, I've got shopping to do.'

'Let me guess,' said Dannie. She felt hostile and made no effort to keep it out of her voice. 'You don't care. It doesn't matter how old I am. You're not mad that I lied. You don't think any less of me. Everything's hunky-dory.'

'Well,' Arn said.

'You don't care, right? What a guy. Guy of the year: Arnold Avery.'

'Should I fly into a rage?' Arn asked. 'I can do that, just let me get some coffee first. Let me wake up a little and then I'll throw some shit around and curse.'

'That might be a nice change,' Dannie said.

There was a long pause then. Both Dannie and Arn tried to stay still, Dannie on the couch and Arn in the kitchen. They hadn't argued before. Dannie knew that part of her irritation was at herself for ever feeling she needed to lie in the first place. What, she was ashamed? She was afraid some dumb kid would think she was old?

It had been an act of impulse, lying, but then she hadn't been woman enough to admit it and laugh about it and it had grown into something compromising.

Arn shifted his weight on the linoleum.

'Let me see *your* license,' Dannie said.

'It's buried at the bottom of one of my bags.'

'Can I see your wallet?'

'Sure, but the license isn't in there.'

Dannie heard Arn walking to the bedroom, then coming back toward her. He handed her the wallet and sat close on the couch. The wallet smelled like the inside of a new car. There was nothing in it but cash.

'When did you get this?'

'Tuesday.'

'What'd you do before that?'

Arn shrugged. 'Pockets.'

'You don't have an ATM card?'

'My account's only a savings account.'

'Well, you need a checking account and you need a debit card and also a fucking credit card. If you want anyone to take you seriously.'

Arn looked at Dannie levelly. 'I don't want anyone to take me seriously.'

'You don't have health insurance, do you?'

'I never do anything dangerous.'

Dannie folded the wallet and rested it on the coffee table and Arn made no move for it. Neither of them said anything for a few minutes and Dannie had no idea if the fight was over and no idea if she wanted it to be.

THE TRAINER

The coyote had been injured as a pup and had been rescued and rehabilitated by an Albuquerque veterinarian, mostly as a publicity stunt. It was decided the coyote would never survive in the wild with his lack of pack training, and so he was gifted to the high school out in Golden, whose teams were called the Coyotes. The coyote never snapped at anyone; in fact, children often had their pictures taken with him. The coyote lived in a spacious room adjacent to the gymnasium where weight room supplies were stored. The man who cared for the coyote, though not a paid employee, had been given the title of 'trainer' by the high school's athletic department. He did his best to look out for the coyote, but still the animal was stolen each year by the rival high school. The last time, they'd dressed the coyote up like a ballerina and put the pictures in their school's newspaper.

The wolf hurled himself through the big glass window of the supply room. He disentangled his legs from the flimsy blinds, stepped over an iron bar, and walked steadily toward the coyote, who retreated a step but didn't cower. The wolf could only imagine the coyote was glad to be put out of his misery. The coyote hadn't been taught by his elders that a coyote's only duty was to survive at all cost.

When the wolf tasted the blood, he saw the trainer's life. The trainer received an amount of money each month that was meant to buy food for the coyote, but instead he pocketed the money and fed the coyote leftovers from the school's cafeteria, the tangy pizza and country fried steak. The trainer was not mentally deficient, but he knew folks thought he was. His brother had died young. His mother was mean. The trainer was addicted to low-stakes gambling and stayed on his computer all night, blowing the dog food money and blowing an allowance he still drew from his grandmother, who loved him but had mostly lost her mind.

CECELIA

She had been distracted, but had not forgotten her hostilities with Nate. She set up a meeting with the leader of the devoted Shirt of Apes fans, at a location of his choosing, which turned out to be the picnic area of a farmers' market. The market was open on weekends but this was a Tuesday, so there was no food to be had, no drinks, no one around.

The guy was waiting for Cecelia, and when she walked up he gestured for her to sit down across from him at his picnic table. His sunglasses were crooked. They looked like they were about to fall apart. Cecelia had never seen this guy without his sunglasses on. He had attended the first month of vigils for Soren, she remembered, he and his gang, but they'd disappeared. Cecelia wondered if they'd quit for ideological reasons or because they'd found something better to do. She'd always been intimidated by him, at the Shirt of Apes shows, but the fact that he'd quit the vigils gave her a sense of superiority.

'I have five minutes,' the guy said. He didn't shake Cecelia's hand or smile at her.

'That should be sufficient.'

'I have something to say first. I think you're beautiful.' He spoke hurriedly and with little intonation. 'Maybe not now, without the band, but on stage you were beautiful. I'm telling you this as a person who takes a keen interest in beauty. The way you looked with your guitar, wearing that dress shirt . . .'

Cecelia wasn't going to blush. She knew not to take the declaration personally.

'Yeah, must've been the guitar,' she said.

'You were an exquisite accompaniment. Reggie couldn't have had a better bandmate.'

'I've never known your name.'

'It's Marc, with a C.'

'Well, Marc, it's the other band mate I want to talk to you about. The third Ape.'

'Nate,' Marc said. 'He was necessary. There wouldn't have been a band without him. Reggie wouldn't have started one. You wouldn't have.'

'He's starting a new band and he's going to use Reggie's songs. Their first gig is tomorrow.'

Marc took this in. He brought his hands above the tabletop. 'We've already had a ceremony, putting those songs to rest.'

'You had a ceremony for Reggie?'

'For the songs. We scored each one out as sheet music and put the papers in helium balloons and released them. No one's supposed to ever play them again. That's the meaning of the ceremony.'

'It's despicable, right? What Nate's doing. It's a crime.'

'Of that, there's no doubt. No doubt at all.'

Marc was starting to stew, but the ball was still in Cecelia's court. She had to be specific.

'What I want is for you guys to do your thing,' she said. 'I want you to show up at Nate's gigs and make sure they don't become popular. Like you did with us – scare everyone off. I don't want Nate making money off Reggie's songs.'

Marc rubbed his earlobe softly between two fingers. He knew

how to enjoy mulling something. 'The situation grieves me, but I cannot do what you ask. I wouldn't take my fanhood lightly that way. I wouldn't fake devotion and I wouldn't ask anyone else to.'

'Just this once?'

'I'm sorry.'

'For Reggie?'

He made a disappointed face at Cecelia, his lips pressed tight, and she knew she wasn't going to ask him again. What he was saying was correct and she knew it. She'd insulted him, maybe. He had no idea what Cecelia was going through and she couldn't tell him – no idea she was being entrusted with new songs of Reggie's by means she couldn't fathom and that she needed to keep the old songs safe for reasons of principle but also because it was important that Nate suffered a loss. She was a curator of the mystical and was also a contestant in a common feud. Another song had arrived that morning, and Cecelia had recorded it on the cassette tape. She'd started to feel like a piece of machinery herself, equipment. She was compatible with a boxy, not-new tape recorder and also compatible with the hereafter. The song from this morning had been bluesy and the lyrics told of a man who'd tried to build his own river. The man digs the river out by hand and constructs docks on the river's edges and rests boats down on the dry waiting dirt and plants thirsty trees up and down the shore. Then he has to wait for a storm. The chorus was whistling, and Cecelia could still hear a trace of her own voice whistling away. She had begun to wonder if this happened to other people, if others received transmissions from higher planes of existence. Why would it only be her? It was tiring to walk around like everything was normal when really you were a participant in a secret supernatural entanglement, but maybe lots of people were living under these conditions. Maybe Cecelia wasn't anything special. Scores of folks were walking around with knowledge they couldn't share and that, if they did share it, no one would believe.

'What are they called?' Marc asked.

'Nate's new band? Thus Poke Sarah's Thruster.'

'I'll remember the name and pray for their failure. That's all I can offer. I can't do more than that. I'm a devotee, not a warrior. And anyway, I can't hear those songs again. If I went to their shows, I'd hear the songs, and that part of my life is over.'

'I'll take your prayers,' said Cecelia. 'I'll take whatever I can get.'

'I'll truly do it. I'll get down on my knees.'

Cecelia asked Marc if his group was following anyone else, if they'd found a new band, and he said they were considering a metal trio that sang half the time to Christ and half the time to Satan. He used both hands to adjust his sunglasses.

'Thanks for meeting me,' said Cecelia.

She got up and walked to her car, leaving Marc at the table. She was not disheartened. She knew it was better if she battled Nate on her own. She knew that. To have help would defuse the prospect of finding out what was inside her, finding out what she would do to win. That's why feuds persisted, so people could test themselves.

DANNIE

She was still in a mood and spent the night cleaning the condo. The furniture was dusty. There was grease on the stove and countertops from all Arn's bacon. It was even on the floor. Dannie wiped down the sticky honey jars and then got up on a chair and threw away a bunch of canned goods the trucker had left in a high cabinet. It felt good to clunk them right in the trash rather than setting them aside to be donated. Arn had tracked clumpy red dirt into the front hall and Dannie vacuumed and then banged a pair of his shoes out on the front stairs. She looked out at the night and there was a weak ring of light around the whole horizon. Dannie didn't know where it came from. She went into the bathroom and got on her knees with a bunch of harsh products and started scrubbing. The only reason the toilet needed cleaning was that Arn couldn't pee straight. There was a bar of soap in the shower drain. Dannie wanted to be pregnant, and Arn was proving no help with that. Dannie had thought she was falling for him, falling in love, but now she couldn't even tell what that meant. It meant fights and secrets, in Dannie's experience. Arn was the one who should've been young enough for love, but who knew what was going on in his heart? Dannie had begun to resent sleeping with him. She could feel the start of that. She wasn't getting pregnant so she was just giving away her body and her roof and her food. The resentment was there. And resentment never did anything but grow.

When Arn got home, Dannie told him he had to be neater in the kitchen and that he had to help out with chores and that she wasn't doing another shred of his laundry. She told him not to drop her soap that had cost eleven dollars a bar at a shop in Pasadena into the drain and leave it there, and also to pull the curtain open after he showered so it wouldn't get mildewed.

He was looking at her with that look like he was about to smile or cry. He was going to do neither. He only said, 'Okay, Dannie.' He hardly ever called her by her name.

'You haven't bought me one solitary gift,' Dannie said. 'It's one of those customs humans observe when they're courting. The male buys the female a gift or two.'

Dannie gave Arn a chance, but he had no idea what to say. He no longer looked like he was about to smile.

'You've never cooked me a meal,' she said.

'I don't know how to make anything good.'

'You have to figure it out. You have to make an effort to learn. You have all night sitting up there doing absolutely nothing.'

'All right,' he said.

'Take your shoes off and leave them outside. Where do you find mud, anyway? We're in the middle of the desert.'

Arn sniffed. He turned around and went back down the hall and Dannie retreated to the kitchen. She sat and listened to the sound of Arn patiently removing his sneakers. He was being patient with her and she didn't know how she felt about having an ignorant child act patient with her, like he was exercising forbearance in the course of dealing with a crazy person. This kid had one important task to accomplish and hadn't accomplished that task. She did know how she felt about it. She fucking resented it.

SOREN'S FATHER

He went to Gee's house thinking that if the opportunity arose to stay the night he would take it. Gee had some of those otherworldly roadrunners stooping here and there in her flowerbeds. She didn't sell them, she told Soren's father. She gave them away as gifts. Gee's house had a big skylight in the roof and a decked-out kitchen with a hundred pots and pans hanging overhead. Gee cooked Chinese food, Szechwan she called it, and while she cut peppers and pounded on steaks that were already thin, she told Soren's father about her son, who was grown and lived in what Gee described as a soulless suburb of Phoenix, where he sold real estate and dated women who sold real estate. When Gee and her ex-husband had split, they'd given the boy his choice of who he wanted to live with and he'd chosen his father and Gee had never forgiven him. The boy had been a teenager then, old enough to know his own mind. Gee and her son had a series of nasty arguments and had become estranged. Gee planned to attempt reconciliation, but it hadn't been long enough for the anger to dissipate. More time had to pass or else something bad had to happen. Someone in the family had to pass away or something like that. Soren's father listened, trying and failing to imagine a scenario in which he would refuse to speak to his son, hoping there was no scenario in which his son would refuse to speak to him.

Gee and Soren's father ate, and once again it was the best food he'd ever tasted. It was better than the food at that chef's house and better than the raw fish. It was absurdly spicy, but somehow he wanted to eat it faster and faster. Gee watched him scarf it down and then gave him a tour of the house. She showed Soren's father the little loft where she worked on her memoir. She had her computer set up where she could talk into it and her words appeared on the screen. She said to the computer, 'Tonight will never make the book. Nobody wants to read about other people being happy,' and the words blinked right up.

To Soren's father's surprise, dessert was a pair of Klondike bars.

He and Gee sat under the skylight with the night above them, the stars tiny and evenly scattered, and Gee, as she often did, began questioning Soren's father in a tone meant to challenge him, to steel him. She'd had quite a bit of white wine.

'Your son might not know you when he wakes up,' she said. 'You might be strangers, making first impressions on one another.'

'Oh, he'll know me,' said Soren's father.

'What if he wakes up when he's thirty?'

'I'll be old, but he'll know me.'

'You'll be alive when the coma breaks,' Gee said. 'That much I can feel. You'll be around to welcome him back.'

'That's right. There I'll be, in my wheelchair.'

'You'll remember me that day. You'll think of me when you get your son back.'

'Where are *you* planning on being?'

'I'm planning on being with you,' Gee said. 'That's how I know I won't be. My plans never work out.'

Soren's father itched his jowl. He was still holding the wrapper from the Klondike bar and he crumpled it small and rested it on the end table.

'I'd like for you to come up and see him,' he said. 'I'd like to invite you up to his room.'

Gee picked up a heavy ink pen and rolled it in her fingers. 'When I pursued you, I didn't think I'd be successful.'

'Well, I'm easy,' said Soren's father. 'I'd hang around with anybody.'

Gee put the pen down and moved her hand toward Soren's father. She stopped short of touching his arm, and he did the least he could, which was to reach out and meet her halfway.

193

MAYOR CABRERA

It was one of those winter days that, from indoors, appears to be a summer day. He was eating a can of nuts as slowly as he could. In front of him, on his desk, was a letter from Ran, the leader of that church that was considering Lofte. Ran was pleased to inform Mayor Cabrera that the decision-making process wasn't far behind schedule. They were hoping to wrap things up in March. The church's taxes were complicated and would tie Ran up for the next few weeks. A couple divorces within the church had to be settled. But March, for sure.

Mayor Cabrera had thought he was going to know Ran's decision before the town council meeting, but it looked like he would not. This would be an unpleasant meeting. Nothing would be revealed that Mayor Cabrera didn't know, likely nothing the other four town council members hadn't sensed, but it was different when you saw it in numbers on paper, when you saw it with other people and had to look at those other people.

Mayor Cabrera ground a hazelnut with his molars, looking vacantly out the lobby windows. He picked Ran's letter up and held it in front of his face. Ran had given Mayor Cabrera homework. He'd asked Mayor Cabrera to answer a single question for him, to answer the question however he saw fit, to write the answer down and mail it back to him. He'd enclosed an addressed envelope, with postage. Iowa.

Mayor Cabrera watched the teenagers spill into the parking lot, disconsolate like only teenagers could be. The Javelina had enjoyed a decent night – the usual loners, an old couple, and then this gaggle of youngsters. There were twenty of them and they'd split themselves between five rooms. Mayor Cabrera always hesitated to rent rooms to teenagers, but he could tell the moment he'd laid eyes upon this group that they would not be rowdy. Upon arrival, they'd milled about in front of the hotel like cattle, their eyes somber. A boy had broken their ranks and come into the office to rent the rooms. He'd explained that they'd driven nine hours to attend a concert in Albuquerque, only to hear on the radio, an hour from their destination, that the concert had been cancelled. The band was from Croatia and they hated touring. They would never come back to the States. This had been it. This had been the teenagers' chance to see them. Last night, about eleven, Mayor Cabrera had walked by their rooms and he hadn't heard a peep.

And here they were again, filing back into their caravan of beat-up SUV's, each teenager with one plain bag. The same boy approached the office. He wore canvas shoes and a diving watch. He came in and gave Mayor Cabrera the keys and settled the bill. Mayor Cabrera offered him some nuts and he turned them down. He extended his arm for a handshake and Mayor Cabrera went along with this. The boy didn't seem ready to leave. He turned to the side and looked out the windows.

'It's no big deal,' he said, embarrassed, aware that he and his friends were being dramatic. 'There will be other concerts.'

'Sure there will.'

'We all saved up for the tickets and gas money and the hotel and everything.'

'I see,' said Mayor Cabrera.

'We were singing their songs the whole way here. No one else at our school has even heard of them.'

Mayor Cabrera exhaled.

'It's still an adventure, right?' The boy laughed falsely.

'Let me ask you something,' Mayor Cabrera said. 'Someone asked me this question and I need an answer: Where do we all go wrong?'

The boy looked out at his friends. He repeated the question under his breath, turning a dial on his watch. 'Thinking that because you want something and it's a reasonable thing to want and you make proper preparations and you deserve the thing, that you're going to get it.'

Mayor Cabrera pushed aside his can of nuts and rested his elbows on his desk. 'That's pretty good,' he said. 'That's not bad.'

Mayor Cabrera watched the boy shuffle back outside, the door dinging as it closed behind him. Mayor Cabrera had never, as a young man, wanted anything. He'd never been as crushed about anything, as a youngster, as these young people here. He'd never made preparations. He'd glided through the years blindly and then lucked into a better life than he'd known existed, his life with Tam. That life had been taken away. Now Mayor Cabrera distracted himself, and when he wasn't distracted he sulked. He'd lost Tam and it was his own fault that along with her he'd lost his sister-in-law and his niece. He was still sulking. He was shuffling around in the hotel parking lot of his life.

Mayor Cabrera understood that he could not pursue Dana, if he was indeed going to pursue Dana, until he made things right with his family. Dana was a woman Mayor Cabrera had fallen in love with, not a quick fix for the ills of his life. He didn't want to use her to patch over holes he'd been allowing to widen for over a decade. Dana would make his days ornate, but at present his life had no foundation. He was as much a drifter as any of the poor dusty souls that bunked down in the motel for a night, cheap whisky in tow, and then disappeared the next day just before check-out time.

Mayor Cabrera hung an OUT TO LUNCH sign on the lobby door. He went to his car, passing the sad teenagers, and pulled out of the lot. He drove to the feed store and got what he needed from inside, waving a quick hello to the owner but keeping moving, and then he drove across town at exactly the speed limit and parked along the curb in front of his sister-in-law's house. He rolled up the windows for no reason. His sister-in-law's mailbox was leaning to one side in a way that seemed precarious. Factions of weeds were jutting up all throughout the yard, looking like scorched bouquets. Part of Mayor Cabrera was afraid to go inside and face his sister-in-law, but now that he'd committed to doing it he could already feel his shame dissipating. The shame wasn't from making a mistake, it was from lacking the fortitude to fix it.

Mayor Cabrera rose from the car and opened his trunk and threw the bag of chicken feed over his shoulder. He marched up to the door, light-headed but certain, and knocked. After a minute he knocked again. She was home. There was no car in the driveway, so Cecelia was gone, but her mother had to be home. The kid had a car and the parent didn't. Mayor Cabrera's sister-in-law had sold her car about a year ago, to a man who lived outside town and bought used cars for no purpose except to collect them. He didn't scrap them for parts or fix them up. Mayor Cabrera thought he heard something inside the house, but no one came to the door. He tried the knob and it wasn't locked, so he pushed the door back a little and called out.

'Who is it?' his sister-in-law asked. She wasn't alarmed, and the matter-of-factness in her voice was familiar to Mayor Cabrera. She'd never been alarmed, in the old days.

Mayor Cabrera found his breath and announced himself. He called out his first name, Ricardo.

After a silence, his sister-in-law said, 'The mayor himself? Gracious, what an honor.' She told him he better come on in, if he was sure he had the right house.

'I'm just looking for a spot to set down this feed,' he said.

He ducked to get the bag through the doorway. He could hear the TV now. The scent of the place was familiar. It didn't smell clean but it smelled wholesome, like old, simple things. Mayor Cabrera paused in the hallway and looked through a half-open door into what had to be Cecelia's room. It was her room, he remembered. There'd once been a crib in it. Now her bed was made and a Rubik's Cube sat on her pillow. The walls were bare. A guitar was lying across the desk, next to a tape recorder.

Mayor Cabrera walked through the living room, nodding hello as casually as he could, and let the bag come down and meet the kitchen floor. He could see the chickens scratching around back there, out the window, working their necks. He'd heard about the birds from his sister-in-law's neighbors, a young couple that had moved out of Albuquerque because there were too many rules and regulations and now seemed to be rethinking their decision. The chickens looked healthy enough, he supposed, or at least they looked the way chickens usually look. Mayor Cabrera stepped back into the living room and leaned over to perform a stiff hug, his sister-in-law sunk into a wheelchair, then he took a seat on the couch. She didn't really need a wheelchair, did she? There wasn't anything particular wrong with her legs. Mayor Cabrera's sister-in-law had him framed in an airtight smirk. He asked her if she always left the door unlocked and she said locking the front door was Cecelia's department.

His sister-in-law was skinny, but Mayor Cabrera had prepared for worse. She wasn't any skinnier than the skinny sister who worked at the gas station. Not that she looked healthy. Her hair was like straw. Her hands seemed heavier. She was the same person, though, the same defiant glint in her eyes. She held the remote for the TV poised, but didn't change the channel. A show about the movies was on. People were waiting to give their opinions. Mayor Cabrera's sister-in-law was looking at the TV, but she wasn't paying attention to it. She was trying not to look at Mayor Cabrera, trying to leave the ball in his court. He wondered if she had any idea Lofte was in trouble, any idea she was a woman in decline living in a town in decline.

Mayor Cabrera asked how Cecelia was doing and his sister-in-law said she wasn't around much. She had her classes, of course, but she'd invented a bunch of other ways to stay away. She'd taken a job on campus. She was in a band, though it seemed like maybe they'd broken up. Mayor Cabrera's sister-in-law didn't blame her daughter. She didn't blame her one bit for steering clear of the house.

'She'll come back to you,' Mayor Cabrera told her.

'One day she's going to drive over to Albuquerque and never come back,' his sister-in-law said. 'She's smart enough to get tired of walking back into this house with me waiting on her. Forget Albuquerque, she's going to drive down into Texas, or worse.'

Now on the TV they were showing pictures of actresses from ten years ago and then the same actresses today. Everyone was agreeing they looked better today.

'You should've been around,' said Mayor Cabrera's sister-in-law.

'I know it,' he said. 'I've handled things about as badly as possible.'

'There's no one else to talk to about the things I want to talk about.'

Mayor Cabrera looked right at her. 'I've wasted a lot of time,' he said. He and his sister-in-law were breathing the same close air.

'Who used their time real well and who didn't is *not* something I want to talk about.'

'A debacle, I think they call it. The last bunch of years.'

Mayor Cabrera's sister-in-law shook her head, as if in bitter disagreement with herself. She looked him square in the face. 'I miss her so much,' she said.

'Just as much as the day of the funeral sometimes.'

'And I have a hard time remembering her face.'

'I try to forget it but I can't.'

'There was no way around missing her but you didn't have to make me miss you too.'

'You reminded me of her. I didn't want to get over her. I just wanted to pout.'

'I know the reason. It's no excuse.'

'I handled things badly.'

Mayor Cabrera was being sincere and it felt good. Absurdly overdue. He wondered, if it weren't for Dana, if he'd have ever been moved to fix any of this. He'd found out he could fall in love again. He'd found out there was hope for him.

Mayor Cabrera's sister-in-law improved her posture, using the armrests of her wheelchair to get settled. Mayor Cabrera noticed that one of the rubber handles of his sister-in-law's wheelchair was chewed up, and he remembered that handle. He realized it: this was his wife's old chair. He couldn't remember letting his sister-in-law have the wheelchair, couldn't recall how she'd ended up with it. He didn't recall a lot from the months surrounding his wife's death. He wasn't angry. Whatever was going on with his sister-in-law, it wasn't her fault. She was off-course, like him.

'Do you remember how she used to eat corn one kernel at a time?'

'I do,' said Mayor Cabrera. 'I used to cut the kernels off the cob with a knife.'

'She was so picky and organized. It was the opposite when we were kids.'

'I never let her cook,' Mayor Cabrera said. 'She'd take too long. We'd have both starved.'

'She was the opposite when we were little.'

'If I let her do dishes, she'd be in there till midnight, holding bowls up to the light.'

'You spoiled her. You were lucky you got to do that.'

Mayor Cabrera thought of his dead wife's tiny, soft hands. They'd felt like cats' paws on his chest. He put his leg up on the coffee table, showing he was going to get comfortable. 'These years have been a pile of crap,' he said. 'It helps to say that.'

Mayor Cabrera's sister-in-law clicked her cheek. She didn't say anything at first and then she said, 'Next time you go to the cemetery, I want you to take me.'

Mayor Cabrera hadn't been to the cemetery since he'd become mayor. He nodded and reached out and touched his sister-in-law's big cold hand.

'We'll make it soon,' he said.

CECELIA

It was eleven in the morning and she was parked on a side street in a fancy neighborhood. The driveway she was observing had been empty and without action for forty-five minutes. Cecelia didn't have one of Reggie's songs in her head, and she decided to leave the radio off and exist in silence for a little while. If she wasn't going to hear music of Reggie's, she didn't want to hear whatever some DJ was going to play.

Cecelia couldn't miss a class doing this. Or work. She couldn't be noticed as absent from anything. Cecelia could see the red tile roof of the house above the pale wall that enclosed the yard. The wall would provide Cecelia plenty of privacy.

Every ten minutes or so a car rolled past on the main drag, mostly women on cell phones guiding glimmering sedans down the center of the street. The houses around her were in clashing styles – Tudor, French Chateau, ranch houses, even an occasional Southwestern spread with all the outdoor fireplaces. Nate's family's house was in some Spanish style. A carpet of lush grass covered the neighborhood. If you saw green lawns in the desert you were either in a cemetery or an exclusive part of town. Here came another one, another woman on a phone, this one in a little coupe. Cecelia couldn't tell their ages. They were older than her but they weren't old.

Cecelia pulled her tickets out and took another look at them – heavy and sharp-cornered and with a shiny red stripe down one side. Nate and his band had booked their first gig already, and he'd left two tickets for her in an envelope up at the A/V booth. The tickets had been printed by a local version of Ticketmaster. Thus Poke Sarah's Thruster would never sell out, but to be safe you could go to a kiosk and get tickets in advance. These had come from the kiosk on campus. The bar was called Antivenin. Cecelia and Reggie and Nate had played there a few times. Cecelia had to hand it to Nate for not wasting any time. His band had a set list, probably composed mostly of Reggie's songs, and now they had a gig, and he hadn't even neglected to taunt Cecelia.

A woman stumbled by up on the sidewalk, yanked this way and that by a dog with bulging muscles. The woman wore a jogging suit and her hair was done. Cecelia bet the dog cost more than Cecelia's car was worth. If you were an artist you weren't supposed to care that other people had money, and that was more proof that Cecelia was not an artist. Not like Reggie had been. Reggie'd had vision, while Cecelia's cobbled-together songs were always blatant and derivative. Reggie hadn't harbored uncharitable thoughts, and all Cecelia could think was that the people in this neighborhood were dense and shallow and didn't deserve anything they had.

A car turned down the side street Cecelia had parked on. She tensed a moment, but the car pulled into a driveway four or five houses up. Another one of these women. This one was wearing a short-skirted business suit. She loaded her arms up with grocery bags, leafy vegetables sticking up out of them like in a TV commercial, and made it to her front door without ever getting off her phone. She had dropped something and it had rolled to a stop under the back of her car. Cecelia watched the woman disappear into the house and then she waited a minute before cranking her ignition. She watched all the warning lights come alive in her dashboard. All fluids were low. Every gasket was worn. Her exhaust was toxic and her belts loose. Her upholstery sagged. Her tires were bald. And of course she knew she had a blown brake light.

She rolled around the corner so her car would be out of view, then shut the engine back off. She was feeling customarily cheated in the big picture, but at least she was going to do something to allay that feeling. She'd been playing by rules in a game that rules rendered pointless. She'd been faking something that now she felt genuinely, a disregard for consequences. The rules of the universe were off if Cecelia had access to Reggie's unknown songs and the rules of Cecelia's life were off now too. She still wasn't hearing a song, was still living in quiet as she had been since yesterday, and a fresh loneliness was building in her.

Nate was at school and his dad was at the restaurant and his mom was off doing God-knew-what, whatever she'd always been doing when Cecelia had gone to Nate's for rehearsal. Cecelia got out of her car and took a gas can from the hatchback. She cut through a few lawns and came up to a side gate, opened it, slipped inside. The gas can was heavy but Cecelia knew it would be light on the way back. She rounded the house. There it was, that hacienda-style barn, that red-roofed play garage.

A rabbit hopped in the grass not far from Cecelia, startling her. It was grazing on the succulent blades.

'How'd you get in here?' Cecelia asked it.

The rabbit only looked at her.

'Might want to back up,' she told it. 'Friendly advice.'

Cecelia opened the door of the barn. The doorframe was strung with little wooden skeletons, a repellent to evil spirits. The skeletons weren't going to work on Cecelia. She was flesh and blood. She looked up and saw the hot tub still hanging inside, waiting up there. She thought about the great number of enemies Nate and his family must have. Cecelia paced the inside walls, dumping gasoline in sloppy glugs. It was getting on her sneakers and jeans, but she had a change of clothes in her car. These sneakers and jeans were putting in their last day of service. It wasn't easy to use all the gasoline. She had to do three laps. She loomed in the doorway a moment and then lit a match and watched the flame flare.

THE TEACHER

He was a vegetarian who owned a pampered goat for the purpose of making his own cheese. He had a shop in his backyard that he'd converted into a creamery and he'd turned his flowerbeds into herb gardens, and the cheese he made he donated to a program that fed the poor. The wolf had left his goat alive.

After the attack, the goat's demeanor softened, as if she'd been taken down a peg. When she had milk she was generous with it. She quit butting the fence posts. She was still fed as well as a human, and now when the teacher arrived with her supper she ambled right over and nestled her head into his palm. Of course the goat had a limp now, her hind legs chewed up as they were. Of course she wouldn't be allowed to stay in the backyard anymore, grazing all night on elk grass, nothing but a short fence separating her from the wild desert.

SOREN'S FATHER

He had a cot in the room. The clinic called it a bed but it was a cot. He didn't use it. He sometimes roughed up the bedding before morning so nobody would know he stayed in the chair all night watching the red tail-lights disappear into the Southern flatlands. He wondered how many of the cars were the same ones night after night, and how many of them had started their journeys somewhere other than the desert and would wind up somewhere other than the desert.

It was at night that he thought of Soren's death, and he could never think a minute past it, like thinking of the end of the world. Soren's father wondered if his son's face would pinch or broaden the moment before he passed away, if his eyes would pull open briefly or if any light he saw would emanate from a place no one could see until they were going there. He wondered if the room would grow perfectly silent, Soren's breath gone, before the machines began sounding off. To not be in the room when Soren came to, when he blinked himself conscious and tried to jerk away from his monitors and probably cried out with confusion, to not be waiting for him when he returned, would be terrible, but to not be in the clinic when his son expired, the thought of that locked up Soren's father's chest.

He looked out the window at the straight road that led into the greater dark. It was the time of night – too late even for the night owls and not yet early enough for anyone else – where several minutes could pass without a car and the cars that did appear were probably on the road because of bad news.

DANNIE

She was going to try. She was going to make a grand effort with Arn. She packed water and a piece of fruit and a stick of lip balm, then she put on a bikini and over that a big sweatshirt and sweatpants, gathered a warm hat and gloves and good sneakers. She positioned the telescope. She located the big rock shaped like a totem pole, the one with the scrappy, twisted pine growing from the top of it, and to the left of that was a wide spot in the trail where Dannie had often seen hikers take rest breaks. Dannie focused the telescope and secured it against the banister and kept it in place with a couple heavy bookends plundered from the trucker's stuff in the extra bedroom. She tightened the wheel that held steady the height of the tripod.

Arn was napping. Dannie had less than an hour to get out there. She wrote a note, telling Arn what time to look and stressing that he not bump or jostle the telescope. She taped the note to the top of his alarm so he'd hit it with his hand when he reached to stop the buzzing.

She got in her car and sped away from town, checking the clock in her dashboard and watching for signs, and eventually she found a spot where she could access the trail, a small parking area with a single exposed picnic table. She got out of the car and felt cold, and that's how she wanted to feel. When she took off her sweats, she wanted her skin alive with goose bumps. When she removed the bikini, she wanted her flesh to sting.

She hiked steadily and without thinking, slightly uphill, losing her breath. Prickly pear stands lined the trail, their fruit still hard and green. Tiny birds flitted this way and that. Dannie was getting there. Though her feet were starting to hurt, she was making good time. The trail was full of stones that looked like they belonged on the bottom of a river.

Dannie drank some water. She adjusted her bikini bottom. She was rounding a bend in the trail that she recognized from the telescope. She had to cruise downhill about a quarter-mile and she'd be there. She'd be to the totem pole rock. She'd paced herself correctly. She had ten minutes, plenty of time.

When Dannie turned the last corner, the big totem rock was right where it was supposed to be. The sun was where it was supposed to be, striking its last pose before it sank away. Dannie's resolve was right there in her chest, where it belonged. The old man wearing a windbreaker and white Velcro sneakers was *not* where he was supposed to be. Dannie didn't know where he belonged, but he didn't belong on *her* bench-like outcropping in the middle of *her* wide spot in the trail. Dannie stopped a few yards from him and put down her satchel, thinking he might take the hint and move on, that he might understand it was someone else's turn to have the bench. He didn't, though. He sat there. Dannie sighed, like she was so glad to have found a place to rest, and the old man kept looking blankly out toward the sun, which was all color now and no brightness. His hair was of a different generation, that parted, water-combed style. Now that it was the real gusting winter, Dannie saw about one hiker a week on this trail, but here was this guy. She didn't know what to do. She had a few minutes, but they were melting fast. Arn was going to wonder why such pains had been taken to allow him to watch Dannie stand next to an old man on a trail.

'Where'd you come from?' Dannie asked.

'What do you mean?'

'I mean, why are you here?'

'Just resting.'

Dannie made an exasperated motion toward the basin with her arm, indicating they were in the middle of nowhere.

'My group deserted me,' the old man said.

'What group is that?'

'Or I deserted them. I guess that's probably the way it happened.'

Dannie glanced back across the expanse of desert. Her condo complex was a raised, brownish stain. 'You really should start heading back,' she said. 'It'll be pitch dark out here.'

The old man folded his arms.

'The temperature's already dropping.'

'Let it drop.'

'You're just going to sit there till you freeze?'

'If I feel like it.'

Dannie looked at the old man's pressed slacks. His eyes were not cloudy or watery. She looked at her watch, knowing what it was going to say. It was almost time. It *was* time. It was too late to panic. The moment was now and it was wrecked. The sweat suit would remain on. The bikini would remain hidden. Dannie's irritation was drying easily into defeat. In a couple more minutes, there wouldn't be enough light for Arn to see anything out here. She leaned against a boulder. What was she even doing out here? What was this? She knew the answer. This was desperation. Out here away from everything, she could see. Whatever she and Arn had, it was running on fumes. When you had to make grand efforts, it was already too late. Dannie was trying to kick-start the relationship with the only thing they'd ever really had, which was sex. Dannie wasn't getting what she wanted, and Arn wanted nothing. They'd lost momentum. Dannie wasn't young. She didn't need to be pulling stunts like this.

She stepped close to the old man and he made room for her on the flat seat of the rock.

'What kind of group?' she said. 'I want to know.'

'Watching birds of prey.'

Dannie looked out through the failing light. She couldn't remember seeing any hawks or eagles. Only buzzards and crows and gulls.

'They give you binoculars,' the man said. 'I couldn't get mine to focus.'

'You just track them while they soar around?'

The man shrugged. 'The whole thing was my wife's idea. To get me out of the house.'

'Yeah,' Dannie said. 'I don't have anything to get me out of the house either.'

'Turns out there's not much worth doing. There's not much out here.' The man was softening a bit. 'I dread the mornings,' he said. 'The whole day out ahead of me, knowing I'm going to drift around.'

Dannie got out some trail mix and the old man didn't want any. He didn't want water, either. Dannie couldn't see the condo complex at all.

'It's not the mornings for me,' she told the old man. 'It's the nights.'

HISTORY OF ARN III

He couldn't get any of the cushy factory jobs, so he ended up doing odd crap nobody else wanted to do. He never kept these jobs long. He always felt like someone was gaining on him. You didn't get off scot-free from smacking your legal guardian in the head with an aluminum bat. It wasn't a live-and-let-live deal. It wasn't boys being boys. If Arn stayed put too long, his past would catch up with him.

Just inside Oregon's border he worked at a mill that produced wooden arrows. The arrows looked exactly like the arrow that kid had shot at Arn in middle school. The mill had a room on the side of it where all the sawdust collected, and once a week someone had to put on a mask and go in there and shovel the whole thing out, filling dozens of tall canvas bags. This was one of the tasks that fell to Arn. Sawdust came out of his nose along with his snot. It came out of his ears when he swabbed them out. Arn's boss would call him into the office, where he would preface whatever complaint he had with an assurance that he was not jumping Arn's shit. 'Now, I'm not jumping your shit,' he would always say. 'I don't want you to think I'm jumping your shit.' There was a woman who did quality control at the mill and one Monday she came in late, looking devastated. At break time she told everyone she'd gone on a bear hunt and three dogs had given their lives to protect her.

In Northern California, Arn worked at a winery. He got picked up in a van every morning. He did not participate in The Crush, which he'd heard so much about. The winery was small time, a couple years old, owned by two brothers who were learning as they went. Arn's sole responsibility, for weeks, was to open bottles of wine and dump them. Thousands of bottles, poured into a steel tub and lost down a drain. Arn never knew what was wrong with the wine, whether it was tainted in some hazardous way or merely tasted funny. When all of it was gone, Arn weeded and painted.

He rented a cheap, clean studio apartment that happened to be smack next to a high school, and this high school was a corral for countless numbers of the most alluring girls Arn had ever seen. The Spanish tutors up in Oregon were homely compared to these Lodi girls. These girls had breeze-blown bangs and movie-star sunglasses and tiny tops held in place by proud little breasts that didn't bounce an inch when the girls walked across the parking lot. The girls who were seniors all went across the street for lunch, to a wholesome deli with tables outside in the sun. Arn started taking his lunch break at the same time they took theirs, started driving into town from the winery every day in one of the company vans to grab a table and eat sandwiches full of pesto and sprouts. He had no problem talking to the girls. He talked to one after the next after the next and managed to sleep with four of them. He would tell the girls, vaguely, that he worked in the wine industry, that he wasn't from around here. There were no other men at this deli. It was like Arn had crashed on an uncharted island. Sometimes he felt like he was being tricked, like a mouse gorging himself on free cheese. He managed to keep himself in Lodi until summer, before losing his nerve and hopping on the overnight train.

In Fresno, Arn found work at an outfit that produced diploma frames. The place was full of lesbians, and a lot of them prided themselves on having been fired from other jobs because of their lifestyles. Arn's task was to cut the backboards of the frames down to size. He had his own area and could set it up as he chose. When he cut a board too small or large, no one bitched. They threw it out and tried another. Arn cut boards and cut boards and ate the free food the company was always ordering for lunch.

He met a woman in Fresno, a bartender. This woman let Arn help out at her bar on weekend nights, extra money for Arn. Each night, after the bar closed, the people who worked there held a low-grade party at someone's apartment. They would drink a little and do some drugs and eventually pair off and go home. At one of these parties, Arn drank a bunch and went out into the yard and looked into the sky and it struck him for the first time that he might be a murderer. He'd never let himself consider this possibility – hadn't been ready to, he guessed. He'd hit the man with a blunt metal object and the man might very well not have survived. The man had

not recovered. They'd rushed him to the hospital and tried everything to save him, but it had been too late. The mother and son
were alone now, more miserable than before. The mother and son
hated Arn. Arn's case wasn't getting buried by fresher offenses. It was
still right at the top. A murderer. Arn's face was probably on posters
back in Washington. He was on a special page of the national fugitive database reserved for real scumbags, his face among the faces of
rapists and such.

In Nevada, Arn spent his days standing on a platform, ears
plugged and knees rattling, feeding strips of scrap plastic into a
grater.

In Phoenix, at a mine supply, he stood inside a huge warehouse
and instead of cleaning and organizing the place, as he was being
paid to, he threw a golf ball back and forth with a bald man who ate
a lot of snack cakes and did calisthenics. No one ever checked on the
two of them. Arn realized his attitude toward work had changed. He
used to want to impress people, to impress himself, and now he only
wanted to reach the end of another day and another week and get
his check. He was an adult, for better or worse. He took naps on
piles of tire tubes. Sometimes he swept. The building was so long
that when Arn threw the golf ball it would bounce three or four
times before it reached the bald man.

Arn's second day in Tucson, he went into a coffee shop to look at
want ads and struck up a conversation with an Asian lady. The lady
was much older than Arn, but you could only tell that by her eyes.
He asked her to meet him for a movie later and she readily agreed.
Arn was glad he'd bothered to put on a decent shirt. The lady left
the coffee shop and Arn switched to a different section of the newspaper, the one with the movie times. There was a theater right

downtown, about two blocks from where Arn was sitting, and this was good because he didn't want this woman to know that he didn't have a car. That was a revelation that could wait.

The Asian lady met Arn for the movie and later in the week for dinner and another day they went for a long walk in a park. The Asian lady did not seem intent on enjoying these dates, was not stymied with the question of whether she and Arn were connecting. She was going on the dates, it seemed, because she knew it was healthy to go on dates and foolish to turn them down. When Arn had been acquainted with her for two weeks he asked her if he could stay with her until he found his own place and she agreed to this.

The Asian lady had plum streaks in her hair and she ate a lot of bagels and did a lot of sit-ups. She had no family in this country. She had graduated from business school at University of Arizona and had applied for a loan to open a sunglasses shop and the loan had been approved. She was about to open a second shop. She didn't say much to Arn, but when she touched him she did so gently, like he was precious. She never said a word about his lack of an automobile. She said nothing about the trouble he was having finding a job. She didn't understand the jokes Arn made, seemed to have no use for them.

One morning, instead of bagels, she whipped up a breakfast of eggs and bacon and toast. When Arn sat down to it, she asked him if he would like to marry her.

Arn set his orange juice down.

'Is this a citizenship issue?' he asked.

'This is a I'm getting old issue. You like me. I'm good-looking.'

It occurred to Arn that you could ask someone to marry you right away, like the Asian lady was doing, or else you had to wait a long time and pick the right moment and be sure of everything. They seemed equally good methods.

'We get married and you manage the new shop.'

'Wow,' said Arn.

The lady laughed. 'You think about it.'

'I will,' said Arn. 'I'll think about it.'

The Asian lady took more bites of bacon, like she was getting comfortable with it, like she'd never eaten it before. 'You think,' she said. 'You say no, I'll ask the man who owns the barbecue place near my shop. He'll say yes, for sure.'

'If I say no, you'll ask someone else?'

She nodded vigorously. 'The guy who owns the barbecue place. He'll say yes right away.'

CECELIA

She had received another song and then another. One whole side of the cassette was full. The songs arrived in flurries or at least pairs, and then there'd be stretches of dead air in between that could go on for days. Probably Cecelia was facing one of these stretches now. The songs never had anything to do with her life – no college, no crappy cars, no arson. She had no idea how many were coming. She could not begin to imagine where Reggie might be. Cecelia had made a deal with herself to try to keep her emotions out of this, to perform her duty of recording the way one did laundry or dishes. Since she'd made this deal, the songs were coming even easier. She'd learned how not to resist them or be delighted at their arrival, to simply receive. The last song had been about an old businessman who goes searching for a girl he'd loved in grade school. As a child he'd shown his affection by throwing the girl's shoes in the lake near their houses. As an old man, he returns to the lake and dives to the bottom, trying to find the little sandals and boots and roller skates.

During the day, Cecelia avoided the house. She'd caught her mother crying one evening, indulging in redundant sobs. Her mother had been standing in the kitchen near the window and letting herself blubber and this had made Cecelia want to yell at her. She hadn't, of course. She'd slipped off, her mother never aware she was there. More than once Cecelia had come home in the afternoon and seen her uncle's car in the driveway and had passed right by. Maybe *he* could help her mother. Or maybe she'd drag him down with her. Whatever they were doing, Cecelia wasn't going to disturb them. She didn't know why her uncle was coming around all of a sudden and didn't care to know.

Cecelia felt both proud and empty when she thought of Nate's barn. She'd kept the clothes from the fire in her car in a plastic grocery bag for days, unable to figure out what to do with them. If she took them somewhere and tried to burn them someone could catch her in the act. She didn't want to throw them away, not smelling like gas. She was being paranoid, probably. Cecelia wondered if the fire department had come to Nate's house. They must've, in that neighborhood. She wondered what Nate's mom and dad thought. She wondered what had happened to the rabbit. Cecelia had seen nothing about the fire in the newspaper, heard nothing around campus.

SOREN'S FATHER

Gee was the first person he'd let in Soren's room who wasn't part of the clinic staff, his first social visitor. She usually stayed about an hour, and while she was in the room Soren's father felt relief from his loneliness but he also felt intruded upon. The clinic wasn't fun or freeing like when they went out to dinner. Gee always went over to Soren when she arrived and again right before she left and pressed her forehead against him and whispered things to him that Soren's father couldn't hear. She never brought flowers, but often she brought food. Today she had éclairs, and though Soren's father wasn't wild about sweets he ate one and made sure to seem he was enjoying it. Gee had also brought coffee. She couldn't stomach the clinic brew.

She finished eating and stood at the window with her short foam coffee cup, a look of certainty on her face that for some reason irked Soren's father.

'Albuquerque is so ugly, it's beautiful.' Gee's coffee cup was making a patch of fog on the window. 'God made this place ugly and humans made it uglier, and that was just what it needed. It needed to be uglier.'

Soren's father knew he wasn't required to respond to such statements. Especially here in Soren's room, he could stay as quiet as he liked. Gee came away from the window and sat. The chairs were orange and the table was small and high. She told Soren's father she was through with the art world. She was through consulting on galleries and she was through with her own art too.

'I'm making the same roadrunner over and over. That's not art, it's craft.'

Soren's father told Gee he'd seen a real roadrunner out the window earlier that day, strolling right down the roadside.

'The real thing is always better than the artifice.'

'Thanks for the coffee,' Soren's father said. He tipped his cup toward her.

'I've had enough food of the spirit. I'm ready to deal with food of the stomach.'

'The restaurant,' Soren's father said.

'I found a space that would be suitable. Not perfect, but suitable. I paid them to hold it for me a couple weeks.'

'You must be about ready to reveal the idea.'

'I am. Asian-influenced chicken wings, served with watermelon.' Gee's eyebrows perked.

'Is that an appetizer?'

'That's the whole menu.'

'Oh, okay,' said Soren's father.

Gee explained that the wings would boast a more complex spice pallet than usual hot wings, and the watermelon was a Southern twist on celery and tasted better than celery. Instead of bleu cheese, she was concocting her own dipping sauce with local goat cheese as the base.

'If you're cooking it, I'm sure it'll be good,' Soren's father said.

Gee gave him a long look but didn't say anything. She was deciding, Soren's father knew, if it was the right time to talk to him about going in with her. She'd talked about it before and she would talk about it again. Soren's father was enjoying a break from loneliness, but he was also looking forward to being alone in the room again. It was a wrong feeling, he knew. Gee was wonderful. That was a fact. He was craving solitude and he also found that for some reason he was looking forward to the next vigil in the parking lot. That was the kind of company he wanted, company that was quiet and didn't know what it was after. Soren's father had purposely never invited Gee over on a Wednesday. She seemed totally unaware of the phenomenon of the vigils and that was okay with him. He didn't care to hear her opinion on the matter.

'Once I commit to this,' she said, 'I'm in for about seventy hours a week. That's doing it without quality help.'

Soren's father set his jaw. He didn't take a sip of coffee or glance over at his son.

'It would be nice to get my memoir in order, but this space won't sit around forever. I guess it's just as well. I'm a chef, not a writer.'

'You're a lot of things. You got enough brains and heart to make four or five women.' Soren's father blinked his eyes clear. 'And here I am this one old man.'

THE GAS STATION OWNER

Walking away from Lofte, he thirsted for the arrival of night and the true cold. He had been close to putting it off again, close to not leaving for yet another day, those days that turned into weeks and into worse, but he had not put it off this time. He'd eaten his last meal from the diner. He'd chugged a beer and slammed the can down and locked the doors of his house. He'd laced up his boots. He'd spat on the tame dirt of Lofte and had put one foot in front of the other. He was scared but he didn't care about that. He headed west, his pack already heavy, his face to the sun. His legs were prickly with exertion. Parts of him were being roused from long disuse. He was doing it, going into the desert. In no time Lofte looked tiny behind him. In no time he had the town in perspective. It wouldn't disappear from view, though. It stayed, minute but stuck on the horizon, until the gas station owner got rid of it by veering north around a hulking dune.

Forty days and forty nights. This was day one. The direction he was heading there were no towns. If he spotted an over-serious hiker or drug lab he would give a wide berth. He didn't have enough food for forty days, and his water would be gone in a week. Forty days and this was day one. The gas station owner thought of all the nuclear geeks shipped over to this bleak land and charged with creating a weapon that could make any land bleak. He thought of these men who'd never wondered about their purpose, who'd fallen asleep and awakened thinking of the same thing always, whose greatest love and greatest fear had been in their brains all along. The gas station owner lived in his body and keeping that body alive would become his obsession. Forty days and forty nights. He knew he was mixing science and religion, but neither had a claim on him. He was going to force the desert to claim him, to claim his life or claim him as an equal.

DANNIE

She didn't want the vigil to end, but as always the hour came when the group naturally and wordlessly felt that it was time to rise. There were seven of them remaining. They'd lost the painter. Dannie had no idea what kind of painter he was, if he whiled away his mornings on corny watercolors or if he painted houses or if he touched up signs for the city. The fewer people that remained, the more it troubled Dannie when they lost someone. Each departure, at this point, felt like a betrayal of the group. They weren't a mass anymore. They wouldn't have been able to field a softball team. Dannie had seen bands with more members. They'd lost the fat hopeful women. They'd lost the guy with the sunglasses. Dannie had singled out one of the remaining vigilers, the college girl who was getting skinnier by the week but only ever wore baggy clothes. This girl would not abandon Dannie. When the others left, as they were bound to, Dannie wouldn't despair. She had the girl. Maybe she didn't have Arn the way she used to, but Dannie had this girl.

Arn had sat next to Dannie and had held her hand for a while, out of obligation, but the quiet charge of intimacy was gone. Now it was simple wordlessness between them. It was like they were relieved to be at the vigils because they *couldn't* talk. They had made love that afternoon and it seemed to Dannie they were performing out of fear, acting. Arn would never admit they were growing apart, and Dannie hated him for that. She was the one who had to initiate anything unpleasant. Like she had initiated everything pleasant. They never raised their voices with each other, which made the idea of breaking up seem unapproachable. She'd never slapped him. He'd never wrenched her roughly by the arm.

Dannie drove them back to Lofte and when they arrived at the condo she said she was supposed to meet an old friend for coffee back in town. She told Arn she'd be home late. He looked at her puzzled but he didn't protest. He went inside and Dannie pulled onto the road and went all the way down to Route 66. She wanted to feel free and aimless. She wanted Arn to be the one sitting at home and wondering.

THE GUIDE

She drove without thinking, hitting the likely spots. She was supposed to be talking about how plants and animals survived in this harsh habitat, but her mind was full of what had come in the mail the day before. She was going to Las Cruces. There wasn't anything for her to do in Las Cruces until the summer, but she was going right away. She was going to lose two weeks of rent, and so be it. She was going to pack her old Subaru to the gills and aim it south on I-25 and not stop until she saw a sign that read NEW MEXICO STATE UNIVERSITY.

This would be her very last desert safari. She had one guest in the jeep, an old guy who was in great shape, who looked like he could still play football or build a barn. His hands weren't knotty. He sat placidly as she motored them across a flat of sagebrush.

'It's okay if we don't see javelinas,' the man said. 'Don't worry yourself.'

She looked at him in the mirror. They'd seen roadrunners and woodpeckers and hummingbirds and several rodents and a big scorpion, but still no javelinas.

'I like the scenery,' the man said. 'The scenery is enough.'

'Oh, you're going to see a javelina,' said the guide.

The man waited. He wore a bright gray jacket the same color as his hair.

'My insurance policy,' the guide told him. She popped open the glove box and removed a gallon-sized zipper-bag of sweet rolls and cantaloupe. 'I don't leave it up to chance. When the little suckers hear the Jeep they'll run out and meet us. There's one that's bigger that sort of leads them.'

'Lucky pigs,' the man said. 'Better breakfast than I had this morning.'

The guide downshifted for a hill and when they crested it she and the old man saw all the light pouring into the valley before them, casting long shadows behind the cacti and behind the carcasses of dozens of miniature hogs. The guide let the Jeep roll halfway down the slope and then held the brake to the floorboard. There was hardly any blood. Some of the creatures' snouts were pointing straight up in the air. They didn't look surprised or scared. They looked as helpless as they'd always looked. The guide could smell the animals. They weren't rotting yet; this was how they always smelled. The buzzards had not yet arrived. This was the guide's last day in the basin, thank God.

She looked over into the old man's steely eyes and could feel that her own were moist. He put his hand on her shoulder. All he said was, 'Jesus, sis, sorry about your pets.'

CECELIA

She had been flat on her back on her bedroom floor, had sensed another song on the way and had stilled herself in order to let it arrive peacefully, but then she'd heard her mother out in the living room talking to someone. She got herself up and went to the hallway to listen. Concerning her mother, this was what she'd been reduced to – spying. Cecelia had never gone back to getting her mother up in the mornings, and her mother seemed to be managing that on her own, rousing herself at a reasonable hour with no help. Maybe Cecelia was doing the right thing, leaving her alone. She needed space. She didn't need an enabler or a critic. Maybe Cecelia's uncle was a good influence. Cecelia made her mother feel guilty, but Cecelia's uncle could talk to her mother as a fellow over-the-hill half-depressed person. Cecelia didn't feel sorry for either of them – someone they loved had died, just like had happened to Cecelia – but her life would be a lot easier if her mother got better.

From down the hall Cecelia could see her mother's stiff, dull hair hanging over the back of the wheelchair. Her mother was ordering something over the phone but she was watching the church channel, not a home shopping channel. Cecelia heard the TV, the guy with the shiny beard and the headset who'd once been penniless but had depended on faith and had been rewarded with a corporation. Cecelia's mother was telling the person on the other end of the phone that she felt her faith multiplying in strength.

'Now where is your organization based?' Cecelia's mother asked.

Cecelia didn't know what to do. She could hear the central melody of the new song in her head. It sounded like one of those lullabies that could fill adults with fear. Cecelia felt weird at how *not* weird it felt to her now, receiving the songs. It was a vested condition of her life. Each song could reasonably be deemed a miracle, and to Cecelia each was only an interesting chore. She wasn't missing Reggie on her own terms, but nothing ever happened on her terms. She listened to her mother ask question after question. Something was off. The conversation didn't seem friendly. Cecelia's mother was asking questions about where exactly her money would end up and she wasn't getting an answer. Cecelia saw a tiny insect bumbling across the wall and she didn't disturb it. She shifted so it could pass. Here came her own voice trilling in her head. Here came the lyrics, something about praying for a drought. She tried not to hear them.

'Money is no object,' she heard her mother say. 'I have a great deal of money.'

Cecelia knew *that* wasn't true. It seemed like her mother was getting transferred, working her way up the ranks of holy tele-marketing. She still wasn't getting answers. She wanted to know that her donation would help people in need. Cecelia's legs were starting to ache. She was hearing the chorus now. *If I can't take your hand for a dance, there ain't no Egypt, there ain't no France.*

'Does it feed orphans?' Her mother was almost yelling. 'Or does it buy your boss a speedboat?'

Cecelia saw now. She got it. Her mother was prank-calling them, harassing them. Cecelia had never heard of a person engaging in solitary pranking and she'd never heard of a fifty-year-old woman prank-calling anyone at all. She ought to be relieved, Cecelia supposed. Her mother wasn't brainwashed. Her mother still had her spunk. Maybe, when she thought no one was around, she allowed herself moments as her old self. Or maybe she and Cecelia's uncle were turning back into the early-twenties punks Cecelia used to hear stories about. Cecelia didn't care if she wasn't the one capable of helping her mother, as long as someone did.

The religious people were trying to get her off the phone and Cecelia's mother wasn't going quietly. She was still claiming to want to donate a large sum, a sum they'd finally become convinced she didn't have. She wanted to sow a significant financial seed, she kept insisting.

Cecelia slipped back in her room and finished getting dressed, still hearing Reggie's song, which was telling her that missing people was a way of giving yourself the sour rewards you deserved. And how else could it work? Cecelia was missing Reggie but she was also missing herself as she'd been when Reggie was around. She was missing having a place in the world, because a world without Reggie didn't seem to want her.

She went out the front door without a sound, her mother more or less in a shouting match now, about to get hung up on. She had an afternoon shift in the booth at work. She drove fifteen over the whole way and jogged in from the parking lot and arrived only a couple minutes late.

She opened the door to the A/V booth and there was her boss, sitting in Cecelia's chair. Her boss held up a finger. She was reading a young adult novel, as she was known to do. It appeared from the cover to be about zombie cheerleaders. No one knew if she herself preferred this brand of literature or if she liked to screen whatever her children were going to read. No one knew if she even had children. No one knew a thing about the woman. She got to the end of a chapter and snapped the book closed.

'Don't put your bag down,' she said.

She stood and faced Cecelia and informed her that her services were no longer required by the Office of Internal Resources. It was that simple. Cecelia's boss thanked her for her time. It didn't seem like Cecelia was getting fired, because the air was not charged, but she was. She was being fired. Her boss wasn't going to be dramatic, but neither would she be unclear. No one ever got fired from OIR. Not even Marie, who missed a shift about once a week. True, everyone else could work the equipment. Cecelia had had plenty of time to learn how, to ask someone to teach her, and she hadn't. She'd remained ignorant.

Her boss held her hand out and Cecelia reached and shook it. This lady wanted Cecelia to leave so she could get back to her zombie book. This lady had never been a bit curious about Cecelia and she wasn't curious now. She was only curious about her undead pep squad. Cecelia had an impulse to tell the woman that sometimes her enemies became victims of arson, that the woman better watch her back, but she stifled it. Cecelia still hadn't heard anything about the barn. Nate hadn't said a word. Nate's parents had probably decided to cover the whole thing up, for whatever reason, and they probably had the pull to do that, to make it like something that was important to someone had never happened. But there was another way to think about it. Maybe the barn was exactly *why* she was being fired. This was the world's next trick, the next step in the dance. She'd taken the barn and now she had to give up her job.

'I can't believe it took so long for you to do this,' Cecelia said.

The woman made a face.

'What's the worst part about being old?' Cecelia asked her.

'I'm only forty-one. I guess that's old to you.'

'You're forty-one but you might as well be seventy-one, and when you were twenty-one you might as well have been seventy-one. Right?'

The woman's face had very little animation, but there was fear in her eyes, if Cecelia looked hard enough.

'I'm broke,' Cecelia said. 'Which means I wasn't in a position to quit a job, so thank you for firing me. It was up to you and you finally did it.'

The woman set her book down on the counter. On the back cover was a terrified crossing guard. 'You're welcome,' she said. 'It was my pleasure.'

'Yeah,' Cecelia told her. 'It turns out I'm not a piddling kiss-ass nerd, so this wasn't going to be the job for me. I'm not like you. I can be miserable and I can be happy. I'm in congress with music from the great beyond. It lands in my brain. It's happening now, in fact. I'm important. I'm needed.'

'I'm not miserable,' said the woman.

'This job is beneath me. I have a higher calling.'

'So I guess this is perfect. Everyone's happy.'

'I'm not happy that often anymore,' said Cecelia. 'But I'm happy right now.'

SOREN'S FATHER

He had sold his remaining three lunch trucks, but when Gee asked him what was new, he only shrugged. He had admitted to himself that inevitably he was going to wind up selling off the whole fleet, and a man selling three trucks was still a man selling a business, while a guy selling one truck was a guy selling one truck. If he let Gee know the business was gone, she'd double her efforts to recruit him to be the cook at her restaurant. The restaurant was going to happen, apparently. She'd even gotten an investor. She'd come to terms with the fact that Soren's father wasn't going to be her partner, wasn't going to come up with any seed money or even an idea or two, and now she wanted him to be her 'wing man'. She'd offered him thirty dollars an hour to learn how to make the chicken and then keep it coming. Then she'd offered thirty-five. If he were going to do it, he would've agreed by now. Soren's father had more money in his bank account than he'd ever had, and the thought of that made him feel lost. It was supposed to mean something, having a hefty sum in the bank, but it felt like nothing. Everything was this way. He ought to have been over the moon to have Gee, but nowadays he felt lonelier during her visits than any other time. None of their talking felt right. He didn't want to talk about the future, about plans, and small talk in the presence of a boy in a coma felt that much smaller. Gee could tell. She was testy. The last time she'd visited, a nurse had asked her if she could wear soft-soled shoes the next time she came to the clinic because her heels clacked and some of the patients slept in the afternoon. Gee had let her have it, a nurse Soren's father had seen around but didn't know yet. Gee had asked her if she thought the patients appreciated the toxic cloud of perfume she dragged into all their rooms. She asked if the nurse had had a run-in with a skunk and was trying to cover it up. She asked the nurse if she owned stock in the perfume company. She asked the nurse if she thought it would be pleasant to be trapped in a flower shop as it burned to the ground.

DANNIE

She'd broken up with Arn. She stood at the front window now, shifting her weight from one leg to the other, an eyebrow resting against the glass, gazing at the empty space where Arn always parked his truck. This time the truck would not be back. The permanently abandoned look of that particular parcel of concrete, this time, was not something Dannie was imposing. The oil stain would dry and fade and get blasted clean by the patient sand, sand that would never be anything but sand and would only grow finer.

There'd been no moment of disbelief. Arn hadn't asked for a reason. He had never made a single demand on her since Dannie had known him and this afternoon had held to form. He'd asked her to stay in the living room, out of his way, and he'd packed all his stuff in a duffel bag in about ten minutes. She had been the one crying, she who'd had a chance to prepare.

Standing at the window now, Dannie felt that she hadn't known

Arn at all. He could be an identity thief. He could be heir to a shipping fortune. Could be dying of a terminal illness. Dannie had watched him from the other end of the hall, stalking around with shirts and underwear in his fists, and he'd seemed ready and willing to be heartbroken but simply unable to pull it off. Emotions were a foreign language. They weren't his element. His face had been empty as he jammed things in his bag and then sat on the bag and then jammed in the rest. It hadn't all quite fit and he'd squeezed through the front door wearing two coats and with a hat on his head and a pair of sneakers in his hand.

Dannie didn't want to keep playing the scene over and over. None of it was her problem anymore. She could quit trying to figure Arn out. She could quit wearing out her eyes on the empty spot in the world where his crappy pickup used to be. She'd had her explanation, her little speech planned out, and he hadn't wanted to hear it. Now she felt like she had to tell it to someone. The words were lumped in her throat. She had to walk out into the desert and whisper them to a cactus or something.

Dannie pulled away from the window and went to the kitchen. She stared vacantly into her pantry. There were about a dozen boxes of crackers, all open. She didn't even look in the fridge. She drank a glass of water and went to the back sliding door and looked out past the balcony. Her condo felt creepy, like a big country house.

Dannie remembered college, high school. She remembered all the breakups, the loss and the freedom. Breaking up back then had been exhilarating, but now she only felt adrift. Even her divorce had seemed positive, but there was nothing positive about losing Arn. Dannie didn't open the sliding-glass door. It still wasn't dark out, the moon a low bloom. Dannie was going to have to start from square one. She'd done it before and she was going to have to do it again. She was going to go to a fertility doctor and she was going to look for an appropriate partner. If she had to move back to LA to find one, that's what she was going to do. She was going to set herself a deadline, and if she didn't meet anyone by then she was going to look into other options. This thing with Arn had been built on deceit. It was a deceitful fling, and now all the deceit was gone, behind her. She was going to sit around for a couple days and wait to get her period. She could feel the start of it. Her periods had gotten worse in recent years. She would bleed like she'd been stabbed. She wouldn't fit into her jeans. She would have horrendous thoughts. She'd be stuck in here alone, like someone coming off drugs.

THE RIVALS

Sometimes the wolf could withstand a series of full days without a song and sometimes he grew demented and out of control after only a few hours. He struck again, a dog and cat who lived next door to each other. The owners of the animals were not on speaking terms, but the pets were close. The wolf had broken their necks and flung their bodies under a shrub. Again he had not eaten his prey. At first look, the dog, an Australian cattle dog that for some reason had never grown to full size, and the cat, a massive tabby, looked to be cuddling, taking a nap.

The owners were two old men who'd worked in the turquoise trade and had each coached many youth baseball teams. Once, they too had gotten along famously. They were both lifelong bachelors. The cat was named Bonnie and the dog Clyde.

MAYOR CABRERA

The council meeting. Lofte had always scrimped and jiggered, but this year a lot of items would be plain neglected. No further magic could be performed on the numbers. There hadn't been a security patrol or volunteer fire crew for some time, but now they would have to close the recreation center. There once had been a commercial alliance that spruced up the main drag every couple months. There once had been a parents' alliance that stewarded the baseball diamond.

Mayor Cabrera had not gone to see Dana last night, the second appointment he'd missed. It had been two months since he'd had his troubles with her. He wondered if Dana thought he'd met someone, that he'd given Dana up for some other woman. Maybe she thought he was having money problems, as if that would've stopped him from visiting. He would've robbed a bank, if it had come to that. It was seeming more and more farfetched, the notion of Mayor Cabrera driving to Dana's villa and propositioning her. Washing his car, slapping on cologne, knocking on her door and looking her in the eye and asking her to fully retire and become his woman – the idea seemed childish. Dana didn't love him. At least at this point she respected him as a customer. Mayor Cabrera couldn't have Dana think of him as pathetic. That just wasn't something he could live with. If his dream of being with Dana was what had caused him to go to his sister-in-law when she needed him, then good had come of his falling for a professional lady. He could think of it that way. He'd only seen his sister-in-law four or five times and her spirits had already risen.

'Hidey there, Mayor,' said one of the council members. 'You with us?'

The town council consisted of four members. One was Lofte's lone lawyer, a guy who always wore a polo shirt and always carried a tape player with headphones for listening to books on tape. One councilman was a kid in his twenties who was a single father. He drove his daughter to Albuquerque every day, to a fancy school. The kid was awaiting a big settlement because a surgeon had messed up one of his hands. There was an elderly councilman who was a crack shot and had a range set up on his property. If you showed up at his house and asked to shoot, he'd lead you around back and load up his arsenal of old rifles and let you have at it, no questions asked. The last member of the council was a middle-aged woman who was loud and grating, but if you knew the facts of her life you couldn't help but root for her.

The council discussed the wolf. The town's pet owners were in a lather. This was a problem something could be done about, unlike the budget. Maybe they could have a vote about it, a town vote. People loved that, when they got to decide something local and immediate. The youngster with the daughter said he knew a guy who sold these rigs that turned regular fences into electric fences. If you had a chain-link fence you could spend eighty bucks and hook up this box that ran a current. The kid presented this information, like most things he said, as an idea to be only lightly considered, a jumping-off point.

'What about the people with wooden fences?' Mayor Cabrera said. 'And what about the pets themselves? The very pets we're trying to protect could get harmed.'

The old man didn't know why they didn't set traps. Bait them with ground beef. You'd get a few coyotes collateral damage, but so what. The lawyer wondered what the proper channels were. Wolves were protected, no doubt. Maybe the state would tranquilize and relocate it. The tutor-woman said that in the old days people would've looked after their own, bundled up in a rocking chair on the porch, shotgun at the ready. To be honest, she added, she didn't give a shit about people's goats and cats. She didn't like when people treated animals like they were family. In truth, she was rooting for the wolf.

Mayor Cabrera hadn't told the council about Ran. He hadn't told anyone at all. He didn't like keeping secrets, but he didn't want folks to get their hopes up and also didn't want to deal with people who'd resist having an enormous off-brand church moving into the area. Mayor Cabrera of course resented that some stranger from another state would determine whether Lofte survived. He felt like he should be doing more to secure Ran's favor, but he wasn't sure what. Maybe he was supposed to fly to Iowa with a detailed proposal, a sales pitch that pointed out the myriad attributes of North Central New Mexico. He didn't have that in him. Not these days. He was also keeping the whole thing to himself, he knew, because if it didn't work out it would seem he'd failed. It would seem that the town had expired not due to population atrophy and dwindling tourism, but because Mayor Cabrera hadn't been able to close a deal. Mayor Cabrera didn't want to fail, nor did he want to perform a miracle. Honestly, he didn't even want to come to another of these meetings. The council had moved on to another topic and Mayor Cabrera again wasn't paying attention. In a few minutes it would be break time and Terry, the old guy, would pour everyone a small cup of the lemony liqueur he was never without.

The fact that Mayor Cabrera had only recently gotten it together to do a proper Internet search on Ran was a testament to his lack of presence when it came to mayoral concerns. During one of the many slow moments at the motel, he'd gotten the lobby desktop fired up and typed Ran's name into a search engine and browsed about a dozen relevant links. What he'd gleaned, and he couldn't tell if the information pleased or dismayed him, was that Ran was unconnected from any serious wrongdoing. He didn't seem to have ever been to prison, didn't seem to have made anyone mad at him, didn't seem to have fled from anywhere. He'd changed his haircut and clothing style, but people did that. He'd changed church denominations – people did that too. What he was, it seemed, was determined. He was a leader. A talented, capable leader.

CECELIA

Cecelia had filled a whole tape, front and back. The latest song was about souls who spoke the same language, and how when those souls were close to each other they could finally see that they'd been banished to a foreign locale for years, alone, squinted at, and now they were home. You could say parakeet or bedpost, viper meat or dry toast. Everything was comprehended. The song talked about clouds being born, which happened when all the winds in the sky spoke the same dialect. The last line was, *When it's about to rain, I know I know you.*

Cecelia was tired of missing Reggie over and over in the same way. She was tired of sloughing on and off the same sadness, no progression, no control. It was all apprehension when a new song arrived now, no joy. The songs were hollowing Cecelia out. They were relentless. They'd proven their point. Each song was beautiful in flight, but they had no regard for the wear they were causing as they landed, song after song, on the same strip of Cecelia's heart.

DANNIE

She had been harboring the irrational hope that Arn would show up at the vigil. The vigils were hers now, something he'd lost in the breakup. Fitting, because they'd been hers to begin with. There were only three of them now. The vigil group had withered week to week before Dannie's eyes but she still didn't know how it had come to this – only three. The college-age girl looked so tired, her face all shadows. And then there was the arrogant man with the pin-covered coat. Both of them had cast strange looks at Dannie when she'd walked up and settled in without Arn. They knew they'd never see him again.

Part of the parking lot had been repaved. When Dannie had first shown up the smell had been overpowering, but now she was used to it. She felt lightheaded. When the time came to leave no one moved. Usually the vigils ended naturally, the vigilers a unit, a herd, but tonight someone was going to have to lead. Dannie hoped she could count on the other two vigilers to show up next week and the week after and the week after, but counting on people was foolish. Worrying about being alone seemed to be a good way to wind up alone. Dannie wondered if the others were hoping she'd stay like she was hoping they would, and she wondered if they felt weak for hoping that, for needing someone else to be alone with.

MAYOR CABRERA

He still had his high school football helmet. He'd never turned it back in – had stolen it, if you wanted to put it that way. The helmet was silver with a green facemask. His high school, over near Golden, had been poor and still was. You could tell the high schools with money by their soft sod fields. Mayor Cabrera's school had a gridiron of mown weeds.

He remembered the bus rides, wondering if he would be a different person in Albuquerque or in Santa Fe. He got to return kicks for a season, when the little slick guy broke his collarbone. Mayor Cabrera always went around the first tackler and through the second. That had been his method. The coaches had always pointed Mayor Cabrera out as an example of heart and toughness, never as an example of speed or agility or power.

Mayor Cabrera was sitting in the basement of the motel, his palm pressed against the cool dome of the helmet. He recalled the feeling of waiting for a kickoff, rocking leg to leg in the calm before the tornado. He remembered getting prepared mentally to enter that closed circuit of chaos, wondering if the chaos, that particular return, would be on his side or against him. And then he thought of Margot, a girl who had taken a liking to him junior year and who would rise to her feet in the stands and cheer Mayor Cabrera's name in the quiet before the ball was kicked. Mayor Cabrera remembered being embarrassed by that, by Margot cheering for him. He could remember fearing looking over and making eye contact with her more than he feared being smacked by a linebacker with a fifty-yard head of steam. This girl Margot had made it where she and Mayor Cabrera were lab partners when they dissected frogs, and he had clammed up and barely said a word to her, standing right next to her for two entire class periods, tiny organs on display in a tray in front of them. This girl had intimidated Mayor Cabrera to the point that he could not discern whether she was pretty. Now, in his memory, with her heart-shaped face blooming up from a turtleneck in the stands, she was angelic. Mayor Cabrera had been frightened of her, and when she'd given him a letter just before Christmas break professing her affection he had made no acknowledgment. He never, in fact, spoke another word to her. In the spring they didn't have any classes together and eventually Margot wound up dating another boy and then during senior year she moved away to somewhere unfathomable like Minnesota. There'd been Margot and then there'd been Mayor Cabrera's wife, some years later, and now there was Dana – the three women Mayor Cabrera would never stop thinking about. Margot had knobby little knees and Mayor Cabrera had always marveled that she didn't fall over when she walked. She had seemed both wiser and more naïve than Mayor Cabrera, back in high school, sage yet also silly, but it was just that she hadn't been afraid. He had no idea what had happened to it, the letter. He kept everything, but he didn't have that letter. He could still see the handwriting, which wasn't cursive but was still bold and loopy.

Mayor Cabrera put away the football helmet. It was the middle of the night but he felt wide awake, so he went up and cleaned the windows in the lobby and dusted the countertops and the desk. He put new candy in the dish and squared up the rug and filed some stray paperwork. Put more paper in the printer. Replenished the coffee supplies. After that he went out front and swept in front of the carport and then, out of tasks, wandered back to the basement and found himself sitting at the big metal table with a sheet of printer paper in front of him. He found himself writing a letter. He dove right in, parsing out the difference between wanting someone and needing someone and which was worse. Nowhere did he write Dana's name. He wrote of the trouble of having his feelings ripen rather than rot. He wrote about the back of her knee when she bent her leg, about her tiny ears. He wrote about thinking of her with other men and having his heart fold up and collapse. Of her practice of wearing a different perfume in each season, and how he hadn't smelled the winter fragrance this year. Other men had, but Mayor Cabrera had not. He wrote down all the nicknames Dana called him and that he'd never once called her a nickname, had never addressed her in a whisper as anything but Dana. He wanted to call her something other than the name her mother had given her. He wanted to call her Love. Mayor Cabrera wrote of the time he'd visited her, going onto another page now, one of his first appointments, when he'd arrived and could tell she'd been crying, her eyes puffy and voice wavering, and he hadn't asked her what was wrong. If he ever saw her again, that would be the first thing he'd ask, what had upset her that day. He wasn't afraid of the answer. He wasn't afraid of Dana's past or her present. He wasn't afraid for his own feelings.

Mayor Cabrera wasn't calming down, but he wasn't feeling as crazy. It wasn't late. It was 11:30. He hadn't eaten dinner. He wrote that the night was an evil time but not when he was with her because then he wanted the night to last forever. Mayor Cabrera felt that Dana was his oasis and he wrote that down too and then he rested his pen. He didn't need to worry if everything in the letter made sense because he wasn't going to send it. It wasn't really a letter. He picked the papers up and gazed at them, as if they held a landscape rather than a frenzy of words, listening to the sand brushing against the high basement windows. He didn't ball the pages up. He folded them in half and then filed them down in the empty garbage can in the shadow of the big table.

THE GAS STATION OWNER

The sun was a sour note lingering in his temples. He got his headache about this time, like clockwork, about an hour after his breakfast of jerky and pretzels and coffee. It was like a visitor, the headache, a companion. It might have been brought on by the arid glare, but it also had something to do with lack of whisky. The gas station owner had brought none at all, and that had been an error, but he would've been out by now anyway. He could only have brought a bottle or two. He'd get past it. He was glad he'd at least brought sunglasses. He'd never used them before, had always considered them womanly, like sandals or scarves, but he'd never been in this much glinting late-winter sun and he'd never quit whisky.

The gas station owner hadn't moved in a week. He'd found water gurgling down a cliff face and had stayed with it as long as he could, burning up seven of the forty days he was going to stay in the desert, but now the trickle had petered out altogether. He had come across a roofless hunters' cabin two mornings after leaving Lofte and had found a jar of sweet pickles in a cabinet. The day after that he'd crossed some kind of old fire road, free of tire tracks but still edged with shin-high berms. But then this spot – he knew it would be the last easy place. There would be narrow canyons with puddles hidden in their troughs. There would be cacti with moist flesh. Rain, with any luck. The desert was asking him to bow out now. He was being tempted, like someone from a Bible desert. Tempted to give up his journey.

He wasn't going to bow out. In the morning he would leave here and wander not in the direction of the basin towns and not in the direction of Albuquerque. He would wander toward nothing. He would find some other water, and some other water after that, or he would not.

He'd killed and eaten a crow, and that was the only action he'd taken so far that felt right, that felt like real engagement. He'd leveled his pistol and intentionally winged the stupid bird. Then he'd gotten a grasp and broken its neck and plucked it and cleaned it in the pure trickle and roasted it over his fire. It was more work than it was worth, but it felt right. It was an action that had startled the desert, that had announced his presence.

He looked out from his half-assed grotto, which gave him shade mostly when he didn't need it, late in the day, and the far-off mountains appeared to be crumbling. The mountains he could barely see, veiled in the blue dust of distance – that's where he would survive or perish, where he would find himself in a type of straight-forward peril men had found themselves in since the beginning of time.

SOREN'S FATHER

He had decided maybe it wasn't a great idea to have Gee keep coming up to the clinic room. Something was wrong and he wasn't interested in figuring out whose fault it was because it was probably his. He hadn't told Gee any of this and had been avoiding her calls. He wasn't sure how to proceed. Everything was his fault. Doctor Raymond had come in that morning to flash his penlight in Soren's eyes as he did every week and then listen to his chest and declare with astonishment, as he did every week, that Soren still didn't need a tracheotomy. Soren's father had asked him exactly what he was looking for with the light and when the doctor said he was watching for any changes, Soren's father cut him off and said there weren't any damn changes and that was obvious and if it was really necessary to keep shining a bright light in the kid's eyes and making useless checkmarks on a useless clipboard then could the doctor come do that when Soren's father wasn't around?

'But you're always around,' said the doctor.

'I didn't say it would be easy,' said Soren's father.

Now Soren's father felt bad about that. He wasn't upset at the doctor. He was upset because he saw he had to face Soren's situation alone. It was one of those things. There were four walls where Soren's father lived and a wasteland out the window, and Soren's father had to figure out how to do the time alone. He had to make peace with the beeps and cycling hums of the machines that monitored Soren. He had to make peace with the clinic food, which he now knew was terrible. He had to make peace with his son's sallow, sinking face. He did not need to be leading on some woman who was too good for him anyway. He wasn't with the living. He wasn't with the living and he wasn't where his son was.

He took magazines into his hands and he remembered to brush his teeth and clip his nails, and he reminded himself that Soren, if and when he woke up, would need him. He saw Gee's weird roadrunners in his mind's eye. On vigil nights, he closed the blinds tight and flipped off the lamp. He did not want to offer the remaining vigilers any encouragement. Before, when his son had been healthy, Soren's father had been happy and the vigilers had been miserable, and now these people were using his son to try and find peace. There were a few left who refused to quit. They didn't want Soren to wake up. They didn't want anybody to be happy.

DANNIE

Something was wrong with her body. Her body was against her, betrayed. No one had forced her to get married. No one had forced her into a job where she never met new people. No one had forced her out to New Mexico. Dannie had to get this period to arrive and get out of her sweatpants and out of her condo. If she could get through this period she could leave Arn behind and make hopeful new plans. Her back was aching. Her hands and feet were tender. She could lie still for hours without falling asleep. She'd been eating nothing but dry sopapilla. It was hard to open the honey jar and tedious to keep dipping the bread. She could make it as far as the balcony, where she could breathe fresh air and keep an eye on the heavens, but every time Dannie came inside she smelled bacon. That smell was never going to leave. It was in the furniture, in her hair.

Dannie managed to make an appointment. She showered and put on jeans and a flannel shirt. She made it down her condo stairs and over to her car. It had rained all yesterday and there was no way to tell. No puddles or sog. The desert was dry and the sky was how it always was, close and distracted. Dannie looked at herself in the rearview. She was stuck smack in the middle of her life. Her hormones were brawling. Dannie kept her eyes on the road, kept the car between the lines.

She parked in front of a low building made of mirrors and found the mirror that was the door. She signed in on a clipboard and then had to fill out paperwork. The other women in the waiting room were nondescript. They were nondescript to Dannie because they were just like her. They were in their thirties, trim and savvy. Except when it came to becoming thirty-five, thirty-seven, thirty-nine years old; they didn't know how that had happened. When it came to knowing where their youths had gone, they weren't savvy at all. Here they were, flipping through magazines, meekly awaiting verdicts.

The doctor was that perfect doctor age, about forty-five. He spoke to Dannie in an exam room. He wore a suit without a tie, no scrubs or lab coat. He weighed Dannie and took her blood pressure. There didn't seem to be any nurses anywhere. The doctor's hands were big and smooth as silk on Dannie's arm.

'You look like someone,' he said. He was puzzled, not happily.

'I don't think we've ever met.'

The doctor tapped his forehead with his knuckle. 'Are you a chef? Do you work at a restaurant?'

Dannie shook her head.

'I'm telling you, you remind me of someone.'

The doctor left her in the exam room. There was an empty hat rack in the corner. There weren't any diagrams on the walls, no drawings of organs, just a photograph of sheep on a hillside.

After a while a woman came in, another doctor, and Dannie learned that she was married to the male doctor. She had stringy hair and pointy-toed shoes. She was the one who gave Dannie her exam. Afterward, she had Dannie drink a bunch of water and pee in a cup, and then Dannie was back in the waiting room. It was a different bunch of women, but they might as well have been the same.

After a time, the male doctor opened the waiting room door and waved her back and she followed him to the same exam room. Dannie saw how the office worked. The wife performed the exams and the husband handled the bedside stuff.

'I thought of it,' he said. 'You know the talent show on TV with the Australian guy?'

'I know *of* it.'

The doctor motioned for Dannie to sit. 'They had a girl on it who throws footballs through tires. This prim thing with manners, and she stands twenty yards away and zip, zip, zip – one after the next.'

'I've never thrown a football in my life.'

'You're not from Texas. This girl was from Texas.' The doctor drew his hand behind his head daintily, and then whipped his arm forward. He held the pose. 'They kept her around because she was an attractive female who could throw footballs.'

'Mystery solved,' said Dannie.

The doctor set the file flat on the desk. He made sure it wasn't too close to his soda. 'So, you're pregnant.'

Dannie looked at him.

'In my opinion, the answer to whether or not you're likely to get pregnant is yes – it's overwhelmingly likely, a hundred percent likely. You can quit waiting on that period.'

Dannie didn't know how to feel. She felt stupid. She was a woman who'd been having sex with no birth control and then her period had been late. Her mind had not allowed itself to consider the obvious. Nothing could happen until you stopped hoping for it. She'd met Arn after she'd decided not to try and meet anyone. She'd gotten pregnant when she'd deemed herself unable. Her womb was not a cobwebby corner in the rafters.

The doctor had a lot of literature for Dannie. She was in a fog. He gave her many phone numbers. He gave her his card. It had his name on it and his wife's. Her name was Marney. The husband and wife would no longer be her doctors. Their duties ended with conception. There were a bunch of foods Dannie was encouraged to eat and a bunch she needed to avoid. There were exercise programs. Dannie looked at the photograph of sheep and it looked different. The sheep looked like they'd been through an ordeal. They looked dumb with gratitude. Dannie was passing back through the waiting room, all those other women. She was out of the building. She was in her car.

She didn't know where to drive. She wasn't going home. When the lights were green she went on through. When they were red, she got into a turning lane. She headed mostly south. It was the middle of the afternoon. She went down past the factories and the scattered, one-story neighborhoods and took a ramp onto an interstate. There was a dairy farm with a complicated irrigation system and then a flurry of signs for a taxidermy museum. She was down into the featureless desert. There weren't mountains down here and there had never been towns.

Dannie felt something unfamiliar and she hoped it was joy. Joy wouldn't feel this complicated, though, this unfinished. People were going to want to help Dannie. They were going to judge her. She was going to be an open book. She had so much to learn. She was about to start a twenty-four-hour-a-day job that was going to last many, many years. Dannie wanted to tell her friends. She would be let back into their good graces because she had a story to tell. That's what was required when you forsook people and disappeared into the wilderness: a story. They would support her. But she wasn't going to tell them until she was ready. Dannie didn't want a bunch of fluttering attention just yet. She had to think things over. She had cards in her hand but the game she was playing was wholly unfamiliar. She was still heading south, the only car on the road. Albuquerque had disappeared from her rearview. The Owl Café was supposed to be down here. Maybe she'd stop and get a greasy burger. She adjusted her visor and opened the window a crack.

Arn. What about Arn now? He *had* held up his end of the bargain, not that he'd known a bargain was ever in place. He was an unwitting donor. He lived like he didn't want to ever be wise and now he was none the wiser. He wasn't ready to become a father. Not even close. He would have a whole different life a few years from now, and Dannie had no right to ruin that life by telling him about this pregnancy. Their time together had been mutually beneficial. She'd given him a fling with an older woman and he'd saved her from the world of sperm banks and adoption. At a sperm bank they had contributions from a bunch of tall guys with college degrees, as if the world wasn't crawling with six-foot college graduates who were complete assholes. Dannie's child was going to look like Arn – there was no way around it – but Dannie was an adult and that meant dealing with difficult circumstances. The child might have Arn's temperament, and that would please Dannie but also make her miss him. She'd be ready for that. She'd handle missing him. She would miss the way his eyes could appear uninterested while his touch was full of passion. She would miss his voice, would miss the way he never cried but always seemed not far from it. People cried too much. Dannie was a mother now. Her crying didn't mean anything anymore. She was a mother and she was going to have to miss all sorts of things.

Dannie saw the billboard for the Owl Café and then she saw the exit and blew past it. She wanted to be in her car. There was something way out ahead of her on the horizon, either low clouds or lofty mountain peaks. They were as far off as her eyes could see, in another state or another country.

MAYOR CABRERA

He walked his sister-in-law out to his car and she lowered herself down into the passenger seat without any help. Mayor Cabrera got them going north on the old Turquoise Trail. His sister-in-law was wearing an actual outfit, a blouse and pants that matched and a coat and shoes that went together. She'd made some effort with her hair. Mayor Cabrera could tell by the way his sister-in-law looked around at the scenery that she hadn't been up this way in a long time. She placed her hand on the dashboard, bracing herself, and Mayor Cabrera slowed down. When they were young, she'd have been egging him to go faster. She and Tam and Mayor Cabrera had spent so many hours in a car, in his old El Camino. They'd burned a whole summer chasing around the state to sites where aliens had been spotted.

At the cemetery they walked at a measured pace, browsing the tombstones. Some of these people had lived in the Old West, Mayor Cabrera thought. The Old West had not been so long ago. Mayor Cabrera asked how his sister-in-law's chickens were doing, which was a way of asking if she was worried about the wolf. She said she couldn't bring the chickens in at night because of the mess they'd make. She hoped there were enough of them to look out for one another, or at least raise enough racket to wake her. She seemed resigned to leave her chickens to fate, which Mayor Cabrera decided to take as a sign of sanity. She seemed a little embarrassed about the chickens, in general. If she could be embarrassed, she was rejoining the human race.

They came to the tombstone they were looking for. Mayor Cabrera had decided not to put dates on his wife's stone. He didn't want her hemmed in that way. There was an engraving on the stone of verbena, her favorite flower. There was a weed the landscaping crew had missed, leaning against the stone like a drunk against an alley wall. Mayor Cabrera reached down and plucked it.

His sister-in-law's cheeks looked blanched, out in the chilly breeze. 'Things have never felt real,' she said, 'without her here to see them.'

Mayor Cabrera knew what she meant. The moment he was in now didn't seem all that real. 'We used to be the best people we knew,' he said. 'We walked around with that. The knowledge that we were fun and tough.'

His sister-in-law's lips became a hard line and then she said, 'I remember. I remember how I was.'

The sun found its way out of the clouds and Mayor Cabrera saw that they were standing in the shade. He hadn't visited his wife's grave in forever but the feeling was nonetheless familiar, the uncertainty about what to feel, about whether he was there for himself or Tam, whether that mattered. Maybe it was good to feel confused. Maybe some people didn't feel anything at the cemetery, and that had to be worse.

'I remember,' his sister-in-law repeated. 'But it was easy back then.'

A small noise issued from behind them, a throat-clearing, and they turned to see an old man approach a nearby grave. He pulled a newspaper out from under his arm and rested it in front of the stone. It wasn't yellowed or stiff, the paper. It looked like today's paper. The old man removed his hat with a shaky hand. He didn't seem to notice anyone else was around, and Mayor Cabrera and his sister-in-law, in order not to disturb him, grew still and quiet.

THE FRESHMAN

He was in ninth grade but was almost six feet tall and had strapping forearms. Each morning he came out before he left for school and fed his rabbit and stroked its ears back. It wasn't a normal rabbit, nor even a jackrabbit. It was some European breed with long hair and a permanent frown that the boy's mother had rescued from a defunct circus. The rabbit looked like a wizard. It had taken the boy's mother one day to realize she didn't want the rabbit inside the house and two days to realize it would make a poor pet. By then, the boy was attached.

When the boy came out, still chewing his last bite of cereal, he saw the buzzards all around and knew what had happened. He didn't know what had happened, but he knew the rabbit was dead. He couldn't see the cage from where he stood because it was tucked against the side of the house in a utility shed that was really only some sheets of plywood. The buzzards had not dared inside. They were building courage. The wolf now knew everything about the boy. The wolf, by this time of morning, was hiding somewhere on the edge of the wilderness. He was hiding but he wasn't worried about getting shot or captured. He was worried because the songs were coming less often and he needed them more and more. The girl in the house with the chickens was failing him. The wolf would have been relieved, somewhere inside him, to have the humans corner him, the same as the pets were relieved in their souls when they saw the wolf's eyes before them.

The boy, the rabbit's owner, was always alone at the house in the mornings because his mother worked early, and for once the boy was grateful for this. He went in and got the shotgun and the paper bag of shells. The paper of the bag was stiff and rough, like it had been rained on and then dried out. He sat himself on a stack of vinyl siding and aimed the shotgun and put even pressure on the trigger. Then he quickly fired the other shell. Then he reloaded. He was so close to his targets, he didn't have to use the bead at the end of the barrel. Each time he shot a pair of buzzards he had to wait for the rest of them to resettle. They would scurry a short ways, flapping and stumbling, wanting to get to safety but not wanting to forfeit their spot in the chow line. The boy didn't want to see the rabbit yet. He wasn't going to school. He was excusing himself. He shot twice and waited, shot twice and waited. The sun ascended shapeless and white. After a half-hour, there were more buzzards, not fewer. Some of them had lost interest in the hidden rabbit and were poking at their dead brethren. The man who lived on the next property came over to see what was happening. When he realized the boy's pet was dead and the boy was almost out of ammo, he allowed the shooting to continue. It was a sight. The yard looked war-torn. The shot buzzards were fifty low, tattered flags from fifty defeated little forces.

In time, the boy had to go look. He saw. The rabbit had beaten its head against the bars. The boy had been right that the cage was sturdy enough to keep out any predator, but he had not counted on an animal that would scare the rabbit to death just to do it. The wolf hadn't wanted to eat the rabbit, only to torture it. It was a lot for the boy to take in.

The man from the next property sent the boy inside. He agreed that the boy didn't need to go to school that day. The man got his pickup truck and tossed every last buzzard in the bed, so he could haul them out in the desert and dump them. He couldn't believe how light they were. Each bird weighed about as much as an apple. He had a tarpaulin cover for the bed and he stretched it on, to keep the rest of the buzzards at bay. He wondered if all the live ones would follow him when he drove off, a grim cloud. He got the rabbit out of its cage and rested it on the seat of his truck, and then he grabbed a shovel. He was going to dig a grave for the rabbit, and the buzzards he was going to dump on the side of a little-used road, to show them what it felt like.

SOREN'S FATHER

He finally answered one of Gee's calls and she told him before he could even say hello that she was only interested, at this point in her life, in getting swept up in a person, and that with Soren's father she had been doing all the sweeping. She wasn't looking to take care of someone. She wasn't misery looking for company. She had given more than she'd gotten all her life, she told Soren's father. All her life. She'd realized she'd wanted to start a restaurant mostly for *him*, to give him a partner and work to do and distraction and self-respect, and so she'd scrapped the plan. The restaurant was off. She was going to work on her memoir full time, something selfish, something for her.

Soren's father had a perverse impulse to beg her not to leave him, to say he wanted to join in on the restaurant even, but he was able to swallow it. She had never been angry with him before.

'I'm sorry,' he said.

'Don't be. Just be grateful. Be grateful for the time you had with me.'

'I'm that too.'

Gee exhaled into the phone. 'This was the last time I was going to try calling you. I'm driving to Phoenix to see my son. Bags are packed.'

'You spoke to him?'

'Not yet.'

'What are you going to do?'

'Drive into his six-month-old neighborhood in my twenty-year-old van and knock on the front door of his mini-mansion. That's what.'

'I'm glad to hear that,' Soren's father said. 'I wish you luck.'

'I can feel that it's time,' said Gee.

Soren's father was grateful to know Gee, but he was also grateful to her for sharing her intentions about seeing her son. It was good news that felt like good news. Gee could've said her little piece about breaking up with him and then hung up the phone. Soren's father felt a burning in his sinuses and realized it was the beginning of tears. He took a greedy breath to hold them back.

'There's going to be a reunion,' Gee said. 'And that occasion will be the final triumphant chapter of my memoir.'

'I'll read it when it comes out.'

'And it *will* come out,' Gee said. 'I've done harder things in my life than publish a damn book.'

'Yeah, you tried to be my girlfriend.'

'I was trying to help myself at first. I thought I needed to get close to Soren or close to you. I thought I needed something, but I don't. I've fixed myself dozens of times.'

'I've never fixed myself once.'

'You don't need a whole lot of fixing. You don't need a complete overhaul. You're just a little lost.'

Soren's father looked over at his son. Whenever he was upset, it seemed to him that Soren was breathing slower, but it was only Soren's father's impatience.

'Let's say I'm lost,' he said. 'What am I supposed to look for?'

'You don't *find* anything,' Gee told him. 'You just be brave. You make that a policy.'

Soren's father had never thought about bravery. He didn't know what his policy was.

'We're friends,' Gee said, 'and I'm going to tell you one thing before I get off the phone.'

'Okay,' said Soren's father.

'Don't use your son as an excuse.'

Gee left the line quiet a few moments. Then she said she had a hell of a drive in front of her.

THE PIANO TEACHER

She had never thought of herself as possessing nerve. She'd thought of herself as a person with endurance, a person who, if she entertained fantasies, did so in the service of her everyday stamina, but here she was pulling past the clinic, past the vigil, already in progress, and hitting the gas rather than the brake. There were only two of them left now in the parking lot, two women, two vigilers.

The piano teacher didn't feel she'd made a decision. She felt as though something had been sprung on her. She hadn't packed a stitch of clothing or even a toothbrush, but here she was cruising right past the final shadowy pair. Here she was rolling by the Mexican market with the happy vegetables painted on the walls. Here she was getting on the empty interstate and bringing her car up to a speed it hadn't achieved in ages.

She would leave her car in the garage and her daughter would have to pick it up. The piano teacher imagined the phone call and could already savor her daughter's outrage. She'd tell her daughter she was staying a week and wouldn't tell her daughter where, and then after a week she'd tell her she was staying another week. She'd have to return eventually. It wasn't a permanent escape. She would run out of money, for one thing, and that's what her daughter would be most worried about. Maybe the piano teacher would spend every penny she had and force her daughter to pay to fly her home.

She exited the interstate. The road that led into the airport was lined with towering terra cotta pots and the pots were imprinted with symbols and drawings that could have meant anything. Wherever the piano teacher ended up, she was going to buy a crappy piano that was all hers and play it just for herself, and she was going to keep it until the day she died. Her daughter would have to ship the thing home and the shipping would cost more than the instrument. The worst piano she could find. Maybe with a family of mice in it. The piano teacher felt a physical craving for her fingers against keys, felt a need to put organized noise into a cranny of the world. The piano teacher would soon be near an ocean, in a place with vines and moss and high-hung fronds, a place that appeared on the verge of swallowing itself. The piano teacher was going to listen to the noise of honest blue waves spending themselves until she couldn't remember the noise of this broken desert wind that, for once, seemed to be at her back.

CECELIA

During the vigils, she never heard songs. She heard only what was meant to be heard, the noise of the sand and pebbles and gravel and whatever else was slight enough to be brushed about by the wind. The gusts came from one direction and then another, as if the wind meant to sweep the world's scattered ingredients into a pile.

Only one other still attended, the elegant woman whose boyfriend had quit. The woman was different than usual. She was focused. She was looking up at Soren's window but Cecelia could tell she wasn't thinking of Soren. Cecelia had stubbornness, but this woman had been surviving ordeals long before Cecelia had, and Cecelia had no idea if she could outlast her. At least Cecelia knew who her most worthy opponent was. Cecelia knew who she had to beat. She had authority over whether she won or lost. Nothing could stop her from showing up here except herself, and she wasn't going to stop. This chick with her pricey coat and soft makeup was in for a struggle.

Cecelia hadn't received a song for many days now, the longest she'd gone without receiving one. She wondered if she'd had control the whole time, without knowing it. She'd made a definite wish not to receive any more, and now she wasn't. She was glad she'd received them, and glad now for a break from them. Maybe Reggie had simply run out. Maybe he was doing something else.

He might be in a good place. He might have a view of a distant bay full of burnished boats, none of the boats having a thing to do with him, all owned by strangers and visitors. In this place, every person has a strong heart and a share of important work to do. In this place, the future placidly becomes the past. In this place, each person feels the dignified solitude of one engaged in a lost cause. And there were realms sweeter than this, realms that would suit Reggie precisely, that Cecelia could never envision. A million heavens waited, a million people scuffling around the desert hoping not to see their heaven too soon, failing to believe in the afterlives that awaited them and would have them in time, whether they kicked and screamed or closed their eyes and sighed, whether they tried to do good and could not or tried to do bad and succeeded.

Cecelia thought of Soren. She pictured him as she always did, with fawn-colored hair, slender and wan, but she knew he could look any way. He could be husky, with a black crew cut. He was losing the happiest part of his life on earth, the part before you noticed what was missing, before you thought in terms of fixing anything. Soren himself needed to be fixed. He might have authored a miracle, but now he was awaiting one.

After the vigil Cecelia headed to campus. She was drowsy so she stopped off and bought a huge iced coffee. She took a sip and balked at the taste – cloying and scorched – then drove the rest of the way to campus with the unwieldy beverage sweating onto her jeans.

The university was deserted except for a homeless guy sleeping on a bench and a few nibbling critters. The dorms, where people might be up and about, were on the other end of campus. Cecelia approached the rehearsal spaces. She'd turned her keys in when she'd gotten fired, but Marie had let her copy the music building master. Cecelia had the key and she had a pocketknife her mother had given her as a child, a pink Swiss Army knife, and she was still lugging the iced coffee, which was wetting down her gloved hands.

She went in and eased the door closed, set her drink down on the floor. The place smelled like insulation. Cecelia looked around the room for cameras, scanning the high corners. She knew there weren't any cameras. She stripped off her jacket but kept on the gloves.

She walked over to Thus Poke Sarah's Thruster's guitars, three of them, one a bass, all leaning at the same angle against a step, and one by one she held them by their necks, business end on the ground, and stomped on them until they cracked in half. The guitars made a low crunch when they gave way, like a bone breaking, and then they hung in one piece by their strings. Cecelia dropped them all in a heap. She went over and did what she could to Nate's drums with the pocketknife, slicing up the taut hides. She got her iced coffee and poured it down into the biggest amp. The liquid drained without hurry down through the machinery and onto the floor. Cecelia had felt her blood humming when she'd come into the room, but now it was stagnant. She didn't feel triumphant or even tough. When she'd burned the barn she'd told herself she had no fear, but now she really didn't. Fear was what made anything worthwhile. Without fear, she was going through motions. She had the sensation that she'd been driving for days without stopping and had forgotten her destination. She felt like a madwoman, but it didn't feel good.

She moved on to the keyboard, her blood tepid. Cecelia stared at the thing. Her eyes had adjusted to the dim light. Cecelia saw the kid's name on the keyboard, in silver marker: T. ANDERTON. She sat down at the instrument. She flipped the power switch and red lights appeared all over the control panel. You could set it to sound like an organ if you wanted or like a synthesizer or like a regular piano. It had a bunch of dials and pedals. Cecelia didn't touch any of them.

She heard footsteps approaching the door outside and it didn't take her long to resign herself to being caught. She was engaging in a criminal act, damaging property, and in a moment someone would catch her. All there was to do was wait and see who that someone was. It could be a security guard who'd be thrilled to finally bust someone for a serious crime. It could be that homeless guy from the bench looking for a warmer spot to bed down.

Cecelia heard the doorknob turning and then a moment later she and a guy about her age were looking at each other with identical frankness. The guy had on a tight-zippered sweatshirt with a hood and long plaid shorts. He didn't pull his hood off. Cecelia recognized him from when she'd spied on Nate's band. He released the knob and the door shut. He was the keyboard player. He looked at the carnage of the guitars and then at the drum set, then he squinted and said Cecelia's name.

'How do you know me?' she asked.

'I don't know,' the guy said. 'I do, though.'

He looked at her coat on the floor, not far from where he stood.

'Are you up late or early?' Cecelia asked him.

'I'm always up at this time.'

The guy looked around again and shook his head, seeming both disappointed and impressed, then he walked over and sat on the bench next to Cecelia. He seemed like a person with a reasonable, fair burden. He understood that things got complicated. He tapped one of Cecelia's gloved hands with his finger.

'Fashion or fingerprints?'

'At first they were to keep my hands warm,' Cecelia said.

'You don't seem drunk.'

Cecelia shook her head.

'You're, like, a badass.'

Cecelia could smell the guy. He didn't smell bad.

'Barry and Sam are going to lose their shit,' he said. 'Those dudes pride themselves on their bad tempers.'

'*You're* not mad?'

'The only thing that makes me mad is when people don't keep secrets, but I can forgive that too.'

'Nate will replace all this stuff,' Cecelia said. 'Probably with better stuff.'

The guy yawned, then he said, 'He's kind of a dickwad, I know. I'm not going to tell on you.' He pulled his hands out of his sweat-shirt, both of them, like he was going to do something with them. 'They don't know I write songs,' he said. 'I come early, when every-body's asleep. I write pop songs. I write songs they can play at the beginning of sitcoms. I'm not a delicate genius.'

Cecelia thought of when that kid had caught her on his screened patio. She could remember feeling confused, about everything. Now she didn't feel confused. Not that she'd figured anything out, but at least she was in charted territory.

The guy told Cecelia he was only in a band to work on his stage presence, to get used to collaborating, access to instruments, rehearsal space. In time he was going to move to a music town like Austin or Seattle.

'You're a slimeball,' Cecelia said.

The guy winked.

He was more savvy than Cecelia and Reggie had been. He was using Nate.

'What does the T stand for?' Cecelia asked him. 'T. Anderton.'

'Terry Anderton is who I bought this from. His parents got it for him, but he wants to be a veterinarian.'

'Then what's your name?'

'It's going to be Nevers. No one knows that. I'm keeping the name secret as long as possible. Don't tell anyone, okay? I don't like when people tell secrets. I can forgive it, but I really don't like it.'

Cecelia reached behind the guy and with two fingers tugged his hood off. He looked upward with only his eyeballs. His hair was red and very short. His red hair and his tan skin clashed.

Cecelia grasped his head with two hands and kissed him. He wasn't ready. He put his hand out to brace himself and sounded a patch of keys. The noise was wrong but interesting, like his hair against his skin. The notes didn't linger; the quiet they left wasn't the same as the quiet from before. The guy, Nevers, tried to catch up, to get as much of Cecelia as she was getting of him. He shifted and pressed himself against her. She felt his fingertips descend the skin of her hip and she pulled out of the kiss. She rose off the bench and snatched her coat off the floor by its sleeve. She wanted to say something before she left, something reassuring. She wanted to tell Nevers that one day soon, when her mind was her own again, she would let him take her out to dinner and then she would sleep with him and then in the morning he might try to play her one of his pop songs.

JOHN BRANDON

THE WOLF

The songs had ceased.

There had been the songs, and when there weren't songs there had been the pets to calm him. The wolf had still not taken a chicken, and that meant something to him. It had become a vow. Now the songs had ceased. The pets would no longer be enough. The wolf could feel that. His hope was dead. The wolf had abandoned the gully near the house with the chickens and had taken up residence at the ugliest spot in the desert, a place where the humans had once produced drugs. There were a couple trailer homes rotting into the earth, stinking of science. The old bristlecones had perished. They'd survived a thousand years in the most discouraging soil in the world but had not survived human fun. Drugs were not merely fun for the humans, the wolf knew. It wasn't that simple. Every creature in the world was laboring to escape the perils of human intelligence, and often that went double for the humans themselves.

The wolf's foreleg had healed and his teeth were stained, but the pets would no longer be enough. Not without any songs. The wolf understood right and wrong now but didn't prefer one to the other. He was living out season after season, endless unconvincing winters.

The humans were on the lookout for the wolf but none had spotted him. All they had were their eyes. There were humans who were paid to look for things and they had never found this place. It hadn't always been the ugliest spot in the desert. There'd been an explosion and a scattered buffet for the buzzards. If there were a human paid to look for the wolf, he would never imagine the wolf so close as the gully and he would never find this bankrupt place, would never smell the chemical-soaked carcasses of the trailer homes.

The chickens may have been the only pets left unguarded in the whole of the basin now. The songs had been protecting the wolf and the wolf had been protecting the chickens. The songs had been made out of something pure, something like instinct. The pets, they gave nothing but momentary glee and permanent knowledge, and knowledge was the worst thing for the wolf. And now he needed the knowledge. He didn't want it but he needed it. Like the humans with their drugs. It was bad for him, knowledge, and he could never give it back once he had it, not a useless shred.

MAYOR CABRERA

Finally Cecelia had come home at a reasonable hour. Mayor Cabrera parked around the corner. He'd already gotten a copy of the key from his sister-in-law, and she'd called him and said Cecelia was fast asleep. Mayor Cabrera opened the passenger door and then reached through and unlocked the driver door and went back around and lowered himself into the Scirocco. He puttered down the block a ways before opening it up. He had a guy on the outskirts of Santa Fe who'd agreed to work at night, a German compact specialist. He'd told Mayor Cabrera there wasn't anything he couldn't fix before morning, except his marriage.

The shop was made to look like an adobe dwelling, like all businesses in Santa Fe. The mechanic sat on an overturned bucket, outside on the driveway, fiddling with a pair of glasses. He slipped the glasses in his shirt pocket and motioned for Mayor Cabrera to pull inside. He shook hands then immediately propped the hood up and began poking around. Mayor Cabrera had no clue how much this night was going to cost him. He imagined a very high figure, so that he wouldn't be shocked. The mechanic jacked the car up a few feet and wriggled underneath.

Mayor Cabrera stepped out the bay door and sat on the flipped bucket where the mechanic had been sitting. It was a brisk night, the sky a brimming void. It felt strange being this close to Dana, being back in Santa Fe. He had told himself he would confront Dana once his family affairs were back on track, and at the moment, so close to the ground with the sky so far above, he felt that he *would* confront her, that he had nothing to lose by doing so, that he was a guy with a couple troubles like every other guy. Things were on track with his sister-in-law and now he was doing something for Cecelia that a real uncle would do.

The mechanic stood back up. 'One step at a time,' he said. 'That's how we climb this mountain.'

The mechanic talked as he worked. He told Mayor Cabrera he was going through a divorce, and that's why he didn't mind being in the shop all night. He was moving into a new place, but it wouldn't be ready for another week. Hotels were too expensive, he told Mayor Cabrera, and Mayor Cabrera did not try to sell him on staying at the Javelina. Mayor Cabrera was not a salesman. The mechanic said he was going to need every dollar he could get for lawyers and furniture. He'd spent a couple nights in the shop and a couple in the garage of his house and a couple in his Caprice Classic.

'I ordered a pizza to the car,' he said. 'I told them where I was parked and they brought over a pepperoni pizza.'

Mayor Cabrera laughed. He wasn't comfortable sitting on the bucket.

'She didn't seem like the type to turn on you,' the mechanic said.

Mayor Cabrera could hear him straining, and then something came loose. 'She's always doing volunteer work and drinking soy milk. Always listening to music you never heard of. She seemed like she wanted to live in the moment and be forgiving. Not the case.'

Mayor Cabrera rose and asked the mechanic if he could bum a smoke from the box on the desk. He said he was going down to the street to smoke it, and left the mechanic clanging around under the car. Mayor Cabrera found his matches. He tried to always carry matches. He stood in the middle of the road and lit up. He hadn't had a cigarette since he'd been with Dana – since he'd been with Dana successfully. He was grateful to be stuck at the shop, his transportation dismantled. That way he didn't have to consider the option of going over to Dana's right now. He didn't have to worry about rushing over there with no plan and pounding on her door and finding her there with someone else, another customer. He didn't have to worry about *not* going to Dana's, about not finding the courage. He didn't have to worry about going to Dana's and deciding not to knock on her door and winding up creeping around in the bushes, a grown man, a mayor, trying to spy on a professional lady.

REGGIE

He had never been blocked before. He had refused to write for a time when he'd first found himself in this mute gray afterlife, when he was new to death, but that had been his choice. What was happening now was something else. He would sit at the piano to compose and it simply would not work. It would not happen. He could feel the plan brewing in his mind, could sense the glorified math of music within him, but at the piano it wouldn't bang out. And now all this music that refused to cooperate, that refused birth, was getting mixed up in his head and he was slipping further and further from being able to write a song. He'd never thought of himself as confident, because he'd never lost confidence. On several occasions he'd stayed in front of the piano for what would have been hours on end if hours existed in this place. He would sit there with these melodic spare parts and half-strategies tangled in his mind, and he'd feel a sneaking pleasure at not being in control of his self-expression. He'd feel a slight, ephemeral thrill at failure, he who'd always succeeded.

He had taken to drink, had become a permanent shadow in the bar that at first he'd had no use for and later had warmed to. It was now his favored haunt in the hall. He wasn't sure whether he could get drunk like living people, but everything was softer once he'd made a dent in a bottle. Sometimes, drinking, he felt the presence of time in the hall, of progress. Sometimes he felt he could achieve real sleep. Sometimes he felt he was learning, becoming wise, but that was what all drinkers thought. He was keeping close to the liquor to avoid a problem of the mind, as anyone might, but there was a practical problem he wasn't going to be able to ignore much longer: the bottles had quit refreshing themselves. The hall had been pleasant enough as long as Reggie had been producing songs, but now that he was blocked there was no breeze for the hammock, the hall was chillier and dimmer, and when he left the bar and took his shirt off and stared at the keys and then put his shirt back on and returned to the bar, the bottles were not full. There had been a few empties, and then the number of empties and fulls had been equal, and now Reggie had only three unopened bottles and a splash left in the bottom of a fourth. Reggie didn't feel he was being bullied or coaxed like before, but rather that he was being neglected. The hall wasn't shrinking, but it wasn't being tended. It smelled musty. There was a crack in one of the walls that Reggie could fit his fingertip in that ran from as high as he could reach all the way to the floor.

Reggie had come to understand that he'd been writing songs for Cecelia. He had not been writing songs he believed she would enjoy, but had been writing songs *about* her, about his feelings for her. He'd come to understand that. He'd learned from his own songs how much he had loved this woman, Cecelia. And when he got down to two bottles, two amber allotments of twenty-six-year-aged St Magdalene scotch, he could see that all the songs he'd written in the hall were insufficient. They were songs of Cecelia that weren't good enough, that did neither his affection nor its object justice. The songs were about love, like all songs, and they were clogged and fettered by Reggie's talent, by his know-how. Talent was perfectly meaningless. He needed to write a song that laid the cards on the table with no cleverness. Not write it, just deliver it. Art was Reggie's trouble. He needed to bring forth a song that couldn't get in the way of itself, a song devoid of style. He didn't know if he knew how to do this but if he couldn't then he wouldn't be here. He'd be somewhere else with some other impossible assignment.

Reggie cracked the next bottle. He'd sensed all this from the first moment he'd been blocked, and that was why he'd resigned himself to the bar. It wasn't only weakness, escape. It was because he had a better chance of stumbling upon the song he needed than of searching it out. It was because this time instead of dividing his love by writing it into a song, he had to let a song be nothing *but* love. Reggie had picked his love into strands and woven it into artifice.

THE WOLF

It had been so long without a song, he hardly remembered what it felt like to hear one. He wondered if he was already dead whenever the buzzards passed overhead like a gathering stream, calling themselves to fresh meat, and he felt no pull to track them to their confluence. His instincts were a ghost town. There would be no end to this accruing of knowledge, this piling on of the hollow wisdom of common lives. He would drag it around the desert until the desert was again a sea.

He felt on the brink of an extinction that could never be complete, a lone wolf in the midst of countless coyotes who got snakebit and tracked by cougars and poisoned by small-time ranchers and who had their young carried off by hawks and were torn limb from limb by their own packs and were shot for fun by the sons of doomed towns.

All this wisdom, it felt familiar. The wolf felt he'd lost his instincts before. He'd gained and lost music before. He was in a cycle as surely as he was in New Mexico. The wolf had always believed the desert had nothing to hide and no place to hide it, but perhaps *he* was the secret. Perhaps he'd been here through all of it. The stitching of the land with train rails. The human borders shifting this way and that. Gold discovered. The wolf had seen human after human lowered into the parched earth in boxes of cold wood. He'd seen them left unburied as expedition after expedition became ill-fated. He had tried not to cower on the night birds of fire chased away the bats and burned the forest to sand. Albuquerque was founded and could have withered like any other town. Orphanages were established. Squash and beans raised. All of it had been bound inside books, all of it but the wolf.

THE GAS STATION OWNER

He couldn't tell if he'd reached the blue mountains because as he got closer they were no longer blue. He had been trying to touch the horizon. His naivety was a comfort, as wisdom is to the young. He had used the pages of the atomic history as kindling for a fire, and then decided that if he didn't have the scientists he didn't want the Bible either. He'd never seen a Bible burned. Something happened to Bibles, otherwise the world would be overrun with them, but the gas station owner had never seen one destroyed. He had burned his cash. He had broken his knife. He was out of jerky and pretzels. He had some coffee left but no water to brew it with. He had a headache from lack of whisky and lack of food and lack of caffeine and there wasn't a cloud to be found in the shallow bowl of the sky.

It had been three days since the last evening shower. There'd been nothing to get under, so he'd stretched atop his pack to keep it dry and had opened his mouth to the heavens and shivered the long hours until the clear black night appeared. He had expected to fall ill but he hadn't. No self-respecting illness wanted anything to do with him. The next day he'd wrung a mouthful of water from the filthy leather of the pack before the desert air stole it all. His little notebook had stayed dry, and he took it out now with the stump of pencil that he no longer had a way to sharpen, and he marked the closing act of another day, the twenty-sixth day, knowing his own closing act was ready to commence all around him.

CECELIA

She headed toward the vigil, her car driving like new, running with a whisper. Her uncle had taken it one night and had every important part replaced. Cecelia didn't know why her uncle had fixed her car. She knew he'd done it for himself as much as for her, to make himself feel better, but he'd still done it. It had cost him money and time. He'd solved one of Cecelia's ongoing and growing problems. Cecelia had been a little jealous that he'd been able to make headway with her mother, but she didn't feel that anymore. She was grateful. And whatever the motives, she was grateful about her car. All the handles and knobs worked. The only light on in the dash was the one telling Cecelia her seatbelt wasn't on. Her brake light was back, she assumed. It even smelled nice in the car, like mint. She'd never missed her uncle, not really, but if he wanted to be good to her she was going to let him. He was an oaf. Cecelia wasn't going to make anything hard on him. She was going to wait and see what he did next, and in the meantime, if she saw him at the house or in town, she wasn't going to avoid him like usual. She was going to thank him. Cecelia pressed the Scirocco to go faster and faster, and the sound of the engine stayed smooth and healthy. Whoever had worked on the thing was a hell of a mechanic.

Cecelia still hadn't received another song. They'd stopped. She could finally settle in to whatever she was going to feel toward Reggie, toward his memory. When he'd died, she'd felt cheated, and then she'd gotten a bunch of him she hadn't expected. She was going to miss him, but she didn't feel as shortchanged. The songs had given her so much practice missing Reggie, she now felt equipped to do it on her own. She hoped Reggie was in that placid place she'd imagined, near the sea, that place with gently bobbing docks and like-minded strangers.

She pulled into the clinic parking lot, the concrete like carpet under her new tires, the clouds disappearing as they crossed the moon. She parked and walked over to the spot where she always sat. After a few minutes, the other woman appeared in her sleek white car. She came over and sat close but not too close to Cecelia and settled in. Cecelia watched the woman gaze into the black yonder above the clinic building. The woman didn't look at Cecelia at all. Cecelia felt doubt. She felt that this woman could outlast her. This woman was better at existing than Cecelia was. This woman was putting forth no effort. She'd lost her boyfriend and it hadn't fazed her. She was preoccupied in a way that could only aid her endurance. She was present only physically, and didn't seem to even realize that Cecelia was competing with her.

Cecelia squirmed so she was facing away from the woman. She tracked a cloud all the way across the sky, and then another. Normally, at the vigil, the world seemed to slow down around Cecelia, but tonight she was the one who felt slow. She felt way behind. She'd been trying to be a jerk and had been succeeding. She'd been a jerk on many fronts, but with her mother especially. Cecelia was mad at her, but that didn't give her the right to avoid the woman like the plague. The world might have been rotten, but her mother wasn't. Cecelia was acting like because she was younger than her mother she shouldn't have to be the adult. What did being an adult have to do with anything? What was an adult anyway? Some people could locate their spirit when it was wandering lost in the hills. Some people could line their unruly energies up single-file and march them. Cecelia could, her mother could not, but what was Cecelia marching toward? She rested her face in her palms. She should've started a new band by now, writing her own songs. She should've gotten another job by now. Months were going by – months that had every right to be memorable. Cecelia wasn't advancing her life. She did not want any more songs. She didn't want more of the fucking things. She wanted to be okay with her mother and to be able to relax at the vigil. There was a happy self in her and she'd been doing everything she could not to find it.

DANNIE

At the clinic, Dannie's thoughts were clear. At home, her mind was mush already, soft around the edges. At home she was leaving milk out on the counter and finding it hours later. She was missing her TV shows and putting jeans in the washer with pockets full of gum. Dannie hadn't told anyone she was pregnant. In her belly was the start of a person who would one day make small talk, who would one day make an effort to eat more servings of fruit, who would have to choose a shampoo out of the hundreds, who would drink coffee on trains.

A cat pawed up to Dannie and the other vigiler, the college girl. Dannie had no idea how many more weeks this girl planned to stick it out. Dannie didn't know what she'd do if she were the last one. It was a responsibility Dannie didn't want. She didn't want to be alone and she didn't want to be the one who let the vigils lapse away. The cat approached the girl and Dannie watched her make no acknowledgement. It was a Siamese cat, but something else was mixed into it. It had the look of an orphan, bored and wily.

Dannie felt childish in this girl's presence. She needed to be an adult now, but she had no confidence that she was. Dannie had grown impatient because she hadn't gotten what she wanted from Arn right when she'd wanted it, because everything hadn't happened according to her timetable, and so she'd run him off. She hadn't been capable of simply being happy and enjoying him. Dannie was supposed to have been the grown-up in the relationship, was supposed to have known what was good for her and what was good for Arn. She didn't know what was good for anyone, and now she was going to have a little son or daughter to guide. She was missing Arn's presence in her future child's life, she understood, but she was also missing the way his breath wheezed when he slept, not quite a snore, and she missed the ropey muscles of his arms and his belly and the way he never gave away his mood with his voice, and Dannie missed Arn's wise, patient innocence, which she thought she could use about now.

The wind gusted and Dannie watched the girl pull up her hood and tug the drawstrings. She had precise fingers. She could do sign language or construct toys. The tepid winds reminded Dannie of the Santa Anna winds. Maybe they'd made it all the way across the desert. Maybe that's how the gulls had made it here from the coasts, riding bands of destined air. Dannie felt antsy. Her scalp felt hot.

Fucking Arn. Dannie still hadn't told her old friends she was pregnant and it was because she didn't want to pretend she preferred being alone, like it had been her plan to use some dope for his sperm and the plan had worked splendidly. She didn't want to have to describe Arn, or make up some fake guy in order to avoid describing Arn. She was angry at him for not coming back, angry with herself for not going after him. She'd been telling herself he was in the wind. She'd been telling herself he was hardened against her, through with her. But maybe he wasn't. Maybe he was missing her too. Maybe he was cursing her this very moment. Arn was another thing Dannie had lost, but what if she hadn't lost him yet? The course of her adulthood had been charted by quitting, and maybe she needed to not quit on Arn, to not quit on something she'd lost but go get it back. Maybe she needed to go find the best part of her life instead of worrying about what other thing she would lose next.

ARN

He had taken to shutting the screens down for hours at a stretch, sometimes all night, and starting them up again minutes before the owner arrived at dawn. He was tired of humoring the owner. The government had an observatory of its own, immeasurably more powerful, rows and rows of dishes a hundred miles to the west, like some huge gleaming sand crop. This job made Arn feel toyed with. He'd worked at warehouses where products were stored, factories where products were made, a bar where drinks were served, a winery that didn't produce wine but at least might've served as a front for criminal enterprise. This observatory had no function whatsoever except to tickle the fancy of the owner. Aliens were not attempting to communicate with us. They weren't. And if they were, they could. It wouldn't matter whether or not we had wired bowls propped up on the desert floor. It wouldn't matter if some idiot were sitting the graveyard shift.

Arn was back to sleeping in his truck bed, and it wasn't so bad this time of year. It wasn't freezing or hot. Arn didn't feel safe sleeping under his topper, but people weren't safe anywhere. Bad luck and aliens – if they wanted you, they'd find you. Arn had a membership at a YMCA in an Albuquerque suburb so he could shower. He sat out at the pool sometimes. There were tan lifeguards in bikinis, but they didn't do much for Arn. The weight rooms were full of fathers. They were all faking being good fathers like Arn was faking being a regular guy who wanted to stay in shape. Not one person Arn saw seemed genuine. Now and then he shot hoops, only when he found the courts abandoned and could shoot in solitude. Just like at the church compound back in Oregon.

Dannie wasn't going to come for him. She wasn't going to have a change of heart. She'd probably found another kid to play around with. Arn knew the only reason he was still in New Mexico was he was hoping Dannie would come. Normally he would've quit this job by now. He would've been in the next state, Texas or Oklahoma. He had no energy for going back on the road, same as he felt no energy for the brown lifeguards in the red suits. New Mexico had been the first state he had not felt lonely in. Dannie had been his friend. Whatever else they may have been or not been to each other, they had become friends. There wasn't a way for Arn to win except to know her again. Whatever cheap motives he'd had at the start, they'd died off. He'd had an ally and had lost her. He missed her skin and the way she rested one fingertip on her chin when she was about to explain something. He wanted to push his forehead against her cheek.

Arn turned a page of the huge poetry book and the next page was blank. There were no more poems. Arn closed the book and slid it to a far corner of the metal desk. Arn hadn't known what any of the poems were about, but he'd enjoyed them. The poetry book was the only book in the observatory that wasn't work-related, that wasn't a radio manual or a history of space encounters. Arn had finished the whole thing, one thin, crinkly page at a time.

Arn saw now that he had been *hoping* all this time that someone was after him, the cops or a private detective or the enraged family of the man he'd slugged with the bat. He'd needed someone to be after him. On the run, he didn't have to admit anything about himself. He was a deceitful orphan. That's what he'd been afraid of being and that's what he'd become. He'd had to keep moving, in part, to not get caught in his lies. They were lies of omission mostly, but you could get caught in those too. He had told Dannie she'd been his first, and that he'd never been to California. He'd acted unfamiliar with bars, unfamiliar with drugs. This was the part he'd played with all the women. Mystery was all he had. And false innocence. He didn't have a self. Everything around him in the observatory was clean and hard, the buffed concrete floor and the metal desk and the molded plastic chair. Nothing had been chasing Arn, and it had chased him far enough. He went to the middle of the room and got down flat on his back on the floor. The concrete felt good against his arms and legs. Everything sounded different when you got down low and still. It reminded him of the vigils he'd been going to with Dannie. He wondered if she was still going to them. Arn was going to miss the boy, the way one missed peaceful places one had only seen in pictures. Some time in the past months Arn had learned that he could be still without hiding. You could just be where you were. He tapped his fingers on the concrete. The aliens were talking around us. They were holding lively conversations just beyond the reach of human surveillance.

Arn was trying to get fired so he'd be forced to leave the area, but he didn't *want* to leave. He didn't have the guts to simply quit. He was sabotaging himself, turning the machine off every night. The machine kept a record, of course. If the owner bothered to check, he'd know right away. But the guy probably wouldn't fire Arn. He'd have a talk with Arn, something like that. He'd write Arn up, as if this were a real company with real policies and protocols. The owner's main concern would be that they'd missed a transmission.

MAYOR CABRERA

A shop that sold musical equipment had been going out of business and he had bought five cases of those space-age tiles you could nail up that were supposed to soundproof a room and improve the acoustics. The guy who owned the shop hadn't been one bit upset that it was going under. The guy had a brand-new tattoo, still under a bandage, and he kept lifting a corner of the bandage and admiring what was hidden underneath. Mayor Cabrera didn't believe the squares could really soundproof a room, but they might *dull* sound, and Mayor Cabrera could make sure never to rent out the unit right next door. There were thirty rooms and he couldn't recall the last time they'd rented more than half of them at one time.

It took him almost three hours and a whole canvas sack of roofing nails. His forearm was numb. The hotel room looked like it belonged on a UFO. Mayor Cabrera was doing the only other thing he could think of for Cecelia. Her car, and now this. He didn't know how to be an uncle. He had no experience with it. He was trying to help her and he was also trying to win her over. She had thanked him, about the car. He'd seen her in town and she'd only spoken to him a moment but he'd sensed a softness toward him. She was like her mother. She could talk herself into being bitter, but it wasn't in her heart. Mayor Cabrera put surge protectors in all the sockets and lined up some music stands against the wall. He dragged the desk out and brought in a big amp. Mayor Cabrera was working on a baggie of jerky and he had a couple more tallboys in his cooler. He was no longer the mayor of Lofte. He'd informed the board and they'd drawn up paperwork and he'd signed it. There would be a special election. Until then, the lawyer was in charge. Mayor Cabrera wasn't Mayor Cabrera anymore. He was just Cabrera. *Cabrera.* The next time they held a council meeting, he wouldn't be there. He was Ricardo Cabrera, private citizen.

He filled the closet with bottles of water and cans of ginger ale, fruit roll-ups, bags of popcorn. He dragged the mattress outside and then the box spring and when he went to move the bed frame he saw something underneath, on the floor. It was one of those magnetic travel chess sets. He opened it and it had all the pieces, all thirty-two. He knew what he'd do. He'd teach his sister-in-law to play chess, whether she wanted to or not. Most of their life together was in the past, but not all of it. Some of it was waiting for them, time waiting to be spent. They were family. They would play chess. Once she knew what she was doing, Mayor Cabrera would get a regular set, carved of wood, with pieces substantial enough to work around in your palm as you parsed out your next move.

Mayor Cabrera had once gone to Sun Studios in Memphis with his wife, and it hadn't looked much better than this hotel room now did. They had a control room at Sun, but other than that it was about the same as this place. Mayor Cabrera began gathering his supplies and tidying up, the extra tiles and his beer cans and such, and was struck with a pang of pure fear. He couldn't stall about Dana anymore. All the amends were in progress. There was nothing standing in his way now. He was a brother-in-law again and was becoming an uncle again and he had to find out what he was going to be to Dana. He deserved her as much as he ever would and she'd either want him or she wouldn't. Nothing could make him pathetic now. He felt able to weather a hardship with dignity.

THE WOLF

The wolf scrambled up the loose rocks and out of the gully. He had returned to the house of the older woman and the girl, the house where he'd once heard the songs. The wolf stopped at the edge of the property and listened hard, as if trying to hear the drifting of clouds. The temperature was dropping. The wolf could feel it in his snout and behind his eyes. There was no space between the wolf and the sheer cliff of his ill mind. His saliva tasted like paper and his paws were stones.

A hard twig was barbed into the wolf's side and he yanked it and then paced toward the chickens. The wolf pressed his muzzle to the fence and the chickens did not hustle about. They kept going about their pointless business. They weren't afraid. They felt nothing for the wolf, considered him harmless. The chickens were skinny and their beaks and feet were the same color as their feathers. They stood with heads high, almost haughty. They were waiting for the next idiot scuffle to break out, for seed to be scattered. When death arrived, as it was about to, they would greedily scuffle over that too.

*

The isolated homesteads. The outposts of the outposts. What he'd done to the chickens had provided the wolf no solace, nor did he feel regret. The wolf had made the chickens thin air, had given them unprofaned existence, and they'd given him back nothing. He'd gained no knowledge. If there existed a more potent apprehension it could be found only in a human, not in a human's lesser companion. The wolf now peered out from a thicket of soft weeds, spying on a mother and a baby. The house was a box of sticks but the porch was grand. The wolf couldn't see the baby but it was there, wrapped down in the cradle. The mother made tender, distracted clicking sounds in her cheek. It was dawn, the world yellowing. The mother rose and stepped inside the house without shutting the front door. She could see the cradle from where she stood, the wolf knew. The mother was recovering from injury and the baby was a baby.

The wolf broke from the thicket, crossing the dirt road and halting at the mailbox. He couldn't see the baby but now he could smell it, fatty and scrubbed. Like he would've in his old life, the wolf washed the base of the mailbox with his urine. If he took another step closer to the baby he wouldn't be able to stop himself. Before he knew it he would have the soft infant in his hard jaws, its limbs flopping as the wolf galloped into the wilderness. He kept his haunch against the post. He wanted the mother to come back out to the porch so he might be able to flee but she was brewing tea. The wolf smelled cut pine and tobacco and the knees and elbows of the baby. He couldn't back away and tried not to move an inch closer. The wolf wondered if he was mad enough now, devoid enough of instinct, that he could be blamed for his actions. Innocence was a silly human notion, but guilt had been around always.

The wolf realized his teeth were bared. He had never in his life tasted human blood. The wolf tried to imagine where he would take the baby, what would happen to it since he was not going to eat it, and of course its unavoidable end was to be ripped asunder by buzzards whose profession was hunger and who didn't distinguish a human baby from a roadside possum. The wolf put his belly to the ground. He was trying to outrace fate but he was going in circles. He had known it all before and forgotten it all before. He could remember being healthy and somehow could remember being even more ill. The baby would not help nor hurt the wolf. The baby was beside the point. The reason to take it was the same as to not take it. The wolf was playing games – taking pets, subsisting on flying insects, waiting around for fixes of music. Making vows. It was not the wolf's job to protect anything. The wolf was afraid he might push the mailbox over. The mother was still inside, feeling secure on a whim as humans always did, and she was right this time; the wolf was not going to harm the baby. The wolf wanted to believe that every last hope for peace had not expired in him. He pushed himself back from the mailbox as if dragging a loaded sled and then raced, stumbling, into the borderless abyss that had to be his true home.

CECELIA'S MOTHER

Whether she wanted coffee or not, each morning she put on a kettle of water. As she ran water in the kettle she got to look out the back kitchen window and see her chickens getting about their business, and early in the morning was the only time she enjoyed them anymore. She got to stand near the warming stove. The kettle was something to wait on, a ritual. And when the kettle started whimpering she would wait still, until the sound grew urgent.

This morning she pushed close to the window and saw no movement, heard no impatient clucking. The ground outside was blanketed white. The rest of the desert was correct, but in Cecelia's mother's fenced enclosure the ground was a downy carpet. The feathers were spread evenly, as if a giant had fixed up a place to sleep for the night. Cecelia's mother pulled the door open but she could only make it down the first step. She didn't want to tread on the feathers. She was marooned on the steps. It was like looking at art, or something more important than art.

By now everyone knew the wolf wasn't killing out of hunger. He was killing to settle a score Cecelia's mother could not fathom. Cecelia's mother had begun to believe that the wolf had passed her over, like in the Bible when all those people painted their doors with blood. Cecelia's mother knew that the chickens had been working against her. She had secretly begun to hate them. If her chickens were tender for some ancient, animal debt, she wasn't going to begrudge the transaction. Some chickens became nuggets; hers had been raised to a higher calling. She wanted to laugh at these thoughts, standing alone on the steps, because they were stark and even silly, but she had no laughter to give.

Something was wrong with Cecelia's mother, but at least she knew it and at least she was working her way out. She wasn't crazy. She missed the chickens. She'd let go of them weeks ago in her heart. She hadn't tossed and turned last night, which was unusual. She'd had dreams, and they'd been empty. Her dreams had been hollow eggs. She hadn't heard a ruckus out back of the house and she hadn't heard Cecelia leave this morning. She remembered the day she'd bought the chickens, one of the last times she'd walked to Lofte's little downtown to go grocery shopping. She'd had her backpack with her, and was planning to grill steaks and pan-fry something green. On her way she'd passed the little Redding property and had not felt like cooking but had definitely felt lonely and the chickens were in the front pen for ten dollars each and Cecelia's mother had made a bad decision because she had the right to. She'd saved the chickens' lives. The Reddings were getting out of the hobby and Cecelia's mother got in. She could have company like everyone else. She could have something going on. She could do something Cecelia wouldn't approve of. She'd come home with live chickens she meant to keep alive rather than dead steaks she meant to put over a fire. She'd never had a pet in her life, probably another reason she'd bought them. It wasn't nuts to have some chickens. It was only nuts to have chickens if you were nuts anyway, without the chickens.

Cecelia's mother looked at the fence from one end to the other, still standing on the back step with the kitchen door wide open, and she saw no breach. The fence was perfect. She realized that there was no blood, not a drop anywhere. The sky in the distance, above the peaks, was stained red. That's where the blood had gone – far off, high above. Cecelia's mother stood there wondering whether she would rake the feathers up. That seemed disrespectful somehow, to rake them up like leaves. Maybe she could pick them all up with her fingers and drop them in a big sack. She could leave them alone, let the wind carry them off a clutch at a time. She didn't know if she wanted anyone else to see this. This was hers, not Cecelia's or the neighbors' or her brother-in-law's. She stood there, her kettle starting to make its noise.

SOREN'S FATHER

There was an open lot not far from the clinic where hot-air balloons launched. The sky was clearer than it had been. Soren's father watched several balloons take shape and cling to the ground until they no longer could and then float out over the flatlands, and now he watched the crew struggling with a lavender vessel that must've had a leak. They could get it only so full before it listed and collapsed.

The nurses had not been permitted to throw out Soren's father's mail, but they'd kept it from him in a canvas laundry bag. They said he had to be the one to empty the bag down the trash chute. There hadn't been near as much mail since the nurses had been stewarding it as back when Soren had first fallen into his coma. The mail didn't nearly fill the bag, but was only something in the bottom that caused the bag to swing when Soren's father carried it to the end of the hall. He watched the envelopes tumbling into the dark, glimpsing return addresses in New Hampshire, Utah, other places.

He returned to his son's room and stood at the window. His eyes traveled from the lavender balloon, which had been cleared off and was being examined by young men with ponytails, to his own reflection. His face was inches away. He was wearing a sweater he didn't recognize. It was the color of hazel eyes. Gee had told him he wasn't brave, as if anyone was as brave as she was. He wasn't a coward, but he knew what she'd meant. He wasn't kind and he had no friends. He wasn't kind or trusting and the worst thing about other people was they were those things. He'd seen the same folks every day at the factories and warehouses, knew their orders by heart, but he'd never known one thing beyond what they liked to eat. He'd had customers and a couple employees and a wife who'd gotten to know *him* but whom he hadn't truly known, a wife he'd never had a fight with, that he'd never cried in front of. Soren had come along and made all that moot. That's what Gee had meant about using Soren as an excuse. Soren's father was worse now. The warmth in his life was frozen and sitting still was his business. He had a space to be alone and he'd defended it against the nurses and doctors and against Gee and he'd even been cold to Soren's piano teacher, the poor woman. There'd been a cousin Soren's father had been close with as a child who'd died when they were both in their twenties. Soren's father didn't know why he was thinking of him now. He couldn't remember if that cousin had been a genuine friend or just a family member about the same age whom he happened to get along with. He couldn't remember why they didn't stay close once they weren't children anymore. Soren's father had been sitting in this room for a long time and he saw that he hadn't been hoping properly, not with a live heart, not in a way that meant anything.

Soren's father took a step back from the window. He was still holding the canvas bag. He thought of the people who had sat and taken time to write the letters he'd sent down the trash. They were better than Soren's father because they could admit they were desperate and try to do something about it. Soren's father folded the bag like a big pillowcase. He couldn't get it to look neat. He rested the bag on the dresser and went over next to Soren and kneeled beside him. He pulled Soren's stiff crossed arms off his chest with a gentle effort and put his ear to Soren's body.

CECELIA

She went out with her guitar and muted the TV and played for her mother, an old Arizona mining ditty that was one of her mother's favorites. It had been months and months since she'd played a song that wasn't Reggie's. She watched her mother's expression soften during the first verse and her posture improve during the second. It was like back when Cecelia was first learning guitar, back when she and her mother were proud of each other. Her mother wanted to know that Cecelia didn't despise or resent her, and Cecelia was letting her know she did not. The song was a peace offering that could open the door for other offerings. The two of them hadn't had it out. Cecelia hadn't said anything mean to her mother, had never raised her voice. They'd both stood their ground long enough that the ground had become worthless.

Later, while Cecelia's mother made them sandwiches, sandwiches that would constitute the first meal they'd shared in way too long, Cecelia went over to the Waller lady's house and bought her mother a bird, a tiny inside bird that lived in a cage. She felt a pure physical relief at buying her mother a gift, as if she'd escaped a building that was caving in. Driving home with the well-mannered bird in her passenger seat, she felt no dread at the thought of arriving back at the house, and she realized in a way she hadn't before how terrible that was, to not want to walk into your own house. There wasn't going to be a tearful reconciliation, but a restoration was in progress, and that was enough for now.

Once home, Cecelia presented her mother with the new pet and they found a spot for it and admired its stately habits. Cecelia promised her mother she'd always be home in the mornings, and she convinced her mother to donate the wheelchair, to make an effort to eat proper dinners. They were both giving in, that was the important thing.

Cecelia offered to clean up the feathers in the backyard and her mother said she wanted them to stay. Cecelia remembered the chickens being dingy, but the feathers were bright as snow. Cecelia didn't tell her mother about getting fired. She certainly didn't tell her about Reggie's songs. For now she was only going to treat her mother like a respectable adult who had a right to her own business, and she could treat herself the same.

Cecelia had no clue whether the new bird was supposed to be able to speak, but she and her mother talked to it anyway. They asked it who the yellowest bird in the whole desert was. They asked it who had the best little birdie manners.

MAYOR CABRERA

Ran was in New Mexico and wanted to meet. No decision yet, but he wanted to meet. He didn't know Mayor Cabrera wasn't the mayor anymore. Mayor Cabrera didn't want to invite him to Lofte and have people wonder who he was and start busy-bodying around, so he suggested a bar out east, out where the old mining concerns used to operate.

It was a good afternoon for driving. The landscape appeared painted in oil, and Mayor Cabrera was putting himself into the painting. To be nervous for this meeting with Ran was the sensible emotion, but Mayor Cabrera mostly felt distracted. He saw that the situation was not urgent, whether he was the mayor or just a citizen. It wasn't urgent in the big picture. Lofte would fail, of course.

It would fail in a couple short years or it would find a way to hang on for several decades, and it didn't matter which. Lofte's story was going to end sadly, whether pretty soon or very soon. People were going to have to find another place to live now or find another place when they were older and had less energy. They were going to have to find another place to get attached to, and what exactly were they attached to about Lofte? Most of the folks Mayor Cabrera knew could use a change. A big one. Mayor Cabrera was one of them.

The bar looked like a log cabin. There was one person inside and this was indeed Ran. Mayor Cabrera sat down at his table. Ran had a soft-looking spike haircut. His hands were pudgy.

'There's a sign up there that says the bartender stepped out for a bit,' Ran said. 'I've thought it over and I'm going back there and mixing us a round of drinks.'

Mayor Cabrera peered back toward the kitchen.

'Stay put.' Ran smirked. 'I don't want you getting involved in this.'

Ran went and found what he needed and mixed the drinks, humming as he worked. He brought the drinks to the table on a tray. They were tan in color, each with a twist of lemon on the rim.

'I don't know why I picked this place,' Mayor Cabrera said. 'Maybe I felt like a drive.'

'I always feel like a drive,' Ran said.

'I could've shown you around town. That would've been the smart thing.'

'I've been to Lofte plenty,' Ran said. He sipped his drink, judging the flavor. 'There's no bar in Lofte. Not really. Not one I'd want to go to.'

'Is that a positive for your church?' Mayor Cabrera asked. 'Not having bars around?'

'There are a lot of positives. Plenty of positives. I've observed you in secret and I like your style. The town takes on the personality of the mayor, in my experience.'

'You observed me?'

'That's how these things are done. I wasn't observing *you* in particular.'

Mayor Cabrera tasted his drink. It didn't taste bad, exactly.

'That's a sazerac,' Ran said. 'They grow on you.' Ran's hands looked even smaller and softer wrapped around his cocktail glass. 'I got drunk on these the other night, with some guy from the History Channel.'

'I watch that,' Mayor Cabrera said. 'We get it at the motel.'

'They're doing a special on cults. We're not a cult, but if you never do these little cable channels then you never do the networks.'

Ran was trying to impress Mayor Cabrera. It was working, a little.

'When will it be on?' Mayor Cabrera asked.

'They don't know. I might not even be in it. They might cut me out.'

'What exactly qualifies a given group as a cult?'

Ran laughed archly. He didn't attempt to answer the question. Mayor Cabrera took a closer look around the bar. There were photographs hanging everywhere of smiling miners. They had soot all over them, but their teeth were gleaming. There were some pictures of the womenfolk, as well. They weren't as pleased.

'That town in Oklahoma is throwing itself at me,' Ran said. 'And you've been doing the bare minimum. Like I said, I like your style.'

'The basin speaks for itself,' said Mayor Cabrera. He wasn't sure what he meant.

The door swung open and a guy came in carrying a jug of mixed nuts. It was the bartender. Ran told him about the sazeracs and the bartender said they were on the house. He said it was against his principles to lock the door during business hours.

'And we'll take another round,' Ran said. He was done with his drink.

'I don't tend the kind of bar that doesn't have nuts,' the bartender said. 'I really hate it when people ask for nuts and I can't give them any.'

The bartender got to work, clinking things together. Ran's face changed, and then he leaned in.

'You see that car outside when you came in?'

Mayor Cabrera nodded.

'That's a 1984 Saab hatchback, red. One hubcap mismatched. Big tear in the passenger seat upholstery.'

'Could use a wash too.'

'That car makes me happy,' said Ran.

Mayor Cabrera waited.

'That's the exact kind of car I had when I was a senior in high school. I found it at a used car lot last month and bought it on the spot. I had to take it to the shop and have them unrestore it. It had been kept too well.'

The new drinks came, and Mayor Cabrera hurried and finished his first one.

'I'm not a sneaky person,' Ran said. 'I'm precisely as corrupt as the world warrants. I wanted to meet face to face in order to invite you to bribe me.'

Mayor Cabrera didn't want to bribe Ran. He didn't think he had anything to bribe Ran *with*.

'It's not my style,' Mayor Cabrera said. 'That style you like so much, bribing people isn't part of it.'

'How can you be so nonchalant?'

'Because this is my last act as mayor. Drinking these drinks.'

'I don't ask twice,' Ran said.

'If you do, you'll be asking someone else.'

'Not an ideal time for a leadership change. We'll be deciding within a week.'

'There's a big hurry all of a sudden?'

Ran grunted. He had an unguarded look on his face that wasn't quite a smile. It said he'd been around the block and wasn't going to get in a tizzy if a meeting didn't go his way. It also expressed an even further deepening of his admiration for Mayor Cabrera's way of handling things. Ran took a big pull on his drink. 'I make these like crap,' he said. 'It's reassuring that there's skill to it.'

'Is the town in Oklahoma going under too? Were you only considering desperate places?'

'That's kind of the way it works,' Ran said.

There was a silence then, not unpleasant, in which it became apparent that Ran was going to be true to his word. He wasn't going to ask again to be bribed. The bartender was wiping things down. The miners were beaming and their women were exhausted with their own thrifty ways.

'I was in love,' Ran said. He looked at his drink, down into the shrinking pool of it. 'I used to drive her around in my beat-up Saab. They say teenagers don't know what real love is, but it's the opposite. Teenagers love harder because they're unaffiliated.'

'I'm working on getting unaffiliated.'

'No hope for me,' said Ran. 'I'm affiliated as hell.'

DANNIE

She had gone southwest the day before, and tonight she was heading southeast. She wouldn't necessarily find Arn if she found the observatory, but she could find out for sure that he was gone. She could confirm that fact and try to move on with her life. The observatory was the only place she knew to look. It wasn't in the phonebook, of course. It didn't have a website. The owner liked to keep a low profile. Dannie pictured the owner with a neat goatee and pricey boots. He probably ate the exact same lunch every day of the year.

Dannie wasn't sure she'd even know the observatory if she saw it. It wouldn't have a sign. It would be way back off the road, might even be disguised. It might be made to look like some shop nobody would ever go in, a pocketwatch repair joint in the middle of nowhere, a trophy store, anything. The observatory would be the same color as everything else by now. You couldn't fight it; out here everything ended up the same color. It could be underground, all but the big dish. That's what Dannie could look for, the dish.

Dannie's baby was the size of a raisin. The sunset was occurring without struggle on all sides of her. None of the birds were flying. All the birds were teetering along the roadside like pilgrims.

Dannie saw a statue of an Indian god, all its arms. The statue wasn't blue. It was that same color. She saw an out-of-business tourist attraction with a sign that said FEEL THE VORTEX. The hills were in their own shadows. A hundred guys on motorcycles flowed past Dannie, going the same direction she was but much faster.

Dannie wanted to see a chain-link fence, a barrier of any kind. She wanted to see an effort to keep someone out of somewhere. She felt safe, but she did not feel lucky. Dannie had crispy bacon wrapped in paper towels in her glove box. She reached and extracted a strip and took a bite. She didn't know whether to use her brain or her gut, whether to follow logic or her blood. She had thought about the fact that it was Wednesday three or four times over the course of the afternoon, that it was a vigil day, had understood in a cloudy way that at some point she would have to call the search off and find a road back toward Lofte and then back toward Albuquerque, that she would have to designate one of these lonesome stretches of road as the last one to be studied this evening, but she had not done this. The sky had turned red and then darker and darker and Dannie was heading farther away from the clinic. Her foot was lightly on the gas pedal, her eyes scanning in what light was left. There had been two signs and here came another one for a diner a couple miles ahead. Because there was nothing else, she had made this her destination. Someone might know something.

A mile from the diner, when she could see a lone light atop a steep roof, she brought the car to a stop at the roadside. She had always wondered how people felt when they quit the vigils. She got out of her car and walked for a minute into the desert. She couldn't see her car but she could see the light on the diner. She had too much freedom. Inside her was something that would be a part of her forever, but outside there was nothing. She was giving up a devotion that was sure and stationary, a boy in a coma who would never know a thing about her, in favor of looking for a boy who knew things about her whether he wanted to or not, and who would've, in time, found out the rest, a boy who needed her and was probably fleeing faster than Dannie could chase.

She went into the diner and no one knew anything for sure. They'd heard of the observatory. They knew it was around. They knew where a defunct chemical plant was. They knew where someone had tried to start a museum for vintage cars. Dannie had been southwest and southeast and so she headed as close to north as she could. She'd covered hundreds of miles of road that all looked alike. What had seemed like the same mountains looking down on her with pity. The same dazed sky. The same tumbleweeds blowing halfway across the desert and then halfway back. There were two soda bottles rolling around in Dannie's floorboard, a banana peel, a cracker box. The bacon was gone. In her purse, a mess of scribbled, contradictory directions. Lipstick. Vitamins.

It was as dark as it was going to get, an advanced phase of dusk that wouldn't give out, and Dannie had been driving farther away from her home and then closer and then farther, the roads seeming absolutely random in their paths, her mind more lost than her car, when the unbroken field of disappointing wilderness Dannie's eyes had been skimming for hours was intruded upon by a squat brick mail receptacle. Dannie knew she'd found it. She knew right away she'd found the observatory. She'd harassed luck until it had wanted nothing more to do with her. She'd turned the day's bad luck to good with pure doggedness. Before she'd even heard the crackling buzz of the elaborate generator set up under a wooden pavilion about a hundred feet off the road, she knew this was the place. It was either the observatory or the end of her looking for the observatory, and she knew it was both.

Most of the observatory, as Dannie had predicted, was underground. The building was painted a faint green color that was somehow ugly. Green in the desert was always pretty, but the observatory was not. She'd turned in next to the little mail house and soon there'd been fence posts but no fence. There'd been a power line from the electrical source. There'd been a soft dirt road that had turned into a hard dirt road that had become a concrete drive, and then she had seen the pickup, and then she'd seen the big lone dish. Arn's truck in sight, real as her own hand. She took her time. She left her car door open and took slow steps into the dusk air. She touched Arn's door handle and looked all around at the bristly shrubs and broken boulders. The sky had no edges. She wandered toward the building, toward the only visible entrance, not quite wanting to turn her back on Arn's pickup. The door to the observatory wasn't locked but was extremely heavy. Instead of a knob, it had a leather strap you wrapped around your hand. Dannie had to yank the door a crack and put her foot down. She used her shoulder to force the door open and slip through, and once inside all she saw was a narrow staircase that descended steeply. The steps were covered in metal studs that were meant for traction but only made Dannie's footing unsure. There was sound coming from the walls. As Dannie grew closer to the bottom of the stairs, a smell like undrinkable water wafted toward her. She came onto flat ground in a plain room that made her think of a newspaper office if you took out the desks. She knew Arn was here. There wasn't anywhere for him to hide. She saw Arn's table over near the controls, saw his water jug lying empty on its side, saw the big poetry book. She went over and righted the jug and sat in Arn's chair. There was a black screen with green cloudy light spread across it. It was like a weather screen, but for sound instead of rain. The green cloud was shapeless but you could tell where it was going. Dannie wondered what would happen down here if a message came through, whether alarms would sound, if the screen would start flashing.

Dannie heard something behind her. She rose and spun around to see Arn standing there, brow furrowed, hands empty and down by his sides. There was a light directly above him, and it turned his hair auburn and his face shadowy. He looked scandalized, confused. His wiry arms hung limp. Dannie came around the chair and took a step toward him. She thought maybe she could smell him, his wholesome, hale musk. The bad water smell had faded from the room. Arn was so still he didn't seem to be breathing, but Dannie could hear something. The noise was Arn starting to cry, and it was the sweetest thing Dannie had ever heard. He sniffed deeply. A fat tear ran down his cheek and then another. He seemed not to be able to move, so Dannie went to him. She didn't embrace him, just took him by the hand and by the shirt. He'd withheld a lot of tears and Dannie wanted to see them roll. This was more than she could've expected. She wanted to see Arn's face betray things it had never betrayed, while his body held still.

They were in the bed of the truck, cozy under the topper. Arn had given himself the night off – a personal night, he called it. There had to be stars out, but Dannie couldn't see them. Tomorrow she and Arn would go and find a place to live together, a new place. Dannie had had enough of the condo. Arn had pieces of poetry for her, from the book inside. *There was a kinsman took up pen and paper, to write our history, whereat he perished, calling for water and the holy wafer, who had, till then, resisted much persuasion.*

'I want to learn how to drive stick tomorrow,' Dannie said. 'I used to know how.'

'You still know how. It's one of those deals like riding a bike.'

'Is it?' Dannie said. 'I like things like that. Things you can't lose even if you try to.'

Dannie gripped Arn by his forearm. She would tell him about the baby in the morning. She wasn't afraid to tell him; she was excited to. But she wanted all his attention tonight. She shouldn't have to share him tonight.

CECELIA

She was the only person in the parking lot. She felt exposed. She was in physical danger, an immediate physical danger that any lone girl would be subject to in this part of town, and also she was in spiritual danger, because the fact that her stubbornness had won out didn't mean she was tougher than the other vigilers. It probably meant she was weaker. She'd wanted this boy to be better than the world because she hadn't wanted to deal with the world, hadn't wanted to deal with Reggie's death, but Soren was the same thing Reggie was, a young person who'd run into bad luck. People had talents. What both Reggie and Soren should have had a talent for was sticking around. They hadn't been so talented at avoiding comas and car accidents.

Cecelia shuddered. She looked up at Soren's window, which was dim but not as dark as the windows on either side. She hadn't brought enough clothing. Spring was arriving, but Cecelia had never been cold like this. The blacktop felt like a sheet of ice under her legs. She was too aware of her position in the universe. She was sitting in the shadow cast by the planet she lived on. She was in the center of a wilderness on that planet. Cecelia didn't know how to stop vigiling. She would be here next week, she knew. She was not authorized to give herself permission to quit. Better or worse, right or wrong, she'd be here next week. Danger or no danger.

No one was breathing near Cecelia, no one shifting on their haunches. The clinic was dead, no one coming in or out, no lights turning on or off. The few cars in the lot must've belonged to the nurses. There wasn't even any wind. The vigils were always quiet, but this was different. There were no trucks roaring by up on the inter-state, no lizards scratching about. Cecelia began to hear all the songs Reggie had written since he'd died. She wasn't hearing them one at a time. Her mind was gathering them up like a shepherd after a storm, calling the songs to her. The old man diving for the girl's little shoes. The young man digging the river. The birth of clouds. The streets that could be terrifying one day and cozy the next. Foreign countries and outer space. The fast tender songs and the slow mean ones. Cecelia had only ever thought of herself missing Reggie, but Reggie had been missing her exactly as much. He'd been figuring his way out of his own trouble. He had not been trying to help Cecelia with these songs, she saw. He'd just been missing her more than he missed anything else. He would miss her always. Cecelia heard all the songs at once and heard them each clearly, until one by one they reached their ends and by degrees the quiet returned.

THE WOLF

The wolf stood in the shadows of one of the ghost towns. All the windows of the buildings were gone, but there was no broken glass.

The glass had become part of the desert. The wolf had lost much of his fur and more than one tooth. The skin of his belly was loose. He had tried everything except nothing, so he stayed at the ghost town through a night and then another. And here came the third night – the gray-pink of evening. The wolf had inhabited this old settlement.

It didn't matter if the wolf was wise to weather, if his senses were keen, if his instincts brought him safety or threat. His story was lingering, weighting the air, not blowing as it should to far-off places. The desert smelled like the inside of a bottle and sounded like nothing. The wolf craved a sign, a call to act. He wanted to taste something new. He wanted to know where he was going before he moved away from the ghost town.

He came out of the shadows, his paws ruined and his heart in a constant weak spasm, and watched a buzzard soar, its course uncertain. The wolf wanted the bird to lead him somewhere. He watched the buzzard as the darkness took over. He watched the buzzard until he saw that its course was not indeterminate, that the creature was flying in vast circles that had begun to tighten.

THE GAS STATION OWNER

He didn't know whether he was resting or quitting. He knew he should be looking for food and water, but when he surveyed the nothingness in every direction he could not get himself moving. His stomach had stopped growling. He held his arm up above his head to make sure he could, then let it fall limp. The sun could no longer burn him. He and the sun had been locked in a petty disagreement since the day he departed Lofte, and they'd grown bored with each other. It was around noon, around what would have been lunchtime if he'd been sitting in the station on his stool in front of the window. The gas station owner wondered how the station was doing, and for a reason he couldn't pin down he began to laugh. He couldn't picture the girls he'd hired to run the place, the girls who'd been waitresses and in time would become librarians. He remembered them as pretty, almost preposterously so, but he couldn't picture them. He thought of enchiladas with green chiles and it was useless, like thinking of a billion dollars. He couldn't smell the sauce or feel warm tortillas in his mouth. This wasn't a hunger he knew anything about. It wasn't in his stomach but in his head and limbs.

The sky grew dim as the lunch hour passed, and the gas station owner was relieved when he saw flashes of lightning in the distance. He waited and waited for rain – it must've been a full hour – but if there was weather it wasn't going to hit him. The lightning stayed in the distance, too far off for its thunder to be heard. It was too much for his eyes, but he watched it anyway, a last show for him, a message he need not return.

He emptied his pockets. In one was the stumpy pencil and tattered scorecard the gas station owner had managed not to lose. Some of his marks were faded and some were trying to hide in discolored creases. The gas station owner flattened the paper on his thigh, which was just a bone now, and made a mark for today, the lightning day, the quitting day. He counted the marks without rushing and came up with thirty-six. He rested, head in his hands, eyes aching, then counted again and got thirty-seven. He thought he had one more attempt in him. He pressed his fingernail against each mark. Thirty-five. From his other pocket he emptied a handful of lizard bones, now not much more than sand. He drew the broken little bones to his nose but they only smelled like his pants, only smelled like him. The gas station owner dug a small hole with the cup of his hand and dropped in the bones and covered them over.

He wasn't going to count the marks on his scorecard again because his eyes were worn out, and he also wasn't going to count them because he wasn't going to reach forty anyway so what did it matter and on top of that he didn't count the marks again because he was allowing himself to admit what had been nagging him half the time he'd been out here: his venture, mission, his test of himself, had from the start been artificial. Great tests, you couldn't assign them to yourself. If the universe didn't want to test you, you wouldn't be tested. You didn't get to decide for yourself how much time you had and what supplies you could bring and you didn't even get to choose your adversary. There was nothing heroic in this challenge. The gas station owner was not nobly and obliviously obsessed. He was more aware of simple concerns than ever, and those concerns were growing by the moment.

It took what felt like an eternity for the wolf to approach, the silent afternoon lightning still flashing steadily from miles away. The gas station owner sat with his knuckles to his lips, taking comfort in the salt. He watched the wolf from when he could've been a coyote and then through the middle distance when he took on his color and eventually the wolf's snout and heavy paws were right there. Burrs were grown into the wolf's fur. His eyes were yellow marbles and his ribs looked like the rotting hull of a boat. His tongue hung from his tight-closed mouth, his snout crusted white. The wolf growled without effort or meaning. The animal was desperate and so it recognized desperation. This was the least silly creature the gas station owner had ever seen.

The wolf had stopped twenty paces from the gas station owner. The wolf knew something had to happen and was waiting. He and the gas station owner could not pass each other, could not go their own ways. Their journeys had brought them to a common spot, and both were spent.

The gas station owner kept his eyes on the wolf but he rummaged behind him into his pack and found the pistol. He had two rounds left. He shifted himself onto one knee and lifted the gun shakily, aiming as best he could. His hand, empty, was heavy to him, and the gun felt like a sack of wet sand. The wolf's eyes failed to flash at the weapon.

The gas station owner jerked his finger and the gun jumped and sounded its report. He missed low, a cloud of dust blooming from underneath the wolf. The wolf wasn't looking at the gun anymore, but straight into the gas station owner's eyes. He'd shot plenty of elk, but he never had to look them in the eyes. The gas station owner put his finger to the trigger again and half-pressed, not enough to fire the gun. He held the trigger static, a hair shy of the firing point, the barrel leveled at the mangy beast before him. He thought he could hit the wolf this time, his aim corrected from the miss. The wolf's growling was even, no threat in it. The gas station owner's brain was telling his hand to fire the gun but nothing was happening. His arm began to quake under the pistol's weight so he braced his gun arm against his leg. He had no idea if he was trying to provide for himself or defend himself. He breathed in sharply and then went ahead and lowered the gun. He looked at the weapon, gray under a gray sky. It had one bullet in it and that bullet would not be used. It wouldn't be used on this wolf or on the gas station owner. It would stay safe in the spinner.

The gas station owner sidled over on his knees and lifted the rock he'd used as a pillow the night before. He rested the pistol underneath it, hiding the gun from view. No human would ever find it. It would remain where it was until the whole world was finally punished. Still on his knees, he edged toward the wolf, closing in on him. The gas station owner stopped at a few paces and held his hand out, his shoulder again quaking. He tried to soften his eyes, to let the wolf know that the fighting was over, that the gun was extinct. He was dizzy now with the effort of this peace offering, with the weight of his hand even without the gun, even in the lightest air in the world, and when the animal took a step toward him it startled him. The gas station owner felt energy, fear. The wolf closed the distance and the gas station owner gave no ground when his hand was hotly sniffed. The wolf seemed more intelligent than the gas station owner. The wolf had known from the start that an understanding was inevitable. He sniffed the gas station owner's fingers greedily. The wolf was long-legged and long-necked and was reaching downward to get the scent he wanted, and the gas station owner resisted reaching out his other hand and petting the wolf on his bony head. He kept his hand raised to the animal, his arm no longer heavy. The wolf started licking the gas station owner then, wetting down the flesh of his hand and then the topside of his wrist, like a bumbling collie, and then the wolf pressed its dry muzzle against the gas station owner's forearm and the gas station owner pushed back to keep his balance. The wolf balked, snorting, and the gas station owner felt the wolf's teeth against his scorched forearm, saw that the wolf's saliva was flowing openly, springing from some hidden source in the wolf's desiccated body and slicking the filthy fur of his front. The lightning was still striking, an empty county away. The moment was changing and the gas station owner, trapped inside it, had no power to escape, no power to change course now after this much wandering, after arriving at this impasse. At the taste of the gas station owner's blood the wolf's tongue became animated and something changed in his eyes. The wolf seemed to remember that he was not afraid of anything. Night would not come at the end of this day. Forty days never mattered, but this did.

The whole meat of the gas station owner's lower arm was in the wolf's mouth and the gas station owner did not protest. The wolf sliced easily into the skin, never biting down all the way. He was merciful, the wolf. The gas station owner wanted an active part in the moment. He would not be victimized. He shoved his arm roughly at the wolf, encouraging him. He felt no pain. Though he felt removed in some necessary way, he could see it clearly when the wolf got hold of the piece of flesh he was after, the veined old muscle the gas station owner would've used to pull the trigger again, had he pulled the trigger again. The wolf paused and shuddered. The gas station owner watched him peel away a full strip of his flesh, watched the wolf retreat several paces and chew and swallow hard.

When the air hit the wound, he could feel it, but the gas station owner had felt worse pain many times. He'd probably had hangovers that hurt worse. He tucked his arm to his side, remaining on his knees and returning the wolf's hollow stare. The wolf didn't look desperate anymore, didn't look special. The gas station owner waited, curious about his life, curious if this was how it was going to end or if there'd be more for him to deal with, and next he was watching the wolf turn away and trot toward the east, toward the coming night. It would arrive, the night. The gas station owner could see the wolf for a while and then could only see the dust the wolf disturbed as he returned to his life, part of the gas station owner inside him, fueling him.

The gas station owner's blood was surging now. His arm was bleeding and his mind was buzzing. He stood and went to his pack, hoisted it off the ground. There'd been nothing in it but the pistol for days. The gun was gone and he was not afraid. He dropped the pack on the desert floor without ceremony and began walking, his mangled arm snug to his body. He wasn't trying to conserve energy or trying to find anything. When his blood slowed, he would walk no more, and he wanted to cover some ground while he could. He would walk for another minute or he'd make it ten miles, to where the lightning was finally giving out, only a late weak flash now and then. There was a point on the horizon where in a couple hours the sun would set, and maybe the gas station owner could beat the sun to that spot.

MAYOR CABRERA

He was visiting with his sister-in-law when the call came from the clinic. They told him Jay Fair had been brought in, worse for wear but stable now, severely dehydrated and torn up a little from a run-in with some coyotes. A young couple had come across him driving back from a remote hike, on a washboard road that sometimes went unused for days. Mayor Cabrera wasn't sure if Fair had asked for him because they were friends, or if he'd been contacted because Fair had no family and Mayor Cabrera had long been the head of the town Fair hailed from. He hoped it was the former. He hoped he was about to drive to Albuquerque on purely personal business this Wednesday evening.

He excused himself from the living room, said goodbye to his sister-in-law with a lingering hug, and dumped the rest of his tea down the sink. He went up the hall toward the front door and stopped at Cecelia's room. He knocked and heard Cecelia's small, clear voice. Mayor Cabrera went in and Cecelia was making her bed, tucking the last corner in tight. Then she stepped over and gave Mayor Cabrera a hug that was stiff but nonetheless felt sweet to him. He asked her if she was still going to the vigils at the clinic, because he had to go there too tonight, to see about Mr Fair, who'd turned up half-dead from the desert. He asked his niece, not whispering but not loud enough that his sister-in-law could've heard from the living room, if she wanted to ride over with him. He knew catching a ride with him wasn't any more convenient for Cecelia, and probably she liked being alone with her thoughts when she went to the vigils. He had no idea how late she usually stayed, but he assured her that he'd be happy to sit with Mr Fair all night if necessary, and was surprised when Cecelia rested her Rubik's Cube in the center of her bed, glanced toward her window in the general direction of Albuquerque, and said, 'Sure.' She asked if he was ready to go right then and Mayor Cabrera said he guessed so and stood by as Cecelia wriggled into a sweatshirt, her face emerging open and calm. She patted her pockets then told Mayor Cabrera to lead the way.

They got in his car and set off and Mayor Cabrera made sure not to act like it was a big deal that Cecelia was riding with him, not to act like it marked a success for him. They opened their windows and got clear of Lofte and onto a two-lane county road that wasn't paved very well but didn't have any stoplights. Mayor Cabrera didn't want to be on the interstate, where you couldn't converse over the whipping wind. The evening was almost warm, the air with weight to it and carrying a scent like grainy crackers.

Mayor Cabrera knew it didn't matter what he talked about. He had to say something. He had to not say nothing.

'I had a dream last night where people kept smiling at me,' he offered.

Cecelia was lost in thought, but she abandoned whatever she'd been mulling. She considered Mayor Cabrera's statement earnestly, as if he'd stated a philosophy.

'Like in a good way?' she said. 'Or creepy, like in a Christian coffee shop or something?'

Mayor Cabrera didn't know about Christian coffee shops. 'No, not in a good way,' he told her. 'It was like they knew something about me.'

'Sinister grins?'

'You could say that. And they were all standing really still.'

Something dashed against the windshield, a large insect or a tiny bird.

'Sorry, fella,' Cecelia said.

'The farther away they were, the creepier it was. I saw one guy grinning at me from all the way across a parking lot.'

'Were you at a mall?' said Cecelia.

'It's possible.'

They turned onto a different two-lane road, this one running quickly through an isolated development that had been abandoned half-built. A few folks lived in it, wondering if they would ever have neighbors. Farther up the road were homes that had always been there, shabby but permanent. There were donkeys in the yards.

'Thank you for the studio,' Cecelia said. 'It's really nice. The car and then the studio. You can stop now. I get the point.'

307

'Well,' said Mayor Cabrera. He knew Cecelia had been over there, because he'd left the key with her mother and then checked back on the studio room each evening. The other day he'd found the equipment shifted around and a gum wrapper in the wastebasket. He hadn't wanted to mention it until she did.

'Is it big enough?' he asked.

'It's plenty big. It's perfect.'

'Any songs you write in there, I get to hear it first.'

'It's a deal,' said Cecelia.

Mayor Cabrera reached over and let the glove box open and pointed to a bag of pistachios, offering them to Cecelia. She shook her head. He didn't want any either, he supposed. He thought he could see the lights from the rooftops of the downtown skyscrapers, but maybe they were just tower lights from one of Sandia's foothills, or low stars appearing. He wasn't driving fast, but he slowed a little.

'What do you think is the best way to woo a woman?' he asked. 'In your opinion.'

'Did you say "woo"?'

'I don't know what it's called anymore.'

Cecelia let the glove box back open and shut it again. 'Who are you planning on wooing?'

'I don't want to say yet.'

Cecelia crinkled her face. 'Fair enough,' she said.

'I'm so out of practice.'

'Yeah, but being out of practice can be an advantage,' Cecelia said. 'Depending on the woman. Sometimes if you're not smooth, that's good.'

'That's a relief to hear.'

'Do it the old-fashioned way. Don't get creative. That's one of the

308

problems with the world. Millions of people want to be creative and only a couple dozen of them are good at it.'

'Which old-fashioned way?'

'Flowers. Overrun her with flowers. Don't get cute, just bombard her with mass amounts of bouquets.'

'Right. I can do that.'

'Leave them in her yard at night. Put them in her car and in her mailbox and hire some neighborhood kids to knock on her door every hour.'

Mayor Cabrera didn't know if there were any kids in Dana's complex. When he thought of her front walk and her door and the hall that led to her kitchen, he didn't feel anxious. He'd wooed Cecelia and her mother, hadn't he?

'How about chocolate?' he asked Cecelia.

'That may be too old-fashioned. A lot of people have funny diets.'

'Perfume?'

They rose out of whatever valley they'd been in and were suddenly crossing numbered streets.

'Does she use perfume usually?' Cecelia asked.

'Yeah, she switches every few months.'

'I don't know about perfume, but I know clothes wouldn't hurt. For you, I mean.'

Mayor Cabrera looked down at his button shirt. The pocket had a fish embroidered on it. 'Like a suit?'

'Sure, a suit would be good. A suit and a haircut.'

'I just got a haircut.'

Cecelia looked over, right at him. 'Your part makes you look careful.'

Mayor Cabrera laughed. He checked himself out in the rearview mirror.

'I burned down a barn,' Cecelia said. 'Some people's fancy barn in their back yard. I dumped gasoline on it and burned it to the ground.'

Mayor Cabrera made an effort to not appear concerned, which probably wasn't working. 'You burned down someone's barn?'

'I'm an arsonist. The kid whose barn it was covered it up. He wanted to have a fair feud.'

'A fair feud?'

'And I also trashed his band's equipment. And I lied to a cop.'

'About the barn?'

'No. It was a white lie.'

'You've been busy.'

'I also mugged a rich kid.'

'You mugged someone? For their money?'

'Not much money.'

'When?'

'Over the holidays.'

This was what uncles were for, Mayor Cabrera knew. This right here. People could tell their uncles things. That was the function of a proper uncle. You couldn't tell an uncle every single thing maybe, but you could tell him a lot, and he had to take it like an uncle. Cecelia knew. She knew how to be a niece.

CECELIA

They had to wait almost forty-five minutes to see Mr Fair. The wound specialist was in there with him. He had just been moved from the ER, and Cecelia and her uncle sat in the hard molded

chairs and succumbed to that exhaustion that always set in as soon
as you sat still in a hospital. For the first time, Cecelia was inside
the clinic, which of course felt odd because she'd stared at the outside for so long. She felt like a little girl inside a dollhouse. The
clinic wasn't cozy like she'd come to imagine. It wasn't especially
high-tech. It looked like all medical facilities, only cleaner. When
Cecelia and her uncle were called in, Mr Fair wasn't really cog-
nizant. He grinned a little when he realized he had visitors, but he
was elsewhere. Tubes were hanging out of both his arms, pumping
him with fluids and probably painkiller. His right arm was band-
aged neatly.

Cecelia's uncle got comfortable. He made no move for the TV.
Cecelia was already late for the vigil. This would be the second week
she'd be all alone out there. She wondered how long was polite to
stay in Mr Fair's room, seeing as he was oblivious, and after about
ten minutes she cleared her throat and said she was going on down.
'Take your time,' her uncle said.

She was free to arrive at the vigil any time she wanted. She would
have the parking lot to herself, no one to witness or judge her. In
another way, she wanted to keep observing the rules. That corner of
the parking lot was sitting vacant and Cecelia was the only person
who had the right to change that. If she was going to vigil, she was
going to do it correctly.

She took the monotonous hallway toward the elevators, thinking
of being outside, of completing another week, fulfilling duty, of
breathing the night air, which this evening had been strangely
humid as it had rushed in the windows of her uncle's car. A few
rooms from the end of the hall a woman wheeled out from her
doorway and called to Cecelia, her wheelchair almost bumping

Cecelia's leg. Cecelia stopped short and the old woman pinched the sleeve of Cecelia's sweatshirt.

'Can you find me a blanket, sweetie?'

Cecelia looked up and down the hall. Not a soul. She couldn't tell what kind of face she was making at the woman.

'I need a blanket and a cola,' the woman said. She opened her eyes as wide as they would go. 'You can't say no to a cold, thirsty old lady.'

'I guess that's true,' said Cecelia. 'I bet that line works every time.'

The old woman dug through a small bag hanging from the arm of her wheelchair. She smelled sick and sweet, like a dessert that had been left out. Her gray hair was thick and lustrous. She tugged a rumpled dollar bill flat and handed it to Cecelia, then explained where the vending machines were. Cecelia was wondering why the woman didn't call her nurse. She probably wasn't allowed to have soda.

'I like you,' the woman said. 'So far.'

'I'll be right back,' Cecelia answered.

She stopped by the nurses' station first and asked for the blanket. There was only one nurse behind the desk. She squinted up at Cecelia and said she had to finish typing a note, that she couldn't save the note halfway through with this new computer system. She didn't know why they'd changed the system again. She hunted and pecked at the keyboard, Cecelia leaning forward against the counter. Cecelia was going to be an hour late for the vigil, she saw. A full hour. She was ready to feel panicked about this, but the panic wasn't arriving. Cecelia could detect run-of-the-mill annoyance at unexpected chores, but even this was not strong. It was mild annoyance. She wanted to help the old lady out. She wanted to exercise patience with this rundown nurse as she dealt with her computer.

In time the nurse sighed and hit the ENTER key with finality. She rose and slipped into a back room, and when she returned she handed Cecelia a blue blanket folded in a sharp square. Cecelia tucked it under her arm and went down a side hall to the vending machines. She found the one that sold soda and fed the old lady's dollar into it and the machine promptly spit the bill back out. Of course it would. The thing was about as limp and crinkled as a dollar could get. It looked like it was going to fall apart completely in the next week or so, a tiny portion of the world's wealth lost. The price for a can of soda was eighty-five cents. Cecelia dug into her pockets and came up with two quarters and a dime. She draped the blanket over her shoulders and squinted at the vending machine. She could go back to the old lady and ask if she had other dollar bills. She could find the nearest open door and ask whoever was inside to borrow a quarter. She had an impulse to just leave the blanket on the floor and escape this floor of the clinic via the stairs, which were at the opposite side of the building than the elevators. This was Cecelia's most familiar impulse, but she wasn't going to follow it. She was going to get this lady her damn soda. She felt in no rush about the vigil, still felt no anxiety as she grew later and later. She had nothing against the old lady or the nurse or her uncle's slow driving. She had nothing against anyone. She had stepped inside the clinic for the first time tonight, and being inside this place, where lives were fought for and won or fought for and relinquished, it made the outside, the vigil, feel like a farce, like make-believe. The vigil was comfortable, Cecelia knew. She'd convinced herself it was some kind of test, but it was a comfortable place where real life was not allowed, where you didn't have to face anything. It would have been easier for Cecelia to descend to her smoothly paved sanctuary, and suddenly she was washed with the anxiety she'd been awaiting. She pulled the blanket snug around her. Letting the vigil slip away was not a matter of worry, but what she had to do instead was. She had to go up and see Soren, had to set eyes on the boy. As she stood in front of these dull-lit vending machines she was breathing the same air as Soren. He was two floors above her. The blanket on her shoulders might've warmed him some recent night.

REGGIE

As soon as he began playing, he recognized the song. He was writing the song but also remembering it. It was the song he'd begun just before his death, that he'd been working on in his pickup that hazy, not-quite-hot day. The notes were there for him, he only needed to give them safe landing. The breeze that had been soothing Reggie picked up into a dry wind as he played. It ruffled Reggie's hair and raised an eerie wail as it passed through the harmonica over on the bureau – a sound like the cry of a cornered animal. At some point Reggie had decided and then gone on assuming that he was in dusk rather than dawn, but now the hall filled with light, pinkish and strengthening, and Reggie felt a longing to see the moon again, the standoffish white sliver of it or the jolly yellow face. Above him the gray clouds had grown heavy, churning faster with the gusts. Reggie's shirt blew off the piano bench and out of sight. He kept his feet planted on the pedals, his back straight. He was farther into the song than he'd written in life, more than halfway through. He didn't allow himself to drag the song out. He harbored no folly. He didn't play louder or soft. He looked at his hands and they did not look familiar. A fly buzzed around Reggie, bothering his eyebrow and then trying to cling fast to the empty music stand. And then it was gone, lost in its own ordeal. The clouds were lower now. If Reggie had stood on the piano and reached he could've touched them. He heard the wind tinking the liquor bottles in the bar, and then heard one of the bottles crash to the floor. Book covers were flying open in the library.

Reggie knew that the pinched calm that filled the spaces between the notes was the sound of eternity. He knew an immediate future awaited, an extended present, and the rest of the song would fill it. He did not hope for unrippled bliss. He did not hope to hear the voice of a god. He did not want oceans or mountains. He was a single note and he only wanted to ring.

SOREN'S FATHER

He parted the blinds with a thumb and still the girl wasn't out there. The last one. It was past the time when the vigil normally began, and even last week, alone, the girl had shown up promptly. The sun had tipped out of sight, leaving a sloppy wake of flesh-colored sky that was fast disappearing. Soren's father pulled away his hand and the blinds closed up. He fetched the wastebasket from the bathroom and scraped the table near the window clean. He hadn't eaten a proper dinner, but he'd polished off five cups of Jell-O. The cups tinked down into the can and then the plastic spoon after them. The only other thing in the trash was a disposable razor Soren's father had used that morning. There was so little straightening up to do in the room. Usually Soren's father had coffee around this time. He didn't want any today.

He moved the orange-upholstered chair right next to the window and drew the blinds enough to see out. He didn't want the vigils to be over. He didn't want cars to reclaim that area of the lot. Whether he wanted to notice or not, that portion of ground, that ration of blacktop, had assumed a sacredness, and Soren's father didn't want a bunch of cars all over it. Soren's father was mildly relieved and mildly lonely now as he accepted that the girl was not coming, and he was capable of letting these reasonable feelings inhabit him. This wasn't a loneliness that would eat at him – instead, one human simply missing other humans. He missed Gee still, and he knew he would hear from her in time and looked forward to that. He missed the last vigiler, the girl. And the relief he was feeling was as much for the girl as for himself. The vigilers had been a target for his frustration, and had also been something reliable to hang his weeks on. None of them had been happy that his son was in a coma. They hadn't been seekers of relief. They were people who longed to be decent. Who knew how to be decent anymore? Soren's father leaned forward in his chair, his face close to the window. No sign of the girl. Nothing but the chollas, in full bloom now. They seemed to glow burnt yellow in the new dark, as if they'd been collecting the sun's power all day.

Soren's father had stopped wishing for Soren to awaken, at least stopped wishing it in a selfish way. He'd wanted Soren to return, all these months, because it would've made him happy, because it would've benefited the father, not the son, would've saved him from grief and confusion. Soren was in no apparent discomfort. Soren's father wanted his son to be in a good place and to come to no harm. That was his pure desire. Whether his son was special was beside the point, but for him to presume that his son was just like everyone else because that would be easier was as wrong as calling him an angel or a prophet. If Soren was special, Soren's father could deal with that. He didn't have to understand everything. Soren's destiny was as open as anyone's, and Soren wouldn't be afraid of that destiny the way his father had always been afraid.

Soren's father stood. Housekeeping had left a vase of fake flowers that matched the orange chairs, a gift from the clinic that every patient had received, a gift from the corporation that owned the clinic really, a gift from no one to anyone. Soren's father plucked it off the little side table and rested it down on the floor where he couldn't see it. He went and raised the blinds all the way. They hadn't been all the way open like that since Gee had visited the room. Soren's father gazed out at the barren territory beyond the parking lot and the neighboring streets, the expanse beyond the precarious civilization, the harsh province that was his homeland, and it looked finished. There was nothing broken, nothing wanting.

CECELIA

She pressed the UP button rather than the DOWN button, held her breath until the doors were closed, and then the elevator jerked subtly and she began to rise. She hadn't been in a tall building since she could remember. The clinic wasn't tall compared to the skyscrapers downtown, but it was tall to Cecelia. The elevator was huge inside, a whole room. Cecelia moved to the back corner. She'd paid respects to Soren for five months and had never been up against the prospect of seeing him. There were healthy elements to her nervousness – awe and pride. No music was playing in the elevator, but

Cecelia could hear something. There was other noise. She knew what was happening. She was getting another song. Now. She'd been sure they were through, that she'd received them all. She could hear the first notes being unchambered, finding their marks. She felt a pinch in her temples, a churn in her stomach. She was dry-eyed. Another fucking song. She settled her weight evenly down through her feet. She was out of practice but she could feel the skill returning to her, the skill of receiving. She could do it again, could usher this song into an out-of-the-way wing of her mind and go about the business of confronting Soren. She wasn't going to bail on this mission. Reggie was still not at peace and she wasn't going to be either, but she was going to face down this kid. Cecelia still had to grapple with Reggie, her ally and her illness, but she would do it later — had to wonder whether he was still writing these songs or whether he was dead and gone and the songs were outliving him, had to wonder if the songs had existed always and Reggie had come along to free them and had screwed everything up by dying too soon. She was losing the threads of her thoughts before they were even unspooled. She was thinking too darkly. Reggie hadn't screwed anything up. The songs were love songs. The songs were Reggie's and Reggie loved her.

A bell dinged as the elevator passed by the fifth floor. There was a poster for a children's gymnasium on one wall and a poster for a seafood restaurant on the other, a big lurid lobster on a mattress of parsley. Cecelia wanted more time, but she wasn't going to get it. She heard the bell again. The opening of the song in her head, which was straightforward and elegant, was intact already. The song was ready to shift into gear, or at least turn a soft corner. Cecelia stepped off the elevator into an empty foyer area. The fourth floor hadn't had a foyer. Cecelia could see down the main hallway. There was no one but a janitorial worker, all the way at the other end, dropping bags down a garbage chute. There was a window in the foyer and Cecelia looked toward it. The lights from the ceiling were glaring off the glass and Cecelia couldn't see anything outside, just her own reflection. It looked right. It looked like her. It looked like a girl who could go through with things.

Cecelia advanced up the hall, stepping stiffly to keep her sneakers quiet. The floor was polished and the walls were bare. The first doors she passed were closed, and Cecelia could somehow sense that the rooms were empty. She walked by a room in which an old couple and some small children were cleaning up from a party, then three rooms that all had TVs going, all tuned to the same program. She knew approximately where Soren's room should've been, from staring up at it. It was nearly all the way at the other end. Cecelia would have to pass the nurses' station.

She tried to appear confident, or at least absorbed in her own business, which she certainly was, and she strode past a few more almost-shut doors, the people behind them negotiating final burdens Cecelia couldn't plumb and her with her own troubles no one anywhere knew, and then straight through the nurses' area, which was occupied only by a young female doctor who paid no attention to Cecelia. Once the nurses' station was behind her, she came up to the staff worker she'd seen before, who passed her by, nodding curtly, and then there was nothing but wide vacant hallway. Cecelia had Soren cornered and she was cornered too. There was nothing she could say to Soren's father that wouldn't sound crazy.

The very last door was a utility closet, so the one next to that had to be Soren's room. The door was open but not enough to see anything inside. Cecelia had to knock. She had to knock and present herself. The door was going to open and she was going to see into this room that for so long had been the border of an eternity of night sky. She wanted to flee, but she held herself in place. She didn't want Soren's father to hear her breathing, to hear a noise from her sneaker and pull the door open and see her standing like a scared ghost. She was hearing the song now as an echo, as if someone in another wing of the clinic were playing it and it was reaching her through the heating ducts. The music had no cousins. It was sad music that didn't know it was sad. Cecelia raised her hand and rapped it against what felt like painted steel, not quite knocking hard enough to push the door open any farther.

The light changed in the room, a lamp clicking on. Cecelia heard the creaking of a chair and then footfalls, manly and even. The door receded and Soren's father was standing in front of Cecelia. He didn't seem surprised to see her. His face was hardly even questioning, as if Cecelia were a small girl who'd shown up at this home with a fundraiser catalog. He had good teeth and a nondescript haircut and he looked manly in a way that matched the reliable sound of his steps on the linoleum. Cecelia was frightened, but less so than she'd been a moment before.

'I'm Cecelia,' she told him.

His face didn't harden. Cecelia glanced up the hall and it was thankfully still empty. She didn't want an audience. Soren's father let go of the door and stood taller. 'I know who you are,' he said. 'I didn't know your name was Cecelia, but I know who you are.'

Cecelia couldn't read him, and she couldn't bring herself to state her desire of laying eyes on his son. She'd gotten this close and she might get no closer. That was the new fear.

'I wanted to wish you the best,' Cecelia said. 'And I think I wanted to apologize too.'

Soren's father looked at the palm of his hand and then put it to the back of his neck. 'I appreciate that,' he said. 'I don't accept your apology, but I appreciate it.'

'I wasn't helping anything out there,' Cecelia said. 'I wanted something I could love that had nothing to do with me.' Cecelia knew she needed to be truthful. She said, 'There are a handful of people I care about. I care about you and your son. I care about you guys, not that I expect it to mean anything.'

Soren's father blinked slowly. He looked back at the window, toward the parking lot, then reached his hand out and rested it on Cecelia's wrist, a gesture more tender than a handshake. 'I never knew what to think, but you were there instead of not there. You were there, and not asking for anything. It *does* mean something.'

Cecelia looked into his face and could see that his soul had been whipping in the desert winds for a long time. He had little left but kindness. Cecelia didn't know what to say next. She didn't want to upset or disappoint him.

'I need to stretch my legs,' he said.

Cecelia waited. Soren's father was wearing a stiff button-up shirt and it occurred to Cecelia that she was underdressed for a visit like this. She'd dressed for a vigil, in a sweatshirt and far-from-new shoes.

'Would you keep an eye on him for a minute?' Soren's father gently tugged his collar. 'Could you do that? Could you watch over my boy while I step out for a quick stroll? I'd appreciate it.'

He'd taken his hand off Cecelia's wrist. Her gratitude was like a liquid rising inside her. She was being trusted.

'Of course,' Cecelia said.

Soren's father leaned toward the hallway, showing he wanted to get by, and Cecelia made way for him. She didn't thank him and he didn't thank her. He slipped past her and with that same even stride made his way down the hall. Cecelia watched the back of him. She didn't feel ready to be without him, like she'd been poorly trained for an important duty. Soren's father didn't glance back at Cecelia. She watched him until he reached the nurses' station and turned a corner.

With the door to Soren's room wide open Cecelia could see a dresser and a chair and a big window. She stepped across the threshold and the end of the bed peeked into view. The air in the room carried the mixed scent of a boy's rest and a man's restlessness, of stale coffee and clean linens. She took another step and could see where Soren's feet were tenting the sheets. Then she saw a closed cabinet that probably contained a TV and she saw a machine that was monitoring Soren and only after she'd found the machine with her eyes was she aware of its whirring, which maybe she'd been hearing since Soren's father had pulled open the door. She was all the way inside the room. She looked at everything else – looked inside the open closet at the neat shirts and pants in there and looked at the little shoes half-tucked under the bed and at some fake flowers that had been stashed down in a corner. Then she let her eyes drift to Soren's face, which was a faultless oval, with small ears and a dimple in the chin. Cecelia went around the side of the bed, the side without the machine, still stepping cautiously as if afraid to awake Soren. His eyes were closed but not all the way. His hair looked healthy and was parted. It looked like someone's project, his hair, one of the nurses'. He wore a pressed gown and the sheets were pulled up past his waist. His hands rested on his stomach, one on top of the other, the fingernails trimmed neatly. It was impossible not to think he was merely sleeping. His skin was not gray, but it wasn't normal either. Cecelia surveyed the length of him, his frail shoulders, the rise and fall of his flat stomach, the shape of his legs under the bedding. He was a little boy. A sick child. He was none of Cecelia's business.

She reached and took one of Soren's hands in her own. It felt like an expensive glove. This was a time for prayer, a time to admit that one could be of no help and possessed insufficient wisdom and had wasted much time, but Cecelia couldn't put words together. She had never prayed in her life and now she had a song playing in her mind that was the prayer of prayers. It was a bad prayer, a prayer for nonbelievers. The song wasn't straining, but Cecelia was straining to hear it. She wasn't keeping it in a back room, it was hiding by choice. She placed Soren's hand back on his stomach and stepped over near the door. She heard nothing in the hallway. She wanted Soren's father to return. She wanted him to reappear and know exactly what to say. Cecelia sat down in his chair. There were two chairs, both orange and stiff-looking, but one had an indentation in the seat. Cecelia couldn't stay sitting. She arose again. The room was so clean. It looked like Soren and his father had moved into it the day before.

Cecelia went to the window. The blinds were drawn. The parking lot was a sprawl of concrete now and not a thing more, like the vigils had never happened. Cecelia had sat out there part of the fall and the entire winter. She put her knuckle soundlessly against the glass. She could not hear Soren breathing, nor the drumming of her own blood. She could hear the song. The music had slowed and gathered power, and Cecelia began humming it. She got through the opening, and with the first frank declaration of the melody her humming grew louder and more inflected. She tipped her head to look up at the night sky. A lot of the stars were missing, but there were still too many to count. She hummed the song even louder as she got about halfway through. The second half she would discover as she went. The bridge was coming to Cecelia. She stopped humming, her throat coming to rest, and the quiet, when it returned, had something wrong with it. Cecelia heard something that didn't belong in her ears and didn't belong in the room, an auditory presence both scratchy and high-pitched. It was coming from behind Cecelia and she could see by the reflection in the window that Soren's father had not returned. No one else had entered the room. The bits of song were spaced and were trying to find their key and Cecelia recognized them as some distortion of what she'd just been humming, of the song arriving from the beyond. Time was not passing, which made it difficult to move. Cecelia turned herself away from the window and looked at Soren. His chest no longer rose and fell smoothly. His eyes were still closed, tightly now, as if in pain. His hands did not move, nor his feet. Cecelia moved away from the window. She saw Soren nestle the back of his head into his flat, thin pillow, tipping his chin and clearing his throat. He gathered a breath and resumed humming. Something was happening with his monitor, a light flashing on the panel. Soren had the rest of the song, the part Cecelia hadn't received yet. She watched Soren's eyes gape open, saw his unsearching cornflower eyes. It was like Soren was looking out at an ocean. Cecelia couldn't tell if Soren's song, Reggie's song, was settling or building, whether it would cease unexpectedly or crescendo. She looked at the door. She wanted to shut it so no one would hear Soren, so she could think, but she made no move toward it. There was a call button somewhere, but she didn't want to involve a nurse. Maybe the monitor had already alerted the station, if anyone was paying attention. She ought to go find Soren's father, ought to track him down in the halls. Soren's hands were animated now, his fingers flexing like someone who'd been lugging a heavy suitcase. Cecelia needed to take action but she needed to hear the rest of the song, needed to hear it from outside of her for once, needed to hear it to the last note.

SOREN'S FATHER

They were on the dock. Soren was throwing nickels into the water, something he relished, as anyone would. He had a roll of them clutched in his fist and was tossing them one by one at the same spot in the darkening sea. There wasn't a sunset in St Augustine. The water went dark and then the sky went dark. They'd been in Florida over two years and the nights still snuck up on Soren's father. The winter had snuck up on him too, because it wasn't a winter at all. Winters in Albuquerque had been mild enough, but the winters here were beautiful. You stood out on a dock in winter. You enjoyed yourself.

'Are fish right down there?' Soren asked.

'Of course,' Soren's father said. 'About a million of them.'

'Big ones?'

'Big enough. I think the really huge ones stay where it's cold, though.'

'Are they going to go to sleep soon?'

'They can sleep whenever they want. They can wait till morning to go to sleep if they want to.'

'Do they dream when they're sleeping?' Soren lofted another nickel. It made no noise at all entering the Atlantic Ocean. 'Do the fish dream?'

'Sometimes they do. If they're tired enough.'

'What about?'

Soren's father placed both his elbows on the warped railing. The wind moving over him and his son was slow and heavy with salt.

'They dream about what they already got,' he said. 'They dream about swimming as deep as they can, down where the whales go, and they dream about watching the boats skimming by up above. They don't dream about being on land.'

'Do they ever have nightmares?' Soren asked.

'Oh, no. No nightmares. They're like you and me. They have so much fun, they can't remember what they're supposed to be scared of.'

After a short quiet, the waves lapping, Soren ran out of nickels. Soren's father watched him crumple the coin wrapper and shove it in his pocket, and then his face changed. There was another roll in there. He'd forgotten about it. He seemed amused at himself, nowhere near his wit's end. He peeled the wrapper back and held the nickels out toward his father.

'You want to try one?' he said. 'You have to throw it right where I always do.'

'You know, if we throw enough of them in there we'll fill up the whole ocean.' Soren's father took a coin from the roll. 'That's the new goal. We're going to fill this sucker up.'

CITRUS COUNTY

John Brandon

Discover the American cult classic of teenage life,
love and heartbreaking drama . . .

The story of a boy, a girl and a devastating secret,
Citrus County was published to rave reviews across the USA.
It is a unique book: at once hilarious, subversive and devastating –
and the work of an author tipped for stardom.

'*Citrus County* is important. It is a read unlike any other.
It is my favourite book of the year'
Huffington Post

'A story that keeps you turning the pages even
as you want to slow to savour them'
New York Times

'Brilliant. John Brandon is a young writer who can –
and probably will – do anything'
San Francisco Chronicle

'Disney's *High School Musical* as remade by Quentin Tarantino'
Daily Mail

978-0-349-12377-6

BC 06/13
KE8V 6/14
KT 03/18